On My Side

QUIBLINGS: BOOK 3

KATIE DUGGAN

Contents

Author's Note

While *On My Side* is, at its heart, a romantic comedy, serious topics are included as well. Life is funny, and life is tragic, and I hope I was able to blend these two facts in a sensitive and empathetic way.

On My Side features graphic, consensual, and kinky sex. I've chosen to include kinks in case any of the following may be triggering to you. The following is done between consenting adults:

- Bondage

- FDom

- MDom

- Audio erotica

- Choking

- Spitting

- Hair pulling

- Praise

- Breeding

- Dirty talk

- Light degradation

Major topics readers may find triggering are:

- Body shaming (on page, by a side character)

- Depressive episodes (on page)

- Ableism (in past)

- Religious bigotry (in past, impacts discussed in present)

- Parental abandonment of a main character (in past)

- Teenage pregnancy (in past, major plot point)

- Slut shaming of a main character (on page)

- Loss of a family member (in past and off page)

Brief mentions readers may find triggering are:
- Past transphobia

- Alcohol consumption (characters are over 21, except for brief mentions of a main character drinking as a teenager)

- Internalized homophobia of a side character

- Discussion of abortion (in past)

While it is my biggest hope *On My Side* brings joy and healing to my readers, I understand that may not be the case for everyone. If you think it may be too much, please take care of yourself and your brain first.

If you have overwhelming thoughts and need someone to talk to, please call 988 if you are in the US, or scan the QR code below to view resources available in your country.

You and your wellness are the most important.

Dicktionary

For readers like me, who search specific keywords on their e-reader to get to the good parts sometimes: I hope this makes it easier on you.

And for those who want to avoid the smut: please know while the following chapters are the ones with on page intimate scenes, sex and pleasure is discussed freely and is a plot point in *On My Side*.

- Chapter 2

- Chapter 7

- Chapter 14

- Chapter 17

- Chapter 18

- Chapter 24

- Chapter 26

- Chapter 38

- Chapter 39

Playlist

While writing and editing *On My Side*, I curated a playlist of songs related to Ren, Audrey, and their love story. The lyrics may not always directly apply, and listening to the playlist is not necessary for the enjoyment of *On My Side*.

Songs are listed before each chapter, and you can scan the QR code below to be taken directly to the Spotify playlist.

You can also find the playlist called "On My Side by Katie Duggan (Quiblings 3)" on my Spotify profile (Katie Duggan).

Quinn Family Tree

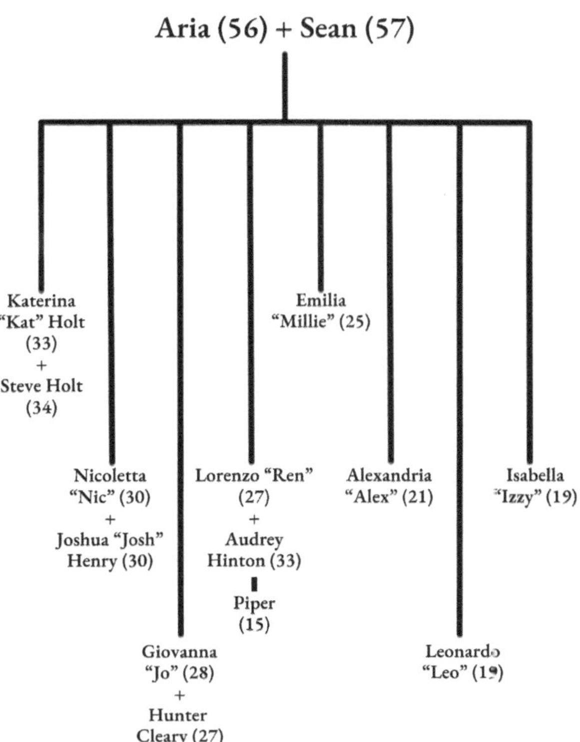

Character Catch Up

While each book in the Quiblings series is meant to be a stand-alone novel, the characters are very intertwined in each other's lives. If you're confused about any of Ren's (many) siblings or their partners, I've included a quick guide to introduce you to those you may not know yet, including identities.

Nic Quinn and **Josh Henry** are the main characters of **From the Start**, which is the first book in the series. It's a childhood nemesis to lovers, sex lessons, black cat x golden retriever story. Nic is autistic, bisexual, and mid-size, while Josh has undiagnosed PTSD, and is fat and queer.

Jo Quinn and **Hunter Cleary** are the main characters of **Back to Me**, which is the second book in the series. It's a second chance, fake dating, roommates story. Jo is a Type 1 Diabetic, fat, lesbian woman, while Hunter has ADHD and is a mid-size queer woman.

There is about a month's overlap between *On My Side* and *Back to Me* (not including the final chapter of *On My Side*).

In regards to future books...there are quite a few hints about tropes, love interests, and more.

Enjoy your time with the Quinns!

To those who feel like everyone eventually leaves, and who try to do everything to get them to stay: may we have the strength and courage to let go when the time is right, and to trust the right people want to stay. We're the right person for the right people.

And to Cait, who holds my hand physically and emotionally when life is too much. Who cheers me on and makes me feel like I'm where I'm supposed to be, with the people who are supposed to be with me. Thanks for being on my side.

Chapter 1

Ren

Playlist: Can I Be Real? | Brynn Elliott

June

I didn't think I'd regret not bringing an extra pair of pants to family dinner this week, but here we are.

"*Shit,*" I hiss, jumping to my feet as my brother-in-law's Coors Light seeps through my chinos.

"Sorry, man," my oldest sister Kat's husband, Steve, slurs, reaching for my crotch.

I slap his hand away. "It's fine." I force a smile onto my face, knowing any other reaction would lead to unwanted conflict. "Accidents happen."

My meager slap doesn't deter Steve, though, and he reaches toward my lap again. This time, I push my chair back and take a giant step away from the table as the rest of my present family stares. I swear I can hear Millie, my younger sister, snickering into her wine glass.

I make eye contact with my dad. "Think I can borrow a pair of pants?"

He nods, lifting his own bottle of Guinness to his mouth and glancing away. Good. If he looks at me too long, the smile gets harder and harder to maintain.

Of course, Ren Quinn, beloved music teacher and golden boy, doesn't get to be a little slutty.

When I re-enter the dining room with my chinos balled under my arm, Leo, my younger and only brother, snickers.

"Where are Nic and Josh?" I ask loudly, trying to get the attention off me. Nic is another one of my older sisters, and she lives in Brooklyn with her partner, Josh. Since they started dating in the fall, they've been coming home more regularly for Sunday dinners. Nic is autistic and struggles with big family gatherings, but since she started dating Josh, she's been more comfortable in her own skin, and with the rest of us.

My mom puts on her reading glasses and pulls out her phone, squinting at the screen. "Your sister said, and I quote: 'there's no flipping way I'm taking the train today LOL. Maybe next week? Love you.'"

"No way did Nic say *flipping*," Leo objects.

Mom peers at him over her glasses. "There's no need for me to repeat what she *did* say."

I pick at my dinner while smiling and answering questions about the impending end of the school year and beginning of summer.

"Are you teaching private lessons again?" Leo's twin, Izzy, asks.

I nervously twirl my linguine around my fork. "No, I think I might help out with summer school this year instead."

My entire family's eyes are on me as the entire room goes silent. Some would call me predictable, but the people in my life say dependable. Since my sophomore year of high school, I've taught private piano lessons during summer break, a job

I took out of boredom and kept out of necessity. I'd heard throughout my time in college how underpaid teachers are, but it's one thing to be told something and another to *live* it. When I graduated, I found myself setting up my classroom with my own money while drowning in student debt. The extra income was necessary for survival.

It still is. The extra income just comes from a different source.

"I thought you loved teaching private lessons!" Mom exclaims, her brown eyes wide.

"I do!" I reassure her, a twinge of guilt burrowing deep in my belly. "The school needs help, and it looks good if I'm able to do it."

It's a lie—I don't love teaching private lessons. Once I graduated college and became an actual, professional music teacher, it felt like the fun that had once come from private lessons was sucked out of it. Instead of being excited for lessons, I dreaded them. The focus became making parents happy instead of doing things at the student's own pace and evaluating their individual needs and wants. Not to mention the moms who think their flirting is subtle and can't seem to control their giggles around me.

So, when a friend from college mentioned in passing last year they were creating a new app and looking for contributors, my interest was piqued.

I don't know what I was expecting, but it certainly wasn't an audio erotica app. I'm sure I appeared shell-shocked as she explained the premise to me: dozens of diverse creators fulfilling diverse fantasies by providing audios with a focus on consent, pleasure, and intimacy.

I was desperate enough for a change that I said yes, and a week later, a box of recording equipment was waiting outside my door. I set it up in my spare bedroom, and recorded a friends-to-lovers dominant scripKadence sent me. I chose Sky as my stage name, and worked hard to perfect his own voice to keep my privacy and anonymity.

Sky is deep-voiced, sensual, and he records audios directed toward all genders.

By he, I of course, mean me.

4Play took off right away, and was one of the top ten most downloaded wellness apps within its launch month. Articles were written, influencers featured our audios, and I began making more money and more audios than I'd ever thought I would. I've been able to pay off most of my student loans, and have more than a year of my teacher's salary in savings. This is important to me because I want to be able to financially support any of my family if they need me to. Even though that hasn't been necessary yet, I'm glad I'm prepared if anything bad happens.

"I should get going," I say, bringing myself back to the present. Thinking about sex work at the dinner table with my family is probably frowned upon, and I have to upload an audio to the drive by midnight.

Mom's face falls, which is how I find myself staying another hour. I could leave sooner, *should* leave sooner, but I can't find it in me to make anyone less than extraordinarily happy.

Finally, I'm at the apartment I share with my cat, Princess Leia. Girl cats get the worst rep, but Leia—named after my favorite fictional general—is the best. Is she stubborn and sometimes rude? Sure, but I was raised with and by strong-willed women and have a soft spot for them. I found Leia by the seawall the summer after I graduated from college; a tiny, screaming calico kitten who was positively offended when I lured her to me with a can of tuna and scooped her into my arms.

"Hey, baby girl," I coo as I close the door behind me. Leia stands from her regular spot on the back of the couch, yawning and stretching like she worked a ten-hour shift. I don't have to worry about feeding her, because I splurged on an automatic feeder when my first check from 4Play hit my checking account. What can I say? I'm a good cat daddy. I scratch behind her ears before heading into the spare bedroom that serves as my recording studio.

I genuinely enjoy being Sky, and I know other people enjoy it, too. More than enjoy if the comments on the "Sky's Sluts" subreddit are anything to go by. AshBash69 commented that I helped her conceive, which is both cool and bizarre as hell.

I sit at my desk and open my current script, an intimate scenario in which I comfort my wife—the listener—after a bad day with light choking, fingering…the stuff that makes my Sluts feral.

I should probably mention they came up with "Sky's Sluts" on their own. I had nothing to do with it, but I use it out of respect for their chosen fandom name. Sky is completely anonymous and offline, with no social media presence or identifying information in order to protect myself and my job.

I stretch my neck and take a sip of water before turning the mic on. As I record, I let go of the man who feels the need to please everyone, and become the man who actually does.

Chapter 2

Audrey

Playlist: Skin and Bones | Cage the Elephant

Sky's Sluts

RebelLady93: omfggggg i just finished listening. Y'all aint ready, he's hotter than normal.

MeetMeInStarsHollow: every time i think this man can't record something hotter, he proves me wrong.

AshBash69: GUYS. GUYS IT HAS THE GOOD GIRL TAG. AND CHOKING.

SkysMainSlut: thank GOD. last week he was subby which is fine but dominant sky is where it's at.

MeetMeInStarsHollow: omgggg not the husband tag i'm gonna die.

MeetMeInStarsHollow: okay i gotta take a listen before i get out of bed. i'll report back later, sluts <saluting emoji>

"You like my hand on your throat and my fingers in your pussy?" he groans into my ear.

I dig my teeth into my lower lip as my back arches, climbing higher and higher toward my release.

"Uh, uh." His chuckle is dark and deep. "Use your words. Do you like my hand on your throat and my fingers deep in your cunt?"

"Mmhmm," I manage to whimper. I'm so close, I'm right on the edge, right on the precipice between heaven and earth. I thrust my hips and turn my head, biting my pillow between my teeth to keep myself quiet.

"I know, baby. I know. Be a good girl and come for me," he coos, triggering my orgasm. I come hard and fast, like I'm falling from the peak I'd been teetering on before. No wonder the French call it the little death—this freefall truly might kill me.

"Good girl, such a good girl when you come for me." His voice is breathy and husky. "God, I could watch you come forever. The way you clench around my fingers is fucking heaven."

I inhale shakily as I come down from my high, and the sensation is too much. I fumble with my clit-sucking vibrator and turn it off.

"I love you," he says, quiet and low, and for a fleeting moment, I let myself believe it. "I always want to take care of you like this."

Then silence, the way it always ends, and I sit up, taking my noise-canceling headphones off and grabbing my phone from my nightstand.

Tuesday is my favorite day of the week, because I always wake up to a brand new audio from my favorite 4Play creator, Sky.

His newest one that dropped today was hot as hell, though to be honest, he could upload a recording of him reading the dictionary and I'd be able to get myself off to it. This one, however, was a scenario where Sky was the listener's husband

and he comforted me after a hard day. There was body worship, light choking, hard fingering...it was a good time.

I force myself out of bed and shrug into my marine blue bathrobe before going to the ensuite bathroom to brush my teeth and do my morning skincare routine.

When I enter the kitchen, Piper, my newly fifteen-year-old daughter, is already at the table, eyes glued to her iPad and a bowl of Reese's Puffs in front of her.

"Morning, Pipe." I lean down and kiss the crown of her head before playfully ruffling her hair.

She squawks and shoves my hand away. "Mom! It took me thirty minutes to get my bangs to look like this!"

"I'm sorry." My apology is genuine. My parents never apologized when I was growing up, and it was something I promised Piper and myself she'd always get when needed. "It looks great, birdie."

"Thanks." Her eyes are on her iPad as she takes another bite of cereal.

I wrap my robe tighter around myself and walk to the coffee maker, scooping in my favorite French roast and pressing the button to brew, the same way I do every morning.

"Do you need a ride to school?" I ask, eyes on the coffee's slow drip into the glass pot.

"No." Her voice is muffled from her mouthful of Reese's Puffs. "I'm riding my bike."

"Sounds good. Don't forget to text me when you get there."

Piper groans and rolls her eyes the same way I did at her age, because fifteen is simply too old for your parents to still worry. "Mo-om." She stretches the word to two syllables, the same way I did.

"Hey, I try to be the cool mom. I don't check your location, but I need you to do your part, too."

She sighs heavily. "*Fine*."

"Thank you." When I was a teenager, I rebelled against my parents to get the attention I never got from them. The only time they paid any attention to me was when I had done something bad enough to warrant their discipline. It started with little stuff, like staying out past curfew, but my attempts became more extreme over time. This is why it's important to me that Piper knows she always has my attention, and I'm never too busy for her. I make it a point to talk to her before school, even if I worked late the night before. Not only to keep her out of trouble, but because I genuinely like the kid, and she deserves a mom who gives her all.

"Don't forget you have OT after school!" I remind her as she pushes her chair backward, the legs making a scraping noise against the linoleum floor. Piper's been in occupational therapy for the past decade or so, learning how to exist in a world that wasn't made for brains like hers. She's learned coping skills, has a sensory menu, has improved communication, and has increased her confidence when it comes to stimming or and her other autistic traits.

I turn off the coffee maker and pour it into a mug decorated with disproportionate, lopsided butterflies Piper painted in second grade.

It's my favorite.

"I know." She exhales a long-suffering sigh. "I'm riding to the office after my meeting with Ms. Santiago."

I turn to her after stirring in cream and sugar, brow furrowed. "Why do you have a meeting with Ms. Santiago?" I have yet to meet Piper's beloved music teacher, Ms. Santiago, mainly because I graduated high school with her husband and I prefer to keep that part of my life locked away in a box.

After my parents kicked me out, my great-aunt Olivia took me in. She was the exact opposite of her sister, my late grandmother, in all the best ways. I lived with her and worked at the inn for three years, until she encouraged me to move out of town to find my own way. I packed up Piper and her things and moved into a shady two-bedroom apartment in Norwalk. It was far enough away I could escape from my past, but could still frequently see Aunt Olivia. She paid for Piper's childcare, and once she was in kindergarten, insisted on paying for me to take classes at the community college.

When Aunt Olivia got sick two years ago, against her insistence we stay where we were, Piper and I moved back into that little cottage so I could be her primary caregiver and take over her work at the inn. I dyed my naturally blonde hair auburn to blend in, and was surprised at how well it worked, how almost nobody recognized or remembered me. Once, I made eye contact with my former best friend's dad over the produce at Stop & Shop, but by the time he did a double take, I was speed walking towards the deli. When Piper was born, I'd refused to give her my parents' last name. Her dad was never involved, so we took Aunt Olivia's last name instead. The Hinton name is one of love.

It's also generic enough that Piper isn't immediately associated with me. If someone hears or sees my name, they don't know it's Audrey Price, the "town whore who got herself knocked up," as my parents lovingly referred to me.

"She wants to talk about summer plans," Piper says breezily, putting her backpack on.

"What summer plans?"

"Exactly. She wants to make plans so I practice consistently and don't lose my skills."

Ever since Aunt Olivia gifted Piper a toy piano for her first birthday, she's happiest when her fingers are dancing across the keys. I surprised her with a baby grand piano for the inn lobby last year, and despite never being able to afford formal lessons, she loves wowing the out-of-towners who frequent Port Haven in the summer. She's self-taught, and has big dreams of being a concert pianist. I wish I were able to provide more toward this dream, but the funds have never quite been there. She's never complained, but I think I'll always want her to have more.

I smile and bring my coffee to my mouth. "Sounds good, let me know what she says."

"Yep." My daughter puts a pair of yellow earplugs into her ears. They're protective enough that she won't get overstimulated by noise on her ride, but not so noise-blocking that she can't hear what she needs to while on the road.

Piper was diagnosed with autism a few weeks after her third birthday. It was a hard diagnosis to navigate, with so much conflicting information, but after fifteen years, we've hit our stride. She has a routine that works for her, and occupational therapy has helped her learn ways to come with the discomfort that comes with existing. Insurance didn't cover OT, but after researching different options, I knew that was the best fit for our family. Aunt Olivia insisted on paying, and I'll always be grateful for her generosity.

She passed away two years ago, and I was shocked to discover she'd left me the inn and most of her money, except for the money set aside for Piper. I knew I had to do something to revive the inn and make it a success beyond the summer months.

I put everything into transforming Port Haven Inn into SandPiper Inn, expanding it and creating space for events. Aunt Olivia would have loved the inn in its current state. Her fingerprints are everywhere.

"Piper Elise, don't forget to wear your helmet!" I know my daughter, and I know she has sensory issues with the chin strap that she's learned to cope with. I know even better she'll try to get away with not wearing a helmet on days she styles her hair.

"Mo-om!" she whines from the entryway.

"Pi-per!" I whine back. "It won't matter how good your hair looks if your skull gets crushed in!"

She grumbles, but I still hear the quiet snap of the chin strap's buckle.

"I love you!"

"You're so annoying!" my beloved daughter responds.

"I know, birdie. Don't forget to text me when you get to school."

She continues to grumble under her breath, and honestly? I don't care. I'm simply grateful she knows she's safe enough to be unhappy. That she's safe to grumble and stim and complain and be a teenager.

"I love you!" I call, knowing she won't respond.

She doesn't, and the screen door closes with a slam behind her. I smile softly and lift my mug to my lips. Piper loves me, but shows it in her own way, like agreeing to wear her helmet and putting her bowl in the dishwasher instead of the sink.

When I finish my coffee, my mug joins Piper's bowl in the dishwasher, and I hop in the shower to get ready for the day. An hour later, I'm wearing my favorite khaki linen pants and a kelly green mock neck sleeveless top with flats. I put on the heart necklace Piper saved her babysitting money to get me for my birthday last year and a pair of Aunt Olivia's earrings. I pull my hair back with a claw clip and quickly apply concealer, blush, lipstick, and mascara to complete the look. On the days I don't do my makeup, a local elderly couple always stops in and the man will *always* make a comment about how tired I look. I'm never in the mood for that. A win for the patriarchy. I guess.

Before work is my weekly therapy session with Eva. Eva's an older white woman with gray hair and brown sparkling eyes that get me to spill every secret. Tuesdays are the best days for my mental health: new 4Play drops *and* therapy.

"Good morning, Audrey," Eva greets when the video call connects. "How are you?"

"Great!" I say way too quickly. Dammit.

Eva raises a brow. "Not good, huh? What's going on?"

I shrug. "Life. Existence. Parenthood."

"Ah, the big three." She smiles softly at me. "How are you coping with the heavy weight of life, existence, and parenthood?"

Lying to her is useless. Eva's been seeing me since I was a severely depressed teenager with a screaming three-month-old in the waiting room. I still remember our first session so clearly; I tried to convince her, and myself, I didn't need to be there, that I wasn't depressed and that I was taking care of myself and Piper just fine.

I wasn't. I'd been getting two hours of sleep and passive suicidal thoughts were constantly in my brain. She saw through me, and sat quietly while I insisted I was fine until I finally broke down into heaving sobs. I admitted for the first time how hard it was, how afraid of my feelings I was, how I loved Piper but I felt like I loved her the way my parents "loved" me, and the idea of continuing that cycle devastated me.

"Sleeping a lot," I admit to Eva, who nods understandingly. "But I'm still making it to work and taking care of Piper."

"How are you taking care of yourself?" she asks, and I grimace.

"I don't know that I am," I admit.

"That makes sense. You're giving so much to others that there's not anything left for yourself. How do you think it will hurt you, Audrey? How will it hurt Piper?"

Damn this woman. She pulled out the big guns by mentioning Piper, and she knows it.

"Try to take some time to focus on yourself. Why don't you go out with your friends?" Eva asks innocently, and I fight the urge to roll my eyes.

"You know I don't have friends." I haven't had friends since B.P.—before Piper.

"Why don't you make friends?" I stifle a groan. I do like people, which makes running the inn a good career choice. But the people I interact with are either my employees or my guests. I love my employees, but the idea of hanging out with them outside of work and work events feels like crossing a line.

"I mean, I really don't want to make friends with people in Port Haven," I say, realizing how true this is. "It's too small, and most people my age...well. They've already made their decision about me."

"Sounds like a conundrum," Eva says, tapping her pen against her chin. "Let's circle back to that and we'll brainstorm ideas. Besides sleeping, how else is your depression manifesting?"

I reluctantly tell her about how exhausting showering is, how cooking, my favorite hobby that usually energizes me, has been stressful and draining. How my bedroom is filled with dirty dishes, food wrappers, cups, and dirty clothes. We discuss baby steps for me to take, and Eva doesn't bring up the friends thing again, thank god.

"Don't think I forgot about you making friends," Eva says at the end of our session. I internally groan. Goddammit. "But," she continues, "we need to get you to a healthy baseline before we add more goals. You're going to be okay, Audrey. And once you're okay again, we'll work on getting you to happy."

"You're going to cure my depression?" I tease.

"I would if I could," she answers earnestly. "But the best I can do is help you find the things that make you happy, the things that make you want to feel better."

God, even that feels unattainable.

Chapter 3

Ren

Playlist: mirrorball | Taylor Swift

Quiblings group chat

Leo

reeeeennnnnnnnnn

Leo

mom's complaining you didn't stop by on wednesday like you usually do.

Leo

stop being such an overachiever and making the rest of us look bad.

Nic

you know what? hell yeah. sunday dinner when you can make it should be enough to make her happy, but nooooo you and kat have to be perfect, local children without boundaries who will do anything for our parents so when we can't it makes us look like assholes.

Kat

sorry for being a good daughter <eyeroll emoji> millie sure isn't going to come through for them, and if ren can't, who's going to? me.

Millie

get fucked. <middle finger emoji>

Kat

sucks being name dropped for no reason, doesn't it?

Nic

trust me, there's a reason.

Jo

how the hell do you people still sound loud in text messages?

Nic

hey! noise complaints are my thing.

Alex

she's right, it's 4am in la and you woke me up with your incessant yapping.

Leo

listen i didn't mean to start a whole thing. I just need you to know i'm home for the summer and if she sighs and stares wistfully out the window saying, "ren is such a good boy" whenever i tell her i'm busy and can't do something for her, i'm going to lose it.

Izzy

and if he's in jail, our twinny connection is going to fritz and i'll lose it, too.

Ren

sorry. i'll talk to her about not comparing us.

Leo

no don't do THAT.

Leo

then she'll know i'm a snitch.

Alex

what's he supposed to do?

Leo

stop being goddamn PERFECT.

Read by Ren

I open the door to Port of Call, the local bar, and am immediately enveloped in the smell of sweat, booze, and deep-fried something. In other words, a perfect recipe for celebrating the last day of school.

When I graduated high school, my dad took me to Ireland, and he ordered me a Guinness. He called it my first "Irish Legal Drink," and I gagged at my first sip while he laughed at me. On my twenty-first birthday, he took me to Port of Call and bought me another pint of Guinness, smirking as he handed it to me. I know he expected me to choke my way through it, and it was the most satisfying thing to watch the smile slide off his face when I drank it effortlessly.

I think about that every time I come into Port Alcohol—as it's known among the locals—how my dad somehow thought I hadn't been drinking in college.

Teachers are scattered in clusters at tables throughout the bar, but I grab a barstool and order a Guinness like I always do. The end of the school year is bittersweet, filled with contrasting emotions of relief and sadness. I love my job, even though it isn't what I always wanted to do.

When I started college, I planned to major in piano performance, but halfway through my first semester, a classmate mentioned they were double majoring in music education and performance. On a whim, I decided to as well, since I'd enjoyed teaching piano lessons during the summer. Learning about music education was illuminating, and I wanted to create the same magic it felt like my own teachers did when I was a kid.

Now I get to bring students joy through music and be a safe person for them. Of course, it's not always magical or fulfilling. There are the days a student throws up while playing a recorder, or one mentions something about their home life that prompts mandated reporting.

There's also the occasional mom who thinks her flirting is subtle. It never is.

It's always overt and obvious and makes me uncomfortable. Comments like, "the things I'd do if I had you for a night," make it clear they want quick and casual, but I found out the hard way that sex without love isn't something I can do. I'm demisexual, and I need an emotional connection to be attracted to someone, and a deep, meaningful relationship is necessary for me to enjoy sex with a partner.

My last sexual relationship was last year with Taylor, a former fourth grade teacher at the school. While I thought it was more than that, it was casual for her, because we never clarified our expectations. When we realized we wanted different things, it ended. My heart was broken, and I was a mess. I refuse to get into that kind of relationship again because I know it'll hurt me. Besides, it's not like I'm lonely or need a relationship. I have my family, my cat, my friends, and my best friend since middle school, Will, who moved home recently.

"Renny!" I glance up in time to see my friend, Jocelynn, wrapping me in a hug. She's the classmate who convinced me to double major, and we've been friends ever since. Ever since we both ended up in the Port Haven school system, we always meet for celebratory drinks after the last day of school.

"Jossy!" I say teasingly, hugging her back. "It's been too damn long." In addition to being the high school band director, Jocelynn actually uses her performance degree by moonlighting as a concert pianist. If she's not at school, she's playing a show, even more so during the summer. I saw her play at Carnegie Hall last year, and I'm not too proud to admit I sobbed watching her performance.

"*Way* too long," she agrees, stepping away and looking me up and down. "Did you get taller? Do you have a girlfriend yet?"

I roll my eyes. "Okay, Nonna. No, I don't have a girlfriend."

She grins and hops onto a barstool. "Did you hear who's pregnant?"

My eyes widen, and I lean further in. This is one of my favorite things about Jocelynn, she knows *all* of the good town gossip. The things she's told me further solidify my rule to not date a student's parent. "No, who?"

"Me!" she shrieks.

"Oh! Wow! And that's good?" I say awkwardly, reeling from the noise.

"I can't get pregnant unless I spend thousands of dollars, so yeah, it's a good thing." She playfully pokes at my bicep.

Warren, Jocelyn's husband, was in Kat's class at Port Haven High School. He came out as transgender their junior year of high school, which caused quite the scandal. He went on to go to medical school and suddenly everyone loves him and genders him correctly. I wish every trans person in town got the respect Warren does. I've had to fight with parents and the principal about referring to my students by their correct pronouns and names.

"Right," I say sheepishly, rubbing at where she poked me. "Congratulations! That's amazing!"

She beams up at me. "Thank you, Warren and I are thrilled. He's so excited to be a dad."

There's a strange sinking feeling in my chest. When Taylor and I had been...well, whatever the hell we were, I'd pictured a life with her. A life where we got married and had kids, and I thought that life was within reach. I know there's plenty of time for me to be a dad and start a family, but it feels like I'm still grieving the life that never existed anywhere but my mind. As a result, it's always weird when someone mentions fatherhood.

"He's going to be a great dad," I tell her earnestly. "When are you due?"

She absentmindedly rubs circles on her belly. She's not showing yet, but she already looks maternal. It's adorable. "I'm twelve weeks along, so baby Santiago-Conley will make their grand entrance around December 22nd. Could be a Christmas baby, isn't that wild?"

"Wild," I agree. "I'm so happy for you and Warren, Joss. This is such great news."

She smiles at her belly. "Thanks, we're thrilled. I've already talked to my principal and with the timing, they've offered to have the assistant band director step up so I can take the entire semester off. I'm not gonna lie, it's tempting."

"You should do it," I encourage.

"Honestly, we'd be fine financially if I don't work a semester."

I don't tell her, but I'm also at a point in my career with 4Play where, if I wanted to, I could stop teaching and still live comfortably.

I don't want to, however, and I can't see her stopping completely, but I think a break would be good for her, which is what I tell her.

"Yeah... but enough about me. When do you start private lessons?"

Barry, the bartender, brings me my Guinness and takes Jocelynn's order. I take a sip before answering. "I'm not doing lessons this summer."

I feel Jocelynn's eyes boring holes into the side of my head. "Yes, you are."

I lower the bottle and raise a brow. "Um, no I'm not?"

"Yes, you are because I told a student you'd be taking her on this summer when I leave!" she throws her hands up in apparent exasperation.

I freeze mid-sip. "Why would you tell a student that?"

"Because I assumed you'd say yes!" She throws her hands in the air again. At this point, she should keep her hands up there. "You always say yes!"

I do. It's a fatal flaw that has led to burnout and more than one depressive episode.

"Wait, what do you mean, when you leave?" I ask in confusion.

"I'm auditioning for philharmonics full-time this summer! And I only felt comfortable leaving her knowing you'd take her on..."

"But you *didn't* know I'd take her on. You *assumed* I'd take her on. That's not the same thing."

"Tomato, tomahto. Please, Ren. Just this one student. She's really special, and I think you two would work together even better than she and I do. She's a rising sophomore and unbelievably talented and dedicated to the craft." She bats her eyelashes and pouts as she clasps her hands beneath her chin. "Pleeeeeeease? For me?"

I want to say no. I don't want to teach lessons, but I always have a hard time saying no to my people. My therapist calls it people-pleasing; I call it peace-keeping. People-keeping, even. If I say yes, if I put my head down and do what's asked of me, I won't disappoint anyone.

"She's autistic," Jocelyn hurriedly continues. "And music is her *thing*, you know? She calls it her special interest. She needs someone who validates and encourages her but also pushes her to her full potential. I think that's you."

Shit. Jocelyn doesn't know my older sister, Nic, was diagnosed with autism last year, so this hits close to home.

I'm imagining my sister as a high schooler: cranky, freckle-faced, and curly-haired. She told me it never felt like she quite belonged in the world, like if she were a robot, she was missing a mechanism that everyone else had.

I wish someone had believed in her the way she deserved before she was in her late twenties.

I sigh. "When is it?"

Jocelynn squeals and claps excitedly. "You're the best! I told her she deserved a two week break, as long as she practices consistently, so you're scheduled Saturday the twenty-fifth at ten a.m."

I pull out my phone and open my calendar, making sure it won't double book me. "Where?"

"The SandPiper Inn."

I look at her blankly. "Where's that?"

"It's the inn on the other end of the seawall."

My brows raise. "I thought that place closed."

"Nope. Piper's mom owns it, and Piper uses the baby grand in the lobby. That's her name, by the way. Piper. And she's great—funny and sarcastic as hell. You're gonna love her."

I frantically type in the information as she gives it to me. Piper, rising sophomore, autistic, adult owns the inn I didn't know existed.

"Did you talk to her adult about payment?" I ask, eyes on my phone.

Jocelynn snickers. "You're such an elementary teacher. Her *adult*. She lives with her mom, and I did tell her to tell her *adult* to expect that discussion with you. But I'm sure Ms. Hinton won't give you any trouble."

"I can't promise the whole summer." My therapist made me promise to set better boundaries, to pay attention to what will energize and make my life better, versus what I'm pressured to do to make other people happy. "But I'll meet with her on the twenty-fifth, and we'll go from there."

"You're the best." Jocelyn leans forward and squeezes my forearm. "Next Guinness is on me."

And there it is. That warm, fuzzy feeling whenever I know I've made someone happy, made things better.

My therapist is going to be pissed.

Chapter 4

Audrey

Playlist: Peach Fuzz | Caamp

"Don't forget about my piano lesson later," Piper says as we're eating breakfast one Saturday morning.

I peer up from the Port Haven Herald crossword puzzle I'm working on. "Huh?"

"My piano lesson." She says it slowly, enunciating each syllable, like the concept of a piano lesson is what's confusing me. It's not. What's confusing is I have no memory of her telling me about a piano lesson. Or I've forgotten to remember. "When someone teaches me technique to help me play better."

"Thank you, smartass." I roll my eyes. "When did you tell me about this lesson?"

"On the last day of school," she tells me through a mouthful of Reese's Puffs. "I swear I told you, Mom—I even put it on the shared calendar."

I pull my phone out, groaning when I see she did indeed put a piano lesson at 10 a.m. on our shared calendar. "I'm so sorry, birdie. I must've forgotten with the events getting canceled."

Last weekend, the inn hosted a bachelorette weekend that ended with both brides pulling a Julia Roberts. I received a call this week telling me the upcoming wedding, which was also supposed to take place here, was canceled. I've been stressed about vendors, and figuring out how we're going to make up the money. I told Piper the brides canceled, but haven't told her about my money anxieties.

"Mom?" Piper waves her spoon in front of my face, flicking drops of milk onto my lenses. "Earth to Mo-om."

I blink, startled, but force a smile. "Of course. Yes. I want to get a few chores done today, is it okay if I pop in toward the end of the lesson?" I take my glasses off and clean them with my robe, mind running wild.

"You're going to let me hang out alone with a stranger neither of us have ever met before?"

Shit.

"Right," I mutter, a headache coming on. I put my glasses back on before roughly rubbing my temples. "That's...right. An obvious thing I should not do."

"I mean. There's gonna be people in the lobby, and I know I can bother the front desk staff if I feel uncomfy."

"That should be fine," I agree, wrestling with the guilt rising in my belly. I make sure she knows she overrides everything else, because my parents never did. I won't allow my daughter to know anything other than a parent who loves her and puts her above any optics. "Sounds like you have a cool as shit mom who ingrained that in you."

"Try annoying as shit," my precious daughter mutters. She gets to her feet, gathering her bowl and spoon. "I'm going to head over to fuck around on the piano."

"Sounds good." I take a sip of coffee and as she puts the dishes in the dishwasher, I have a thought. I hurriedly swallow, the hot liquid scorching my throat. "Wait, maybe don't say fuck in front of your new teacher. At least on the first day. I don't want another repeat of the conversation I had to have with Mx

Asher." I look at her pointedly, reminding her of the call I'd gotten from her English teacher right before Thanksgiving.

"Holden Caulfield *is* fucking obnoxious, though!" she whines.

"You're absolutely right. But keep in mind some adults find teenagers cursing to be fucking obnoxious. And remember your poor mom has enough going on." I stick out my lower lip, giving her a pathetic puppy dog pout.

"I'll do my best," she grumbles, shuffling toward the front door. "No promises I'll be perfect."

"Love you, birdie."

"Yeah, yeah, yeah. I love you, too. Doesn't mean you're not annoying, though."

I chuckle as the door closes behind her, and pick up my phone from the table. I have time to kill, and I decide to make the most of it with self-care with my favorite guy. I know exactly what audio I want, the one he posted around Christmas that's childhood friends to lovers with soft, slow missionary under the glow of the lights on the tree.

Either that one, or the one he posted last month with impact play and degradation.

I contain multitudes.

When I open 4Play, I'm surprised to see a brand new audio from Sky. He does this sometimes, surprise drops an audio. I scan the tags: mutual masturbation, roommates, dirty talk, consent checks, praise...

I'm pulling my robe off and heading to my room before I even finish reading, or before starting a load of laundry.

When I get to the inn, I hear them before I see them. It's a beautiful day, the sunshine brightening the dark wood of the furniture through the bay windows. Most guests are at the beach, so the lobby is relatively empty except for my staff, Piper and the man sitting next to her.

She's playing a piece I'm unfamiliar with, and I can tell he's paying close attention to her, taking her seriously. It makes my heart swell. Since Piper's autism diagnosis, I've seen people handle her like she's fragile. My Piper is anything but fragile. Her autism doesn't make her any more breakable than anyone else. This seems to be a common misconception, even among caregivers and professionals.

I'm brought back to the present by piano keys clanging loudly.

"I *suck*," Piper groans, loud enough for one of my managers to glance up from the front desk.

"You don't suck," the man next to her reassures. "You're better than I was at your age, and you're learning and doing your best. That's the opposite of sucking."

I grin, pleased at how he's interacting with her, how he's treating her.

"I don't want to learn," Piper whines. "I want to *know*."

The man laughs, a bright, bold sound that warms me from the inside out. This laugh feels familiar, comforting, like a hot shower after a hard day at work. Like hot chocolate and your favorite blanket after being out in the snow. "Don't we all? Knowing is constantly learning, so you're on the right track."

My daughter groans again and rests her forehead on the piano keys, the random combination of notes echoing in the lobby. "God, you're *such* a teacher."

There's that laugh again, and this time, I'm disconcerted how safe this stranger's laugh feels. How if this stranger laughed during a conversation with me, I'd tell him my deepest darkest secrets. Hell, maybe I'd even give him a set of keys to the cottage.

Piper turns her head, eyes meeting mine. Her face lights up, and she waves. "Mom!"

The man next to her looks over his shoulder and oh my god, he has the most beautiful green eyes I've ever seen. Fair skin with faint freckles across the bridge of his nose and dark wavy hair that's falling into his eyes. Not only does he *sound* safe, he *looks* safe. Hot as hell, too. He's the generically attractive man I picture when listening to Sky.

I avert my eyes, attempting to avoid his gaze, but I can feel his eyes on me as I straighten my back and stride fearlessly across the lobby.

At least, I hope it appears fearless. I do not feel fearless.

"Hi, birdie," I say, eyes fixed on the carpet. When the hell was the last time we had this cleaned?

"Audrey?" My neck snaps up at the sound of a deep. My eyes meet Piper's new teacher's. He's gazing at me like I'm a surprise, but not an unpleasant one.

"Audrey Price?" He repeats my name—my *old* name—and it feels like I've been doused with ice water. I stumble backward. He knows me.

"Who the hell are you?" I demand, probably with more intensity than is necessary.

His face falls, and I almost feel bad, but the hard work I've done to protect Piper and me is being unraveled by this... this... this pretty white boy.

"You don't recognize me?" he asks, and I manage to shake my head no. "I mean... yeah. That makes sense. It's been a long time. His eyes go to Piper. "Fifteen years, I think."

"Are you my *dad*?" Piper asks, eyes wide.

"No!" he and I exclaim at the same time.

His eyes meet mine again. "No...I'm Ren."

I blink at him. "Ren."

"Yeah. Ren Quinn."

Ren Quinn? Who the hell is Ren—

I reel back as the realization hits me like a wave when you're facing the shore. I'm forced under the surface, lungs filling with salt water as my body's tossed around.

"No," I say simply, shaking my head. "No."

The Quinns were like family when I was a teenager. Mr. and Mrs. Quinn remembered and celebrated my sixteenth birthday when my parents forgot. I spent every moment I could at their house. They had eight kids so there was no lack of shouting, love, laughter...

Oh, god. The laughter.

For a long time, I'd wanted a family like theirs. I'd find someone who loved me as much as the Quinn adults loved each other and have... well, maybe not eight kids. But enough kids that our home was always *loud*.

He blinks at me. "No?"

"No," I repeat, forcing myself back into the present. "You are not Kat's annoying little brother. No."

His cheeks flush, and I want to scream because god *dammit* how did I not immediately recognize him as a Quinn? He literally looks like the image that would come out if you put pictures of his parents into an AI generator thing, but without the questionable ethics. His mom's dark, wavy hair and strong nose. His dad's freckles and eye color. Kat's lips...

"Oh, *god*," I say, taking a step back. "You *are*. You need to leave."

"*Mom*," Piper hisses.

Ren continues to stare at me, all evidence of his smile gone. I feel like I'm too big for my body, somehow. Like my skin is too tight and is stretching beyond its limits to accommodate me.

"I can leave, that's fine," he finally responds, his voice even and the exact opposite of my shaking vocals. It's disconcerting how unphased he seems to be at seeing me. He's a ghost from my past, one of those bad, scary ones, and he has no idea.

"No, wait!" Piper's on her feet, frantically looking between the two of us. "He doesn't have to actually leave, right, Mom?" Her eyes are pleading, desperate, *sad*. My god, I'm embodying *my* parents. Foregoing my child's joy and wants for selfish reasons.

"No, no, I'm sorry," I stammer, trying to save this. "I meant *I* have to leave. I have a thing today." I'm lying out of my ass, of course. The only "thing" on the calendar for today is laundry and this lesson. I spin on my heel, trying to convince myself I'm imagining the disappointment on both of their faces.

"Mom?" Piper's voice echoes through the cottage a few hours after I fled the scene of the crime.

"In here," I answer feebly.

Her lesson ended two hours ago, and she's just now getting home. I didn't even bother looking at her location—I knew she was going to need space, and honestly, I didn't have the energy to care *where* said space would be taken.

I burrow deeper into my blankets. Fuck, I'm a bad mom.

I sense Piper in the doorway before I hear her. That mother's intuition people talk about? Turns out it's not complete bullshit.

Piper walks across the room, and slowly peels back the covers, the same way she has since she was tall enough to do so. The same way she has every time I've hidden from the world.

"Hi," I whisper, closing my eyes to avoid the inevitable anger I know she's feeling.

She has every right to be pissed at me. I was a *mess*.

"Mama, are you okay?" I open my eyes, surprised when her face is filled with concern instead of the anger I'd expected.

"Would you believe me if I said yes?"

The corner of her mouth tips upward. "Hell no."

I sigh and scooch backwards, lifting the blanket with my arm. "Want to come in?" I ask, the same way I have since she was little. It's been a while, though.

She hesitates for a moment, but then she's nodding her head yes and climbing into bed next to me. She snuggles into me, and I kiss the top of her head, fighting the urge to roll my eyes. Her hair smells like coconut, meaning she's been stealing my good shampoo. Again.

"Mr. Q gave me a three hour lesson." Piper's voice is barely audible.

I blink, surprised. "That was nice."

Piper sighs heavily. "He said he wouldn't be able to continue teaching me, so he wanted to give me extra time..."

"He said *what*?" I gasp, lifting my head to stare at her. She reminds me so much of myself when I was her age, both in physicality and personality. My hair and eyes, my stubbornness and disdain for humanity at large. "Why would he say that?"

She stares at me, her expression saying, *Really, Mom? Why do you think?* I sigh and comb my fingers through her hair. "Is it because I demanded he leave and pretended I didn't?"

"*Obviously*. You were weird, and he was uncomfortable after that and told me he didn't think you'd want him teaching me. I came home to yell at you, but you're hiding, so I think you're punishing yourself enough already. Why do you hate him?"

"I don't hate him. I don't *know* him. I *knew* his family before you..." I start to explain.

"Were they mean to you when you were pregnant?" Piper asks gently. Damn, this girl knows me too well.

I sigh. "His older sister was my best friend when I was your age, but she and her family were Catholic and... and they didn't go out of their way to associate with me." I don't tell her how much the Quinn family had meant to me. How much their absence hurt when I was pregnant. How I'd hoped and wished and prayed they'd reach out and check in on me. How long it took me to realize that wasn't happening. How much it hurt that the love they showed me was conditional, just like everyone else.

"Assholes," Piper grumbles, snuggling closer into me. "I don't want to take lessons from his slut-shaming ass anyway."

"I mean... he's like six years younger than me, so there's not a lot to blame him for. He was a kid. It's just... weird to see him again."

"Wait," Piper lifts her head and narrows her eyes at me. "The Quinns? As in Jo?"

"Yeah. Jo's his older sister." I'd heard through the grapevine Jo came out as a lesbian a few years after Piper was born. When I got the email from Jo this spring and realized she wanted to use the inn for the now-canceled wedding events she was planning... it felt like there was a mutual, unspoken understanding between the two of us. We both knew what it was like to be ostracized by this town. "They were kids."

"Like you, Mama. You were a kid, too."

"Yeah, I was," I agree, trying to swallow the lump in my throat.

It's disorienting being a parent and remembering how the adults in my life treated me when I was expecting Piper. The lack of love and care—I can't imagine not supporting Piper or *anyone* through what I had to go through alone. "But I don't want my feelings about his family getting in the way of your lessons. I was watching you two, it seems like you clicked."

"Yeah, he was challenging me on hand placement and was asking questions about things I hadn't thought about before. He's funny, too. He mentioned his sister's autistic when I told him I was, which made me feel better. And he doesn't see autism as a superpower or anything, but he asked what he could do to accommodate my sensory needs. We took breaks when I needed to, and he didn't mind when I put my earplugs in toward the end."

Images of the Quinn kids run through my head like movie credits. Which one of them is autistic? Though I know it's not my business, it makes me feel better to know Ren cares about and loves an autistic person in his own life.

"I think you should continue lessons with him," I say slowly, like if I say it slowly, I can take it back if I change my mind. "I think it'd be good for you."

"No. I choose you over piano lessons," Piper says decidedly, and I smile. She's so fiercely loyal, my sweet girl.

"But there doesn't *need* to be a choice. I'm an adult, and I just didn't expect to come face to face with my past."

Piper searches my face. "It's a small town," she says, and god, don't I know it. "You couldn't hide us forever."

"I know," I admit reluctantly.

"He didn't give me his information, but he mentioned he goes running on the beach most mornings. Like at five a.m."

I stifle a groan. "I'll email Ms. Santiago and see if she can give me his information." There's no way I'm getting up at five a.m. to accost him about my kid's piano lessons.

Chapter 5

Ren

Playlist: Doin' Time | Lana Del Ray

In. Out. In. Out. In. Out.

I keep my breath steady as my feet hit the sidewalk, my favorite classical playlist blaring in my ears. I can't stop thinking about the events of yesterday: helping my sister's ex try to win her back, finding out it worked, and seeing my childhood crush look at me like I was a threat.

Audrey Price. Or Hinton now, I guess. I hadn't thought about her in a *long* time, but god, she was the love of my young life, and her mere presence distracted me whenever I practiced scales on the piano in our living room.

I was *never* distracted while practicing scales. My siblings used to make fun of me, saying I could be struck by lightning and not miss a single note. Something about the rote movement and predictability of scales almost put me in a trance, similar to how running makes me feel.

I run the same route every day, at the same time, and so do most people who are awake and out at this time. I pass a group of the tamer moms, on their daily hot girl walk, as they call it, where they talk about whatever spicy romantasy book they're currently reading. I always wave to Mr. Moody as he walks Scooter, his rambunctious golden retriever puppy. I nod politely at Father Gilligan when I pass him on his rosary walk, and I greet Derek, a waiter at Queenie's, the diner in town, as he sweeps the outdoor stairs.

I immediately notice when someone I don't see every day is sitting on the seawall and slow to a stop. I also can't recognize this person from fifty feet away. As I walk closer, their head moves, and I think they're looking at me. Around ten feet away, the blurriness caused by not wearing my contacts clears, and I stop in my tracks as recognition sets in.

"Hi, Mr. Q." Audrey Price...I mean Hinton...is sitting criss-cross applesauce on the seawall, auburn hair piled on top of her head and a star-shaped pimple patch on her chin. She wears round, wireframe glasses, and a Port Haven High School t-shirt with shorts that show me the pale skin of her thighs, and the faint, silver, stretch marks painted across them.

I clear my throat. "Ms. Hinton, hi." Nailed it.

She uncrosses her legs and gets to her feet, not spilling a drop from either mug in her hands, but her glasses slip just slightly down her nose. "You... um. You can call me Audrey, if you'd like."

God, she'd scamper away if she could hear how hard my heart is beating. My vital organs have zero chill around pretty women. Or men. But this seems excessive, even for me. "I think it's more appropriate if I call you Ms. Hinton," I say. "Or Mrs. Hinton."

"I'm not married," she clarifies, and we fall into another awkward silence.

Yesterday had been awkward as shit. I'd been having a great lesson with Piper, quickly learning how to best critique her and give feedback in a way she would respond positively to. She waved to her mom and in walked Audrey, grown-up and fucking beautiful. Long legs and bouncy hair and bright smile, and it felt like my world was closing in around me.

Now, Audrey and I stare uncomfortably at each other, both waiting for the other to speak first.

It isn't going to be me.

Finally, she lifts one of the mugs she's holding. "I brought you coffee."

I blink at her in confusion. "Oh. Uh, thanks?"

"It's cold now."

We continue to stare at each other.

"This is weird," I tell her.

"Very," she agrees, holding out the mug to me. It has a T-Rex holding a grabber tool in each hand, the words "what now bitch" above the image, and dammit. It makes me chuckle.

Her silvery gray eyes brighten. "Funny, right? Mother's Day gift from Piper this year."

My heart flutters a smidge. That's cute as hell. I take the coffee from her, surprised when the mug is still slightly warm, probably from the sun beating down.

"I remembered you're lactose intolerant, so I used oat milk," Audrey continues.

How the hell did she remember I'm lactose intolerant? *I* don't remember I'm lactose intolerant most days.

I stare at her and lift the mug to my mouth. I'm drinking cold coffee with the woman my nine-year-old self was certain he was going to marry. After running ten miles. There really is a first time for everything.

"Do you wanna walk?" she asks, motioning her head towards the direction I was running in.

I nod, and we begin to move.

"I want to apologize for yesterday," she says after a few moments of silence. "I freaked out and probably freaked you out, and I'm sorry."

"So you decided to interrupt my run?" I try to say it teasingly, hell, maybe even flirtatiously, but she winces.

"I know it's probably another thing I should apologize for, but I'm impatient, and I couldn't sleep last night because I felt ashamed of how I'd acted and...I'm so sorry, Ren. Mr. Q. Whatever..."

I stop walking, but she doesn't notice and continues to walk. I watch in amusement as she continues to ramble about how bad she feels for about thirty seconds before realizing I'm no longer in step beside her. The stunned expression on her face as she turns around makes me laugh again. At my laughter, Audrey's face reddens, and she bites her lower lip. God, even prettier than I remembered.

She shuffles back to me, an exaggerated scowl on her face. "Wow, way to prove you're still the same dweeb you always were."

Way to prove I'm still wondering what your lips would feel like against mine.

If I were still a practicing Catholic, I'd need to go to confession and recite a few Hail Marys to be absolved of lusting over her.

"Sorry," I say. "But I think my weird behavior makes up for yours yesterday. You have to stop feeling guilty, or else I do too."

She blushes again, and I want to trace the color with my thumb. I want to find out if her skin heats when she blushes like that, if she'd lean into my palm and let me find out what else makes her blush. Where *else* she blushes.

"That's oddly sweet. I think," she says.

I shrug. "I'll take it."

She takes a deep breath, and averts her eyes to her mug. She's staring into the coffee like it holds the secrets of the universe. "I still want you to teach Piper. If... if you want to. I'll stay away and won't bother you again, but she was so happy during your lesson and I don't want to hold her back..."

"Parents are welcome to attend class whenever they want," I interrupt. "If any teacher tells you otherwise, that's shady as hell."

She bites her lip again, and I want to get to my knees and beg her not to do that if I don't get to bite it, too. "I just want you to know that if you don't want to interact with me, I completely understand. This is for Piper, and I'll do anything I can for that damn kid."

"If you're okay with it, I'm happy to continue teaching her, and you'll have an open invitation. I think Piper would appreciate that, too. She talks about you like you hung the moon. Kind of like how you talk about her."

She smiles into her coffee. "She's the best mistake I ever made. I can't even see it as a mistake anymore," she says softly. "She's too amazing."

I want to ask her more about what happened all those years ago, but I know that's too personal a question to ask. "She is," I agree instead. "She's talented as hell, too. I was shocked when she told me she'd never had any formal training."

She straightens her back and looks at me. "That's why I think this is important to do now. She wants to be a professional musician, and she wants guidance. How much do you charge per class?"

I stare at her. "No."

She blinks at me. She'd always been tall and elegant, and while her body is softer, fewer sharp angles and lines, she's still taller than any of my sisters. I'm six feet two, and she's probably around five feet ten. "What do you mean *no*?"

"Audrey, I can't charge you for piano lessons. You're *you*."

She averts her eyes. "That doesn't mean anything. How much is your regular rate?"

I wince and tell her my hourly rate. She doesn't answer and instead stares silently out at the water. On clear days, you can see Long Island across the sound. When we were kids, my siblings and I would always wave to our Nonna and Nonno, too young to understand they most definitely could not see us. We've stopped walking, and she's covered in the golds and oranges and pinks of the newly-risen sun.

"Oh," she finally says, fingers anxiously tapping the side of the mug.

It's a lot of money, I know this. But it's a pretty standard rate for a teacher of my expertise in the area.

"I don't want to charge you." She turns to me and opens her mouth to argue. I'm filled with the urge to kiss her to keep her from doing that, but speak over her instead.

"I wasn't going to teach classes this summer. I used to love it, but parents kind of suck, and they took the enjoyment I used to get from teaching kids one-on-one. But I really like Piper and want to work with her, and I don't think you'll make my existence miserable. If you promise to not tell anyone we're doing this so no one else asks me to do it, that's worth more than any payment."

"Are you sure?" she asks, voice barely louder than a whisper. "I don't want us to be a charity case."

"You wouldn't be. You'd be helping me more than I'd be helping you."

I can't help it. I watch her neck as she swallows. Fuck. It's a great neck. The perfect size to cup with my hand and...

"Thank you." I'm forced out of my horny stupor by her quiet thanks. "This is kind of you, much kinder than I deserve."

My stomach twists at her self-deprecating comment. Instead of arguing, I lift the mug to my lips again. Her eyes follow the movement, and it makes my cock twitch.

I need to *chill*.

"Is the coffee okay?"

It's gone cold. It's fine, but she doesn't need to know. "It's perfect," I assure her. "Thank you for making it."

She beams, her entire face brightening and back straightening. "It was the least I could do since I was interrupting your run."

"Can I have your number? So you don't have to go through the trouble of waking up early and bringing me coffee when we need to talk?" I'm damn anxious asking her this. We have a professional relationship, so it makes sense we'd have each other's numbers. But I still feel like a stuttering highschooler asking his crush to prom.

"Oh!" Audrey stops walking and pulls her phone out, holding it in front of her face to unlock it. "Why don't you send yourself a text?" she suggests, holding her phone out to me.

I freeze as our fingers brush, feeling like I touched a live wire instead of another human's hand.

Her breath hitches and eyes widen, and I want to ask if she felt it, too.

Instead, I type my number into her phone and text myself before handing it back. I avert my eyes as she puts it back, hoping to hide my feelings.

"I, um, I think I'm going to finish my cooldown," I say, staring over her shoulder.

"Ren." My head snaps up, and our eyes meet.

"Yeah?" I breathe, heart pounding harder in my chest than when I had been running.

"Thank you," she says. It feels like my soul is visible through my eyes, and she's searching it to see if I'm safe, if she can trust me.

"You're welcome," I say earnestly. "I'm happy to do it. And here, I can't steal your favorite mug."

She smiles softly, taking the mug from me before walking towards the inn.

My heart is caught in my throat, like it's blocking breath and intelligent words. I don't experience this heavy lust often, if ever. I felt it for Taylor after we were together for a while and for a few friends turned friends with benefits. But there's something about Audrey's softness, her vulnerability, that has me wanting to chase after her and ask her to stay and continue walking with me.

But she still sees me as Kat's little brother, and I don't want to ever get close to a parent. So, I turn around and finish my cooldown. I don't turn my music back on, as my mind is occupied with soft smiles and auburn waves, stormy gray eyes and fidgeting hands.

Chapter 6

Audrey

Playlist: The Prophecy | Taylor Swift

July

Ren's been giving Piper piano lessons for three weeks. I know he told me to stop by, and he wouldn't ever ask me not to, but there was something about the way he looked at me when he gave me my mug back on the beach that made me hesitant to attend. Maybe it was the unexpected aching between my thighs.

I don't want to acknowledge the reality that making eye contact with my ex-best friend's younger brother makes me desperate for a touch I haven't received in over a decade. Desperate for a touch I've closed myself off from experiencing again.

I'm in my office at the inn early on a Monday, when an email arrives from Hunter Cleary. She and Jo Quinn—Ren's older sister—were vendors for the almost-wedding that was supposed to be hosted at the inn until it went to shit. Hunter emailed me two weeks ago to tell me she and Jo were opening an event planning firm in Port Haven. They'd been together for like two weeks. It was the most precious—and gayest— thing I'd ever seen.

I like Jo and Hunter, and I love their vision, so I offered office space for them at a discounted rate. We also discussed the inn being a featured, preferred vendor, which could be huge for business.

Ding.

I do a double take when I look at the computer screen and see another email in my inbox, one from Lorenzo Quinn.

From: Lorenzo Quinn <lorenzo.quinn@gmail.com>
To: Audrey Hinton <HintonA@sandpiperinn.com
Subject: Piper's progress and a few questions

Hi, Audrey. <smiley face emoji>

I found your email address on the inn's website. I hope it's okay to contact you this way.

I wanted to tell you I'm impressed by and proud of Piper's progress. I can tell she's dedicated and practicing frequently, and teaching her reminds me of why I love what I do.

I've noticed you haven't stopped by for any lessons, and was curious if I could do anything to make you more comfortable? I think it would mean a lot to Piper, and it would mean a lot to me, too.

Next month, there's a concert at Yale I think Piper would really enjoy. I don't want to tell her about it until I get your permission to take her, or if you would want you can tag along? I think

immersive experiences like that would be benefi-
cial for her.

I also want to offer additional lessons if Piper
wants, and again, check with you first before
telling her. I'm not sure if she told you, but she's
decided her goal for the summer is to master
"Clair de Lune." It's a complex piece, but I think
with her tenacity and dedication, she can do it.
It might be helpful to have a second lesson every
week for her to complete this goal (no charge, of
course).

Thanks for your time, and for letting me hang
out with your kid.

Lorenzo Quinn (he/him)

I feel a myriad of emotions as I read the email. Shame, because
he's right. I haven't stopped by. It's not that I'm uncomfortable
with him. It's just that...fuck. I don't want to face the past. I
don't want to risk being found out and having all my hard work
go to shit.

But, what if Piper thinks I'm staying away because of her?

I take a deep breath and hit reply.

From: Audrey Hinton <HintonA@sandpiperinn.com>
To: Lorenzo Quinn <Lorenzo.Quinn@gmail.com>
Subject: Re: Piper's progress and a few questions

~~Hi Ren,~~
~~Correct me if my memory's wrong, but didn't we~~
~~exchange phone numbers?~~

~~Ren,~~
~~Why did we exchange phone numbers if you~~
~~were just going to email me?~~

~~Mr. Q,~~
~~Haha I forgot your name was actually Lorenzo.~~
~~Does your mom still use it when you're in trou-~~
~~ble?~~

I groan and close my mailbox before putting my head in my hands. Why can't I be normal with this man? It's just a little crush.

"Mom?" I jump when I see Piper in the doorway. Shit, she was supposed to be babysitting today.

"Hey, birdie," I say shakily, glancing towards the clock. "You're home early."

She flops into the chair on the other side of my desk. "Got bored and left the kids to take care of each other." She says it so casually and naturally that if she didn't say the same thing after every babysitting gig, I might actually think she left the kids alone.

"Teaches them responsibility. Good work." I nod solemnly at her. "What's up? I have therapy in a few minutes so I'm going to have to kick you out."

"Nothing. I'm gonna practice and thought it'd be cool of me to say hi first."

"Cool... yes." The wheels in my mind are turning, and I wonder if I can do this without Piper figuring out what or who I'm talking about. "Pipe, you're like... young and cool, right?"

"I *was* until you had to ask." Piper looks disgusted with me. I'm *such* an embarrassment to her.

"What does it mean when someone who has your phone number emails you instead of texting?

She narrows her eyes at me. "This feels like a trap."

"It's not a trap," I assure her. "Your mom's a clueless old lady."

"Have you texted them before?" Piper asks, fidgeting with the hair tie she took off her wrist. "Because I wouldn't email someone if we'd texted."

I shake my head. "Not other than a 'hey, it's so-and-so' text when we exchanged numbers."

"So-and-so? I don't even get a name?" Piper pouts.

"It's... Elmo. He's an accountant I connected with online," I lie.

"Maybe it means he has a weird name and doesn't want to come across as too casual or familiar," Piper suggests. "Like a professional relationship."

I don't know why her words make my stomach sink. She's right, Ren and I have a strictly professional relationship, a relationship that wouldn't exist without my daughter.

"Do you have a crush on Elmo?" Piper asks, and it takes me a moment to realize why she's mentioning the red monster from Sesame Street.

"I... what?" I stammer, cheeks heating. Goddammit. "Of course not!"

"Oh my god, you *do*!" Piper gasps, leaning forward. "I've never seen you with a crush!"

"Yes, you have!"

"Luke Danes does *not* count."

I scowl at her. "Alright, that's enough from you. Mama has therapy."

"Tell Eva I say hi!" Piper calls before closing my office door.

When I sign on to therapy, I surprise myself when I launch into telling my therapist about Ren.

And Eva, bless her, follows along perfectly.

"You and Kat were..." she prompts.

"Friends. Just...friends," I say, hoping she stops asking about Kat.

Luckily, she does. "Got it, and Ren is her younger brother and Piper's piano teacher, and we don't like him... why?"

"That's the problem," I admit. "I *do* like him."

Eva closes her notebook and leans on her elbows toward the camera. "Oh, *this* is interesting."

"What is?" I ask in confusion.

"Are you attracted to him?" she asks point-blank.

I gape at her like a fish. "I... he has brown floppy hair! He's objectively attractive... *and* Piper's piano teacher!"

Eva doesn't say anything.

"Okay, fine. Maybe he's a *little* attractive, but we both know I'm not about to dive into dating. It just freaked me out, being recognized by someone I knew before."

"And he's sticking around, too, right? Teaching Piper's piano lessons?"

"Yeah, he seems... good. To Piper, at least. And I don't know, I've always thought Piper deserved more genuinely *good* people in her life, people who see her for who she is and like her for that."

"And you don't deserve that?"

I scowl at her. "Okay, isn't our session over yet?

"I'm just saying, he might be a good person to try to begin a friendship with."

I hate the idea. Thinking about Ren makes me think about the entire Quinn family, and thinking about the entire Quinn family makes me think about everything I used to want from life.

I always wanted to get married and have a big family. I wanted four or five kids, and a house with a big backyard and pets and chaos and a partner who kissed me whenever they came home from work. I wanted to fall asleep in someone's arms, knowing they loved me, and the life we built together.

I went on a single date when Piper was a year old. A guy I met at a bar a few towns over and went home with. I don't even remember his name, or if he told me. He was in college and a few years older than me, and the fact he wanted me was thrilling. Until I was topless in his dorm. I'll never forget the expression on his face. Or the way he stammered as he handed me the bra he'd taken off me moments before. He remembered he had an assignment due in the morning, and I should probably get going. He didn't look at me until I was completely covered, and even then wouldn't meet my eyes. My breasts sagged from breastfeeding Piper and were adorned with stretch marks, darkened areolas, and large nipples. I've never forgotten the way his rejection felt and the struggles with my body that followed.

All I'd wanted was to be more than a mom. My life and body belonged to Piper, and I wanted to feel like I was still a woman, still complete on my own.

The opposite happened, and the damage it left is still poignant.

"It's scary, isn't it?" Eva agrees. "Relationships. Letting people see, know, and love us." I nod in response. "Audrey, I think it's time for some exposure therapy."

"No, thanks," I respond quickly.

"Nothing terrible, I want you to open yourself up to the possibility of friendship. That's our new focus in therapy: making friends. We'll start small, though. Your homework is to email Ren back."

"I don't *want* to email Ren back!" I whine. God, it's concerning how much I sound like Piper.

"I know. You don't have to be best friends. The first step is to stop avoiding him and be an active participant in Piper's piano lessons."

I want to stomp my foot and refuse.

But I want to make Piper happy even more.

"I hate you," I grumble.

"I know," Eva says with a smirk. "I'll see you next week."

Chapter 7

Ren

Playlist: Sideways | Carly Rae Jepsen

Quiblings Group Chat

Nic

JO OPENED A BUSINESS? WITH HER GIRLFRIEND OF LIKE A DAY????THAT'S THE GAYEST SHIT I'VE EVER HEARD.

Leo

['ha, gay' gif]

Jo

['what happened to hello' gif]

Ren

wait, what??

Nic

i thought i was pretty clear

Millie

okay wait shut the hell up that's so gay and cool <happy tears emoji>

Alex

no, literally so fucking cool. congrats, jo!!!

Jo

wow, you're the first one of our delightful siblings to congratulate me <eye roll emoji>

Jo

but thanks al <heart emoji>

Izzy

the first quibling with their name attached to a business!!!! watch out world! we're adults and goddamn menaces

Kat

did you forget i made partner last year?

Leo

GODDAMMIT

Izzy

HAHAHAAH i win

Nic

> wait win what? i wanna win

Leo

> izzy and i made a bet as to when kat would mention being partner and i said it would be her third text, but iz said it would be her first.

Kat

> what? It's true! jo isn't the first or only business owner in the family!

Jo

> okay but like did you have to make it about you so quickly???

Jo

> also you're partner at our parents' law firm. you're literally a nepo kid

Millie

> kat, be nice and congratulate jo.

Seen by Kat

"Say please, angel," I breathe into the microphone. "You know how much I love it when you beg for me." I pause for a few seconds for the listener's hypothetical response before continuing. "Fuck, you're so pretty when you're begging for my cock. So perfect for me on your knees."

I yawn and stretch my arms over my head, grateful for the magic that is an editor. I take a quick gulp of water and push my wireframe glasses up the bridge of my nose before continuing.

I unbuckle the belt I keep in the booth for sound effects before slowly unzipping a sparkly pencil pouch I got on clearance while back-to-school shopping last year.

I was surprised when I realized how easy it is to detach from my emotions while recording. When Kadence first asked me to work with them for 4Play, I was hesitant. Casual sex is physically painful to me.

But unlike me, Sky isn't demisexual. He isn't *real*.

"Open," I instruct into the microphone. "Are you ready?" I pause for a beat, then chuckle. "That's my girl." I squirt some lube on my hand and stroke my forearm to mimic the sounds of a blow job. I moan and whimper, knowing how much Sky's Sluts love when he does that. "*Fuck*, baby, you take me so well."

It took me a while to get comfortable with acting out sex scenes. Until last year, when my mom asked me to grab her Kindle, and I made the mistake of opening it, discovering the world of cowboy romance. While that was obviously traumatizing, it introduced me to the world of contemporary romance. My sister Nic's boyfriend, Josh, and my older sister, Jo, both love historical romances and are always trying to get me to read whatever book they're currently obsessing over. While I've been avoiding it, Sky's Sluts have been begging for a regency audio on the subreddit, so it may be in my future.

So far, I've done exclusively contemporary audios, and reading contemporary romance has been helpful in regards to writing scripts and, to be honest, dirty talk.

This means I know way too much about my mother, but goddamn, no one does dirty talk like a fictional cowboy. The things I've read make *me* blush.

Not that it's hard, considering I got my dad's Irish appearance instead of my mom's Sicilian complexion.

I continue to moan, to praise the listener. After a bit, I make sure my movements and breath become jerkier, rougher, more desperate.

"Look at you, letting me fuck your face like the perfect slut you are." I close my eyes and lean my head back, the image of an auburn-haired woman with curves that could kill me taking me into her mouth.

"You are, aren't you?" I say, going off-script. "Perfect for me. God, you could eat me alive, and I'd beg you to do it again."

Imaginary Audrey pulls back my foreskin and swirls her tongue around the head of my cock, silver-gray eyes intent on mine. I swear to god, I can *feel* the warmth of her mouth.

I rip off my headphones and push away from the desk. I'm breathing heavily, heart pounding, and, *Jesus Christ*, I'm hard as hell.

I can't help myself and reach into my shorts, wrapping my already-lubed hand around my aching length. The way I'm frantically jerking myself achieves the horniness I try to embody while recording.

I'm on antidepressants, and usually, it takes a little while to come. This has served me and my partners in the past, but tonight it takes *maybe* thirty seconds to feel the hot stickiness of my cum on my hand.

I try to steady my breath, to inhale deeply and get a hold on myself.

Because what. The fuck. Was *that*?

I tuck my softening cock back into my pants before going to the bathroom to clean myself up.

When I'm back in the office, I leave the door open so Leia, who's currently dozing on the back of the couch, can join me if she wants. I keep her out of the room while recording, because if I *don't*, that's when she decides to sing the song of her people.

And since masturbating completely ruined the mood I want to be in while recording, I decide to call it a night. I sit back at my desk and grab my phone to text Kadence and let them know I won't get the audio to them on time, but get distracted by the texts on my lock screen.

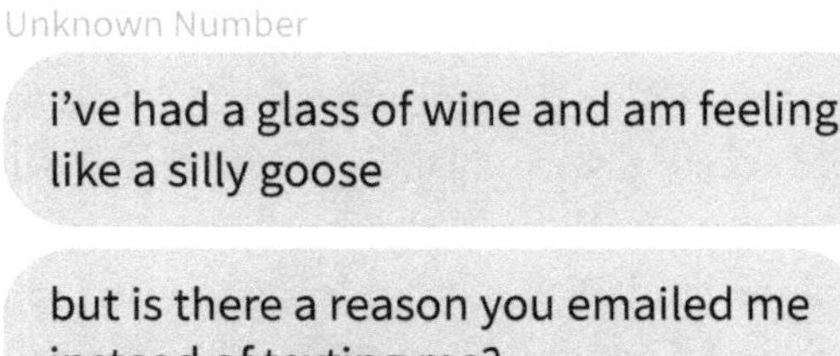

I rub my eyes, my knuckles bumping my glasses as I frown at the phone screen, trying to remember who I've given my number recently.

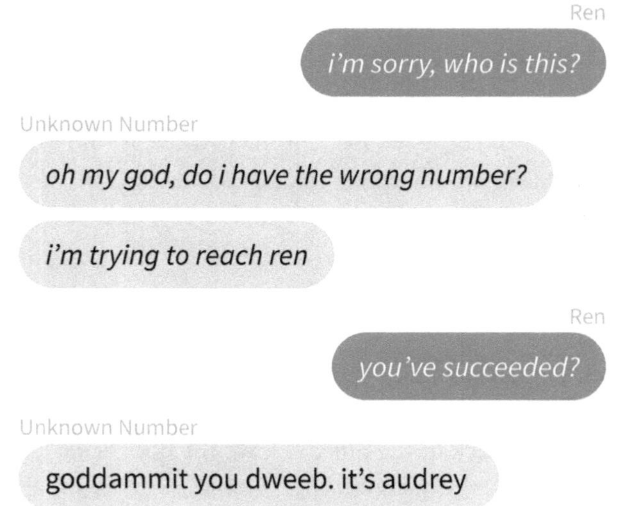

I bark out a laugh at the sheer insanity that is receiving a text from the woman whose image I masturbated to less than five minutes ago.

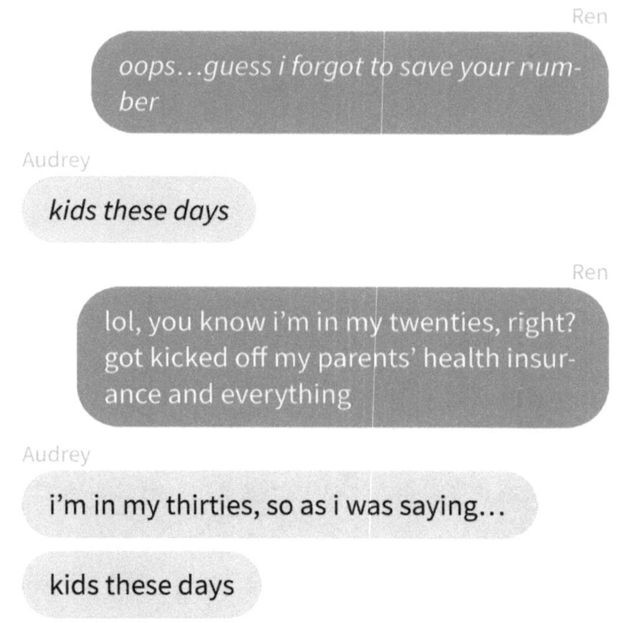

I'm embarrassed by the blush creeping along my cheeks. Not only is Audrey a goddamn smokeshow, she's funny too. Talk about the girl of my dreams.

I bite my lip as I think of the right thing to say. What's a nice way to say, "Well, you've been avoiding me when I'm teaching your kid, so I thought texting would come across as too familiar, and that's the last thing we are, you and I. Familiar."

Ren

as you can see, I forgot to save your number

Audrey

oh. i thought you hated me or some-thing

Ren

hold up, you thought i hated you?????

audrey i haven't heard a peep from you since that morning on the beach, despite seeing your daughter at your business on a weekly basis

even if i had saved your number, i doubt i would have used it because things feel WEIRD

I watch as the three dots appear and disappear and reappear as she, I assume, figures out what to say.

Audrey

i'm trying to figure out what to say

I laugh again before responding.

Ren

i figured

Audrey

sorry i'm weird… piper always says i'm embarrassing as hell and goddammit i think she's right

Ren

okay well that's not what i said. it just feels like you don't want to interact with me

Audrey

it's not that i don't want to, it's that i don't know HOW to

like my therapist told me today my homework is to MAKE FRIENDS because i'm a friendless loser with abandonment issues that affect how i interact with people beyond a professional basis!!!!

and you were this annoying little kid the last time i saw you and now you're not…idk. betcha regret emailing me now huh

Maybe I'm the problem, but I don't know if I fully believe her.

Audrey

> if i were you i'd tell me to go to hell and block me. but if you could not give up on piper… she's my kid, yes but she's also really incredible on her own and only the best of me…unless you consider how stubborn and angry she can get, but that's besides the point.

Ren

> i'm definitely not blocking you, or giving up on piper. can we talk in person?

Audrey:

> …i'm supposed to take baby steps in friend making, talking in person seems like at least a toddler step

Ren

> maybe sending this text was the baby step, and the next step is eating solids! and to celebrate you meeting that milestone, we should meet at queenie's at 9 tomorrow. we can even get smoothies if you don't feel ready for solids just yet

This might be the worst idea I've had in a while. Getting *closer* to the woman giving me uncontrollable amounts of lust simply by existing?

Audrey

ok, we can do that

Ren

see you then <smiley face emoji>

When I fall asleep an hour later, I dream of myself in assless chaps and a cowboy hat, and Audrey in Daisy Dukes and cowboy boots embracing in a field.

Because of course I fucking do.

Chapter 8

Audrey

Playlist: Make This Leap | The Hunts

Sky's Sluts

SkysMainSlut: ladies, is my internet acting up or did Sky not upload this morning.

AshBash69: WHAT

AshBash69: NO

MeetMeInStarsHollow: okay, lets keep calm. He's never missed a tuesday draft before. Maybe the drop is just happening later today?

RebelLady93: Adam uploaded, and so did Lucky.

RebelLady93: literally all of the tuesday regulars did except him.

SkysMainSlut: i'm going to scream

AshBash69: the emotional pain i'm feeling is worse than the physical pain of pushing a baby out of my vagina.

MeetMeInStarsHollow: i'm holding out hope it's just a glitch and he'll upload later. <prayer hands emoji>

I don't know why I'm sitting in an old vinyl booth at the only diner in town.

Especially when I definitely drank too much last night.

I'm not a big drinker, but Piper was babysitting and Mama needed to unwind. Instead of unwinding, I *unraveled*.

"Can I get you anything, ma'am?" the waiter asks. He's bald with light brown skin and a nametag identifying him as Derek.

"I'll take a coffee for now," I say, forcing a smile. "I'm waiting on someone."

When Derek leaves my table, I pull my phone out, double checking the time Ren suggested we meet. Yep, nine a.m. It's not nine yet, and I'm definitely just a nervous wreck. But I double check 4Play and scroll quickly, disappointment filling my gut.

Sky didn't upload an audio today. I'm not the only one who noticed either. There were multiple threads about it in his sub-reddit, which I had checked earlier upon realizing he didn't upload. I may or may not have added my own unhinged replies to these threads.

A bell rings as someone enters the diner, and I don't have to look up to know it's Ren. His aura is *that* powerful.

"Hey," he says, sliding into the booth across from me. "Thanks for meeting with me."

He sounds winded and out of breath, and it makes me squeeze my thighs together. Is this what he sounds like when he's fucking someone? When he's thrusting into them and telling them how good they feel? When he...

Whoa. Where did *that* come from? Ren and sex should never be on the same wavelength in my brain.

"Hey," I respond, staring at the paper placemat and refusing to meet his eyes. If he knew what I just thought about him, he'd think I was one of those creepy moms without any boundaries.

Oh, Lord. I *am* a creepy mom without any boundaries.

I peer at him, and a wave of relief washes over me when I see he's studying the menu. The Quinns have been coming to Queenie's regularly since Kat and I became friends in middle school, and probably even before then. I'm sure he knows what he wants, but I appreciate him pretending to pursue the options nonetheless.

"Do you know what you're going to get?" I ask, flipping over the menu like I'm actually reading what it says.

I'm not. It's all Greek to me.

Truly, they have something called a Gyro Breakfast Burrito.

"Probably the Gyro Breakfast Burrito," Ren answers, and I can't help but giggle.

He looks up with a smirk. "What?"

My cheeks flush and I duck my head, staring intently at the menu. "Nothing. It's silly."

In my peripheral vision, I see Ren put the menu on the table, rest his elbows on the surface, and place his chin in his hand. "Tell me. I love silly."

Somehow, that is as sexy as Sky begging me to come for him.

I force myself to meet his eyes, which is a mistake. He's looking at me like he's absolutely captivated by what could come out of my mouth next, like he truly loves silliness...loves *my* silliness.

"I was looking at the menu and made a joke in my head about the Gyro Breakfast Burrito, and then you said you were getting it."

"What was the joke?" He seems like he's on the edge of his seat waiting to hear this silent joke I made about a breakfast item.

"I've never seen something like that before. A Gyro Break-fast Burrito. And it's funny because a gyro and a burrito are somewhat similar in the way they're both proteins wrapped in a type of bread… but they belong to widely different cultures, so I don't understand what it's trying to be." I shrug my shoulders. "I guess it's all Greek to me."

Ren's laugh is beautiful, and it brings me back to the first time I heard it a month ago. Familiar. It felt so familiar, like the happiness of having a friend and a family.

His laugh is full-bodied, his shoulders shaking as he buries his face in his hands. It's *not* that funny, but god, it feels good to know I'm the reason he's laughing so hard the older couple at the booth behind us is glaring at us.

"It's… it's not that funny," I say, fighting back a smile.

"I *know*. I don't know why I find it as funny as I do, but *fuck*. That got me."

"It's probably because you work with literal children and are used to having to laugh extra hard at things that aren't actually that funny," I suggest.

He meets my gaze, a twinkle in his eyes. "Maybe you and I have the same sense of humor."

"Piper rolls her eyes at your jokes, too?" I tease.

"Oh, at least once every other minute." He laughs again and how weird would it be if I asked if I could record it to be my alarm sound? Waking up in the mornings wouldn't be so bad if that was what I was waking up to.

I grin. "Sounds like Piper."

Derek appears and places a steaming cup of fresh coffee in front of me before fist bumping Ren.

"How did Zariah like her first year of middle school?" Ren asks him.

"It was her first year of middle school, so it wasn't easy," Derek says. "But you know what a tough kid she is. She really tried to make the best of it and joined a few clubs and is in band. She took up clarinet, if you can believe it."

Ren's face positively lights up, and for the first time, I understand exactly what that phrase means. It's like he's a light source, eyes bright and face glowing with what looks like pride and excitement. "I *can* believe it," he replies excitedly. "She loved the woodwind unit."

How is this man so precious with everyone he interacts with? Derek is beaming as Ren asks more about his daughter and there's a simultaneous twinge of envy and admiration for his ability to make people feel so important, so seen.

Ren is mid-laugh when he suddenly freezes and his eyes widen. "Derek, it's been good to see you," he says, sliding out of the booth. "But I have to run."

He makes eye contact with me, and my heart sinks. "I'll text you, okay?" he says smoothly, before shaking Derek's hand, spinning on his heel, and striding towards the exit.

Derek and I both stare at Ren's retreating form in silence, and I'd love to say it doesn't bother me, but it does. I rarely go out in Port Haven, out of fear I'll be recognized because of my past. And if I were Ren, I wouldn't want to befriend someone with a reputation like mine, either.

No, that's not true.

I'd never make someone feel less than, or that they don't deserve my company because of what they might say about me.

I force myself to smile at Derek before pulling out my phone, surprised when I already have a text from Ren with more coming in.

Ren

i. am. so. sorry. a parent of a student walked in and she's highkey my sleep paralysis demon. she told me during parent/teacher conferences she wishes i was her husband and father of her kid

i think it was a joke but i still had to talk about it in therapy. if you want to order to go breakfast is on me

Audrey

it's okay, we can reschedule if you want

Ren

i was excited for our breakfast honestly

Audrey

we can take it back to my place if you want to hide from any more feral mom sneak attacks

Ren

i'll send you the money, can you order me the gyro burrito with home fries?

He proceeds to send me fifty dollars, which we both know is way more than a diner breakfast costs.

But I can't think about the fact I'm pretty sure I currently have less than one hundred dollars in my bank account, and while I have a safety net in savings, I shouldn't use it for breakfast. I'll ask him if he wants the change later, but it was generous of him to treat me to breakfast.

He seems to be a genuinely generous and thoughtful person. It's throwing me off.

When our food arrives in to-go containers, I go to the front counter to pay. "Are you in line?" someone behind me asks, and I fight the urge to roll my eyes. I'm waiting directly behind the customer who's currently paying... what else would I be doing here?

"Mmhmm." I'm proud of myself for holding myself back and not answering sarcastically the way I'd wanted to. I spin my debit card between my fingers, and unfortunately, I do not have the same dexterity as my daughter, because I drop it. I curse and bend down to pick it up, knocking heads with the owner of the voice behind me.

"*Ow!*" the no longer disembodied voice complains.

We didn't hit heads *that* hard, but I'll let them have their dramatics. I grab my card and we both stand.

That's when I make one of the biggest mistakes of my life. My eyes lock with none other than Celia Bryan, one of the people who made my senior year at Port Haven High an actual living hell.

I quickly turn back around, praying in my head she doesn't recognize me as memories of the rumors she spread play in my head. According to her, I ran out of boys in our class to have sex with and resorted to seducing teachers, which was blatantly untrue. But the adults in the situation seemed to buy it. They started to hate me, instead of the person spreading rumors. No matter what I did, I was the seductress, I was the one that was wrong, I never got a chance to defend myself. I was always the one they chose to hate.

"No. Way. Audrey Price?"

Fuck.

Changing my last name allowed me to stay relatively anonymous in this ridiculously chatty small town. Add me dying my hair to the mix, and I'm pretty much a completely different person.

"It is you, isn't it?" Celia continues, a hint of amusement in her voice. I turn to face her and she slowly scrutinizes my body with her eyes. "Didn't think we'd see your pretty face around here again." Her tight smile tells me what she's really saying: *"Ballsy of you to show your face again, slut."*

"Hi, Celia."

She ignores my greeting, eyes continuing to roam my body. I cross my arms in front of my chest, shame spreading in my chest like a black hole. "Almost didn't recognize you," she finally says after her perusal of my body. "You look... older."

"Well, people's appearances tend to change as they age," I respond, awkwardly shifting from foot to foot.

"And you know, babies ruin your figure, though I didn't find it too hard to lose the weight," she continues, once again ignoring my contribution. She meets my eyes and smirks, "But not everyone has the discipline. I heard it was a girl?"

I hate how much it still can hurt. How this woman can find each scar and reopen the wound so the shame I've tried to contain floods out.

I'm not ashamed of Piper. I never could be—becoming her mom is the greatest thing I've ever done. But that scared, ostracized teenager is still inside me, huddled in a dark corner and begging to be seen, to be protected and taken care of.

"Aud!" I don't know if hearing Ren's voice makes the situation better or worse.

"Mr. Q!" Celia squeals, her voice a much higher pitch than from when she was talking to me. "I thought I saw you earlier!"

"Good morning, Mrs. Davidson," Ren says in an overly formal voice. "I didn't realize you and Audrey knew each other," he continues, and I force myself to look up. Celia is twirling her hair while batting her lashes at Ren. The corner of his left eye twitches.

"Audrey?" Celia asks innocently, tilting her head to the side. I internally roll my eyes because, girl, he *just* saw you talking to me. From Ren addressing her as Mrs. Davidson, I also assume she's married and changed her name. Unfortunately, nothing of substance seems to have changed about her, though.

"Audrey," Ren repeats as I glance at him. We make eye contact and I want to melt into the floor. "Didn't realize you knew her. Can you believe she's never had a Queenie's Gyro Breakfast Burrito? I had to make sure she got one. Right, Aud?" He throws his arm over my shoulders and my heart skips a beat at the shortened name.

That seems to bring Celia out of whatever Ren Quinn-induced stupor she's in. She quizzically looks between Ren and I. "Aud?" she repeats.

"I'm going to pay so you and Celia can catch up, okay?" Ren says. I open my mouth to remind him he already sent me the money on Venmo, but he silences me with a single arch of his brow.

The power this man exerts over me is concerning to feminism.

Of course, Celia has nothing more to say to me now that she has an audience, opening and closing her mouth wordlessly, like a fish you make fun of at the aquarium.

"How do you know Ren?" I ask innocently, crossing my arms over my chest. I already know she's the wine mom he ran out of the building from, but I'd love to hear it from her.

"He... my kids. Music teacher," she says. I like to think she's so intimidated by me she can't form full sentences, but if I'm being honest with myself, I think it's the fact Ren was short with her, and gave me the attention she obviously wants from him that has her so taken aback.

Whatever, I'll take what I can get.

"Ready to go?" Ren asks after paying for breakfast.

I nod, keeping my eyes on Celia. "Mmhmm. Good to see you, Celia."

"You... you too," Celia stammers, eyes following us as Ren and I move toward the door. I stare directly ahead, because I know if I make eye contact with him, I'm doomed to dissolve into either laughter or tears.

Chapter 9

Ren

Playlist: 1996 | Wild Child

Mom

Hi, love. Do you mind stopping at Stop & Shop and grabbing some ground beef? I want to make Bolognese for dinner, which of course you're welcome to stay for.

Ren

i'm pretty booked today, any chance kat could do it?

Mom

Kat and Steve are on a couple's retreat in Mystic this week, and I have meetings with clients.

Ren

what time do you need it by?

It's around a ten minute walk from Queenie's to Audrey's home, a small white cottage tucked behind the inn. I spend ten minutes trying to figure out what we have in common to talk about so it isn't awkward.

"Piper!" I exclaim as we climb up her front porch steps. The white cottage is tucked away behind the inn, the sky blue shutters and doors popping against the white. Purple and blue hydrangeas line the front porch, and the *porch*. I don't know when having a front porch became my lifelong dream, but god. I'm in love with it.

The porch is scattered with mismatched chairs and a table, all different colors and styles. But despite that, everything looks like it belongs. It's welcoming and cozy, and I hope she's okay with me never leaving.

Audrey stops walking and stares at me. "What?"

"Piper," I repeat. "Your daughter."

She blinks at me a few times. "Yes?"

"She's cool," is the response I land on. Great work, Lorenzo. Real smooth. Making her think you're unintelligible is one way to reiterate the fact I'm just a kid to her.

Strangely, Audrey doesn't seem weirded out by my sudden outburst about her child's coolness. Quite the opposite, actually. A slow, proud smile spreads across her face, and it's like the sun coming out from behind the clouds.

It's devastating.

"Yeah. The coolest," she says, pulling her keys out from her oversized bag. "She's my favorite human on the planet, and like, yeah, it's probably because she's my kid, but I'm so lucky she's mine."

And somehow this woman, who I thought couldn't be more beautiful, is even more exquisite while talking about how much she loves her kid. Cool. Cool.

Get yourself together, weirdo.

"Do you want coffee?" she asks, pushing the front door open.

"Sure." I already had a latte at my parents' this morning, as is my post-run tradition. It started when Millie moved out of our parents' house a few years back and instantly missed their fancy espresso machine. She mentioned how she snuck into the house in the mornings to get her fix, and the next morning, I showed up, too. Over time, more people joined in our criminal activity until we were discovered. Except it turns out my dad woke up early to unlock the door for us and knew the whole time, which I personally thought would take the thrill out of it, but it's still a special routine for us, and our numbers continue to grow.

I should've known my parents knew what was going on the moment oat milk appeared in the fridge.

I step into the house after Audrey. "I sort of made a guess when I brought you coffee on your run. How do you usually take it?" she asks, closing the door and locking it behind me.

However you'll give it to me, sweetheart.

I have zero chill.

"Oat milk and sugar," I respond, grateful she can't read my mind.

She nods towards the food in my hand. "Should we warm it up?"

"Probably wouldn't hurt."

I follow her into the kitchen, and if I was obsessed with her front porch, I'm whatever is one step above obsessed with her kitchen. The furniture and cookware are all mismatched again, and artwork, pictures, and graded assignments make it so no part of the fridge door's surface is showing.

I find myself drawn to one in particular, an old photo held to the fridge with a Brooklyn, NY magnet. In the center is Audrey the way I remember her from all those years ago. Next to her is an older woman with a bright smile and crinkles around her eyes. Her aunt, I assume. On her aunt's lap is a little, blonde human with a grumpy scowl on their face, and my heart lurches when I realize this picture must have been taken soon after Piper was born. She can't be more than a few months old.

"It's weird seeing her that tiny now she's a terrifying teenager," Audrey says from behind me.

"That's your aunt? The one who left you the inn and cottage?" I ask, pointing to the woman in the picture.

"Aunt Olivia. The woman, the myth, the legend," she confirms. "I miss her every day."

"Tell me about her."

"Oh... I..." she stammers, face reddening. It's like she didn't expect me to ask any follow up questions, and it hits me like a wrecking ball that maybe no one ever asked any. "She was my favorite family member when I was a kid." she says, looking away. "She was my mom's aunt, and never married. My parents didn't like her, but she always gave me candy and seemed to be interested in what I had to say."

I watch Audrey bustle about the kitchen, turning the oven on to preheat before facing me. "No one ever listened to me. Not like her." There's a soft, fond smile on her face, one that exists solely when she's talking about Piper. My heart aches for her, for her loss and for the way she spent her life thinking she didn't have anything to say that was worth listening to. "When I was a teenager, I stopped seeing her because... I don't know. I was too busy fighting with my parents and getting grounded and sneaking out. When she found out I was pregnant, she came to my parents' house. Somehow she *knew* I needed her, and she showed up for me."

I inhale through my nose and look at the fridge again. "She sounds like she loved you like you love Piper." I examine a report card on the fridge, a strange sense of pride coming over me when I see Piper got all As this past year, except in English, where she got a B. She's a smart cookie.

"She did love me like that. Piper, too. One of the only few people who cared."

I lean back against the counter, shoving my hands in my pockets to keep from reaching for her. "What do you mean?"

We cared. I remember my family caring about her. Then one day she was suddenly gone.

Audrey sighs, digging through her cutlery drawer. "Getting pregnant as a teen doesn't make you any friends. Or have you already forgotten how Celia treated me just now?"

"No, I remember. I saw your face through the window. No one deserves to be alone with that woman. But isn't that just Celia?"

Audrey scoffs, pushing the drawer closed with her hip. "No, that's pretty much how everyone treated me. Especially then, hence the new name and new hair color. I'm sorry, by the way."

I feel my brows furrow into a scowl of confusion. "Sorry for what?"

"That she recognized me. You shouldn't have to be seen with me. I'm worried she'll start spreading rumors."

My eyes drift back to that one photo on the fridge. Audrey is smiling, but it doesn't meet her eyes. The Audrey I remember had eyes that seemed to always glisten, like she knew a secret no one else did.

She always seemed so... *alive.*

It's ironic that creating new life is what took that gleam away. Or rather, how she was treated while pregnant.

"I really don't care about any rumors Celia tries to start. I'm not embarrassed to be seen with you."

The timer on the oven beeps, but before she turned her back to me, I saw the fleeting look on Audrey's face. A little bit of shock, a tiny glimmer of hope. But she brushes it off, replaces it with doubt.

"Ready?" Audrey asks, handing me a mug of coffee—one that says, "Best Mom Ever" over and over in various fonts—and my plated gyro breakfast burrito.

We go out onto the porch, and she takes a seat in a wicker rocking chair, curling her legs beneath her. She places her own bacon, egg, and cheese sandwich on the side table and lifts her steaming pink ceramic mug to her mouth.

"So," Audrey says, lowering her mug. "The concert."

I clear my throat. "Yeah, Yale's symphony is doing a summer series and there's one right before school starts back up that's a John Williams tribute..."

Audrey furrows her brow. "John Williams?"

"Famous movie score composer. *Star Wars...*" I trail off, looking at her expectantly.

"That's the only score he's composed?" she asks.

"Well, no." I admit, feeling my cheeks flush. "He's done other stuff, but I can't think of any off the top of my head."

"Hmm," Audrey says, staring intently at her coffee. "Do you like *Star Wars* or something?"

My cheeks redden deeper. I've loved *Star Wars* since my dad brought me to the movie theater in Milford to see *Attack of the Clones*. It was probably the most transformative experience in my young life.

"They're good movies..." I start to say, but stop short when I notice Audrey's shoulders shaking. I narrow my eyes at her. "*Wow.*"

"I'm sorry," she wheezes.

She doesn't sound even a little bit sorry.

"I'm sorry," she repeats. "You used to sleep with that robot plush..."

"His name is R2-D2."

"And if you weren't watching *Star Wars*, you were playing with those toys or or you were playing 'The Imperial March' on the piano or..."

"Thank you, I get it," I interrupt. Curse these Irish genes, I can *feel* the heat radiating inward from my face. "First of all, they're collectible action figures. Second, I was *going* to tell you I bought you a ticket, too."

Her laughter stops short and she stares at me. "You... what?"

"I got you a ticket to the Nerd Concert."

"But... I don't..." She bites her plush lower lip and looks around, like people are listening in to our riveting conversation about me being a giant ass nerd. "I don't know music. I don't know if I'd fit in..."

"It's open to the public," I say before she can finish her self-deprecating sentence. "It's not going to be a bunch of like… high brow patrons of the arts."

She stares at me like I'm absurd. "It's *Yale*."

"Hey," I say, softening my voice. It seems to affect her somehow and she blinks at me repetitively. "I bought it because I thought you'd be more comfortable if you were there, too, and… and I want you to come." My face is burning again.

She's surprised by this. "You do? Why?"

"You were a part of my life for a really long time, Audrey. I don't know why you stopped coming around, and yeah, you were mean and scary but you never told my mom about the Princess Leia picture you found under my bed and… I want to get to know you. You're not as terrible at interacting with people as you think you are." Saying it out loud sounds so silly, so inconsequential and unimportant.

"You couldn't take Piper alone?" Audrey asks, and it feels like she's pleading with me.

"Think of it as therapy homework. Baby steps to being friends."

"You can be alone with Piper and still be my friend," she insists.

"Audrey, I refuse to be alone with students, ever. In private, in school. The other option is you taking her alone."

She stares at me. "That wouldn't be fair to you, though. You bought the tickets."

I shrug. "Either the three of us go, or I give you the tickets for you and Piper to go, if you'd rather. But Piper and I going alone is off the table."

She inhales shakily. "Okay. I'll go with you guys to your damn nerd concert."

Both of us have finished eating, so the next natural step is for me to thank her and head home. But I don't want to leave; I want to stay and keep talking to her, keep learning about her. I want to ask about her aunt's death, and Piper's first word. I want to know her.

"I, um. I have to get to the inn," Audrey says. "I hate to kick you out."

"Can I at least wash the dishes?" I ask.

"You don't have to do that."

"I want to do it."

She smiles softly, but like the Audrey in the photo, it doesn't meet her eyes.

I wonder what it'll take for her eyes to glimmer again, for her to remember the secret that only she knew.

I don't know, but I'm determined to find out.

Chapter 10

Audrey

Playlist: Guilty as Sin? | Taylor Swift

August

Sky's Sluts

AshBash69: okay, i think i'm pregnant again after that cne. Anyone else?

SkysMainSlut: oh me, for sure. Probably with twins. how is this man SO HOT???

MentallyInStarsHollow: that moan at 15:43??? immaculate conception.

AshBash69: the way i made note of the time stamp so my hubby can listen and replicate it.

SkysMainSlut: you lucky bitch.

MentallyInStarsHollow: no seriously, i will NEVER be satisfied by a real man again. and honestly? If his drops keep being this good, I don't think i mind.

I fall back against my pillows, lightheaded and chest heaving, as I pull my headphones off and turn my vibrator off.

It's a quiet Saturday morning, and it's been over two weeks since Ren and I had breakfast together. Over two weeks of me actually showing up for Piper's lessons, interacting politely with him, and picturing Ren whenever I masturbate to Sky's audios.

I know it's wrong to visualize this man when I mastur-bate...but when I close my eyes and touch myself, it's Ren I see. Green eyes hooded, full lips parted, waves stuck to his forehead with sweat as he talks me through it.

Hell, it almost even sounds like him. The way he laughs...

My eyes fly open and I stare at the ceiling fan as the entire room spins along with it.

His *laugh*.

I sit up against the headboard, my heart still pounding from my climax, and slip my headphones back over my ears.

I know it's probably a coincidence... but still I scroll through Sky's audios, choose a random one from three months ago and press play. It takes three minutes for his laughter to fill my headphones.

I could swear it's the same laugh, just deeper. The same breathy gasping sound that sounds like it's coming from deep in his chest.

I keep scrolling and starting random audios, heart pounding harder than it was after my orgasm.

The same deep laugh, over and over again.

Until I find his very first audio from a year ago.

I hesitate when I go to press play. This feels like a sort of breach of privacy. Crossing a line, even though it shouldn't be.

Ren isn't Sky.

Sky isn't Ren.

And this was a good one, anyway.

"Oh my god, hi. I didn't expect to run into you today. Yeah, I know, we haven't seen each other since... that night."

This doesn't sound like Sky. His voice is higher, brighter.

Like Ren's.

"Yeah, your brother told me about the promotion. I always knew you had it in you."

"No, no, no, no," I chant, pulling my knees to my chest.

And then he laughs.

I'm so startled by the fact it sounds like Ren's laugh directly in my ear that I rip my headphones off and throw them across the room like they're on fire.

Ren is Sky.

Sky is Ren.

"Mom?" Piper calls. Shit, she usually isn't awake this early. "Are you okay?"

"Fine, birdie!" I wheeze. "I'm great."

She buys it, I guess, because she doesn't push it further.

I, meanwhile, am spiraling.

Why? A small voice inside me asks. *Why are you freaking out over Ren and Sky being the same person?*

The thought gives me pause, because why *do* I care? Ren is allowed to do whatever he wants, and Sky is one of the few 4Play creators with zero social media presence. That made me think he had a personal life he didn't want associated with the work he did for the app.

I mean. I was right. And he deserves that privacy.

But I ruined it.

He'll never know, that one voice says again. *You'll keep it together and not embarrass him or yourself and never say anything.*

God, one can only hope.

Chapter 11

Audrey

Playlist: Close To You | Gracie Abrams

I spend the next few hours staring blankly at the ceiling. I don't want to go to Piper's lesson. I don't want to look into the eyes of the man who's made me come every night for a year.

If I act differently than I have the past few weeks, both Piper and Ren will know something is wrong. But after Piper leaves for class, I force myself out of bed, showering before making Ren's coffee with sugar and oat milk in one of my favorite mugs.

It's strange, knowing Ren is Sky. Sky is Ren. I look at Ren, and I see Piper's piano teacher, a man who genuinely cares about her and her success and talent. But I listen to Sky and... fuck. He's pure sex.

I wonder if it has anything to do with the pesky butterflies that arrive in my stomach when he glances up from the piano and his face brightens as he takes the mug from me.

"You're a godsend," he says.

"No, you," I say, and immediately wish I didn't, because yikes.

He blushes. "If you insist."

"I do..."

"Are you two done flirting yet?" Piper interrupts, a bored expression on her face. She leans her elbow against the keys, the loud clang echoing through the lobby.

"*Piper*!" I hiss as Ren chokes on his sip of coffee, his face somehow turning even redder.

"What?" Piper asks, looking between the two of us. "Are you not flirting right now? When Luke and Lorelai do it, you say..."

"Can we talk for a moment, birdie?" I ask, not waiting for an answer before reaching around Ren and wrapping my hand around Piper's bicep.

She sighs heavily and gets to her feet. "That's your 'I'm giving you the illusion you have a choice, but you and I both know you don't have one' voice."

I ignore her, pulling her across the lobby and into the back offices.

"Mo-om!" Piper whines, pulling her arm free. "You're embarrassing me!"

"Piper. Sweetie. My darling baby girl. You cannot say shit like that about your mother and your teacher."

She widens her eyes and slowly blinks them. I narrow mine and point at her. "Stop with the puppy dog eyes, you monster."

"Why is it flirting when Luke and Lorelai do it, but not when you and Mr. Q do it?" she asks, sticking out her lower lip.

"Because... because..." Goddammit, this is what I get for forcing her to watch *Gilmore Girls* with me so often. "Because I said so!"

"Ah-ha!" Piper points her own finger in my face and I swat at it. "You promised you'd never use that as an excuse!"

"That was before you decided to be a little shit."

"Hmph." She crosses her arms over her chest. "Sounds like bullshit. You told me when Luke and Lorelai talk like that to each other, they're flirting. Why is it any different?"

Piper learns a lot about how social interactions work through media. We've spent her entire life pausing TV shows, movies, dog-earing books, and talking over commercials on the radio to talk about social interactions she didn't understand. It makes sense she understands flirting through the lens of Luke and Lorelai.

What *doesn't* make sense is her thinking Ren and I were flirting. Because that isn't what we were doing. At all. I mean. Maybe I was flirting a *little* with him, but he certainly wasn't flirting with me.

"I didn't mean to come across as flirtatious," I say slowly, making sure I get the words right. God knows she'll remember if I don't. "I'm sorry for confusing you."

She shrugs. "Okay."

"That's it? No more interrogation?"

"Do you *want* more interrogation?"

"No," I respond quickly. "No, I don't."

Piper steps around me. "Then you're off the hook." I exhale in relief too soon, because she glances over her shoulder at me with a smirk. "For now."

"You're treating this like a date!" Piper groans. She's currently spread starfish on her back in the middle of my bed.

"I am *not*," I argue, pulling a black dress from my closet and examining it.

I'm lying. I totally am.

It's been a week and a half since Piper accused me of flirting with Ren. I've wanted to make myself scarce the last two lessons, but I'm trying to keep a normal routine with both him and Piper, trying to pretend everything's normal and I don't know an extremely intimate detail about him. But since I can't interact with this man like a normal, adult, human being, I've been giving him his coffee, commenting on how great Piper's doing, and excusing myself under the guise of having to put out a fire somewhere in the inn.

Piper certainly doesn't buy it, and if Ren also doesn't, he's kind enough to not say anything.

Ren texted me this morning offering to drive, using terms like "economical" and "environmentally friendly." Personally, I think it's a terrible idea for us to be in such close proximity for the thirty-ish minutes it takes to get to New Haven, but it would make me sound like such a terrible person to refuse his offer.

"Move," Piper commands, elbowing me in the side. I yelp, jumping out of her way. When did she stand up? "You don't get nights out, so you don't know how to dress for a night out."

Ouch, but fair judgment. No one roasts you like your teenager.

She throws an emerald green dress I wear once a year on St. Patrick's Day at me. "This one."

I hold it up and eye it skeptically. "You think?"

"It'll compliment your hair," Piper explains, bending down and rummaging through my dress shoes. "You'll look like a pretty leprechaun."

"I'm not certain looking like a leprechaun is quite the vibe I want."

"You don't know what you want, Mom," she says, and again, *ouch*. She stands up with a gold kitten heel in each hand. "I'm making you pretty so you can flirt with a hot, rich Yale dad."

I bark out a surprised laugh, "Piper!"

"What? You should meet someone, and they might as well be rich." She holds the shoes out to me. "My very own Daddy Warbucks, if you will."

"I absolutely will not." I roll my eyes and take the shoes from her.

"Rich and entitled isn't your type?" Piper asks as I pull my robe off. Both my bra and underwear are at least five years old, and I wince when I catch the beige-ish colored fabric in the mirror. "Say," she continues, "what *is* your type?"

"Good try, birdie." I laugh, pulling the dress over my head. "We're not having this discussion."

"Lorelai and Rory do!" she whines.

I smooth the skirt down and look in the mirror. Curse this troublemaking, possibly matchmaking offspring of mine. The color does compliment my hair.

"Well?" I ask Piper, spreading my arms out and twirling, the skirt swooshing satisfyingly around my legs.

"If you *were* flirting with Mr. Q—which I know, I know, you're *not*—he'd totally flirt back."

I scowl at her. "I'm changing."

Of course that's when there's a knock at the front door. Piper has a shit-eating grin on her face.

"Oh *no*," she says theatrically. "It's too late. Guess you'll have to stay in the hot cougar outfit."

"What did you say?" I ask, mouth agape as she literally skips from the room.

She, of course, doesn't answer and I hear the click of the door unlocking. I sigh and fluff my hair before grabbing my purse. I just *know* she didn't check the peephole before she opened it.

"Hi, Mr. Q!" she says with an excitement I've heard maybe twice in this child's life. Maybe it's because she's excited for the concert, which I'm sure she is.

But I have a hunch she also has some questionable match-making goals for the night. And what happens if she's successful? I let Ren in, and he rocks my world in bed obviously, and when Piper and my life is too much, he leaves and breaks our hearts?

"You can do this. You're casual friends who are doing this for your favorite fifteen-year-old with questionable intentions," I tell myself in my mirror, running my hands over the curves and dips of my body. "You're doing this for Piper. You can keep a healthy distance." I nod determinedly at myself in the mirror before spinning on my heel, throwing the bedroom door open, and immediately realizing I'm screwed.

Ren in his workout clothes is sexy as fuck. Ren in the khaki shorts and college t-shirts he wears while teaching piano lessons is gorgeous.

But Ren in chinos and a sky blue shirt with the top buttons undone and sleeves rolled up to his elbows?

Holy *shit*.

This man is the beauty standard for men.

The blue makes his eyes pop, and I swear his lips are plumper than usual, his hair even curlier. I can't help but wonder if he styled it differently, or if this unbelievably gorgeous outfit of his just makes it look different.

Or maybe I am as slutty as everyone said.

The Piper-induced anxiety is still there, but accompanying it is a different, and frankly unwelcome feeling: good old-fashioned horniness.

I'm debating turning around and making retching noises to fake being sick when he glances up from Piper and meets my eyes.

Maybe I'm delusional, but I swear to god, this man does a double take before his eyes do a once-over. I watch with a mixture of emotions as he swallows, his Adam's apple bobbing in his throat.

It's been a minute since someone looked at me like I was something lovely to behold, something they don't want to take their eyes off.

Okay, I don't think it's actually *ever* happened.

Until tonight.

Ren's gaze meets mine again, and the corners of his eyes crinkle as he smiles.

How the fuck am I supposed to get through tonight?

Chapter 12

Ren

How the fuck am I supposed to get through tonight?

I was already anxious at the idea of spending the night in such close proximity to Audrey when I'm obsessed with her, and now she comes into the living room in a dress that looks custom made for her body. I've seen morning Audrey in her pajamas, glasses, and messy top knot, the poised and professional work Audrey, mom Audrey who always has something from Piper on her person... but this?

This feels like Audrey, no adjectives needed.

And Audrey *shines*. The dress cascades over her curves, making them even more evident, and god, I want to lose myself in them; to find every dimple and roll and become so lost I forget my own name.

"Hi," I wheeze. Good *god*, why do I sound like an unnerved caveman? It's my job to bring people to their knees by talking to them, and I'm ridiculously close to falling to mine and begging her for whatever she deems me worthy of. I clear my throat and try again. "Hi, Audrey. Good to see you."

She smiles. "Good to see you too. Thanks again for doing this for Piper."

Piper. Right. This is for Piper. Her child. Who is currently right beside me. Right.

"Yeah, um. Of course. Thanks for agreeing to come," I say awkwardly, rubbing my thumb along the links of my gold chain hidden beneath the collar of my shirt. If I didn't know better, I'd say Audrey's eyes follow the movement.

Unfortunately, I do know better.

"Can we get ice cream after the concert?" Piper asks as I open the front door.

"As long as it's okay with your mom," I respond.

"Fine by me," Audrey says, skirt swishing around her gorgeous legs as she walks past me and through the door. I'm immediately hit with the scent of coconut I've come to expect on her, but also something new. Jasmine, I think.

I shake myself out of my horny, scent-induced haze and close the door behind me. Audrey locks it while Piper is already clamoring into the backseat of my Corolla. I try to keep my eyes off Audrey, but my nose betrays me.

She turns around and her brow furrows. "What's wrong?"

"Nothing. Why?"

She shakes her head. "Sorry, your face... I don't know. I'm sorry."

I exhale heavily. I could lie. I *should* lie. "No, uh, sorry. It's... you smell different. I was trying to figure it out."

What a creepy thing to come out of my mouth.

Audrey doesn't freak out the way I think she should, and instead begins to panic for a different reason. "Is it too much? I never wear perfume but Piper saved her money and bought it for me for Christmas and insisted I wear it tonight and..."

"Fuck, I'm sorry." I should be embarrassed I cursed in front of a parent, but it doesn't feel wrong in front of Audrey the way it feels in front of everyone else.

So many things should and don't feel wrong with her.

"It's not too strong... I was trying to figure it out. You know, six sisters. They... uh... smell different."

I am *such* a dweeb.

This calms her though, and she exhales.

"I like it," I say, inexplicably. "A lot," I add because I'm a glutton for humiliation.

But then her eyes brighten, almost like she knows a secret no one else does, and she blushes. It may be the greatest accomplishment of my life. "Thank you," she says softly, averting her gaze to the ground. "It's jasmine, I think. God, I was nervous about wearing it. About wearing all of this." She waves her hand around her body, as if indicating she's nervous about everything on her body.

"You look great," I say earnestly, and she glances up again. "Do you feel great?"

Her blush deepens as she bites her lower lip. "I do. I feel... pretty." She whispers this like she's confessing a sin.

"Good." I motion to the car with my head. "Shall we?"

She nods and maybe, just maybe, she can't take her eyes off me, either. "We shall."

Audrey is silent the entire drive to New Haven.

Contrastingly, her child says more in the thirty minutes it takes for us to get to the theater than she has over the entire summer. How excited she is to get back to her daily routine, what classes she's looking forward to, her favorite people in school, her least favorite people in school—Annika Gardner can kick rocks—and which lunches are the most edible.

"We're going to continue our piano lessons, right, Mr. Q?" she asks after catching her breath.

"Uh," I say, honestly not sure what the answer is.

Usually private lessons end when the kids and I go back to school, but I love working with Piper. She's hardworking, and watching her progress has been amazing. She reminds me of myself when I was a kid.

"I don't think Mr. Q does summer lessons in the fall, birdie," Audrey says, breaking her apparent vow of silence.

"Oh." I hear the disappointment in Piper's voice. I see her reflection slump against the seatback. She crosses her arms over her chest.

I make a mental note to talk to Audrey about it at some point, because I would genuinely like to find a way to continue teaching Piper. I wouldn't be able to continue two times a week the way we are now, but I could make at least a weekly class work.

We all climb out of the car and start our short trek to the theater. It isn't until our tickets have been scanned and we've taken our seats that anyone speaks again.

"Kind of chilly in here," Audrey says, wrapping her arms around herself.

I immediately jump from my seat. "I have a sweater in the car."

Audrey stares at me. Piper, I notice out of the corner of my eye, is smirking at her mother.

Am I... being *Parent-Trapped* right now? Am I childless Dennis Quaid? I'll never measure up to Nick Parker.

No. Piper's probably a normal teenager who enjoys seeing her mother in minor discomfort. My sisters were always like that at her age.

"You don't have to..." Audrey starts to say.

I turn around and squeeze by the neighboring patrons before she can continue her refusal.

By the time I get back, gray and navy striped sweater draped over my arm, the lights have dimmed and the symphony is taking their places. I make it back to my seat just as the opening note to "Theme from *Jurassic Park*" plays.

"Here." Audrey sits between Piper and I, which seemed fine when we took our seats. But as her fingers graze mine when she takes my sweater from me, it's decidedly not fine.

"Thank you," she whispers, pulling the sweater over her head. I'm of course devastated to see that beautiful dress and the way her body looks in it covered by a sweater I've had since college, but she already seems more comfortable. Somehow, Audrey when she's comfortable is even more beautiful than Audrey when she's dressed fancy.

"Mom?" Piper says, barely loud enough for me to hear. "I forgot my earplugs."

My stomach sinks. Piper wore earplugs for some of our lessons, and I know how helpful they are for her. I lean forward to peer around Audrey just as she reaches to grab her bag from the floor, and our knees press together.

Fuck. Me.

"Sorry," Audrey murmurs, rummaging through her bag. I grip the edge of my seat, holding myself together after such a simple touch. She pulls out a small round case and hands it to

Piper, who immediately takes the earplugs out and hands the empty case back to her mom.

"Thank you," Piper whispers as the song reaches its crescendo.

As Audrey goes to put the earplug case back in her bag, her hand brushes against mine. Her breath catches and she yanks her hand away like I've burnt her. My heart is in my throat, and I can't help but think, for just a moment, that the simple touches are affecting her as much as they're affecting me. Her eyes meet mine, and god, it's dim in the theatre, but she's still the most beautiful woman I've ever seen.

"Sorry," she whispers.

"You're saying sorry an awful lot for someone who has nothing to be sorry for," I tease gently, attempting to ease her obvious discomfort.

Her responding smile is forced, and then she lowers her eyes to the case in her hand, but makes no movement to put it in her bag.

I'm not sure what's going on right now, and frankly, I'd bet good money she doesn't either. Is she so afraid of touching me again she's going to spend the rest of the night staring at an empty earplugs case?

Applause erupts around us as the song ends. Neither she or I clap, but I feel the applause reverberating in my chest, my heart pounding in time with it.

As the symphony transitions into the next song, the legendary *Star Wars* theme, I hesitantly hold my hand out to her.

She looks at it for a moment, before gently placing the case in my hand. Instead of pulling away, her fingertips graze the sensitive skin of my palm, and this time, my own breath catches.

She pulls away and clears her throat, her eyes trained on the stage. I lean forward to slip the case into my pants pocket, close enough to her that her scent—that intoxicating jasmine perfume—is unnerving. My breath on her neck must be as intoxicating for her, because she makes a tiny gasping sound as her breath catches, and she captures her bottom lip. I follow her lead and fix my eyes on the symphony, casually leaving my hand palm up on the arm rest between us.

I don't think she'll do anything. If she were to do anything, what would she even do? Hold my hand? We're not in middle school...

I nearly spring from my seat when her hand touches mine. I don't know who starts it, all I know is our fingers intertwine and *oh my god are we holding hands*?

We must be in middle school, because holding hands with Audrey Hinton is the most thrilling thing to ever happen to me.

I rebelliously allow my thumb to gently stroke her hand, earning that delicious breath catch again. When I turn my head towards her, she's still looking straight ahead, but there's something different about her.

She's smiling, eyes shining like she knows a secret no one else does.

Chapter 13

Audrey

Playlist: I Want to Hold Your Hand | Kate McGill

A little over fourteen years ago, Piper took her first steps. She'd kept me up all night, screaming, and refusing to settle. Out of pure desperation, and a need to get out of the house, I carried her to the beach as the sun rose over the sound. When she'd pushed herself to her feet and swayed, I'd gotten to my own feet and taken two steps backward, just to see. To my surprise, this wobbling little creature took two tiny steps forward before falling back on her butt. She'd stared up at me expectantly, like she had done it because she knew I needed it. Knew I needed something to remind me life could be good.

While nothing will ever beat that moment, my hand enveloped in Ren's for the entirety of this concert is a new moment I'll remember on the days when the darkness is too much. When I need help remembering there is some good in the world, and it's happened to me.

As the lights come on at the end of the concert, he and I get to our feet like everyone else in the concert hall. Unlike everyone else, we aren't clapping. And despite my expectations, his hand is still firmly clasping mine, filling me with a warm feeling I've only ever dreamed of.

"Did you like it, Mom?"

I am the worst mother in the world. I almost forgot my kid is next to me.

I quickly glance at our clasped hands and pull mine away. I pretend not to notice the way he flexes his hand before he shoves it into his pocket. I quickly turn away and face Piper.

"I did!" I tell her, an all-too-real smile on my face. "It was great."

"Which score was your favorite?" she asks.

Oh. That's... not what made the concert enjoyable.

"Hey," Ren leans across me and grins brightly at Piper. "Did you like it?"

"I *loved* it!" Piper squeals, clasping her hands together. "It made me want to watch the movies they're from! The music told a story all on its own."

"Yes!" Ren says enthusiastically, and I don't know, being sandwiched between these two adorable nerds may be the second best thing to happen tonight. "That's what a good score or soundtrack should do. John Williams is one of the greats, for sure."

Ren gives Piper her earplug case back as we file out of our row and into the lobby. Ren excuses himself to run to the restroom, and Piper and I wait in the lobby.

I'm checking my work email when she clears her throat. I raise a brow. "Yes?"

"You never answered my question," she says, crossing her arms over her chest.

I sigh and slip my phone into my bag. "Remind me again what the question was?"

"Which score was your favorite?"

"I'll always love the *Indiana Jones* theme," I say, remembering it definitely was played.

Piper's face falls. "Damn, I'd been hoping you were making out with Mr. Q and weren't paying attention."

"You *what*?"

"Hey," Ren slips in next to me, and I almost jump out of my skin. "I'm sorry to cut this short, but my landlord called. The apartment above mine flooded, and they're worried about a leak."

My stomach flips. I've dealt with flooding at the inn, and the worst part is dealing with any damage done to the room below.

"I have to bring you home so I can get my stuff out," he continues, jaw clenched.

"Where are you going to stay?" Piper asks, eyes wide and voice laced with concern.

Ren blinks at her, and fidgets with the gold chain around his neck. He's flustered, like he hadn't thought about it yet.

"I... uh. I have family in town. I'll see if one of them can... will let me..."

"You should stay at the inn! Mom can comp you a room!" Piper exclaims.

I try to express the murderous feelings in my chest to her silently, but her eyes are locked on Ren.

This child, I swear to god.

Ren is even more flustered and taken aback by Piper's offer. "Oh no, I couldn't."

"Sure you could," Piper says breezily, walking towards the doors. "Since you taught me for free, I think it's the least we could do."

I glare holes in the back of her head. She could at least *try* to matchmake subtly.

"That would... uh..." Ren stammers as he and I trail after Piper. "That wouldn't work. I have a cat..."

Piper spins around, eyes wide as saucers. "You *do*? I love cats! Mom keeps saying she'll get me one, but the fact I am still cat-less is one of the biggest disappointments of my life. Why don't you take the room and I'll cat sit for you? I have references."

Ren looks at me, and I know he's giving me the opportunity to think of a reason Piper's plan wouldn't work out. But, I could easily comp him a room for a few days until he can go back to his place. Frankly, she's right, he's done so much for us... it really is the least I could do.

"I'd be happy to comp you a stay, if you want," I say quietly, averting my eyes. "Piper can watch your cat, if you're okay with it."

"That's... Audrey." He grabs my wrist as I start to move toward the door, and I'm sent back to fifteen minutes ago when he was holding my hand in the dark theater. "That's way too much to ask of you."

I smile, and beg my stomach to settle itself. "You're not asking, I'm offering."

His eyes search mine. "Would you have offered if Piper didn't volunteer your generosity?"

"That's not fair, I just didn't think about it right away. You can pay me back by telling all the moms they have to book a weekend. Your endorsement would be more effective than a damn billboard."

A slow, soft smile spreads across his face. This man has several different smiles, and they seem so genuine, so real. It's baffling.

"Promise?" He releases my wrist and holds up a pinkie. I'm flooded with memories of me doing the same thing to him one time when he caught me sneaking out of Kat's room one night. Little Ren Quinn with a suspicious expression on his be-spectacled face, pinkie-promising not to tell anyone as long as I got him a chocolate-covered banana milkshake from Queenie's. We'd both made good on our promises, and I think we can do it again.

"Promise," I say, hooking my pinkie around his.

Piper and I wait in the car when Ren goes into his apartment to gather his belongings.

"I know what you're doing," I say, not looking up from the text I'm shooting the night manager on duty. "You're not slick, missy."

"What am I doing?" she asks from the backseat, voice saccharine and one-hundred percent untrustworthy.

I pause my typing for a moment. "I'm not sure *what* you're doing, but I'm certain of *why* you're doing it. You're not Lindsay Lohan, and Mr. Q isn't your dad, weirdo. Why are you *Parent-Trapping* us?"

I hear Piper unbuckle her seatbelt and feel her breath on my ear as she leans forward. "Mr. Q? Don't you mean Re-en?" She sing-songs his name, dragging it out so it has several syllables.

"You're the worst," I grumble, playfully thwacking at the hand she planted on my shoulder. She moves it quickly enough that I end up hitting myself instead.

"When should I start calling him 'Dad'?" she wonders aloud.

"Whenever he adopts you, 'cuz I'm done with you," I fire back.

She cackles.

I fight back a smile, and fail. This damn kid.

"Piper, where is this coming from?" I ask gently, unbuckling my seatbelt and turning in my seat to face her

"You seem happy when you're together—I didn't know you could smile this big, Mama." Damn her, she knows calling me 'Mama' is a foolproof way to make me tear up. "And you both look at each other like... like Luke looks at Lorelai the whole damn series."

"Real life doesn't work like a TV show," I say quietly, reaching back and brushing a rogue strand of hair out of her face. "You don't just... find your person at a diner and become happy."

"You're right. Sometimes you find them teaching your daughter piano."

I sigh. "Piper..."

"Why don't you want to be happy, Mama?"

"I am happy, birdie. I'm always happy with you."

"You literally have depression."

"And you think dating your piano teacher will cure me?" I ask, voice laced with confusion.

She sighs heavily. "No. You're happy enough, but you deserve to smile all the time the way you do when he makes a crappy joke. You deserve to be looked at like you hung the moon. The way he ran to get his sweater for you? You're the one who always runs to get your sweater to give to me."

"Birdie," I reach for her hand and she takes mine with surprising speed. "I love you. So much. And I'm grateful you want me to be happy and be treated well. But Ren and I don't have any sort of relationship beyond him being your piano teacher. But Eva wants me to make friends, and I could see Ren being one. But that's it, nothing more."

"All I'm saying is I wouldn't be mad if you became more," she says quietly, squeezing my hand. "I think you're *trying* to set boundaries with me as your kid, and failing terribly, and that's cool. I'll respect that. But I don't know. You're allowed to be more than my mom. You're allowed to be Audrey and to find happiness that isn't me. You're my favorite person in the world, you know? I want you to be more than happy."

I blink back the threatening tears flooding my eyes. "What's more than happy?"

She squeezes my hand again. "You'll know it when you see it."

The door to Ren's apartment building opens in my peripheral vision, and he comes out holding a cat carrier, a backpack strapped to his back. "If you say so, birdie."

She doesn't respond, just lets out a high pitched squeal as she pushes the door open and tumbles out. "Is that your cat?" Piper asks Ren excitedly.

"Yep," Ren says, holding the carrier so Piper can peek in, similar to a proud father holding his baby's car seat up. My stomach twists as that image forces itself into my brain. Ren with a baby—*his* baby—with a beautiful partner next to him, reaping the rewards of the hot dad forearms he'll inevitably have.

I hate this hypothetical human.

"What's her name?" Piper asks, pulling me out of my maladaptive daydream.

"Princess Leia, but I only add the Princess when she's gnawing on my snake plant." I try to stifle my giggle behind my hand. Of course this dweeb named his cat after Carrie Fisher's character in *Star Wars*.

"Mom does that too, adds the 'Elise' when I'm in trouble," Piper informs him.

He grins. "When I'm in trouble, I *still* get the 'Lorenzo Christopher' treatment. Hate to tell you it never goes away."

"Can she hang out in the back seat with me?" my daughter asks, seemingly ignoring his anecdote.

"Sure thing, Pipe," he answers, handing her the cat carrier. "She might be shy at first, but she's sweeter than pie when she's used to you."

Meanwhile, I'm becoming a pile of goo at hearing him call Piper "Pipe." No one else calls her that besides me, and maybe I should be jealous, like he's inserting himself in my relationship with my daughter.

But I feel bright *joy* washing over me at the fact Piper has someone else who wants to shorten her name, like they might be different, they might want to stick around.

Is this what Piper meant by more than happy? This light, airy feeling of joy and security and gratitude that exists simply because of Ren shortening her name?

If so, I'm fucked.

Chapter 14

Audrey

Playlist: Lay It on Me | Vance Joy

Ren parks his car in the inn parking lot and I'm filled with an uneasy sense of disappointment. This was as close to a perfect night as I've ever had.

Except for Ren's apartment flooding and Piper's apparent audition for Yente, the matchmaker from *Fiddler on the Roof*. Those things were less than perfect.

"They know you're coming," I say, averting my eyes. I don't want to face him, face the midnight of this Cinderella-like experience. "Show your ID at the front desk and Nia will give you your key."

"Thank you," he says quietly, and I dare to glance at him out of the corner of my eye. He's studying his hands in his lap, like he's avoiding my gaze, too.

I clear my throat and unbuckle my seatbelt. "I hope you have a good stay. Let me or any of the staff know if you need anything."

"I will," he answers as I climb out of the car. Piper is out, cradling Princess Leia's carrier securely in her arms.

"Let's go, I have to set up her litter box," Piper says solemnly, walking towards the cottage.

"*Shit*," I hiss as I come to a stop. "We don't have a litter box."

"Yes, we do," Piper calls over her shoulder.

I stare at the back of her head. "Why on earth would we have a litter box?"

Piper stops walking and turns around, eyebrow raised. "It's called *manifesting*, Mom. And yes, I have the actual litter and a scoop, too."

"Where are these alleged cat supplies?"

"Under my bed, duh."

When I was her age, I was hiding romance novels I got from the library under my bed. I'd tell the librarian I was getting them for my mom, and looking back, she *had* to know I wasn't. Meanwhile, Piper is keeping a litter box and the supplies that go with it under her bed as an attempt to manifest a cat in her life.

When we're in the house, Piper springs into action, setting up the food and water bowls Ren provided in the kitchen. She fills them and we head to her room where she sets up the litter box before crouching next to the carrier and unzipping it.

Leia's little calico head pops out of the opening, curiously taking in her surroundings.

"Hi, pretty kitty," Piper coos, a huge smile on her face. Goddammit. I'm gonna have to get this kid a cat, aren't I?

"Be gentle with her, Piper. She's in a strange place with strange people so give her time to..." My voice trails off as Leia gingerly climbs out of the carrier and into Piper's lap. She kneads Piper's thigh, a purr as loud as a motorbike reverberating through her little body.

Piper looks at me smugly. "You were saying?"

I roll my eyes. "Okay, cat whisperer. You got everything under control?"

"Yup." Piper pops the 'p.'

"Great. Wait, what's that Leia?" I cup my ear and lean in. "You want to hang out with Piper's very cool mom? Flattery isn't necessary, but…"

"Oh my *god*," Piper groans, rolling her eyes at me. "Don't you own an inn? Shouldn't you be busy with something? Your new grand-kitty and I are *bonding*."

I lean down and press my lips to the crown of Piper's head, and this time, it's my turn to roll my eyes. "I love you, stop stealing my good shampoo."

"I didn't!" Piper exclaims, way too quickly to be innocent.

"I have a nose, birdie."

"It makes my hair shiny!" she whines.

I stroke the back of her head. Damn, her hair *is* softer than usual.

"We'll talk later. Tomorrow, maybe, when you hang out with your very cool mom." I kiss the top of her head one last time before walking to my room.

I close the door behind me and wait until I hear Piper's bedroom door close, too. Now that I'm alone, I'm surrounded by the memory of Ren holding my hand. How strong and soft he felt, how his breath felt on my neck. How if he had leaned over merely a few inches more, I could have felt his mouth on my neck. I shiver, squeezing my thighs together.

What would Ren feel like on top of me? Saying the words Sky says and making me feel the way he has for so long without knowing?

It's because he's Sky. It wasn't like this before you knew.

I slowly run my hands over my dress, feeling each and every bump, every curve and roll. I'm hot, needy—all because of the memory of him.

I don't bother taking my clothes off, instead burrowing myself beneath the blanket fully clothed. Sky released a new audio a few days ago, but I haven't had time to listen yet, which is opportune considering how desperately I need a quick release. Plus, it'll be a good reminder that this overwhelming attraction is solely because of Sky. Sky is the one doing this to me, who makes my body ache and thighs quiver. Sky is the one I want.

Sure, Audrey. Whatever you say.

Shut up, brain.

I put my headphones over my ears and pull my fully charged—thank *god*—clit-sucking vibrator from my night-stand, sliding it beneath my skirt.

At first, I don't turn the toy on, teasing myself along my inner thighs with it before pressing play on the audio.

"Good morning, beautiful."

I want to be able to disconnect Sky from Ren, to disconnect my goddamn *attraction*.

"Waking up next to my beautiful wife never gets old."

My eyes fly open and I grab my phone with my free hand. Fuck, it's a *married* audio. Those always get me. Being called *wife* gets my gears turning, maybe because it's not something I'll ever be called.

"I know we just got married but..."

Sky's laughter fills my ears and I relax. That's not Ren's laugh. It's Sky. Sky isn't real. Ren *is* real.

I close my eyes and slip my vibrator under my panties as I turn it on.

"Oh, you like it when I call you that? My wife. My wife. My good, beautiful, sexy wife."

My back arches as I place it over my clit, the sensation over-whelming my body.

"Yeah, I'm hard already. You try sleeping next to your naked wife and not waking up hard."

I try to imagine Sky the way I'd imagined him before know-ing his real identity. Before I knew he was Ren. Faceless and tall, maybe some tattoos, because who doesn't love a bad boy. Growly voice and forearms that make me want to scream. Brown curly hair and green eyes that make me want to get lost in a forest and...

That's Ren. I'm literally imagining Ren hovering over me, thrusting into me at the perfect pace, because somehow this man would know how I like it better than I do.

"Fuck, baby. Your pussy is heaven," Sky says.

"You're not broken," imaginary Ren whispers in my ear. *"You're not damaged goods, no matter what they say. Your body is so good. You're fucking good."*

I jackknife into a sitting position and violently yank my head-phones off my head.

What the *hell*?

Is that the dirty pillow talk my subconscious wants? To be wanted even when I'm known? That the things I've put so much energy into hiding are beautiful and worthy of light?

Why can't I be into light degradation or something? Nope, I need my sexual partner to fucking therapize me.

I snatch the vibrator I'd dropped and turn it off. Somehow, I'm even hornier than I was before, and also have *zero* desire to continue, because who knows what other bizarre kinks will be unlocked. Who knows how else I'll picture Ren.

I swing my legs over the side of my bed and get to my feet.

Ren is a person. A human being. He's not a concept and not automatically tied to Sky and I shouldn't know he is. He ob-viously doesn't want people to know, probably so his student's invasive moms don't get off to him.

Ren is a person. A good, generous person. He's not a fantasy. I have to keep reminding myself of that.

I take a deep breath and swap my contacts for glasses. I change into bike shorts and a t-shirt before leaving my room and grabbing my keys.

"Come in!" Piper calls when I knock on her door.

"Hey, birdie." I poke my head into the room. She's turned her fairy lights on and is snuggled under her weighted blanket, her iPad leaning against her giant metal cup on her nightstand. Leia is curled into a donut shape beside her, on top of the blankets. The feline meets my eyes and I narrow mine at her.

Stop it! I tell her psychically. *I know! She needs a goddamn cat! You don't have to make me feel bad about it!*

Leia stares at me, unblinking.

"What's up?" Piper asks, pressing pause on whatever she's watching.

"Nia texted, and she locked herself out of the system and needs me to reset it," I lie. "I'm going to run to the inn for about an hour, are you okay on your own?"

"Yup," she answers, pressing play on her iPad. Familiar music plays from it.

"Are you... watching *Star Wars*?"

"Yes. Leia wanted to see her namesake and since I've never seen it, I thought it was the perfect activity for this evening."

I shake my head. "Mr. Q is a bad influence on you."

I can't see her face, but I know this little brat is smirking. "Sure, Mom."

Ten minutes later, and I'm knocking at room 215, a stack of towels tucked under my arm.

When Ren opens the door, I literally drop them.

Like, literally. It's embarrassing.

He's freshly showered and wearing an oversized t-shirt and forest green boxers that match his eyes. His hair is wet and he's drying it with a towel. He must have brought his own shampoo and soap, because he doesn't smell like the subtle cotton and tea tree oil of the toiletries we provide, but instead like sandalwood and sea salt and... is that peppermint?

"Oh, shit," he says, bending down to grab the towels at the same time I do. Our heads collide with a loud *thwack*. My phone falls from my hand, and we simultaneously groan and pull away from each other.

"Ow," I groan, covering my forehead with my hand. *That's* going to leave a bruise.

"I'm sorry," Ren sounds truly contrite, or maybe he's in pain. "I was just trying to..."

I start to laugh, because god. It's ridiculous. We smacked our heads together like it's some poorly-written meet cute in a Hallmark Christmas movie.

He starts to laugh too, and my entire body is flooded with warmth at *Ren's* laugh. This laugh I've come to love and be comforted by.

"Okay, okay," he wheezes, wiping at his eyes. "Don't move. I'm going to grab the towels."

I raise my hands to show my obedience as he bends down. "Yes, sir."

The speed at which he stands up straight, towels still on the ground, is almost comical.

"What did you just say?" he asks, face red.

Huh? What did *I just...*

Oh my god.

Oh my god.

Okay, Audrey, play it cool. It's nothing. You didn't mean it in a sexual way.

Even if he obviously interpreted it as sexual.

I laugh nervously. "What, no one ever calls you sir? Kids these days have no manners."

He laughs, but this time it's strained. "You can't say stuff like that, Aud."

I feel lightheaded as he bends over again, collecting the towels in his arms and reaching to grab the phone that landed by my feet.

Aud.

Pipe.

He's *comfortable* with us. He's shortening our names like he's *ours,* like we're his.

He stands, avoiding my eyes. "Do you want to come in?" he asks, and I nod. He holds the door open and I squeeze past him, shivering when my breasts brush against his chest.

This! Is! The! Worst!

I clear my throat and glance around the room. It looks like every other room in the inn. King sized bed in the middle of the room, beachy, brown and blue photography and art against off-white walls. I wanted it to be modern and cozy and beachy and, not to toot my own horn, I did a damn good job at it.

Well, the interior designer I hired did.

"So," Ren says, closing the door behind him. My shoulders tense. I'm alone with this hot as hell man in a hotel room. This feels intimate. "How's Leia doing? Adjusting well?"

I laugh. "Oh, she's doing great. She and Piper are thick as thieves already. Good luck getting her back."

He laughs and places the towels in a messy pile on the desk, my phone beside them. He sits in the desk chair and puts on a round pair of glasses.

Fuck. Me.

"You wear glasses?" I squeak.

He eyes me skeptically behind his bronze wireframes. "So do you."

Sure, but they don't make me look like the hottest human to ever exist. *My* glasses make me look like an exhausted mom.

"I *knew* something was missing. Now the exterior matches the nerdy-as-hell interior." Is that too mean? I'm trying to be casual. Friendly. I'm awful at this.

"Ha, ha," he responds dryly, crossing his arms across his broad chest and stretching his legs out in front of him. I'm filled with the disturbing urge to bite his thigh.

I gulp and motion to the pile of towels he placed on the desk. "I brought you towels."

He lifts the one in his hand. "Thanks, but there were some in the bathroom when I got here."

Goddammit. I'd been hoping my staff made a mistake with the last minute reservation, but no, they have to be too good at their jobs.

"Oh," I say. I need to come up with better words. Better excuses. Because this is humiliating.

I reach over him and collect the towels in my arms. "I'm going to put these in the bathroom for you. In case you need them," I say awkwardly.

He's still avoiding my gaze, which makes sense. I'm being a fucking weirdo. "Right. Thanks."

I shuffle in the bathroom. It smells *so* much like him, the scent heavy in the air like a dense, incredible-smelling fog. I stand on my tiptoes and put the towels on the shelf next to the sink.

When I lower myself to my feet, I quietly pull back the shower curtain.

I *have* to know what this man washes himself with. I'm pleased when I find out he's not a 3-in-1 guy, but has separate shampoo, conditioner, *and* body wash. That must be his secret.

"La la la la la la."

I should be rushing out of the room at Piper's text tone, the la la la's from *Gilmore Girls*, but I'm not.

"I'm fixing a few things in here," I call to Ren, carefully flipping the top of his body wash so it doesn't make any noise. "But that's Piper. Can you check to make sure everything's okay for me? Password is 0504."

"May the Fourth be with you," Ren says as I inhale the scent. What a fucking nerd.

"Piper's birthday," I respond, soaking in the soft smell of sandalwood and sea salt.

"Damn, a dream birthday," Ren says, voice wistful. "I'll read the text."

I take another whiff. God, I wish this was something I could get high off. Maybe it is, I *feel* high. Light headed and floaty and...

And did I ever close 4Play?

I freeze, dread filling my body. 4Play is open on Sky's newest audio and I gave Ren my password and...

I shove the body wash haphazardly onto the shower shelf and lunge towards the door. "Ren, wait—"

My heart is pounding when he glances up from my phone, the screen reflected in his lenses—the blue and gray bubbles of mine and Piper's text thread.

"Piper wants to know if she could eat your Cherry Garcia if she replaces it tomorrow," he says, holding my phone out to me.

I take it, hand shaking. "Did... did you text her back?"

"I have six sisters, Audrey. I know better than to give away someone's ice cream," he answers.

I try to search his eyes, but he looks away as he grabs his own phone. I watch in the reflection as he goes to his alarms. "I don't mean to be rude, but it's been a long day and I'm tired…"

"Right," I interrupt. "Right, I'll get out of your hair."

This time, he meets my eyes and I swallow, fighting the urge to blink.

"You're not in my hair," he says quietly. "You're not… you're not a bother, if that's what you're insinuating."

I force a laugh. "Please, I know myself well enough to…"

Suddenly he's on his feet and taking a step towards me. "Don't finish that sentence," he whispers, eyes intent on mine. "Please, don't finish whatever you were going to say. I don't think I can take you talking shit about yourself tonight."

I stare at him. "I'm not…"

"Yes, you are," he interrupts. He reaches his hand out, and softly tucks a strand of hair behind my ear. When I freeze, he pulls his hand back with urgency. "You talk about yourself like you're the worst person in the world, and you're not, Aud. You're a good person. A good mom. It breaks my heart to hear you talk about yourself that way."

"You never talk about yourself that way?" I ask, mouth dry. He's staring at me with an intensity of a total eclipse, and similarly, I know looking at him like this is just as dangerous.

"That's not what we're talking about right now, sweetheart."

"You—you called me sweetheart," I whisper.

His cheeks flush, like he hadn't realized he said it. "I won't say it again. I'm sorry…"

"What if I want you to say it again?" I ask.

He slowly lifts his hand, cupping my cheek. "What are we doing, Audrey?" he asks, voice husky. "Why did you come to my room?"

"I told you, I wasn't sure if..."

"Right, the towels," he interrupts. "If they weren't in my room, I could have called the front desk. You didn't have to leave Piper and come to the inn, but you did. Tell me why."

I want to lean into his touch. To tell him the truth, that I wanted to be close to him. I *want* to be close to him.

But I can't.

I take a step back and his hand falls to his side. "I'm sorry," I whisper, "I shouldn't have come."

He steps back and inhales shakily. "Okay."

"I'm sorry," I say again.

"Okay," he repeats.

He's avoiding my eyes and I want to take it back, to rewind the tape and not let his hand fall.

But I can't.

"You probably want this back," Ren says, giving me my phone.

"Thanks. Sleep well."

"Goodnight, Audrey."

When I get home, I bring Piper my pint of Cherry Garcia and bury myself beneath the blankets. It's not till then I finally let the tears fall. I feel such *shame* for rejecting him, for hurting him. But it's for the better, because if he knew how damaged I am, he wouldn't want me. It's better to shut him down altogether.

The upside is he doesn't know I know he's Sky.

Despite that, the darkness still covers me, a familiar companion pulling me into the depths again.

I cry myself to sleep.

Chapter 15

Ren

Playlist: I Did Something Bad | Taylor Swift

I was awake all night tossing and turning, restless because of this infuriating woman and what I discovered.

I didn't know when I unlocked her phone, it would open to an app I'm intimately familiar with—literally.

She was listening to my most recent audio, the one I uploaded a few days ago. She'd made it a few minutes in and...

Audrey listens to my audios.

I've worked hard to keep Sky anonymous, to keep myself separate from Sky. I felt nauseous, wondering if she knew.

Maybe she didn't. Sky is one of the most popular creators on the app, and 4Play is one of the most downloaded apps in its category. She could not know.

But she came to my room... instead of finishing the audio. Then she pretty much fell out of the bathroom in a panic, eyes wide and chest heaving. While I wanted to believe it was simply because she realized the possibility that she'd be outed as a consumer of audio erotica, there's something inside me telling me she was afraid I'd know what she knows.

I'm feeling so many emotions at this realization, but mostly confused because *how* would she know? I change my voice to stay anonymous, have never shown my face and Sky has no social media. Her knowing should be an impossibility.

But Audrey is nothing if not an impossibility.

I wanted her last night, and I let myself believe she wanted me, too.

I think she *did* want me, too. I haven't wanted to be physically intimate with someone in a long time, and I want a lot more than a quick fuck with Audrey. Every time she lets me into any part of her life, I'm insatiable. I want more of her. More of Audrey's life, more of Piper's sarcastic comments and drinking coffee from Audrey's mugs.

But she pulled away from me.

I finally fall asleep at four thirty, and my alarm wakes me a whopping three hours later. On Wednesdays, Will and I lift at the gym, so I force myself out of bed and get dressed.

My landlord texted me to let me know that miraculously, there was no damage to my apartment and I can come back later today. At least one thing is going my way.

I decide to leave Leia with Piper a little longer, and send Audrey a text to ask if that's okay.

She responds with a thumbs up, like she's my dad.

"Damn," Will says when I find him at the dumbbells. "You look like hell."

"Thanks," I say sarcastically. But when I examine myself in the mirror, I think he may have been too generous. "Yikes."

"Late night for Sky?" Will asks, taking an earbud out of his ear expectantly.

"In a way," I grumble, not wanting to continue the conversation. While Will is the only person in my life who knows about

Sky, I haven't talked much about Audrey, and I don't really want to.

"Hmm," Will says thoughtfully, grabbing two forties from the rack. "You haven't looked this rough since Taylor. Is she back in town?"

I sigh and sit on the bench, shoulders slumped. "Worse. There's someone else, and she doesn't want me."

Not talking about Audrey lasted all of ten seconds. I'm pathetic.

Will hovers over me, dumbbells still dangling by his sides. "Are you okay?" he asks empathetically.

I stare at the ground, at the sweat-stained tiles, for what feels like forever until I finally shake my head.

"What's going to help?" Will asks.

I inhale shakily and get to my feet, striding to the rack with purpose.

I can fake it until I make it.

Because the only thing that might help is lifting weights heavier than the heaviness in my heart.

I'm both relieved and disappointed when I get to the cottage and Piper informs me Audrey's at the inn. Relieved, because of last night. Disappointed, because of last night.

The rest of the week speeds by, and I'm back at my parents' for another Sunday dinner. It's a big, mandatory one. At least for everyone in driving/short train ride distance. The twins' birthday was a few days ago, *and* they're headed back to college tomorrow. Our mother could not be happier.

"We're spending the weekend at the shore after we drop Leo off at Rutgers," Mom says excitedly, red wine sloshing over the lip of her wine glass.

"Mother, you are a mess," Jo says, handing Mom another napkin.

"Respect your elders, Josephine," Josh quips.

"Respect my fist in your face, Henry," Jo says without glancing in his direction.

Nic snickers. "Ooh, burn."

All of my siblings are at dinner, including Alex via FaceTime; she's currently propped against a bottle of Chianti. It's not rare for random friends to join us on Sundays; sometimes it's Josh's cousins, other times Will is able to make it, or Millie's best friend, Poppy. But Finn, Izzy's best friend, hasn't missed a Sunday dinner since he was eight years old and moved into the house next door. That is, until he chose a college out of state.

"You excited to go back to Oregon?" I ask him. Finn's starting his sophomore year at the University of Oregon, where he's studying marine biology.

He looks at me, pushing his glasses further up the bridge of his nose. "I miss class and the work I get to do, but I do get homesick."

"Ask him about his girlfriend," Izzy whispers, peeking around him.

"You have a girlfriend?" I ask.

Poor Finn is more flustered than I've ever seen him, and that's saying something. "I... no. It was... no. We...no."

Izzy snickers, and nudges him with her shoulder. "You're doing great, Finny."

He scowls at her. "One day I'm not coming back."

"Your boundaries are valid," my youngest sister responds serenely, taking his plate and spooning baked ziti onto it. "How are you feeling about vegetables today?"

"The same way I feel about you harassing me over a non-existent girlfriend," he grumbles.

"Gotcha," she nods.

After dinner, Nic and I are on dish duty.

"So," she says. "You're acting weird,"

I glance at her out of the corner of my eye. "Am not."

"Are too. You're less smiley than usual."

Shit. Am I? I mentally berate myself for this, though maybe nobody else noticed. Nic is annoyingly observant and can tell the slightest shift in the way someone behaves, even if she can't quite tell what it means.

"It's that time of year again. Preparing for the start of school is exhausting." I make sure to tack on an extra-wattage smile at the end.

"Hmm," she says skeptically, and I wait for her to continue. She doesn't.

I guess that's that.

Once I'm back at the table, I pull out my phone.

Ren

hey, was just wondering when you were free to discuss piper's lessons for when school starts?

"Spoons?" Leo says hopefully, slamming his hands on the table.

"*No*," Nic growls at the same time Kat exclaims, "Yes!"

Nic glares at Kat. "No. We can only play during holidays. That's literally the written law on the fridge."

"It's a useless rule," Kat argues.

"It's a *rule* because you gave me a black eye two years ago," Nic shoots back. "Because you lose what little humanity you have while playing and are certifiably a wild animal."

My phone dings and I look at it.

Audrey

> probably not anytime soon. we're really busy preparing for school. sorry.

Ren

> you don't need to apologize. i want to make a schedule so piper knows what to expect if she still wants to continue taking lessons.

"You're just upset because you never win," Kat says to Nic.

"*You're just upset because you never win,*" Nic mimics.

"Oh my god, you're a child."

"*Oh my god, you're a child.*"

I rub at my temples.

"Wait, let's check the log book. I've definitely won before." Nic pushes away from the table and heads towards the family room. Kat follows her, their bickering loud enough to still be heard across the house. I glance back at my phone to see if Audrey's texted back.

Audrey

> she does, saturdays still work for us if they work for you.

Ren

> can you and i meet in person, please?

Audrey

> i don't know if that's a good idea.

Ren

> okay.

I lean over my plate, grabbing my bottle of Guinness before slumping against the chair and taking a generous swig out of frustration. I shouldn't be drinking while depressed, but right now I want to feel *less*.

I'm not going to push Audrey's boundaries. I'm not going to make her talk to me.

But I think I can get her to listen to me.

Chapter 16

Audrey

Playlist: Look What You Made Me Do | Taylor Swift

Ren

hey, sorry it's last minute, but i'm not going to be able to do a lesson tomorrow. can you apologize to piper for me?

Audrey

oh

Ren

first week of classes was harder than i expected.

Audrey

> ren, i know i'm acting kind of weird, and while i'd love to explain i don't know that i can. But please don't take it out on piper. I'll meet with you, we can talk. This is important to her, and it's important to me and i'm sorry i'm a mess and immature and a fuck-up.

Ren

> well, i definitely didn't say THAT. but i do wish you'd agreed to talk to me sooner.

Audrey

> what does that mean?

I'm staring at my phone, waiting for a response to Ren's cryptic comment.

I don't get one.

It's my first day back at work in over a week. After the incident with Ren, I spiraled. Fast. I found myself in bed until Nia texted me that we were understaffed today and they needed backup.

So I brushed my teeth and took a shower for the first time in forever, and here I am, in my office at the inn and wondering what my child's piano teacher is talking about.

I'm on medication. I go to therapy. I try to use the coping skills I've learned over the years and I still have week-long depressive episodes where all I do is sleep and watch TV. It makes me feel like such a failure. Eva reminds me being diagnosed with major depressive disorder literally means it's chronic and these episodes will come and go, but still. Shouldn't I know how to handle them after over a decade of treatment?

I try to focus on my work throughout the day, but I find my mind constantly wandering to Ren. Ren who held my hand through a symphony, for no discernable reason besides the fact he'd wanted to. Ren, who gave me his sweater and listened to me like what I had to say was important.

Ren, who possibly knows I listen to audio erotica. *His* audio erotica. Ren, who's been reaching out and trying to connect while I continue to push him away.

Ren, who probably hates me because I've refused to communicate with him.

It's probably for the best. We'd be awful together. He's beloved by the community, and he should be with someone who is equally beloved, not the depressed single mom who spends a week in bed, barely eating or taking care of herself. He saw how Celia treated me at the diner, and that's just a snapshot of what our future would look like if he chose to be with me.

He deserves someone he can brag about, someone who doesn't send her employees to the town meetings to avoid interacting with townspeople. Someone who doesn't drive twenty miles to Norwalk to grocery shop. Someone he can introduce with pride.

That will never be me.

While he may not understand why, me pushing him away is the biggest kindness I could show him.

I fear my heart's already too soft to have quick, meaningless sex when he's come to mean so much to me.

To Piper, too. God. Piper. I probably ruined everything for her.

Because that seems to be what I do lately. Ruin good things.

I put my phone on the front desk and answer the ringing phone, taking a quick note of what the guests in room 33 need: toothpaste and shaving cream. I collect the items and give them to our runner before helping the guest waiting to check-in for a two-night stay.

Around an hour later, Piper's text tone goes off, so I pick my phone up again.

Well, there goes my multi-hour streak of not thinking about Ren. Except for when a toddler started banging on the piano in the lobby earlier. When I looked, I swore it was him on the bench. I caught myself thinking of him again when I was on hold with one of our suppliers and *Für Elise* was the hold music. Or...

Fine. I *tried,* okay?

I groan and fight the urge to slam my head against the desk. He *did* cancel. He gave a reason, but I can't help doubting his excuse. If he wants to avoid me, fine. He can have his space.

I'll continue to ignore the fact it hurts my heart to think about him not being around.

I need to masturbate, to someone who isn't Ren. I'll try a new performer tonight and I'll forget about Ren Quinn and Sky and we can go back to being maybe friends and I won't wonder what his beard would feel like on my neck as he sucks on my pulse point.

Because normal people don't think that about friends. At least, I won't. I refuse.

But what *would* it be like to have him that close? To have his hands on my body, giving me relief with more than his voice and words? Pleasuring me with his hands, his tongue, his...

I jolt as the phone rings. "Front desk, how can I help you?"

I take notes for what this particular guest needs, trying to ignore what my body is screaming *I* need.

When I finally get home, it's almost ten p.m., and I'm exhausted. I stop in to see Piper, who's on her iPad. Then I head directly for my bedroom, unbuttoning my top as I go.

While removing my contacts, I tell myself over and over I'm going to get myself off to someone new. Someone who isn't Ren's alter ego. Someone who will get me to stop fantasizing about this man I should have nothing to do with.

I strip down to my underwear and climb onto the bed. I lay back against my pillows, hair splayed across the white linen and open 4Play.

I promise, I'm going to explore the other creators. I'm going to listen to someone new.

But the first thing I see is Sky's new release. Sky doesn't usually release on Fridays, and it's simply titled, "For You."

I'm a weak, foolish woman, because I'm pressing play before I even look at the tags, my stomach fluttering like this man made this for me.

"Hi, sweetheart." Sky's voice surrounds me through my headphones, followed by a deep chuckle. See? I can do this. I can get off to Sky and forget he's Ren. I can separate the two and it'll be fine. *"Can I call you sweetheart? It feels right to call you that, and you said you might want me to."*

I spread my legs and plant my feet on the mattress as I reach for my favorite vibrator.

"It's been a minute, huh? You're not talking to me, so I decided to get through to you in a way I knew would work."

I turn on the vibrator and place it over my clit, inhaling sharply at the sensation. *Fuck.* I've been horny all day and I'm desperate for an orgasm.

"I don't know if you realize it yet, but this is a little different. A little improvised. A little... personal."

God. It's no use. When I close my eyes, it's Ren I see. Ren leaning over me, asking if he can have me like this. Ren pushing me against the wall and kissing me until my lips are swollen. Ren kissing me awake and kissing down my body...

And *that's* where my sexual fantasies have gone. Soft intimacy, not with some faceless performer, but with *Ren*.

I *want* Ren. In more ways than I should. In *all* the ways I shouldn't.

"I hope your head's okay, I had a nasty bump on my forehead for a few days."

My eyes fly open and the hand that was pinching my nipple through my bra flies to my forehead, where I covered a quarter-sized bruise with concealer this morning.

"And if you're thinking I'm not talking about you, not talking to you... you're wrong, sweetheart. I'm talking about you, to you. Because I'm always fucking thinking about you."

I slowly sit up as my vibrator falls to the mattress, buzzing against the sheets. My head is swimming, my stomach sinking.

No.

No.

"You're getting it, aren't you? You're getting I know *you knew I didn't need towels. And it's clicking I know you know my secret. And I know yours, sweetheart."*

I pull my headphones off my head.

"What the *fuck*?" I say, probably too loud.

But really, is there too loud a volume for this?

Because honestly, what the *fuck*?

I get to my feet, grab my glasses, and pull out a pair of bike shorts and an oversized t-shirt. If he gets to be absolutely unhinged, then I do, too.

Chapter 17

Audrey

Playlist: Don't Blame Me | Taylor Swift

Sky's Sluts

SkysMainSlut: GIRLS did you see the surprise drop?

AshBash69: I orgasmed as soon as I saw it omggggggggg

RebelLady93: have you listened to it yet?

AshBash69: no, why?

RebelLady93: it's sfw.

SkysMainSlut: WHAT

AshBash69: oh my god my day is RUINED.

RebelLady93: it was kinda weird, honestly. It was direct to listener, but it was like... very specific. Very personal. It was hard to feel like he was talking to me.

SkysMainSlut: i can't believe my man broke my heart like this.

AshBash69: we just have to get through the weekend and monday, and then it's tuesday. Hopefully he'll be back to his normal content by then. <fingers crossed emoji>

SkysMainSlut: i hope so. I need something unhinged and sexy in my life.

It's *way* too easy to get inside this apartment building. If I weren't so pissed, I'd tell Ren about the faulty lock.

But I am indeed pissed, so he can be murdered in his sleep for all I care.

After knocking on three doors, I was finally given Ren's apartment number by a random dude. Again, the odds of him getting murdered in this building are very high.

Now I'm standing at his door, banging on it with my fist.

Ren's eyes widen behind his glasses when he opens the door, like he didn't expect to see me. I fight the urge to roll my eyes. He's going to make an erotic audio about me, or at least directed at me, and act surprised when I show up at his apartment that I definitely didn't know the location of?

Preposterous.

"Aud…"

"I'm coming in," I interrupt, shouldering my way into the apartment. When I step in, most of my gumption disappears because this man has a lightsaber mounted on his wall and a LEGO *Star Wars* spaceship I don't know the name of encased in glass but also, it has that sage and peppermint scent and it makes me want to pull my hair out.

"What are you…" he begins to ask, closing and locking the door with a click.

I won't even tell him how that lock's probably broken too, so it's not the safety measure he thinks it is. But instead I let my emotions take the wheel.

"No, absolutely not." I spin on my heel and take two large steps toward him. "You do *not* get to ask any questions in this situation."

His brows furrow in confusion for a moment before relaxing with realization, a smirk lifting those pouty lips of his. "Ah, you opened a certain app, I see."

"What is *wrong* with you?" I hiss.

He takes a step toward me. He's so close I can see the flecks of gold in his eyes, and he can probably feel my hardened nipples against his chest.

Please, nipples. Chill out.

"I was *thinking* I didn't have another way to get through to you," he says, eyes narrowing at me. "And we need to talk."

I laugh in disbelief and step away from him. "Unbelievable. Instead of coming to see me like a mature adult you made a goddamn erotic audio? What the *fuck*, Ren?"

"How long have you known?" he asks abruptly, voice cold.

I blink at him, taken aback. "I said no questions..."

"I never agreed," he interrupts, crossing his arms over his broad chest. "How long have you known?"

I force myself to meet his eyes. "I don't see what that has to do with anything."

He laughs, a short, harsh sound. "You don't see why you knowing incredibly personal information about me and *keeping* that knowledge from me has anything to do with you being called out about it? Really, Audrey?"

My cheeks heat. "You don't get to be angry about this. What if people I know listen, Ren?"

"I didn't give any identifying information," he argues, throwing his arms in the air. "I wouldn't do that, and you know it."

"I don't know *what* I know," I counter. "I didn't think you'd use fucking 4Play to get in contact with me!"

"How long have you known?" he asks again.

"I don't..." I shake my head, like it's an Etch A Sketch and I need to reset my brain. "It was a few weeks ago."

"How *many* weeks, Audrey?" he says, and the sternness in his voice makes me want to withdraw into myself, hide my body in my shell like I'm a reptile. But it also makes me clench my thighs together and that is *not* something I want to unpack today, thank you very much.

"Three weeks. Tomorrow," I tell him, mouth dry.

I try not to watch his Adam's apple bob as he swallows. I promise, it's a valiant attempt.

"How did you figure it out?" he asks, turning his head away from me.

"It's... it's silly," I stammer, cheeks reddening. "I didn't know at first, you disguise your voice really well," I assure him.

He's silent, arms crossed across his body and eyes downcast, his posture reflecting the way I feel inside. Ashamed.

"It was your laugh," I blurt out. "It's usually different but in... in that week's audio it sounded familiar, and I went back to your first audio..."

"Before I got the Sky voice right," he finishes, tilting his head to stare at the ceiling and exhaling heavily. "*Fuck.*"

"I'm sorry," I whisper. "I didn't mean to..." Mean to what? Call him out? Show up at his apartment and accuse him? I meant to do *both* of those things.

I can't find the courage that brought me here to be honest with him. That bravery that had me asking strangers for Ren's apartment number is long gone, replaced instead by shame.

"It's a nice laugh," I say smally, like that will make him feel better. "I like it better than your Sky laugh."

Shut up, *Audrey.*

That gets Ren to glance at me. "I'm not him, you know," he says softly. "He's a part I play. It's a job. One I enjoy, but I'm not..." He huffs out a laugh and shakes his head. "I'm actually demisexual, you know. I need an emotional connection to feel sexual attraction and... and it's a farce. I'm not this sex god like him."

I must be a twelve-year-old boy because I actively have to stifle my giggle at Ren saying the word *sex*. I try to school my face, because he just came out to me, and I know that means something. He shared a part of himself he hadn't shared previously, trusted me with a new piece of the puzzle that is Ren Quinn. "Okay."

"I get that you want him," Ren continues, dropping his arms to his side and lifting one hand to run his fingers anxiously along his gold chain. "Who doesn't, right? Have you seen the subreddit?" He laughs nervously as I blush and duck my head, face giving away the fact that I have indeed seen the subreddit. "I don't blame you for cutting me off when you realized it was me. I can't live up to him."

"Ren," I take a step towards him, "No. I haven't been able to get off to a Sky audio since..." I trail off, too afraid to admit it to him, to myself.

"Since when?" he asks quietly.

Since I realized how amazing you are. How generous and kind and my fantasies started including you staying for breakfast and being my person. Since I realized Ren was infinitely better than Sky, and I couldn't have either.

"It doesn't matter," I shake my head and look down again. "I... shouldn't be talking about me getting off."

I can hear his quick intake of breath. "Why did you come?"

"I came to give you hell and I don't think I'm doing a very good job at it," I say helplessly.

"Sweetheart, you're doing a wonderful job giving me hell," he reassures.

"No, you don't get to do that." I meet his eyes again and point a threatening index finger at him. "You don't get to call me pet names like I mean something to you."

"You think you mean nothing to me?" He reels back, like I told him the pope isn't Catholic. "Of course you mean something to me."

"Not like that," I say, throat dry. "Not in a sweetheart way."

"Audrey, come on. I can't keep playing these games where we dance around each other and our feelings."

I flush. "Ren, no…"

He takes a step toward me and my breath stutters from being closer to him. There's still around a foot of space between us, but he's *closer*.

"You're going to tell me you don't feel this? You don't feel whatever the hell this is between us?"

I squeeze my eyes closed, unable to look him in the eye. "Yes. I… I don't feel anything."

"Bullshit," he says simply, and I hear the floorboards creak as he takes another step towards me. "I'm calling bullshit."

"We can't," I whisper, eyes opening and heart pounding in my chest as I peer at him. I take a shaky step back. "Ren…we can't. *I* can't."

"Because you don't want to? Or because you don't like what I do for a second job?"

My jaw drops and I notice the sadness in his eyes. "Ren, I swear, I don't care about that. That isn't a deterrent."

"Then what is?" He takes another step forward, and I take one back, my ass pressing against the door. "Because I know how much *I* want you. I know how you make me feel. I know I can't stop thinking about you, even when I'm recording."

A shiver dances down my spine at the knowledge he imagines me the way I imagine him.

"I feel like I'm losing my mind because I've never wanted anything as much as I want you. So what is it, Aud? Tell me."

"Ren, you were a kid when I got pregnant," I say shakily, and he takes another step towards me. I can't take my eyes off of him, and I should feel cornered, trapped...but I don't. "But it was bad. You saw how Celia treated me at the diner. If we were together, you'd get that too. You deserve so much better."

His brow furrows, and he lifts his hand, tucking a piece of hair behind the earpiece of my glasses. "I don't want better, Audrey. I want you, however you'll let me have you."

For a moment, all I hear is our heavy breaths. I don't think I've ever been wanted for me before. I *know* I've never been looked at this way. Like he's stuck in the desert and I'm fresh water. Like I'm the moon and he's the tide. Like I'm *necessary* to his very existence.

"We shouldn't," I manage to whisper, and my heart clenches as he steps back.

"Okay," he says, shoving his hands in his pockets and avoiding my eyes. "I'm... I'm not gonna push you."

"It's not that I don't want you..." I try to explain.

"It's that you think you don't deserve to be wanted the same way you want," he finishes, and I'm taken aback by his words.

Is he right? Is that what I'm thinking?

He wants me, and I want him, and god, it'd be such a mess. I've done fine on my own and will continue to do fine.

But I think I want more than fine. I want something heart stopping and passionate and incredible, something that makes me more than happy.

I want him.

"Fuck it," I hear myself say, taking the two steps it takes to get to him before wrapping my arms around his neck and pulling his mouth to mine.

Chapter 18

Ren

When I was twelve, I lost control of my bike while going downhill. I knew in the moment I should be afraid, because a crash was inevitable. But I felt invincible, like I was flying and it was going to last forever. And sure, I crashed into a parked car and broke my wrist, but before that? Pure bliss. I've never felt that pure rush of being alive since.

Until Audrey Hinton gave up her resolve and kissed me harder than I've ever been kissed. Hard enough for me to know she's been fighting this as much as I have.

Her lips are soft, yet firm, as she kisses me like she's searching for something specific, like she knows exactly what she wants and is going to find it. I hear a strangled groan, and it takes me a moment to realize that was *my* strangled groan. I place one hand on the back of her head, and the other on her hip, pulling her flush to me. God, she's so soft and lush and her body against mine is exhilarating. Her hands are in my hair, running her fingers through them, and it feels too fucking good.

She pulls away and cups my face in her hands, eyes searching mine.

"Do you want to stop?" I ask in a voice I barely recognize.

"No," she whispers, voice breathy. "No. Please... please don't stop, Ren."

I capture her lips with mine, and gently run my tongue along the seam. She opens her mouth with a soft whimper and her tongue meets mine, just as eager as I am.

My hands are everywhere: her face, her hair, the back of her neck, the small of her back, her hips... I want to touch every part of her. To memorize it and make a mental map so I know exactly where to go when I come back.

Audrey grinds her pelvis against me and I almost fall over. I'm aching for this woman.

We're so desperate for each other, and I gently push her against the door. She surprises me by breaking our kiss and swiping her tongue along my jaw, hooking her leg around my thigh.

I press my forehead to hers, the metal of our glasses clinking, our chests heaving. "I want to see you come," I gasp, trying to lower my voice. But doing my Sky voice when I can't catch my breath is nearly impossible. "I want to be the one to make you come undone. Is that okay, sweetheart?"

"Ren, no," she says, quietly. She reaches up, and at first I think it's to push me away, but instead she lifts her hands to my face. She gently removes my glasses, folding them and slipping them into my sweats pocket. "I want you. Only you."

It takes me a moment to understand what she's saying. That she doesn't want Sky, but me.

It's soft and lovely of her, and I want to cry. Instead, I attempt to swallow the lump in my throat. I turn my face to press a kiss to the palm of her hand. "Ah, sweetheart. You have me."

She gently urges me to look at her. "Sky's made me come so, so many times, and it's been good." Her eyes are wide and earnest, shining like sea glass. "But I want Ren to make me come tonight. Is that okay?"

I grind my cock against her center and she gasps, leg tightening around me. "More than okay," I groan. "A million times more than okay."

I want to take my time with her, to savor her. But I can't. Everything about this is fast and desperate and god, how could I expect different when I've spent a summer doing nothing but wanting her?

Her fingers dig into my shoulders as she clings to me, her hips grinding in a circular motion against me.

"You... you make the prettiest sounds," I grit out against her mouth. "Don't stop."

She moans, her head falling back against the door. "You feel so good," she whimpers as I kiss down her jaw, her neck. My hand brushes against hers and she intertwines her fingers with mine. I lift our hands, pinning them next to her head. Her free hand grabs my ass and god, I need her to consume me. To take so much of me that I only exist with her.

I move my hand from her hip up her rib cage, tracing the side of her breast. I'm startled when her hand moves from my ass to push it away as she breaks the kiss.

"Please... I..." Her breath is shaky, and for a moment, she seems afraid. "I don't... I breastfed. They're misshapen..."

"Hey." I squeeze her hand. "You don't need a reason. If there's something you're uncomfortable with or don't want me to do, I won't do it."

"You're okay with not touching them? Or seeing them?" she asks cautiously.

"Sweetheart, I'm certain they're lovely. But it's your body, and what you say goes. I'll touch you wherever *you* want me to."

She grabs the back of my head and pulls me in for another kiss. "Thank you," she whispers against my lips, our hips grinding against each other again.

"Don't thank me for doing the bare minimum, sweetheart."

She doesn't answer, but her head falls back against the door again, teeth digging into her lower lip.

"Close," she whimpers. "I'm... I'm close."

I drop our hands and dig my fingers into her full hips. She has me acting like a wild animal, and I fucking love it.

So does she, judging by the way she ruthlessly digs her fingers into my shoulders.

"Come on, sweetheart," I pant, eyes fixated on her. "Give it to me."

Her breathing becomes quicker, her movements more frantic, and on a sharp cry, her entire body tightens and her head falls back against the door.

It's the most breathtaking thing I've ever experienced.

Her body softens in my arms and she exhales on a moan and it's too much.

I bury my face in her neck and it takes three more thrusts before I come, hot and sticky in my pants.

I don't think I've ever come this hard in my life, and my legs are weak. I lose my balance and with a loud yelp, I take Audrey with me as I fall to the ground.

She lands on top of me, and I swear, I think I'm already hard again, simply from the sheer pleasure of her body on mine.

She groans and rolls off me. I fight the urge to pull her back, to hold her to me and beg her to stay with me, to keep touching me. I reached completion while fully clothed with this woman, and it only made me want more with her.

I turn my head to look at her, taken aback when I see her hands are underneath her glasses and covering her eyes, body shaking.

My stomach sinks as I roll to my side and slip my own glasses back on. "Aud, talk to me. Are you okay?"

She slowly lowers her hands, and a wave of relief washes over me. She's laughing.

She turns her face and meets my eye, laughing harder.

I can't help it, I start to laugh too.

And wouldn't you know? There *is* a sound better than her laughter—*ours*, woven together into the perfect melody.

Chapter 19

Ren

Playlist: Hey Girl | Stephen Sanchez

"So," I say.

"So," Audrey responds.

Then silence.

"Oh my god," she groans, burying her face in my Death Star throw pillow.

After we finally stopped laughing, we got to our feet. She told me she had to leave, and I told her we had to do aftercare. When she insisted she didn't need it, I had the pleasure of admitting *I* need aftercare after physical intimacy with a partner.

We're on opposite sides of my couch, Leia licking her ass between us, and Audrey's face buried in a pillow, groaning loudly.

Suddenly, my cock is at attention again, because I'm fantasizing about Audrey's face buried in the same pillow. Her making that same noise while I have her bent over the arm of the couch and—

"Can I go now?" I think that is what she says, but her voice is so muffled that the odds of her actually having said, "candlelit ghost," are pretty high.

"What?" I ask, making sure she's not asking after Casper.

She sighs and lowers the pillow from her face. "Can I go now?"

"I mean. If you're going to make it clear you want to leave, you might as well."

"Ugh, I'm sorry. It's such a cliché, but I promise it's not you, it's me. Can I overshare with you? Maybe some light trauma dumping?"

I glance at her out of the corner of my eye. "Uh... sure?"

"I haven't had sex in sixteen years," she says before burying her face in the pillow and groaning once again.

I stare at her. "You... what?"

"You heard me," she grumbles.

"I just... what? How?"

She lifts her face again and turns her neck to meet my eyes. "Piper's dad ended things moments after we conceived a child because he didn't want to be 'tied down' in college. Which was fair, I never thought we'd be together forever or anything like that. I went on a single date when Piper was a year old and I'll never forget the way he stared at me when I took my bra off. It was like seeing someone experience Paris syndrome in real life, being disappointed by something you build up in your head... I did everything I could to never repeat that experience, and haven't been on a date since."

My heart sinks. That's why she didn't want me to touch her breasts. Some asshole made her feel like shit about her body. Now she's convinced herself he was right and not simply a loser whose idea of beautiful breasts were what he'd seen in porn.

"I never stayed when I had sex with Piper's dad," she continues. "We'd have sex in his car and he'd drop me home and that was that. Neither of our parents knew we were having sex, and I think that was why we slept together. The thrill of being bad, you know? Sneaking around like that made me feel alive."

She lifts her eyes. "But now I'm stunted because I have no idea what's supposed to happen next."

I chew on my lower lip, trying to find the right words to say. "I'm sorry," is what I settle on.

"You don't have to apologize," she says earnestly. "I wanted... that. You didn't do anything wrong, and you didn't know..."

"Sweetheart, I *know* you wanted it," I interrupt her. "I'm apologizing because I'm genuinely so sorry that someone made you feel shitty about your body."

Audrey doesn't say anything, staring absently at Leia as my cat daughter cleans between her toes. "What happens now?" she asks, voice barely louder than a whisper.

"I'm not sure," I admit. My experience with relationships and sex and love is complicated, to put it mildly. "I think we get to figure it out."

"I have a crush on you," she blurts out suddenly before burying her face in the pillow again.

"I mean... we dry humped like teenagers. I'd *hope* you were attracted to me."

She throws the pillow at me, but I catch it before it makes an impact.

"Come on, sweetheart. I have seven siblings and you thought you could catch me off guard by—" I'm cut off when a Millennium Falcon pillow collides with my face.

"And I'm a mom. You think I haven't perfected the art of taking people by surprise?" she asks in a saccharine voice.

I don't doubt it. She constantly takes me by surprise, and not only because she nailed me with the second pillow.

"Since you told me you have a crush on me, I guess I should tell you I have one on you, too. Always have, actually. You were the first girl I had a crush on. God, you were prettier than

Princess Leia—" Audrey makes a strangled choking noise, but I keep talking. "Like I was kind of obsessed."

"Oh, Ren." She slides closer to me, and my heart inflates. She's touched. Honored.

I turn to face her. "Yeah?" I try to keep my voice steady, so as to not give away how giddy I am.

"I'm gonna hold your hand when I say this..." She picks my hand up and squeezes it. "I know."

I stare at her. "I mean... like I had a crush on you as a kid, not just in the present," I clarify.

She smiles sympathetically. "I know. We all knew. It was a little creepy, to be honest."

"Creepy," I echo hollowly. This can *not* be happening.

"You were nine and wouldn't stop staring at me, or playing love ballads *while* staring at me. You insisted on learning how to play that song from *Titanic* and would sing and stare at me whenever you practiced. One time, you muttered, 'I love you,' at Sunday dinner."

"Ah, yes, see, that was a misunderstanding. I was quoting *The Empire Strikes Back* and hoping you'd finish the quote for me," I defend myself—quite convincingly, I think.

She tilts her head and raises a brow.

"Fine. I was literally in love with you," I say quickly. That look she gave me could get me to reveal the things I kept secret even from Father Gilligan when I still went to confession.

She laughs and I decide it was worth making a fool out of myself to hear that again. "You're lucky you grew up to be so handsome," she says.

I grin. "You think I'm handsome, sweetheart?"

Her eyes widen. "I didn't say that."

"You just did! And if you were to check the transcript, the record would show..."

She playfully shoves my shoulder. "You're an asshole."

"I cannot believe you had the *audacity* to call *me* creepy when you somehow got into my apartment building *and* figured out which apartment was mine. That's like, proper stalker behavior."

"I mean, if you want to get *technical* about it…"

I laugh, and I try to pretend I don't notice how her eyes brighten, like she loves the sound of my laughter as much I love the sound of hers.

That's dangerous thinking.

"What do you want to happen next?" I ask her.

"I don't know," she responds quietly. "I mean… I know I want that to happen again, obviously." I'm pretty sure my chest puffs out with pride, like I'm an exotic bird. "But I don't think I'm relationship material."

My chest deflates like a balloon, complete with the squeaky sound and everything.

I've had sex outside of relationships before, because I thought I had to, or because the other person was showing interest and I felt like I had to return that interest. I felt weird, because while most of my friends were having casual sex, I found I truly didn't even *want* to have sex if I wasn't in a relationship. One of my friends mentioned they were demisexual, and I remember being intrigued, because what they described, attraction only occurring when there's an emotional connection, was something I relate to. After some research, I realized I'm pansexual, too. Someone's gender has never hindered my ability to be attracted to someone, and it felt freeing to find labels I identified with.

After that, I only had sex in serious relationships, or at least what I *thought* were serious relationships, in Taylor's case.

That relationship did such a number on me that I've refused to even download an app to try to get back out there.

I should tell Audrey it won't work. That her needs are valid, but I can't be the one who fulfills them. That sex can never be purely physical for me.

But I want her, any way I can have her. And who am I kidding? She's already holding a delicate, breakable part of myself in her hands.

"Ren?" she asks slowly, somehow dragging out my three-letter name.

"Audrey?" I respond.

"Would you... want to be friends?"

I blink at her. "Are we not already?"

"No. I mean, yes. I don't know. I don't have friends. I haven't since high school. I don't really let people in, you know? Since everything happened."

"Understandable."

"I think you're like... a mom friend. But not a mom friend because you're not a mom. But we're friends because I'm Piper's mom. And I think... I think maybe I'd like to be friends beyond that? Friends not because of Piper... but friends because of us?" She peers up at me, eyes so full of hope, and I'm willing to ignore the fact friends don't usually make out and grind to orgasm.

"Is that what you want?" I ask slowly. "Do you want any... benefits?" I want to run through a damn wall. I don't *do* friends with benefits. For me, sex is a commitment. It sounds like something my Nonna would preach as she shook her rosary at us, that sex is sacred, blah blah blah.

It's not a morality thing, rather that for me personally, physical intimacy is woven together with emotional intimacy.

"I mean..." She eyes me, and suddenly, I want to hide myself. I feel raw, exposed. "I don't think that's a good idea. You're in Piper's life, too, and I don't... I don't want anything you and I do to impact her."

"I understand." I nod slowly, watching the hope of something more with her float away. But being friends means she wants that emotional intimacy with me, too. "I'd love to be your friend, Audrey."

Chapter 20

Audrey

Playlist: Heart Attack | Demi Lovato

"So." Piper scoops a heaping spoonful of Reese's Puffs into her mouth. "Where'd you go last night?" she questions, words muffled by the sugary cereal filling her cheeks.

My cheeks heat. I guess she didn't buy the excuse I gave her before I left.

"I told you," I say, trying to keep my voice even. "They had some booking issues at the inn so I went to help."

Piper makes a noncommittal grunting noise.

I lift my mug and take a too-large gulp of coffee. It scalds my throat as I drink.

"I'm just saying it's okay if you went to Mr. Q's last night," she says casually.

I sigh heavily and put my mug back on the table, a little rougher than I intended, the heavy thud echoing through the kitchen.

"Whoa." My daughter seems both impressed and uncomfortable at my sudden show of emotion.

"Sorry," I apologize, guilt washing through me.

"Fuck," she says casually, spooning another pile of cereal into her mouth. "You must *really* like him."

"Piper, I love you, and I am setting a firm boundary right now," I say, using the tone of voice I reserve for when I need to make it clear I'm not being silly. "You joking or asking about anything between me and Mr. Q makes me uncomfortable. Please don't do it again. If I were to have a partner, I'd tell you when I was ready."

Piper's face falls, and I feel bad for a moment. But the reality of autism is that sometimes, because of her difficulty with sub-text and nonverbal cues, being blunt is the best way to communicate with her.

"I'm sorry," I tell her. "I don't want to hurt your feelings, but I need you to hear me, birdie."

"It's okay," she says quietly, staring intently at the handful of cereal still floating in her bowl of oat milk. "I didn't realize it bothered you."

"I know, and I should have told you sooner. I'm very sorry for waiting such a long time and for hurting your feelings."

I reach across the table for her hand, but she pulls away. I wince. Fair enough. "You didn't hurt my feelings," Piper tells me, still staring at her bowl.

"Okay, but if I *had*, it would be okay. I wasn't kind, and *if* your feelings were hurt, which, I know, I know, they aren't, that would be valid."

"I'm sorry for disrespecting your boundaries," she answers, voice shaky.

I scoot my chair closer to her, and my whole body relaxes when she lets me wrap an arm around her shoulders. "I know, birdie. But I wasn't clear on my feelings about it, so maybe this is something you and I can work on together? Communicating effectively with each other?"

She sighs heavily. "I guess."

I kiss the top of her head. "I love you, and part of my boundary is not asking Mr. Q any questions about me or himself, either." I quickly add, realizing I hadn't specified that.

Piper looks up at me, gray eyes mischievous and lips pursed to hold back a laugh. "That's suspicious."

"Piper Elise."

"Okay, okay. I won't say or ask anything," she groans, shrugging off my arm.

She gets to her feet and shuffles out of the kitchen. She's leaving for her lesson with Ren soon, so I take this slight reprieve to pull my phone out and text him, surprised when he's already texted me.

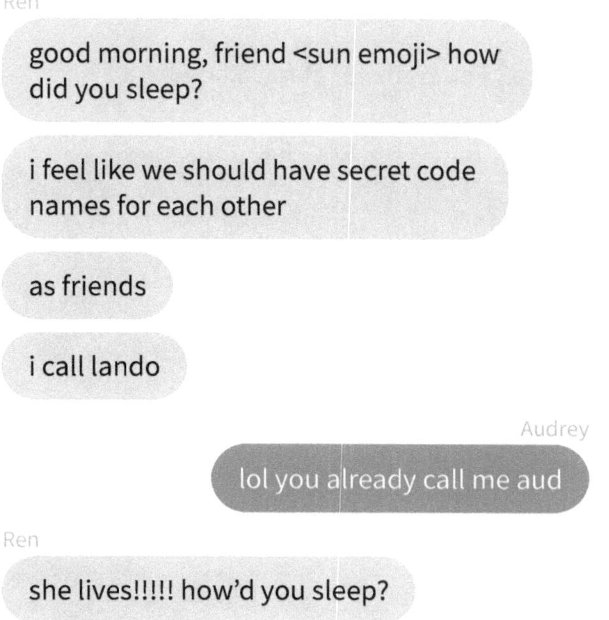

How'd I sleep, he asks? How'd I sleep after dry humping with the most attractive man to ever exist to completion?

Best night of sleep I've had since becoming a mom.
I wish I was kidding.

"Bye, Mom!" Piper yells, the screen door closing behind her.

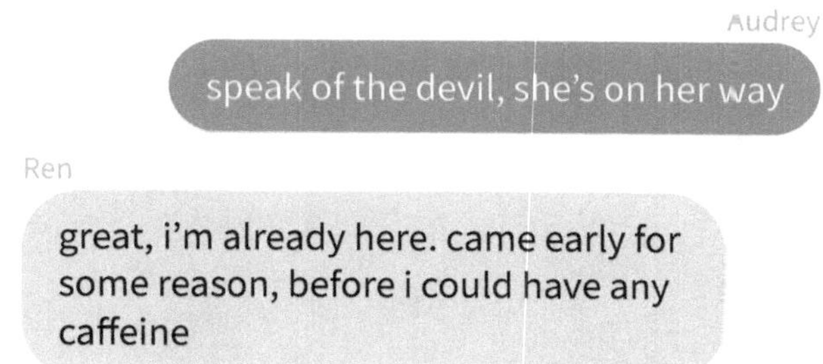

I read his message over and over again before deciding to send the message I'm concocting in my brain.

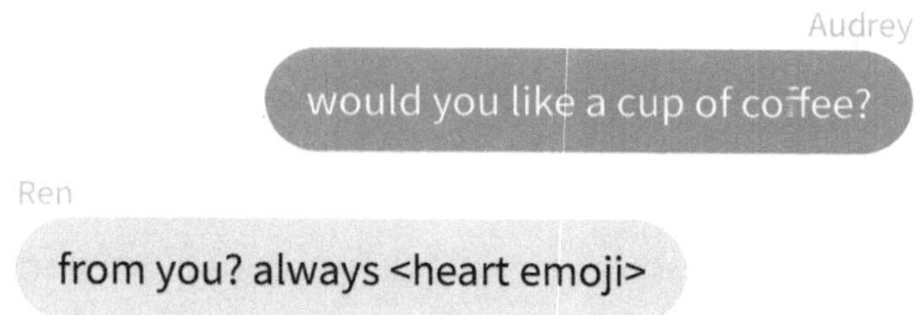

I roughly place my phone face down on the table and scrub at my face. It means nothing. That plain red heart means nothing, and why isn't my heart getting the message?

We're friends. Just friends.

To prove it to myself, I grab my phone again and open the text thread between Eva and I.

> i'm not sure what the protocol is about like reaching out over the weekend.

> it's not an emergency, but i want you to know i am KILLING it at this making friends thing we talked about. i did it! i made a friend!!!! is he piper's piano teacher? sure. did we dry hump last night and is he also my favorite audio erotica creator? maybe. but we're friends!!!!!

Is it oversharing if it's with your therapist? Maybe, if it's a text out of the blue on the weekend.

But I want her to know Ren and I are friends. I did it. I made a friend. I think that's passing therapy in my case.

But there's a problem.

Friends who feel this way about friends don't stay friends. And I don't know if I could take losing another friend.

I'm pulled out of my rumination when my phone dings with a text message.

Eva

> Let's move our session up to Monday.

Chapter 21

Ren

October

Eight weeks.

Eight weeks since school started, two months of Audrey bringing me coffee, two months since Audrey and I made out. A month and nineteen days since Audrey started joining me for the last mile of my run, always with a cup of coffee for each of us. Eight weeks of surface-level conversation and eight weeks since I promised myself I would *not* jerk off in the shower to the thought of her mouth when I got home.

Seven weeks and six days since I broke that promise.

I'm pathetic.

"So, what are you doing tonight?" Piper asks one Saturday in late October. Her tone is casual, but I've gotten to know this pipsqueak enough to know she's rarely casual.

"Why?" I ask suspiciously, narrowing my eyes playfully at her.

"According to my mother, it's *Gilmore Girls* season. She makes us marathon the beginning of season one and we make homemade pizza and we hang out and even though the show sucks, it's kind of fun." She inhales deeply after finishing her run-on sentence.

"It sounds fun," I tell her earnestly.

"We've been doing it since Aunt Liv was alive," she continues, tapping casually at the keys. "I hate the show, but it's Mom's favorite." She looks up at me suddenly, eyes widening to a comically large size. "Wait, you should come over!"

"Oh, I... I couldn't do that," I stammer, feeling my cheeks heat. Audrey and I have done a fantastic job at staying out of each other's spaces and staying in neutral, public areas. The beach for our walks, the lobby of the inn... and everything between us has been surface level.

We've talked about our favorite colors—hers is a gray-ish lavender, mine is yellow—and our favorite and least favorite parts of our jobs. Whenever we get anywhere close to personal vulnerability, she changes the subject so quickly it gives me whiplash. Being in her home, even with Piper there, feels too real, too vulnerable.

But god, I want real and vulnerable with her.

"Why not?" Piper demands, narrowing her eyes at me. "Aren't you and Mom friends?"

How the hell do I explain to this child that while, yes, her mother and I are friends, it's the most painful friendship I've been a part of? That every part of me screams she and I are meant to be more than friends, but more than friends simply isn't in the stars for us.

"We are..." I start to say, but Piper is waving frantically across the lobby.

"Mom!" It feels like my entire body was somehow doused in lava and ice water simultaneously. I can smell the soft strawberry and coconut wafting off her, feel the shift in energy when she's near.

"Hey, birdie," Audrey says. I feel like I'm intruding by watching her stroke Piper's hair with so much care and love.

God, she's such a good mom.

Why is that so hot?

"Hi, Mama," Piper says, turning and wrapping her arms around Audrey's middle. "I've missed you."

My heart could melt at the sweetness, but the same cannot be said for Audrey, whose eyes narrow as she takes a step back out of her daughter's embrace.

"What did you do?" she asks flatly.

"Nothing!" Piper insists, her voice still dripping with sweetness.

"Piper," Audrey says sternly. "What did you do?"

Piper and I speak over one another, two trains colliding.

"Nothing wrong!" she exclaims

"She invited me to dinner and your *Gilmore Girls* marathon tonight."

The absolute betrayal on Piper's face almost makes me laugh.

"Oh," Audrey says, glancing between Piper and I. "I... oh."

"No need to sound excited," I say teasingly. I immediately regret it when her face falls even more somehow.

"No, no, you're welcome to join us," she stammers.

"I was actually telling Piper I have plans tonight, but thank you for the kind invitation," I say, plastering on my brightest smile. The smile I put on when my parents are complaining about one of my siblings. The smile I put on when one of my siblings complains about my parents, or Kat, because everyone's always complaining about Kat. The smile that makes people think I'm fine, that I'm happy to do it for them.

That I'm not aching for someone to offer to lighten the load for me, for once.

"Actually, you told me you didn't have any plans," Piper corrects me matter-of-factly, and I fight the urge to slap my hand over her mouth.

"Right-o," I say, my smile unshakable. "I *did* say that. But alas, I was..."

"Ren, I want you to come." I don't know who's more taken aback when the words leave Audrey's pretty lips, me or Piper.

"*Really?*" the two of us say, voices laced with glee and confusion, respectively.

"Really," Audrey says. Her smile doesn't quite meet her eyes, and it worries me. "It'll be nice to have someone who doesn't talk shit about my favorite TV show the entire night."

"Mr. Q is a smart man," Piper says. "He's gonna hate it, too."

"Well, I guess we'll find out tonight," I say. "Can I bring anything?"

"Princess Leia." Piper's response is so quick I'm convinced getting my cat to come over was her plan the entire time. "And her food. And whatever else she needs for a *Gilmore Girls* marathon."

"Is that okay with your mom?" I ask cautiously, eyes meeting Audrey's again. Now, her eyes are sparkling, and she's resting her chin on her open palm, covering what I *know* is the most beautiful smile.

"That's fine," she says, voice shaking with her hidden laughter. "You and Princess Leia and her cat food and whatever else you want to bring are more than welcome to join us tonight."

I arch my brow and hope my face is expressing what I want it to.

Challenge accepted.

Later that evening, I'm standing on Audrey and Piper's enviable front porch, Leia's cat carrier slung over my shoulder, and an apple pie I spent *way* too much time figuring out how to make in my hand.

"Where is she?" Piper says, whipping open the front door and squatting so she's eye level with the cat carrier. Leia begins to purr in greeting. "My baby!" Piper squeals, taking the cat carrier from me without asking. I don't mind, I think the way she loves my cat is the sweetest thing ever.

Although, to be completely honest, I live in fear Leia will be catnapped. Or is it catnapping if she goes willingly?

"Mom's in the kitchen," Piper tells me, not taking her eyes off the cat carrier. "She got a *bunch* of ingredients for pizza, including dairy-free cheese because apparently you're lactose intolerant, which is sad because does that mean you can't have ice cream?" She takes a deep breath before continuing her monologue. "And then Mom got worried maybe you were a vegetarian or vegan, so we have fake meat and veggies and..."

"Piper, breathe," Audrey calls from the kitchen. "Why don't you come make your pizza and let Mr. Q and Princess Leia get settled?"

Piper's face falls. "But I haven't gotten to show Leia the toys I got her!" she whines.

"Why don't you go show her and get her settled, and make your pizza in five minutes?" I ask, squatting so I'm her height.

She smirks at me, and I realize it's probably a different experience for a teenager than to the elementary school students I interact with on a daily basis. I clear my throat and stand to my full height. "Is that okay with you, Aud?"

"Yep!" Audrey responds, "Five minutes, Piper. I'm setting a timer."

Piper zooms off with my cat, presumably to show Leia her new toys.

I shuffle into the kitchen. "Hey," I greet Audrey as I place the pie on the counter.

She looks over her shoulder at me and smiles. She has flour smudged on her nose and it's walking the line between precious and sexy as hell, considering I want to lean forward and lick it off. "Hey! Glad you made it."

I look around to make sure Piper can't hear before taking another step towards her. "I'm sorry if I'm intruding. I can fake a stomachache or family emergency if you want it to be a you and Piper thing."

"Ren, if you take that cat away from her, I'm definitely being put in a nursing home."

I laugh. "Fair. It's kind of cute how much they love each other," I say, stepping forward to reach around Audrey and grab a black olive from the buffet of toppings.

Of course, Audrey takes a step back from the counter at the exact same time, and before I know it, her ass is nestled into my crotch.

I hear the sharp inhalation of her breath, but we don't jump apart like we should. Which is both wonderful, because touching and being close to her is wonderful, and awful, because there's a zero percent chance she can't feel my erection, which is growing at an alarming speed.

"Well," she breathes, "hello, there."

"General Kenobi," I wheeze.

I one hundred percent just cock-blocked myself.

Or… maybe not. She's still not moving. Should I be the one to move? I don't want to pull away. Her ass is soft and she's so close and smells delectable and—

Beep.

We jump apart as her phone alarm goes off and I pull out a chair at the kitchen table, sitting in an attempt to hide my now painfully-hard cock.

"That's… that's five minutes, Pipe!" she stammers, fumbling with her phone. Her cheeks are pink and her front teeth are digging into her lower lip. But she doesn't seem uncomfortable, which I'm counting as a win for me.

Piper slides back into the kitchen in socked feet, Leia securely in her arms. Damn, this cat only lets me hold her when Mercury is in Gatorade or something, but she's happy as a clam to be carried by Piper.

Audrey barks out a laugh. "Is that…"

"A Princess Leia Halloween costume?" Piper finishes proudly, holding out my cat who is indeed dressed as her namesake, complete with a hat made to look like her famous buns with holes cut out for the cat's ears. "Yep. I think she likes it more than the toys I got her."

I eye Leia warily. Son of a bitch, she's literally being dangled in a dress and hat and she's *still* purring. The disrespect children show their parents these days.

"Do you like it, Mr. Q?" Piper asks, hope shining in her eyes.

"I love it," I say, taken aback when I realize it's true. I *do* love it. I love how safe and comfortable Leia is with Piper, even in a Halloween costume, and how happy that makes Piper. "More importantly, I think *she* loves it, too."

Piper beams with pride and pulls Leia closer into her, nuzzling her head with her cheek. Leia's purrs increase in volume as she returns the nuzzle, making Piper giggle.

"How about you direct me while I make your pizza so you don't have to put Leia down?" Audrey asks, grabbing a pizza pan and spreading out one of the balls of dough on it.

Piper starts listing ingredients and I try to focus on what she's saying. Pineapple. This child likes *pineapple* on her pizza. You're Italian, Lorenzo, channel your distant cousins' dismay for the fruit on pizza. Think of how hilarious they'd be yelling about it, how fast they'd be talking, and how chaotically their hands would move. Pineapple on pizza must be considered a mortal sin in Italian culture...

Great. Now I'm thinking about this fantastic piña colada I had last summer which is making me think about how Audrey's hair smells like coconut which makes me think about how soft it had felt running through my fingers when we...

This backfired.

"Want to make yours, Ren?" Audrey asks after putting Piper's pizza in the oven.

"No," I answer pathetically.

Piper is on the floor with Leia, playing with a feather attached to a stick I've never seen before. I assume it's one of the new toys Piper got for Leia.

Audrey's eyes lower, like she has X-Ray vision and can see through the kitchen table.

"You did this!" I try to scream at her through my expression. *"You did this, so you should* fix *this."*

I'm my own worst enemy, because I'm thinking of Audrey fixing the problem with her hand and mouth.

I stifle a groan and rub my hand over my face. It's gonna be a long night.

Chapter 22

Ren

Playlist: So It Goes | Taylor Swift

"What do you think?"

Three women stare at me expectantly—Audrey, Piper, and Leia. We finished our fourth episode of *Gilmore Girls*, and I know no matter what I say, I'm going to disappoint someone.

"I liked it," I answer, immediately looking at Audrey and internally fist pumping when she beams at me. "I especially liked the pilot and how it introduced the characters."

"Ugh," Piper groans, slumping back against the couch. "I should have known you'd betray me."

"What did you think about Lorelai's outfit for the first day of school?" Audrey asks, sympathetically patting her daughter on the top of her head. "Have any parents worn something like that when dropping their kid off?"

"Honestly, the weirdest shit I've seen has been during private lessons. I haven't seen anything that memorably strange at school but..." I trail off when I realize both Audrey and Piper are staring at me again. "What?"

"You can't bring up weird shit happening during private lessons and leave it at that!" Piper exclaims.

"She's right," Audrey agrees, turning to face me. "Now you gotta tell us the weirdest things you've seen during private lessons."

I look around cautiously, like I could be caught telling a salacious story by someone. "This one family had a nanny…"

They both groan in disappointment. "The dad and the nanny?" Piper mutters. "How predictable."

"No, no. Not the dad and the nanny," I correct, leaning in towards them. "The *mom* and the nanny."

They both gasp with the appropriate amount of drama for the plot twist. "Oh, that's much better," Piper responds, a glint of mischievous glee in her eyes. It's a really good thing this kid likes me.

I give them the sordid details, or at least as many as I can give that don't give away the family's identity, and what's appropriate for a teenager. They eat it up. We then watch another episode of *Gilmore Girls* before Audrey and I clean up after dinner. She washes the dishes, passing them to me to dry while Piper and Leia lounge on the couch.

"Thanks for indulging me and pretending to enjoy my show," Audrey says, putting a pink ceramic dish into the dishwasher. When she straightens, she's so close her damn coconut shampoo overpowers the smell of the cleaner she wiped down the counter with.

"I wasn't pretending," I say earnestly, putting the pink ceramic dish into the cabinet. "I enjoyed it."

She ducks her head, but I can still see the smile on her face. "Even if you're lying, thanks for giving that to me. Piper has made her hatred of the show crystal clear since the first time we watched it. I wonder if she *actually* hates it, or if she enjoys the show, but enjoys the ritual of hating it even more."

"Knowing Piper, either option seems plausible."

"Very true," Audrey agrees, closing the dishwasher and starting the cycle. "Thanks for getting to know her and teaching her, by the way. She's always talking about you."

"It's honestly nothing. She's a damn cool kid."

She meets my eyes, and my knees are wobbly. "Um," I say, voice as shaky as my legs. "I was thinking since tomorrow's Sunday and Piper's having such a good time with Leia... maybe she could spend the night? If that's okay with you?"

Her smile grows. "Shared custody?" she teases.

"I figure if I voluntarily share custody, your daughter's less likely to kidnap my cat," I say, and Audrey laughs that goddamn laugh, making my heart skip a beat. Maybe I should see a doctor about that, it can't be good for my cardiac health.

"That's fine with me," she says when her laughter quiets. I miss the sound immediately. "Wanna go ask Piper?"

"*Yes!*" Piper screeches when I ask her, leaping to her feet.

"*Meow*," Princess Leia says, presumably in agreement with her new favorite human.

Piper starts rambling about how she'll take such good care of Leia, how she won't overfeed her and will play with her and will snuggle her all night, unless she'd rather sleep alone.

I'm listening, but I can't help but peek over her shoulder, at Audrey who beams while leaning against the doorway. She meets my eyes, blushes, and god, I'm glad to know I make her feel *something*, though I don't know what it is exactly.

"Okay, Piper," Audrey eventually says, pushing off the door frame. "Why don't you and Leia start getting ready for bed? I'm gonna walk Mr. Q out."

I'm thrown off balance—literally—when Piper throws herself at me and wraps an arm around my waist.

"Thanks for letting my best friend sleep over, Mr. Q. And hanging out with me and Mom—you made *Gilmore Girls* almost bearable."

I have no idea how to respond. Usually when a student hugs me, I'll hug them back, but they're also usually much younger than Piper, and I'm not obsessed with their adult.

But her adult *is* right there, looking at us wide eyed, like she's as taken aback by this as I am.

I wrap my arms around Piper and hug her back. "Make good choices, pipsqueak," I say, awkwardly patting her on her back.

"Birdie, next time ask before touching someone," Audrey says, like it took her a moment to find her voice.

"Is it okay if I hug you, Mr. Q?" Piper asks, voice muffled.

"*Meow*," Leia says, dangling from Piper's arm.

"Yeah. It's okay if you hug me."

Finally, Piper pulls away and skips off to kiss Audrey on her cheek. Audrey's brows are furrowed in what I assume is confusion.

"Thanks for letting me crash girls' night," I tell her, putting on my jacket.

Audrey unlocks the door and we both step out onto the porch. "Thanks for coming. You chose a strange night to come—someone swapped brains with my child."

I laugh. "Why do you say that?"

"She was so... touchy-feely. I can count on one hand the amount of times I've seen that child initiate physical contact with someone who wasn't me or Aunt Liv."

There's a lump in my throat. "I... oh." How the hell do you respond to that?

"I'm afraid I've passed on my general distrust of people to her," Audrey continues, adjusting the fall-themed wreath hanging on her door. "Nobody really stuck around for me, especially after I was pregnant.

"No one was on my side. It felt like it was me and a tiny little creature in my body against the world. I don't... I don't want Piper to ever think she has to be a certain way to deserve love. I've worked hard to keep her safe and affirm the things that make life more difficult for her, but I'm scared of how capable people are of causing hurt."

"You're a good mom, Aud," I whisper, voice thick. "Piper's an incredible kid and you can tell it's because of how much you love her."

She wipes away a tear. Fuck, I don't want her to cry. "That's a kind thing to say."

"It's a *true* thing to say," I insist. I clench my fists by my side instead of lifting my hand, cupping her cheek, and wiping away her tears like I so want to.

"What if I held her back? What if by trying to keep her safe, I was the one to hurt her instead? What if... no. I *know* she'd be better if I were better. If I had my shit together instead of... this mess." She lifts her arms and lets them flop to her sides, as if motioning to the so-called mess.

"But then she wouldn't be that incredible human inside." I take a step closer to her. "Piper is who she is because of who *you* are. Because of every choice you made over the course of your entire life. Yeah, it led to the shitty stuff too, but parents hurt their kids. Sometimes intentionally, but most of the time not. Most of the time, I wouldn't say they're bad parents. They're just human, and personally, I'm glad you're human," I finish my monologue anti-climatically.

Audrey stares at her feet and nods. "I keep thinking you don't know me, you don't know us. I've successfully manipulated you into thinking I'm not a piece of shit and I feel guilty because I didn't *mean* to manipulate you and..."

"Audrey," I say gently. "Look at me."

She reluctantly lifts her watery eyes. I want her to believe she's not the horrible person she's somehow convinced herself she is. That she didn't deserve the way people treated her in the past.

"You mentioned you see a therapist before. Do they know you feel this way?"

She laughs emptily. "Oh, Eva is *well* aware of the shitshow that is my brain. Depression is a bitch, just so you know."

"Trust me, I know. That's why I run so much. Running, bi-weekly therapy, and sixty milligrams of fluoxetine are the best treatment for me. My brain tells me the same things about myself, and sometimes I believe them, too."

She's staring at me like she's never seen me before, which is impossible considering she's the only person who *actually* sees me.

"Do you have any hobbies or anything you can do when your brain is an asshole?" I ask her.

Her cheeks flush. "Unfortunately, my normal form of stress relief is off-limits now."

I furrow my brow. "Why?"

Her blush deepens under the faint glow of the porch light, and I can see the tear tracks on her cheeks.

"I can't listen to 4Play anymore," she says, shrugging in a way I'm certain she's trying to portray as nonchalant, but really looks like she's carrying the weight of the world on her shoulders.

I'm taken aback by her revelation. I'd thought she'd been listening, so I'd been careful to not think about her while recording, or do anything directly for her.

Which obviously meant I thought of nothing but her while recording. I imagined doing the things I talked about to her. Imagined what she would look like while I did, while she indulged in her pleasure.

I want her to see *me,* the way she sees Sky. I want to share this side of me with her, share these experiences with her. I want her to understand that I'm the one who wants her, not Sky.

"Why?" With that one word, the world is turned on its axis. Her eyes flash, my entire body heats, and my boner from earlier is back.

"Come on, Ren," she says, forcing a laugh. "You know why."

I shake my head. "No, I don't. Tell me." Because if the reason she's not listening is the same reason recording has been a completely different experience, I may pass out.

"I don't know. It's not you. Or your scripts. But whenever I try to listen, and Sky... I mean, you start speaking, it's not the same. It doesn't give me what it used to, and I can't..." She trails off, avoiding my gaze.

Can't what? Get turned on? Orgasm? Stand the sound of my voice? Can't *what?*

I take another step towards her and lean in until my mouth is next to her ear, just to test something. I'm a data-driven man, and I need proof before I act.

"What if," I breathe into her ear, "I told you recording them doesn't feel the same anymore, either?" Her breath hitches. When she doesn't step back or shove me away, I take it as a good sign.

"What would you do if I told you I think of you when I'm recording? That when Sky talks about the filthy, terrible things he wants to do, I wish it were *me* telling you the things I want to do to you. Not Sky. Not a listener. Me and you. What would you do if I told you I think about the sounds you made when you came, as I fuck my hand in the shower? What if I told you that maybe I'm a bad guy, because I love spending time with you and being your friend, but it's never enough for me? I want so much *more* with you."

Audrey stumbles backward and I reach out and grab her forearm to steady her. Once she's stable, I let go and take a step back, shame washing over me.

Too far. I misread the situation and made her uncomfortable and ruined everything and...

"What would I do?" she asks. "If you told me that? You want to know what I'd do?"

I rub my St. Anthony medal between my fingers, staring at the one of the few pumpkins scattered on the porch. I *really* fucked up. "Audrey, I—"

"I'd tell you to prove it."

My neck snaps up and I meet her dilated eyes. Her chest is heaving, and I almost come in my pants again when she swipes her tongue along her lower lip. "You'd... what?" I wheeze.

"I'd tell you to prove you meant what you said," she says, taking a step closer to me. "You say pretty words all the time to countless listeners, and I need to know it's more than words. I need to know I'm not a faceless listener to you. I need to know it's me and you."

I don't know if it's her voice, which is somehow steady and needy at the same time, or her saying my name that breaks my resolve, but something does. I take a step forward, cup her waist and pull her close enough our noses brush.

Please mean it. I internally beg. *Please don't want him. Please want me.*

"Prove it, Ren," she whispers, and it's game over.

I press my lips to hers and god, she's so ready for me, immediately kissing me back with the same fervor as that night two months ago. She tastes like the cinnamon and nutmeg I used in the apple pie, feels like sin and heaven coexisting. She brings her hand to my cheek, running her thumb along my jaw bone as I nip at her lower lip. Her mouth parts on a gasp and I take the opportunity to let one of my hands slip beneath her shirt, the warmth of her lower back a stark contrast to the chill of the autumn breeze. I can hear the waves crashing on the shore in the distance, and I could never write a script as good as this.

I break our kiss and press open mouth kisses down her jaw, and her neck. She moans softly and fists my hair, pulling enough it hurts fucking *good*.

She lifts her free hand to her collarbone, pulling back the collar of her oversized Luke's Diner t-shirt to expose more soft skin. "So Piper can't see."

I pull away and meet her eyes, breath heavy and cock heavier. "You want me to..."

"Mark me. Please, Ren," she breathes.

My mouth is on the soft skin between her collarbone and shoulder blade before she finishes saying my name. I want to give this woman everything she wants, but especially this. Especially something that will make sure she can't pretend this didn't happen, that this isn't real. Her gasps and sighs while I suck at her skin egg me on, and I'm not embarrassed to say the odds of me coming in my pants again are high as hell.

Until the sound of glass shattering echoes from inside the cottage.

Audrey loosens her grip on my hair, and I freeze, mouth still on her skin.

"Uh, Mom?" Piper calls nervously after a few moments of silence.

"Be right there!" Audrey answers as I groan and straighten, taking a brief moment to admire the hickey already forming before she adjusts her collar. "I'm sorry, I have to…"

"Hey, no need to apologize," I promise, cupping her face and briefly pressing my lips to her forehead. "It's fine."

She quickly pecks me on the cheek before spinning around and going back inside the house.

I stare at the wreath on her door for a good ten seconds, trying to process what happened because holy shit.

Holy *shit*. She wants me. *Me*. Not the concept of Sky, but *me*. Her friend.

The smile spreading across my face is gradual and bright and before I know it, I must look creepy as hell, a full grown man beaming at a door.

I spin on my heel and pump my fist because Audrey fucking Hinton wants *me*. Then I'm leaping off the stairs like a ballerina and ending on a twirl and…

Audrey's holding the door open and staring at me, eyes wide.

I clear my throat and shove my hands in my pockets because I am manly and cool about this.

"Um, Piper broke your pie pan," she says after a few moments of silence.

"No worries, it was thrifted." Is my voice gruff? I hope my voice is gruff and she never mentions what she saw because that would be embarrassing as hell. I have to keep some of my dignity.

But her smile is as bright as the stars above us and she's giggling. Her eyes glisten—not like she knows a secret no one else does, but because she and I are the only ones who do. "Me too," she says, and I stare at her in confusion. "I feel like that, too."

My smile is as bright as hers and our happiness seems to reflect each other's.

"Good night, Ren," she finally says.
"Good night, Audrey."
I smile the entire drive home.

Chapter 23

Audrey

Playlist: So High School | Taylor Swift

Halloween has always been my favorite holiday. I love wearing a costume and the candy and the scariness of it. And, lucky for me, Piper loves it, too. Every year, we dress up, stop by the inn for "impromptu" trick-or-treating, and then drive to a nearby town for "real" trick-or-treating. I always pick one of the bougie towns in Fairfield County, where they always have elaborate decorations and hand out full-sized candy bars.

When she was younger, Piper got overstimulated by the Halloween festivities, but over the years, we've learned what works to make it easier: trick-or-treating before it's dark and the scary costumes come out, earplugs, loose costumes she's comfortable in, and a safe word if she needs out.

This year, I have a boring teenager who decided last year she's too old for trick-or-treating. We stayed home and I introduced her to the *Scream* franchise, but *this* year, she was invited to her first Halloween party.

I know I should be happy. She's growing up, finding her own way, blah blah blah blah. But it's hard to be happy when I'm sitting alone on my porch in the same witch costume I've worn for a decade.

When Piper told me yesterday she was going to a party, I realized with sadness the two bags of candy I bought for us to enjoy would have to be used for trick-or-treaters. Last year, we'd left a bowl of candy on the porch for trick-or-treaters to watch the movie uninterrupted. But what am I supposed to do this year? Watch the *Scream* franchise *alone*? That's basically how Drew Barrymore got *murdered* in the first film.

So now I'm the pathetic mom sitting on her front steps in a witch costume—complete with green and black striped thigh highs, of course—coming to the sad realization the little cottage behind the inn is *not* prime trick-or-treating real estate.

"Have fun," I tell Piper, trying to put pep in my voice. I want her to be a teenager, to go out and have fun and not spend all her time with her mom. That's normal and good development! I'm the abnormal one.

"I will," Piper says, fixing the toga she has wrapped around her. Her choppy blonde hair is curled and she's painted her nose pink.

"What are you supposed to be?" I ask, opening my third Kit-Kat of the night.

"Pig Latin," she says with an eye roll, like it's the most obvious thing in the world.

"Right, right, of course," I say. "How silly of me."

She condescendingly pats me on the head and reaches into the bowl for a pack of Reese's Cups. I try to pull the bowl away, but alas, I am too slow.

"What happened to not trick-or-treating, missy?" I tease as she rips open the packaging.

"I didn't say trick-or-treat, did I?" she counters before shoving the entire peanut butter cup in her mouth.

"Are you biking to the party?" I ask as she skips down the steps.

"No. I'd have to wear a helmet and my hair looks too good," she mumbles through the chocolate. "It's a few blocks over on Jefferson."

"Sounds good. Remember to text me when you get there with the address and parents' names, please. And be home by eleven, but I want a text at ten. And do *not* turn off your location."

"Got it! Bye! Don't be *too* embarrassing!"

I wave her off and pull out my phone to open my e-reader app. I've been reading for an hour, with zero trick-or-treaters, when I'm surprised by the first text I've received from Ren since our makeout session a few nights ago.

Yep, this man kisses me like I'm the air he needs to breathe, gives me a hickey, pirouettes off the porch, and doesn't text me for multiple days.

Granted I didn't text him, either, but we still kept our routine of me joining him with coffee for his cooldown mile.

It's been... different. I'd been hoping he'd pull me into the wooded area at the bluffs where people sneak away to smoke and drink and ravish me for real, but alas. We don't have a secret tryst—instead, we walk and drink coffee and make useless small talk.

Ren

taking a page out of your playbook!

I grin like a fool at the picture of his TV with the *Gilmore Girls* logo on it. My heart does a couple, flips too.

Audrey

i'm so proud. <happy crying emoji>

Ren

what are you and piper doing tonight?

Audrey

ugh, my way too cool for me daughter is at her very first high school party while her loser mom sits on the porch with an almost full bowl of candy and no trick-or-treaters in the past hour.

Ren

ouch. <grimacing emoji>

Audrey

yeah, your night sounds way more fun. I might give up and call it a night.

Ren

i'm sorry. You can come over and join me, if you want.

My belly clenches with a myriad of feelings—desire, anxiety. After all, this is the man who got me off while fully dressed. Also the man who released a mask kink audio this morning.

Audrey

> thanks for the invite, but i told piper i'd be home, and i want her to know where i am.

> i know that sounds helicopter mom-ish, but if something happens i want her to be able to come home and know i'm here.

> like she *said* the parents would be home, but you know how many times i told my parents the exact same thing at her age? And there's probably alcohol and weed and like… i trust her. But i want her to know i'm home if she needs me.

Ren likes my last message, and I wait a few minutes for an actual reply, but not even the little typing bubbles appear. I sigh, closing my texts to reopen my e-reader app, hopeful that he's distracted by the shenanigans in Stars Hollow.

I don't turn off my notifications, though. Just in case.

One hour and four chapters of omegaverse smut later, I finally call it quits and go inside. I've been checking Piper's location, and she's exactly where she said she'd be. I *hate* that I'm paranoid, but this is a new experience for Piper and I, and we're still learning the ropes.

I'm settling down with a mug of tea to turn on the first *Scream* movie when there's a knock at the door.

I sit outside for *hours* and *now* they decide to trick-or-treat?

I sigh and force myself to my feet. I shuffle across the floor in my green and black striped stockinged feet before opening the door.

"Trick-or-treat!" I blink in surprise at Ren, who wears a tan tunic with a brown robe over it. He has a bottle of wine in one hand, and some sort of cylinder in the other.

"I... what?" I say intelligently.

"You said you weren't getting any trick-or-treaters, so. Here I am!" He lifts both arms and does a cheesy little bow.

I cover my mouth with my hand to hide my smile. This is better than a text response by far.

"And you're in costume and everything!" I say, taking in his ensemble. "You're obviously..." I trail off, hoping he'll finish the sentence.

"Luke Skywalker, of course!" Ren says with a wink that makes my belly flip.

"Of course," I agree, biting my lip. It's concerning that this full-grown man can be wearing the equivalent of a nerdy potato sack and still make me want to take my clothes off.

"I thought we could watch *Gilmore Girls* together. I grabbed some wine, too, in case wearing full Jedi regalia wasn't enticing enough." He lifts the wine bottle.

I nod towards his other hand. "And what's that?"

With a flick of his wrist, Ren is holding a fucking lightsaber.

I snort. "Incredible. Absolutely incredible."

"That's what I said!" he responds empathetically. "Kat told me the other night this is the reason I'll never find a nice wife to settle down with. Literally. That's the exact phrasing she used."

I'm not completely certain why my stomach is flipping at this second, but it either has to do with hearing Kat's name, or him using the word wife.

I've heard Sky use it a bunch of times, but Ren saying it is different. What kind of woman would he want to spend the rest of his life with? Who would he want to integrate into his already large family? Who would take his name and have his babies and wake him up by getting him off and...

"Can I come in?" Ren asks, jolting me out of my fantasy.

Oops, went off the deep end there.

"Sure," I say, cheeks hot.

"I like your costume," he tells me as I close and lock the door. "It's a classic."

"Mm, that's one word for it," I tease, turning to face him.

He raises a brow. "What's another?"

"Boring."

He laughs. "Okay, but I had *fifteen* students wear witch costumes today and not one of them had cool stripey stockings like that. So you're beating at least fifteen elementary school students, which must make you feel cool as hell."

I lift my skirt a little to show a bit more of the stockings and stick my leg out, toe pointed. "Oh, these old things? They're my potion-making stockings."

"Are they magical, or are you?"

I meet his eyes, and his crooked smile has my belly feeling like jello. How dare he insinuate I'm magical when I'm pretty much the equivalent of three racoons in a witch's costume! "It's them," I say definitively, pulling my leg back in and letting go of my skirt, the fabric falling around my legs. "Definitely the stockings."

Ren makes his way to the couch and I go to the kitchen to get us wine glasses, which is how I discover I don't own any wine glasses. God, I'm more of a loser than I thought, and I already thought I was a pretty big one. I usually drink my wine in a mug, so I grab two and re-enter the living room to Ren staring at the paused TV screen.

"Why don't you pull up *Gilmore Girls*?" I ask, reaching across him for the bottle of wine, and realizing I didn't think to grab a bottle opener.

I hope I have one of those, I usually just buy cheap screw-top wine.

"Were you watching *Scream*?" he asks, eyes on the TV.

"Oh, yeah. Kinda my guilty pleasure..."

"Do you remember when you and Kat told Millie and I it was a funny movie and made us watch it, and I had nightmares for a year?"

I attempt to cover my responding laugh with my hand. "Oh, god. Did we? Are you sure it wasn't Kat on her own?"

"Yup." He points the TV remote menacingly at me. "You traumatized me."

"I'm sorry," I giggle. "I wasn't the most... thoughtful teenager."

"Yeah, you were an asshole," he says dismissively, turning his attention back to the TV. "But so are all teenagers, so don't beat yourself up over it too much. Nic punched me in the face and broke my nose on her seventeenth birthday because I tried to wake her up to surprise her, so she's got you beat."

I laugh nervously, teeth digging into my lip.

"Can we watch it?" Ren asks, turning his body to face me.

"*Gilmore Girls*?"

"No, *Scream*."

I stare at him in confusion. "You want to watch the movie that traumatized you as a child?"

"Yes," he says simply, folding his hands in his lap. "Call it what you want: exposure therapy, facing my fears. But I think it's time. Plus, if I watch this *and Gilmore Girls*, you really can't say no when I eventually ask you to watch *Star Wars*." He looks at me pointedly.

I laugh before going to the kitchen, relieved when I find a bottle opener. "If you're sure it won't give you nightmares again..."

I'm joking, but what *if* he has nightmares? What if he wakes up sweaty and scared and *alone* and I'm not there to...

There to what, *exactly?*

Never mind.

When I return to the couch, Ren presses play on the remote and reaches into the bowl of candy I left on the coffee table. I sit next to him, and try not to creepily leer at his hands while he rips open the Butterfinger wrapper. But I can't help but track the way his long fingers move and flex, and the way his veins decorate his skin.

This "not being able to get myself off" thing is a true tragedy.

"Wait," Ren says, pointing his candy bar at the TV as the movie plays, "is that Drew Barrymore? Of *The Drew Barrymore Show* fame?"

I laugh and reach for my own candy bar. "You're ridiculous."

"Oh, I'm guessing you know her from E.T. since you're a billion years old?"

I get on my knees and cover his mouth. "Lorenzo, the movie's playing."

His eyes widen comically, bouncing between my face and Drew Barrymore cooking popcorn on the screen.

"*Augh*!" I yelp, pulling my hand away from him and shaking it. "Did you just *lick* me?"

Ren shrugs and takes another giant bite of candy. "Maybe. And stop pretending you didn't like it, weirdo."

I sit and pretend I'm not thinking about how desperately I want his tongue pretty much everywhere besides my hand. Hell, maybe in a different context I'd even accept him licking my hand. I'm a desperate harlot at this point.

We watch the movie in silence, and I watch him out of the corner of my eye when Drew Barrymore, of *The Drew Barrymore Show* fame, is brutally murdered.

"Brutal, huh?" I say as the movie logo appears on the screen after Drew's character's violent demise.

"What?" Ren says, staring straight at the screen.

"Your favorite talk show host just died, Ren."

"Oh." He shakes his head, like he's trying to shake out whatever's in his head. "Sorry, I, uh. Wasn't paying attention."

I sigh and press pause. "*You* insisted we watch it."

"I know."

"And you're not watching it?"

"I tried... but I kept getting distracted."

I blink at him, confused. "Distracted by *what*?"

He laughs incredulously. "Oh, I don't know, Audrey. You're sitting next to me in your hot-as-hell witch costume with striped stockings, and our legs keep brushing so I have to pretend I'm watching this movie when all I want to do is find out if the stockings are thigh-highs because I'd very much like to take them off with my teeth if they are and—"

"Yes," I interrupt, face heating.

His fingers rub at the base of his throat, rubbing his chain that tucked under his costume. "Yes, what?"

I take a deep breath and pinch the fabric of the skirt between my forefinger and thumb, slowly pulling it up my thigh to expose more of the stockings. "Yes, they're thigh highs, and yes, I'd like you to take them off with your teeth."

He freezes. "Seriously?"

"Depends," I squeak.

"On what?"

"On if you were serious, too."

I yelp in surprise when he rotates his torso and grasps my hips in his hands, pulling me on top of him so I'm straddling his lap. I'm not thin, but this man's ginormous hands almost span the entirety of my hips and it's incredible.

He pulls me down further on his lap, and I gasp when his rock-hard cock grinds against my aching core.

"I'm serious," he says, eyes intent on mine.

Neither of us move.

He laughs, and I love laughing with this man in our horny hazes. "Should I prove it again?"

I nod. "Yes, I'm data-driven and I need more physical evidence."

He thrusts his hips upward, and I groan as his cock grinds into me again. "You can feel it. I know you can, sweetheart. Look at how you're moaning for me."

I don't think I've ever been this turned on in my life, which is baffling considering this man has made me come in my pants like a teenager *and* gave me a hickey when I asked.

Yet I'm somehow even hornier.

If I didn't have an IUD, the odds of me getting pregnant again would be embarrassingly high.

He grasps my hips like if he loosens his grip, I'll disappear. Like the idea of me getting away is absolutely unacceptable to him.

"Will you touch me?" I ask, surprised at how breathless I sound.

His touch is gentle as he reaches up and grasps my witch hat by the brim, tossing it absently behind me. "How?"

Being celibate for a decade and a half meant I had lots of time to fantasize about dozens of different ways having sex again could go. And now that I'm here... I don't know.

"Why don't we figure it out as we go?" he offers, brushing my hair off my shoulder. It's like he can sense my anxiety, my hesitation.

I cup his face in my hands, searching his eyes and finding the same things I always do when we've been here: lust, passion, patience, kindness. I trace his lips with my thumb, enjoying how his breath hitches. It feels like he wants me as much as I want hi m.

"I'll be so good to you, Audrey," he whispers, and I believe him. I tilt his face and capture his mouth with mine, taken aback by how gentle and soft it is compared to the previous times. I want to ravish him, for him to ravish *me*. I want it hard and fast and rough and to take my pleasure, but he knows I *need* it like this. It's as if he's telling me, *it's just me. I've got you, I promise. I want us exactly as we are.* It's gentle and intimate and it makes me want to sob.

He's the first to break the kiss, and his breath is heavy. "Will you take me to bed?" he asks, and I want to scream because how is he unbearably sexy and fucking warm and soft at once? "I want to see where you touch yourself to Sky."

I groan, suddenly bashful, and bury my face in his neck. He chuckles and moves his right hand from my hip to cup the back of my head, softly threading his fingers through my hair. "It's alright sweetheart. We can stay right here if you'd rather. We can rewind the movie and watch Drew Barrymore's violent demise again, if that's what you need."

I smile against his neck. His patience around sex heals the scared teenager within me who saw how quickly sex could ruin everything. The devastated girl who learned how drastically sex could change lives, the young woman who felt unworthy of it, and the adult who has avoided it ever since.

I lift my head and nod. "Okay."

"Yeah?" he asks, his hand moving to cup the side of my neck. "You'll tell me if something isn't okay?"

"Yes," I promise him. "And you'll tell me?"

He nods. "I will."

I move to stand and he frowns at me, hands grasping my hips again. "Where the hell do you think you're going?"

"I'm taking you to the bedroom?" I say, confused.

"Bold assumption I don't want to carry you."

I laugh. "Ren, you can't. I'm heavier than I look. I—*agh!*" I shriek and wrap my arms and legs around him as he suddenly gets to his feet, easily lifting my more than two-hundred-pound body.

I need to stop thinking he can't get hotter, because I'm *wrong* every damn time.

"Kiss me," he breathes as he carries me down the hall.

I do. Hard and desperate this time with scraping teeth and tangled tongues and moans and grunts as he stumbles through the house, bouncing off walls and into picture frames. It's so good and—

"Oh god, Piper," I gasp, pulling away.

His brow furrows. "It's, uh, Ren actually."

I bark out a laugh and press my lips to his jaw, his stubble rough against the sensitive skin. "No, no, I haven't checked my phone in a while. I want to make sure she's okay and I left my phone on the table..."

"Hey." His voice is so soft I can't help but peer up at him. "I don't want to tell you how to parent... but you're allowed to enjoy yourself. Piper's a smart kid, and I'm sure she'll call if she needs you."

I bite my lip. He's right, yet I'm still nervous. What if this is the one time she can't get through? What if I'm having wild, animal sex and she gets hurt? What if...

"I'll put you on your bed and get your phone," he says gently. "We can keep it on the nightstand, face up if that'll make you feel better. Okay? We can take breaks for you to check and..."

I swallow his words with another hard kiss. He's not telling me my anxiety is unfounded, or that I'm a helicopter mom, and he's not letting me spiral or deny myself either. He's meeting me exactly where I am. I always thought putting Piper first would mean I would never be able to give myself to someone else besides her.

Maybe I was right, because until him, no one accepted me exactly as I am, but now, Ren has me thinking that one day, maybe I can try.

Chapter 24

Audrey

Playlist: Teenage Dream - Acoustic | Bailey Rushlow

Sky's Sluts

LadyRebel93: so who else is asking their hubby to pick up a mask on their way home from work cuz god DAMN.

AshBash69: my husband said no, so catch me listening to sky fucking my brains out in a mask while he sleeps on the couch.

LadyRebel93: fair enough.

LadyRebel93: i shouldn't be surprised i'm into it. i'm into everything sky does.

SkysMainSlut: god it was so fucking good. i listened to it twice before getting ready for work.

AshBash69: can you imagine ACTUALLY being fucked by him? like this man has the biggest dick energy ever

SkysMainSlut: it literally makes me nauseous to think about him having sex with someone else.

LadyRebel93: have you heard of parasocial relationships

AshBash69: i mean considering i listened to his audio the day my kid was conceived, he's pretty much my baby daddy.

AshBash69: but to be real, if anyone is actually fucking him, i hope she knows i fucking hate her.

Ren and I crash through my bedroom door and I blindly slap at the wall in search of the light switch. I take too long because then I'm on my back staring up at Ren, who's barely visible in the dark as he hovers over me.

"Don't. Move," he breathes. "I'll be right back."

Suddenly he's gone, and I miss sharing space with him so much my chest aches. He's back in less than a minute, flipping the light switch on. "Light on?" he confirms.

I sit and shake my head, reaching to my nightstand to turn on the bedside lamp.

He sighs heavily, turning the big light off before his hands move to the brown, leather-looking belt around his middle. "I thought I told you not to move."

My tongue darts out between my lips. "Sorry," I say breathily. God, I didn't know I could *sound* breathy.

He climbs onto my bed, sitting on his knees in front of me as he drops his belt to the side of the bed.

I try not to laugh at the fact I'm about to have my world rocked by a man currently dressed as a Star Wars character, and fail.

"What's so funny?" Ren asks.

"You're such a nerd," I giggle.

My laughter is short lived however, because he reaches forwards and grabs my thighs, spreading my legs as he pulls me to him. I fall on my back with a gasp.

"You know, nerds get overlooked," he says, like he's not currently situated between my thighs with my legs draped over his arms. "We make the best lovers—we're good with our hands..." he squeezes my outer thighs and I squirm. "Passionate..." he dips his head and takes my thigh-high between his teeth. He snaps it against me and I cry out as the burn radiates to my center.

I think I like it? That's new.

He leans over me again, and I feel like he's bending me in half. I'm learning so much about myself in so little time. Apparently, I'm flexible enough to be folded in half. I grasp his shoulders. "And?" I breathe as he lowers his mouth to my ear.

"I'm sure there's more, but now I'm intent on getting you to make that sound again," he breathes into my ear. "Can I try to get it from you?"

"Please," I gasp, needing to clench my thighs, but unable to because this man is currently mistaking me for a paper crane.

"I've been tested since my last partner, and everything came back negative," he breathes.

"They did a full testing panel at my annual a few years ago, and my last partner was Piper's dad. Everything was negative."

He nods once before his eyes drift to my collarbone. "Show me where I marked you." His voice is husky and needy and god, I'll bottle it and bathe in it because it makes me feel as beautiful as starlight. "Please, sweetheart. I've been imagining it for over a week."

I oblige, pulling the collar of the cheap costume I got five years ago just enough that he can see it. It's faded a bit, but is still visible. He groans, and my stomach clenches knowing we both know exactly what it represents—how needy I am for him.

"Touch me," I beg, pathetic and not caring.

"Tell me where."

"Everywhere."

He tenses. "Are you sure? Last time you didn't want me to touch your breasts. Has that changed?"

My stomach clenches and I don't want to be embarrassed, but I am. Breastfeeding changed the appearance and shape of my breasts and I know there's nothing wrong with them but... I still feel self-conscious. I still see the way that guy looked at me so long ago. I still beat myself up for not "bouncing back" the way magazines and celebrities said I was supposed to. I have a hanging belly with sagging skin and stretch marks and breasts with nipples that point to the floor.

I've worked hard to treat my body with kindness, because I know how Piper sees me treating and talking about my body will be how she treats and talks about her own.

But alone, I still grieve the body I thought I would have, and I hate myself for it.

"No," I finally say. "No, that hasn't changed. Is that okay?"

"Of course," he promises, voice gentle. "I'll give you whatever you need, sweetheart, however you need it."

I pull him into another kiss because how could I not? He keeps meeting me exactly where I am, and more than that, lessening my *shame* for being where I am.

"I'm gonna reach over you to put your phone on the nightstand, okay?" he murmurs against my lips.

I nod frantically. "Yes, and then you'll touch me?"

Ren's grip on my thighs tightens and *god*, I hope I have his fingerprints imprinted on my skin. His touch leaves my skin as he reaches over me. "Face up?"

"No, face down," I answer before pausing. "Wait, are we talking about me or the phone?"

He laughs. "The phone."

"Face down," I say definitively. I trust Piper. I trust *myself*. I deserve this.

He chuckles again as he straightens and adjusts himself so he's kneeling between my legs again. "You're keeping your eyes on me tonight, sweetheart. I'll take you from behind another time."

He pulls his tunic over his head in one smooth movement and nothing, I mean *nothing*, could have prepared me for the sight of his bare chest. He's tattooed in the places that weren't visible in the clothes he's worn, and my toes curl as I drink in the sight of him. His torso is muscular, a heavy dusting of the same chestnut hair as his head and face. A gold chain with a small medallion hangs around his neck, and it takes every bit of willpower to not reach out and run my fingers along it like he does when he's nervous. My eyes drift downward, following the strip of hair that extends from his navel to the very hot, very sexy V of his hips, and farther still under the waistband of his pants.

I think I'd be salivating no matter what he looked like naked. Because it's him, and he's fucking beautiful.

"You have tattoos," I say, tracing the floral lightsaber piece on his side.

"Yeah... Millie needed to practice when she was an apprentice, and I wanted to help." He points to one on the inside of his left shoulder blade. "See that? Her very first one."

I squint my eyes. "What is it?"

"A butterfly. It somehow looks more like SpongeBob with three eyes." His smile while speaking about it is radiant. He's so obviously proud of his younger sister. "The first dozen or so were *rough*, and she's since covered them. I won't let her touch this one, though."

I softly trace the misshapen butterfly, my heart so full it could burst. "It's special, because it was her first one," I say softly, thinking about how special Piper's firsts were to me.

"Can I touch you, Aud?" he asks, voice raspy.

"Please."

I lift my skirt as I scooch backwards to make room for Ren to spread out. I have a king-sized bed, because Piper has always been a kicker when asleep. I've never been more grateful for it than right now, as Ren lays on his belly and grabs under my knees, lifting them over his shoulders. He's so close I shiver at his breath on my inner thigh.

"Hmm," he says, hooking his finger into the top of my thigh-highs "Well, I'm having second thoughts. Maybe I should leave the stockings *on.*"

"Striped stockings do it for you?" I tease.

"*You* do it for me." He pauses before adding, "But yeah, the stockings are doing it for me."

I jolt as his teeth sink into the bare skin of my thigh. He soothes it with an open-mouthed kiss before continuing to kiss up my thigh until he gets to the edge of my underwear. He lifts his eyes to mine. "Okay?"

I nod frantically, weaving a hand through his hair. "Don't stop," I beg trembling from the level of need I'm feeling for him. I'm fucking gone I don't even care I'm wearing my usual high-waisted cotton underwear I buy in bulk from Costco. The tenderness with which he slips his finger beneath the elastic makes me feel like I'm wearing silk.

"Your skin's so soft," he muses, resting the side of his head against my thigh.

"Moisturizing body wash," I gasp as he snaps the elastic against me. Then I want to smack myself because I'm certain this man does *not* care about my skincare routine at this moment.

He hooks his finger in again, this time pulling the fabric to the side. I don't have time to be self-conscious about the fact I have a full bush and I pushed an eight-pound human being out of my vagina before he's pressing his lips to the crease between my thigh and vulva. "The body wash works," he muses, mouth moving against a part of me no one has touched so intimately before. "And smells like heaven. Give me the brand later so I can write a review." I grin at the ceiling. "But I have to be honest with you Audrey... your pussy smells like sin."

"Oh my god," my smile is gone, and my teeth are digging into my bottom lip, holding back what I'm sure would be an obscene moan.

"Promise me one thing," Ren says, lifting his head. I fight the urge to shove his head back to where I need it.

Instead I inhale shakily and hold his gaze. "Okay," I whisper.

"Don't hold back on me, sweetheart." My wish comes true as he ducks his head and parts my pussy with his thumbs before flicking my clit with his tongue.

I jolt and my grip in his hair tightens. "Shit!"

"Just like that, beautiful," he murmurs against me. "It's my turn to hear you."

He flicks my swollen clit again and truthfully, his moans may be overpowering mine. I keep my promise, letting myself react the way my body needs to and my god, *he's* enjoying this as much as I am.

"Can I put a finger in this pretty pussy?" he asks, voice muffled.

I nod eagerly before remembering he's currently covered by the fabric of my costume. I arch my back and lift my ass to try to pull the skirt up so I can see him. But he's faster, gripping my thighs and pressing me into the bed. I give up and raise the fabric, uncovering him, and lifting myself on my elbows for a better view. "Yes, please," I answer.

He lifts his eyes for a moment before pulling away from me. I whimper at the loss of contact, but it's replaced instantaneously by a moan as he slowly presses a finger into me.

"Christ, Aud. All this for me?" he muses. "Were you always this wet when Sky made you come?" He curves his finger against my G-spot, and I cry out.

"Yes!" He returns his mouth to my cunt, this time taking my clit into his mouth and sucking softly. "God, I'm always wet for you, Ren. Even before I knew it was you."

He groans, and his eyes meet mine again. He brushes another finger against my opening, and I nod encouragingly. I want more of him, *need* more of him.

He pushes a second finger into me and I feel so *full*, so overwhelmed.

It's so good, so, so good. I want to come for him as much as *he* wants me to come, and he's doing everything right.

But after a few minutes, my stomach sinks and my mind wanders. *Has Piper texted me? Should I check my phone? Shouldn't I have come by now? I'm taking too long. What if something happened? What if I can't come? What if I've actually never orgasmed and only thought I orgasmed? What if...*

"Where'd you go, sweetheart?" Ren asks softly, pulling away.

Angry tears prick in my eyes, and I blink rapidly to fight them back. Sometimes my meds make it hard to come, and no matter how hard I try, I can't come. I've masturbated to the point of soreness trying to orgasm, and sometimes it still doesn't happen.

Why does it have to be happening *tonight*?

"Hey, hey." He's suddenly pushed himself up so he's sprawled out on his side next to me. He wraps his arm around me and pulls me into him, and that's when I realize I lost the battle against my tears. "What happened? Did I—"

"No." It comes out a sob. "No, you didn't do anything wrong. It's my fault. I should have told you."

He's rubbing my back in calming circles, kissing the top of my head, my temple. "Told me what?"

"I know I told you I have depression," I try to say, but I think it comes out as a strangled stream of syllables.

"Oh." I hear understanding in Ren's voice, but he doesn't get it. It's not only my emotions, but it's what my goddamned meds do to me. "What med are you on?"

I lift my head in confusion, my eyes meeting his. "Zoloft," I say quietly. "Since Piper was eight weeks."

"Oof," he says simply, brushing a strand of hair from my eyes. "The side effects can be a bitch, huh?"

I feel like he's lifted a ton of bricks off my body and inhale shakily. "Yeah. And I keep worrying about Piper. I know I'm overreacting but..."

"You said it's her first party, right?" I want him to be annoyed. Make up an excuse as to why he has to leave and never hear from him again. Because him being this kind and understanding is making me soft, and I've worked hard for the past decade and a half to put on armor to protect myself. "It makes sense you're nervous. Why don't you text her and I'll grab you water. Maybe a few pieces of candy?"

Tears continue to fall, but this time for a different reason. He *has* to be too good to be true. "Then what?" I ask. "Are you going to leave?"

"If you want me to."

"Do *you* want to leave?" I ask.

He rests his chin on the top of my head. "No, Audrey," he says quietly. "I really, really don't want to leave."

I shakily wrap my arms around him, inhaling his scent. He smells earthy, like herbs and peppermint tea and safety. "I really,

really don't want you to go, either," I admit, ignoring the glaring chink in my armor.

He pulls back and cups my face in his hands, brushing away my tears with his thumbs. "Then I'm staying."

He presses his lips to my forehead and my eyes flutter closed. Everything within me is telling me to toughen up. To not let myself be taken care of by him because the only person I can rely on is myself.

But I'm tired, and he's strong and kind and maybe he could let me rest and take care of me and Piper and...

He pulls away again and swings his legs over the side of the bed. "I'll grab you some water. Why don't you check in with Piper? I think it'll make you feel better."

"Then what?" I ask.

"Whatever we want," he answers with a crooked smile. "I don't care what we're doing, Aud. I just want to be with you."

Before I can reply, he's gone, closing the bedroom door behind him.

I pick my phone up and breathe a sigh of relief when my screen has no notifications.

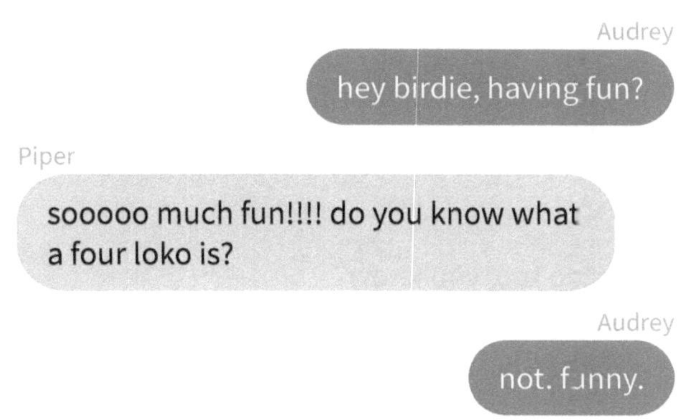

you're right it wasn't funny

it was HILARIOUS

Audrey

<eyeroll emoji>

if the party gets busted make sure you can walk in a straight line okay? i'm not bailing you out of jail

Piper

1) rude 2) in all seriousness, i'm having fun. it's a little loud, so i have my earplugs in, but i think i'm having fun? part of me's waiting for it to go wrong

it feels too good to be true, like i'm not supposed to be having fun. is that bad?

Audrey:

i think everyone feels like that sometimes. you deserve to have fun and be happy. i'm proud of you for going outside of your comfort zone!

Piper

you do too, you know

Audrey

Piper

> yeah I think i'm learning that, you little shit

aggressive for no reason, jeez.

okay i'm gonna go before everyone realizes i'm the loser texting her mommy.

Audrey

> i love you, text me when you're leaving, and call me if you need a ride

Piper

i will

I exhale shakily as Ren slowly reopens the door and pokes his head in the room. The heat that had faded between my thighs reignites.

"Can I come in?" he asks, like his head wasn't between my thighs a few minutes ago and his mustache isn't still glistening with my arousal.

I bite my lip and nod. "Yeah."

He enters the room and closes the door behind him with his hip, hands full with water for us.

He climbs back onto the bed beside me and gives me a glass, which I gratefully take.

"Do you want me to get dressed?" he asks as I drain the glass. Not orgasming is a *workout.*

"Uh... is it weird if I say I want to try again?" I ask nervously.

"Not weird at all. Is it weird if like... I'm still turned on after this?"

I laugh and shake my head. "Maybe, but it's certainly my brand of weird."

He's my brand of everything.

Chapter 25

Ren

Playlist: Hold My Girl | George Ezra

This has been simultaneously the weirdest and best night of my life.

"So this is where you listen to Sky," I muse, taking the opportunity to look around her bedroom. It's spacious and decorated in sky blues and greens, reminding me of sea glass. There's a picture on her nightstand of her in a hospital bed holding a red-faced, screaming newborn, and a dresser with a mirror across from the bed. In the corner stands a bookshelf with a few books, but it's mostly filled with artwork by and pictures of Piper through the years. It's a pretty unassuming room, but it's so cozy, so welcoming, so *Audrey*.

"Yep," she says, popping the 'p' and somehow snuggles in closer to me. "Every release day, sometimes more often." She pauses for a moment before continuing. "Most of the time more often. Can I ask you about him?"

"About Sky?"

"Yeah."

I shrug. Honestly, I'd rather be eating her pussy again, but I can be patient. "Sure."

"What made you decide to... to..."

"To work with 4Play? To create audio erotica?"

She nods against me. "Yeah."

"The founder is a friend from college who reached out when they were developing the app and asked if I was interested. I was struggling to make ends meet just teaching and… I don't know. It sounded interesting.

"I'd recently gotten out of a rough situationship I thought was a relationship, I was hurting, and it felt like something just for me. Something no one else knows about." I glance down at her, and find her eyes on me already. "Except you. And my best friend, Will."

She smiles softly. "So that's why you use a stage name?"

"I use one for a lot of reasons. I don't want my family knowing I'm involved with sex work, for one. And I'm a teacher. I love teaching, and I don't want to jeopardize my job. When I record, I'm not Ren Quinn, or Mr. Q. I'm Sky, a man who's safe to be open in his sexuality and exploration of it."

"Why did you pick that name?"

My face heats. "Oh, god. I can't tell you that, you'd never stop making fun of me."

"Ren." She tilts my face. "I promise I won't make fun of you."

"That's sweet, but you shouldn't make promises you can't keep."

She scowls at me. "I'm serious!"

"So am I. You're *going* to make fun of me. You should accept it."

"I can't believe you have such little faith in me!"

"Fine, I'll tell you. But remember this: I told you so."

She rolls her eyes. "Drama king."

"In my mind, Sky's last name is Walker."

She blinks at me in confusion.

I sigh heavily. "Sky… Walker."

It takes her a second before her face gives way to understanding. "Oh. My. God."

I sigh. "There it is."

"As in *Luke*?" she squeals.

"Yup." She literally has her hand slapped over her mouth. "I told you so."

She laughs, loud and hearty and full and bright and, you know what, I'll make a fool out of myself whenever she wants, as long as I can get that laugh.

"I'm sorry, I didn't expect that," she wheezes.

"Quite frankly, that seems like your own damn fault."

She giggles and stretches out to press a kiss to the corner of my mouth. "I love it."

"You're not embarrassed you got yourself off to a guy whose name is a *Star Wars* tribute?"

"I don't think I could be embarrassed about anything about you. Everything I learn makes me like you more."

That's a win for nerds everywhere.

"I like you, too," I say quietly, turning my face to press my lips into the center of her palm. "If it wasn't obvious."

"Ren?"

"Mmm?"

She pauses and shakes her head, dropping her hand. "Never mind, it's silly."

I furrow my brow. "Well, now you *have* to tell me."

She's quiet, and for a moment I think she's not going to budge. "Do you think a universe exists where we work out? A universe where people wouldn't judge you for being with me? Where we could just be happy?"

It feels like someone reached into my chest and cut my heart out with a dull, rusty knife. "What do you mean?"

"Ren, I'm not someone you can bring home to your family. I'm not someone you can be with in public. I'm *me*."

"I like that you're you," I say so quietly I'm not even sure she hears. It's *because* she's her that I so desperately want her in my life. Not in spite of her past, but because everything she went through created the most extraordinary woman I've ever known.

"And you're... god, Ren you're perfect. Everything about you is good and kind and wonderful and I'm the exact opposite."

Somehow the pain in my chest gets even worse. "I'm not perfect, Audrey. I work really hard to make people think that because it's easier for everyone if I don't need help, or if I'm fine on my own or able to come through for everyone else.

"You're the only person I can simply exist with. I love my family, but Jesus Christ, they're a mess. Someone always needs something and that's fine... but they know I'm the one who will come through. And of course I will, because everyone else has their own thing going on, but I can come through for them. I show up. Because I have to. Because..."

I choke on my words, realizing it's the first time I've said this out loud. "Because if I don't show up, if I'm not perfect, I'm nothing."

"Ren," she says, voice hushed. "I didn't... that's not true. You could never be nothing."

I don't know if I believe her. "All of my siblings have a role in the family. Mine is being exactly who they need me to be. I'm the one no one has to worry about and I don't know what happens if I'm not who they expect me to be."

She exhales shakily. "Yeah. I get that."

My stomach sinks. "Fuck, I didn't mean..."

"I know." She smiles at me but it's watery. "I wish I could tell you they love you for who you are, not who they want you to be, but in my experience that's not how people are."

She snuggles into my chest, and I wonder if she can feel the way my heart is beating for her. "But I think maybe I was wrong. Maybe there are people who aren't like that."

My stomach feels like I'm on an intense roller coaster instead of in bed. A roller coaster with inversions and loops and big drops and...

"I know I said I wanted to keep going..." Audrey's voice is quiet, but not quite a whisper. "But would it be okay if we stay like this?"

This is Audrey with her head on my chest, her fingers mindlessly playing with my St. Anthony medal. *This* is my arms wrapped around her, holding her close and feeling so understood by her.

"Yes," I respond, hoping she doesn't notice my voice cracking. "Let's stay like this."

I don't tell her I also want us to grow, to change. To get to a place where we can love each other and our lives can intertwine, because I think that might be everything I want.

But for now, I'll be happy with this.

Chapter 26

Audrey

Playlist: Emergence | Sleep Token

November

Ren and I entered uncharted waters on Halloween. He stayed until Piper texted she was leaving the party, kissing me on the porch before going home.

When I wake up the following morning, I realize he left his lightsaber in my room. I take a mirror selfie of myself holding it in my glasses and pajamas—a white tank top and purple flannel shorts—with my unmade bed in the background, to make it extra spicy.

Audrey

missing something, mr skywalker?

Ren

oh my god

oh my GOD?!!?<sweating emoji>

please tell me I can masturbate to this. please please please please please please please

this is the longest-lasting fantasy i've ever had.

Audrey

me holding a lightsaber?

Ren

uhhhh, sure. you holding a lightsaber

Audrey

??? what else would you fantasize about me doing with a lightsaber???

Ren

...nothing

Audrey

wait

WAIT

EW

NO

Ren

I'M SORRY

Audrey

tell your dick to chill out please

Ren

why don't you tell him yourself? <smirk-ing emoji>

Audrey

...

Ren

you know saying that was a gamble, and i now realize it was a bad one

Audrey

lmaooo you're ridiculous

also, did you know your sister and her hyperactive girlfriend are hosting their launch event at the inn? hunter told me at 10000 words a minute this morning and I think I retained like one detail. it's gonna be really gay

Ren

hunter's a talker, but she's talked about how much she likes the inn lady a few times at dinner that makes me sound like someone's 75 year old crotchety aunt

now that i'm smiling like a fool at my phone during my prep period… when can i come get the lightsaber from you?

piper will probably be home tonight.

got it, no worries. We can try to do a sneaky pass-off on saturday.

i was GOING to say maybe i can tell her i'm going grocery shopping for a few hours and bring it to you… wearing a different pair of thigh-highs for you to play with, if you want.

<wide eye emoji>

i don't know what that means

<wide eye emoji>

are you broken? Did i break you?

Ren

<wide eye emoji>

Audrey

is that a no?

Ren

<thumbs down emoji>

Audrey

is it a yes?

Ren

<thumbs up emoji>

Audrey

you've lost the ability to compose words and have to communicate via images like a caveman?

Ren

<thumbs up emoji>

Audrey

poor baby lol. see you this evening <winking emoji>

Ren

<thumbs up emoji>

"Hello?" I answer Piper's call on the first ring, like I always do. She rarely calls, and her calling me during school has me nervous.

"Can I go to Annika's for dinner?" she asks, sounding calm and unaffected.

I blink a few times. "You called me to ask if you can go to your archnemesis's house for dinner?" I ask, confused by the situation.

"We're friends now, Mom." She lets out a long, suffering sigh. I rub at my temples. I could barely keep up with my *own* social goings on when I was a teenager, and I'm expected to be in the loop about my daughter's?

This seems unfair.

"Okay," I say. "That's fine. Maybe I should meet her parents, though. If you guys are going to be hanging out..."

"I'll kill you," Piper interrupts.

"Okay, I'm not a fan of that. But can you give them my number and ask them to reach out tonight? I won't make the first move and embarrass you!"

"That might be *more* embarrassing."

I sigh. I don't feel a need to be buddy-buddy with the parents of everyone she hangs out with, but I should at least confirm they're like... not evil humans? That's got to be an okay thing to do.

"I want you to go to dinner, birdie, but I need you to work with me. I need to know you're with safe people."

"Ugh, fine," Piper groans, and I internally pump my fist. I got an "ugh, fine!" A win for moms everywhere!

Hunter is suddenly standing in my doorway, knocking repeatedly on the door.

"Okay, baby," I say, "I have to get back to work. I love you."

"Love you too. Bye." She hangs up with a click.

"Ooooh, who do you love?" Hunter sing-songs, a glimmer of mischief in her sapphire blue eyes.

I roll my eyes. "My child?"

"Ah yes. Doting mom and all that." She nods her head approvingly. "Good job."

I look at her questioningly. "Thank you? Is there something I can do to help you?"

She sighs long-sufferingly. "No," she answers, slumping against the door frame. "I'm just bored. Event planning is boring, and Giovanna is better at it, so I've left our launch event in her sexy, capable hands."

I try to fight back a laugh. "Ah, yes, yet you started an event planning firm."

She sighs like a Victorian woman plagued by consumption. "The things we do for love."

Hunter leaves my office after distracting me for a few more minutes, picking up every single item on my desk and asking me about it, like she's a weird archaeologist finding ancient artifacts, and not a blonde troublemaker with a penchant for rambling and losing focus.

Once she's gone, I pull my phone out again.

Audrey

hey, piper's going to a friend's house for dinner tonight

does that impact our plans? i don't know how to parent, i don't have to be responsible for children unless i'm being paid.

My ovaries are currently screaming at me, like I didn't literally have an IUD shoved up my cervix and into my uterus to keep me from getting pregnant. Like he didn't say he doesn't know how to parent. But the idea of Ren with a tiny baby sleeping on his chest, his forearms flexing while pushing a stroller, tears streaming down his cheeks when a screaming newborn is placed on my chest...

Great. I'm getting horny over non-sexual intimacy again.

If the way I'm squeezing my thighs together under my desk is anything to go by, it's a good thing we have plans tonight. Maybe I'll get lucky and reach that orgasm I couldn't quite get to last night.

no, but do you want to come to the cottage instead?

to be completely honest, that might be best. i have an annoying af cat who will likely try to cuddle us if we leave the door open, or will sit and scream bloody murder if we lock her out sounds like piper when she was a baby.

come over, i'll make dinner. AND i still have the bottle of wine and the candy

Ren

you're all the candy i need

Audrey

you just gave me the ick

Ren

yeah that's fair… am i still allowed to come over?

Audrey

only if you never refer to me as candy again

Ren

DONE

When Ren arrives, I've just pulled the horribly burnt chicken pot pie I'd decided to make for dinner out of the oven.

"Did you follow a recipe?" Ren asks, going around the cottage and opening the windows to air out the smoke.

"Yes! I also realized I didn't shave my legs so I had to jump in the shower and Mom Brain kicked in and I forgot about it."

"Kitchen safety at its finest," Ren teases, coming back into the kitchen. "Next time I come over, I expect you'll be running with knives." He comes up behind me and wraps his arms around me, pulling me into him. It's soft and tender. I want to melt into a puddle of goo. He gently tucks my hair to one shoulder, kissing up the side of my neck.

"W-what?" I say, all thoughts blissfully erased by his touch.

He chuckles against me, a warm breeze on my skin that gives me goosebumps all over my body. "Don't worry about it, sweetheart. Take me back to bed."

He grips my hips and roughly turns my body until my breasts are pressed against his firm chest. He tilts my chin up and captures my mouth with his, stealing my breath as well. I wrap my arms around his neck, desperate for as much of me to be touching as much of him as possible.

"Can I tell you what I want to do tonight?" Ren asks against my mouth.

"Yes," I gasp, already so undone by this man.

"I want you to take me back to the room where you made yourself come to my audios, and then I want you to show me how you did it."

His lips are back on my neck as my brow furrows in confusion. "Huh?"

"I want you to touch yourself. And I want to watch. Do you think you can do that for me, sweetheart?"

That is the hottest thing I've ever heard in my life, hotter than anything he's said in his audios.

"Why?" It comes out as a moan as he gently nips my neck with his teeth.

"*Why?*" He says the word like he can't possibly fathom why I would be asking. "Because I want to know what feels good for you. So I can try again. So *you* can get the release you didn't get last night. I've pictured you spread out on your bed, legs open for me, as you moaned Sky's name and came to his words. I desperately want to see it."

I moan as he grinds himself against my soaking center. He's so hard, so needy for me.

I love it.

"Yes," I gasp, and suddenly, I'm back in his arms and we're headed to my room. He gracefully deposits me on the bed and climbs onto the mattress next to me.

"Do you use your fingers? A toy?" he asks, sitting on his heels at the foot of the bed. He's so excited he's practically bouncing, like Christmas came early, or he found out *Star Wars* is actually a documentary. It's so adorable, and wildly seductive knowing how much he wants this.

"I keep my favorite toy in the drawer—" I don't get to finish that sentence, because as soon as I vaguely point in the direction of my nightstand, Ren is scrambling to reach over my sprawled-out body to open the drawer.

At first he doesn't say anything—just stares wide-eyed into the open drawer.

"You okay?" I ask, turning on to my side to face him.

"Give me a sec," he wheezes, squeezing his eyes shut.

I furrow my brow in confusion and move to look into the drawer, too. It's exactly the way I left it, my favorite clit-sucking vibrator and a half-empty bottle of ibuprofen, some lube, and the weighted sleep mask I got from the inn's white elephant exchange last year. Body wipes and disposable toothbrushes I use when getting out of bed feels impossible, a light I use during the winter to help my mood, and a few loose, unidentifiable pills. Nothing to garner… whatever he's doing right now.

"Ren?" I prompt. "Do you wanna continue?"

"Give me a second," he repeats. "Let me enjoy this."

"Enjoy *what*? What's happening?"

He groans and rubs a hand over his face. "I'm looking at your *sex toy*."

I stare at him. "That's it?"

"That's *it*?" He stares at me completely befuddled. "Audrey, I've imagined every single detail of what you looked like when you got yourself off. I imagined a *wand*. But now I'm staring at this pretty metallic pink clit-sucking monster machine that's made you come and *not* a wand and…"

"Uh, babe?" I say cautiously, placing my hand on his cheek and turning his head so he's looking at me. "I think you're spiraling."

He nods solemnly. "Yes. Quite right."

"Would you like me to use the pretty metallic pink clit-sucking monster machine while you watch?" I ask. "I've always tried to be quiet when I came, but I wonder if I'm loud if I let myself just *feel*, you know…"

Ren doesn't let me finish that thought before he's shoving the toy into my hands. "Fuck," he says simply, eyes wild as they roam my body. "Fuck," he reiterates, in case I didn't get it the first time.

"You gonna be a good boy and watch?" I ask him, raking my fingers through his never-neat curls. They're always wild, making him look well-fucked all the time.

Maybe that's just what I think.

Or *maybe* it's why the moms of Port Haven want him so bad.

My stomach flips as I realize those women with all the money they have to get nice clothes and makeup... he chooses to be with me. In my bed. In *my* life.

Ren nods eagerly in response to my question. "I'll be so good for you, sweetheart," he murmurs before pressing his lips to mine. It's a slow, scorching kiss, and I can't help the whimper that comes from somewhere deep in my chest when he tugs on my bottom lip with his teeth. "I'll be so good *to* you," he adds, and those six words warm my entire being from the inside out.

He cradles the back of my head as I recline against the pillows at the head of the bed. He hovers over me as I lower myself, keeping our bodies connected. Once I'm laying down, he shuffles backward and gently takes my left ankle in his hand and spreads my legs, situating himself between them.

"I like this skirt on you," he tells me, clutching the hem of my forest green corduroy pencil skirt between his forefinger and thumb. "You're gorgeous in green."

I bite my lip, face flushing. Ever since the night at the symphony, I'd known he liked the way green looks on me. I like it, too. I especially like it because it reminds me of his eyes, like a lush forest. I carry a piece of him with me when I wear the color.

A safe-for-work hickey, if you will.

"Thank you," I breathe. "I know you do."

He laughs and meets my eyes again. "Wore this to try to work me up, did you?"

I smirk. "Did it work?"

He leans over me again, clasping my chin in his hand. "Sweetheart, you don't have to try."

He kisses me again, and I swear I can taste the certainty he wants me as much as I want him. I run my hands over his shoulder blades, feeling the taut muscles of his back. He's sturdy, like a house that was built to keep a family safe. Like a house built to last. He feels *right*.

Him kissing down my neck, avoiding my breasts like I asked, and bunching up my skirt as I lift my ass, feels right.

"Wet for me already?" he murmurs, brushing his fingers over my fabric-covered cunt.

I'm sure I say something intelligible and seductive in response, and not the garbled string of noises my ears trick me into hearing.

"Do you want me to take these off?" He traces the seam with his fingertips and my hips jerk in response.

"Please," I beg, wanton and desperate.

This time, I wore a newer pair of underwear, a pair that can still pass as white, and not gray-ish brown. I should invest in nicer lingerie if he's frequently going to be between my legs.

He hooks his fingers into the elastic waistband and slowly inches them down my legs, over the thigh highs and off my body. He keeps his eyes on mine as he brings the fabric to his face, deeply inhaling the scent. It's one of the most erotic moments of my life, and I squeeze my thighs together in a vain attempt for relief.

"Keep those pretty thighs open for me, sweetheart," he says. His words are dominant, but his voice is gentle and soft. "I want to see everything." He sits back on his heels again, eyes fixed on mine.

I take a deep breath, trying to push through the sudden vulnerability I feel in this moment. My stretch marks and cellulite are front and center, but I try to focus on the fact he doesn't seem to care. That he *wants* to see me.

I bend my knees and plant the soles of my feet into the bedding, opening myself—easier access for me, and easier viewing for him.

He wants to see you. I remind myself. *He isn't faking his hard-on.*

I press the button on my toy and it comes to life with a steady *buzz.* I hear Ren's breath hitch as his eyes follow the toy as I bring it between my legs. I suck two fingers into my mouth, and use those fingers to spread myself so I can access my clit. Ren and I both moan as I gently brush a finger over my already-swollen clit.

"You're beautiful, Aud," he chokes out, bringing his eyes back to mine. "How is it possible for you to be this beautiful?"

I blush from the top of my head to the bottom of my feet. I turn my head to the side to try to keep him from seeing how much his words affect me.

"Please don't hide from me, sweetheart." His voice is heart-achingly tender, so much I feel it in my soul. I glance back at him, and he smiles softly at me.

I've never felt so exposed yet so safe at the same time. Like I'm slowly breaking down the walls I'd spent years strengthening, and instead of being horrified and disgusted by what I tried to keep hidden, he keeps asking to see more.

Finally, I place the suction directly over my clit, and we sharply inhale in unison.

"That's it, sweetheart," he praises me, eyes on my pussy. "Take what you want. You deserve it."

I swear to god, if this man makes me cry while I masturbate, I'm going to have a conniption.

Ren watches my movements like he's trying to memorize them. "Like what you see?" I tease breathlessly, unsettled by the silence. I'm not *used* to masturbating without a voice in my ear.

"Like feels too small," he says. "You're perfect, Audrey."

My nipples harden, and I fight the urge to pluck at them. If I were alone, I would, but this is one wall I'm not ready to let down yet. Although, for the first time ever, he has me thinking it might be a matter of time. That he'll look at the breasts that grew and changed and lost shape with pregnancy and breastfeeding and find them beautiful, too.

"Can you kiss me?" I ask, voice shaky. I'm nowhere close to an orgasm, and to be completely honest, I don't know if I'll come tonight. But he's here, and I feel *good*.

Part of me feels bad asking him to move from the show he's earnestly enjoying, and another part of me feels bad for needing him closer.

But the part of me that needs his touch, anything he can give me, *him*, overrides the guilt.

Instead of responding, Ren stretches out next to me and kisses me. My heart beats faster at his touch, and he snakes his arm under my neck, gently drawing patterns on my shoulder.

"Can I touch you like this?" Ren asks me, placing one hand on my belly. I wonder if he can feel the butterflies inside.

I've always been self-conscious about my belly, despite trying to love it. It looks the way it does because my body created and grew my favorite human. But it's jiggly and it has stretch marks and dimples. It's soft, not like his.

Now? His touch is like a balm to the years I spent hating it, wishing it looked different.

He's gentle, his thumb stroking just below my belly button. He breaks the kiss, burying his face in my hair, and it feels like he's surrounding me, protecting me the same way my walls did for so long.

Maybe that's why they begin to crumble.

I moan as I edge closer and closer to the peak. I'm surprised at it happening, and beg my brain and body to let me have this. To let *us* have this.

"You can let go sweetheart," Ren promises, his breath hot against my ear. "I've got you, you're safe with me."

I know I am, and my body does too, because I come on a sharp cry.

I can feel his smile against my neck as I fall apart. "There she is."

He holds me while I fall apart, hips jerking and voice hoarse from my moans.

I shakily turn the toy off and drop it next to me on the mattress. I use that same hand to bury my fingers in Ren's hair, pulling his face to mine to kiss him long and slow. He feels so right next to me like this... I wonder if he feels the same way.

"Fuck, Audrey," he says after pulling away. He kisses the tip of my nose. "You're radiant."

I feel radiant. Like the sun slowly coming out from behind the clouds, or a piece of long awaited art on display for the first time.

I feel treasured.

Chapter 27

Ren

Playlist: Like Gold | Vance Joy

I've never seen a sight quite as breathtaking as Audrey in her post-orgasm glow. I shifted us so she has her head resting on my bare chest, alternating between combing her fingers through my chest hair, and toying with my St. Anthony medal. It's quiet, but a comfortable silence. A satisfied silence. She's peaceful, and I can tell her mind is still.

She traces the tattoos on my chest with her fingertip, following the lines and patterns of the designs. For the most part, I keep my tattoos hidden, and Millie's the only member of my family who knows. They're a physical representation of the parts of me I try to keep my family from seeing. The less-than-happy, less-than-perfect parts. The me parts.

Audrey likes them, or at least touching them, and I like who I am with her. It's like I'm finally able to relax and not act like who people expect me to be. Not Sky, the audio erotica performer, not Ren, the perfect eldest son who never disappoints his family—just me. The imperfect man who's realizing all he ever really wanted was to be seen.

Audrey's hand wanders lower, and my breath catches.

"Can I touch you?" she asks quietly. "I want to make you come, too."

I have never wanted anything in my life the way I want her to touch me.

I cover her hand with mine and guide it until it's cupping my straining cock through my jeans. We both moan, and I bury my face in her sweet-smelling hair.

"I'm not gonna lie to you," I wheeze. "If you want to touch me, you're going to have to do it quickly, because I have about a millisecond before I come in my pants again."

She hums thoughtfully, and gently squeezes my cock through my jeans. "What if I liked it when you came in your pants?"

"*Woman*," I hope the word comes across as a warning, and not like a plea.

She giggles and turns to press a quick kiss to my forehead. "My needy boy."

It was a valiant attempt.

I unbutton my jeans and undo the fly, her hand slipping beneath the waistband of my jeans and boxers. My back arches off the bed at a concerning angle when she wraps her hand around my cock. "*Aud*," I groan.

"Take off your pants."

Fuck fuck fuck. I love bossy Audrey.

No, wait. I like her. Wait, no I—

Oh, fuck.

Oh, *fuck*?

Do I fucking love her?

Personally, I feel like it's not the most romantic thing in the world to realize you love someone when they're giving you a handjob for the first time, so I tuck it away to process later. Maybe I can overshare with Will, he loves that shit.

I lift my ass off the mattress and we shimmy my jeans and underwear off, my straining cock bouncing to attention.

"*Fuck*," she and I breathe simultaneously.

"You're so big," she says, voice full of wonder, and I feel my ego grow three sizes. She uses a single finger to trace over the head, smearing the pre-cum that's collected there, and gently pulling down the foreskin. I fist the sheets in my hand and try not to pass out when she makes eye contact with me, bringing her finger to her mouth and sucking it between her lips.

This is it. This is how I die—naked in Audrey's bed, while she touches me and tastes my pre-cum.

I'm a lucky bastard.

On her knees beside me on the mattress, she wraps her hand around my cock, her eyes intent on her movements.

"How do you like it?" she asks softly.

"Wetter," I tell her honestly.

"Then spit on it."

My cock twitches in her hand and she grins. "You like when I tell you what to do?"

"Apparently," I wheeze.

"I think I like telling you want to do. But I also like it when you tell me what to do."

"Great. I'm gonna spit on my cock," I stammer helplessly. I'm strung so fucking tight I feel like I'm going to snap any minute.

I push myself onto my elbows and do what she told me, watching as the string of my saliva drips onto my shaft.

"Such a good boy," she praises, and my cock throbs yet *again*. Her strokes are firm and methodical, periodically tracing her thumb over the head.

"Twist... twist your hand when you get to the head," I tell her. She obliges and I curse, my head falling back against the pillows. "God, sweetheart. You feel so good."

Her breath is heavy, eyes intent on her movements, and thighs rubbing restlessly together.

"Can I touch you?" I'm not ashamed that it sounds like I'm pleading.

I open my eyes, surprised when she's already staring at me. "Please," she whispers, and it does something to my heart that she's as needy and desperate for me as I am for her. It feels good not to be alone in this.

"Do you want me to use your toy?" I ask.

She shakes her head, slowing her movements. Thank god. I wouldn't be able to continue a coherent conversation if she kept doing that. "Too sensitive," she responds.

I slip my hand beneath her skirt and nudge her thighs apart as she begins to pump me again. We both moan when I find her cunt, still swollen and wet. When I press my fingers into her, they slide in with barely any resistance. I curl them to massage her G-spot, and her hand tightens around me. She twists her body, leaning down to kiss me. She cries out when I gently flick my thumb over her clit.

"Keep doing that," she gasps against my mouth. "Please."

For a few minutes, the only sounds are our labored breaths, heavy and wanting. Until she speaks again.

"I want you in my mouth."

I sputter, face turning red. "I... you don't have to."

"I didn't say I *have* to. I said I *want* to," she clarifies matter-of-factly.

I whimper, pathetic and so far gone. "That's fine, but only if you want... *fuck*."

I don't get to finish my sentence, because at the speed of light, Audrey shifts so she's leaning over me, and taking me into her perfect mouth. I put my hand into her hair, gently fisting at the root. She moans around me and the vibration makes my legs tremble.

"Christ, sweetheart," I gasp. Her eyes meet mine, wide and sparkling. "You love this, don't you?" She nods eagerly in response, eyes watery as she takes me deeper. "God, you're so beautiful like this. My cock in your mouth and my fingers in your pretty, pink pussy."

Her eyes flutter closed with a moan. I curl fingers in her cunt, and she pulses around me. She hums again, and both our movements become more frantic as our pleasure heightens.

I pull her hair close to the scalp, trying to guide her off me. "Audrey," I choke out. "Sweetheart, I'm gonna come."

She wordlessly responds by opening her eyes and meeting mine, arching a single brow and I know she's taking the challenge I unintentionally gave her.

Audrey with my cock in her mouth, her eyes wild with her own pleasure and determination... might be the single hottest view I've ever had in my twenty-six years of life.

As I topple over the edge, I feel her pussy clench around me, a muffled cry as my cum fills her mouth. Her throat bobs as she swallows, but still some dribbles out of her mouth and onto my stomach.

Eyes still on mine, Audrey lifts a trembling hand to her face to wipe the corner of her mouth. I beat her to it, clasping her chin in the hand that had just been inside her, careful not to smear her own arousal on her face. "Let me?" I ask.

She nods in agreement, and I swipe at her mouth with my thumb. She lets out a guttural moan when I slip my thumb into my mouth. I keep my eyes on her as I replace it with my two middle fingers savoring her sweet, musky taste.

I pull her on top of me so she's straddling my lap. I bring her face to mine, capturing her mouth and slipping my tongue between her lips. She moans into me, and I wonder if it's because she can taste us together, and the idea of us together in any way possible turns her on as much as it turns me on.

"Stop being so hot," she murmurs against me, wrapping her arms around my shoulders.

I smirk and pull away. "No, you."

She throws her head back in laughter, and I take the opportunity to nip at her exposed throat, which quickly transforms her laughter to another moan.

"I don't want to go," I admit, soothing the bite with my lips. "I want to stay with you."

Audrey stiffens in my arms. "You can't. Piper can't see you."

I swallow the lump in my throat that grew from the instant rejection. "I know."

Tell me you want me to stay, even if I can't. Tell me you feel this and you want it, too. Tell me you want to fight for whatever the hell this is because I think this is the shit men go to war for.

She's silent, and my heart constricts with disappointment. I clear my throat and pull away. "I'll head out."

Audrey watches from the bed as I find my discarded clothes and pull them back on.

I spiral from the quickness in which Audrey rejected my desire for intimacy, how quickly she made it clear that at the end of the day, I'll always be a dirty little secret to her.

I thought I was more to her than the voice who got her off, but it turns out I'm nothing but a physical manifestation of Sky.

"I'll walk you out," she says quietly, climbing off the bed.

I shake my head. "That's not necessary."

"I need to lock the door behind you." I feel like someone punched me in the face, but nod curtly.

We're silent when we head out the door, and once I'm outside, I expect to hear the click of the closing door behind me, but instead Audrey encircles my wrist with her hand. "Ren," she says quietly. "I hurt you. I'm sorry."

I want to tell her it's fine so I don't hurt her feelings, but I've spent my entire life being dishonest to fit how I want people to see me. I thought being honest with her meant that she wanted the truth from me, but I guess it just means she knows how to hit me so it hurts.

"Yeah," I admit, staring at the grain of the wooden porch. "You did."

"I'm sorry," she repeats.

I pull my arm away. "I think I need space," I admit. I think ripping my heart out and feeding it to Leia would be less painful than this.

"Okay," she says quietly. "That's... okay. What should I tell Piper?"

"Nothing. I told you nothing would change with me as her teacher if things changed between us, and I meant it. I'll see her on Saturday. I need space from *this*."

Her sharp inhalation of breath is like a stab in the heart. "Okay. Um, have a good night, Ren."

I'm still staring at the ground when she finally closes the door.

Chapter 28

Ren

Part of me hoped Audrey would meet me for the last mile of my run the next morning, as has become routine. Maybe I should be grateful she's taking my request for space seriously, but that last mile felt like torture without her and the coffee I didn't know how much I enjoyed.

The following week, it feels like there isn't a moment I'm not thinking about Audrey. When I record, when I shower, when I run, when Leia screams at me for keeping the door closed too long, when I pass the part of the seawall where she waited for me with cold coffee for the first time all those months ago...

I told her I needed space, and now I'm haunted by her ghost.

On Saturday morning, the idea of passing that spot for the fourth time since I told her I needed space seemed so awful I asked Will to meet me at the gym instead. He happily agreed, insisting we have brunch at his place after.

"You seem... pissed." Will's words are slow, like if he says them at a slower speed, they won't piss me off even more.

It doesn't work.

I grit my teeth. "Didn't get enough sleep last night."

Will squints at me suspiciously and hands me a plate to dry. "You usually seem monumentally *less* pissed after working out."

"Yeah, well," I mutter. "Shocking news, endorphins don't cure you of having to deal with shit."

I immediately regret referring to what's going on with Audrey as "shit." It seems to minimize everything between us.

"Have you tried getting laid?" Will asks casually, and I'm so taken aback I almost drop the plate.

"I... don't do that," I sputter, face heating.

"Ah." Will nods his head. "So you were hooking up with someone and the sex was good and then you remembered why you don't hook up and you're mopey about it because you really like the person... but they thought it was casual?"

I stare at him in shock. "What the hell? Have you been spying on me?"

"I'm your best friend," he says simply, rinsing his hands and turning off the sink. "Even when I lived in LA, I know you enough to know when something's off. I knew it with Taylor, I knew it when you and that guy were fooling around in college, I knew it when you tried to keep your sex god alter-ego from me..."

"Okay, I get it," I interrupt, leaning against the counter and folding my arms across my chest. "We can't keep secrets from each other."

Will clears his throat, and looks away. "Exactly. So stop trying. Why don't we sit and you tell me all about it? Pretend I'm your therapist."

I roll my eyes. "I have to go home and get ready for the private lesson I have in a bit."

"Speaking of, why are you doing private lessons again? I thought you hated them and were making enough money with 4Play?"

"Just for this one kid," I mutter. "She's talented and actually cool as hell. She's a high schooler, and wants to be a concert pianist." *And I think I'm in love with her mom, but we'll explore that part of the equation at a later date.*

"What are you doing for yourself?" he asks.

The fifteen year old inside me wants to answer with "her mom," but I bite my tongue. Because I'm not anymore. I haven't reached out to her, she hasn't reached out to me. What would we say if we *did* talk? *Hey, I know you're super protective of your kid, and I get it the world's been awful to you, but also it makes me sad please let me love you.*

Pathetic.

"Do you have time for a quick round of Mario Kart before you go? Maybe it'll make you feel better?" Will asks hopefully.

I agree, and we play like we did as kids. It unfortunately doesn't do too much for my mood, and because I'm so distracted, he beats me for what I'm pretty sure is the first time ever.

When I get to the inn, Piper is already at the piano, tapping out *Chopsticks* on the keys.

"You know I *hate Chopsticks*," I grumble as I slide beside her on the bench. I mean it to sound playful, but I'm pretty sure it comes across as cruel by the way her face falls and her hands drop to her lap.

"Why are adults such dickheads lately?" she complains. "First Mom, now you."

"Sorry." I exhale heavily, rubbing my chain between my fingers. "Long week."

"Mom said the same thing," Piper says casually. "Seemed the same length as usual to me."

"Ha, ha," I say humorlessly. "You're hilarious."

"I'm gonna run to the bathroom, and then we can play some non-*Chopsticks* bullshit, okay?" She gets up from the piano and pats me on the head, like I'm a well-behaved dog.

I scroll on my phone as I wait for her to return.

And wait. And wait.

After fifteen minutes, I decide to look for her, concern a tight knot in my stomach.

"Piper?" I knock on the single bathroom. "Are you okay?"

"Go away!" she shouts tearfully.

I immediately begin to panic. "Pipe, what's going on?"

She doesn't respond, but I can hear her crying through the door.

"Hey, Pipe." I try to calm myself, though it's not working. Did I *break* Audrey's child? She'll never love me now. "You're scaring me. Can you tell me what's going on?"

"I want my mom," she cries, and my heart shatters.

"Okay, okay. I'm gonna call her," I say, pulling my phone out of my back pocket. "It's okay."

Five seconds later, I get Audrey's voicemail.

I have to call two more times before she finally answers. "What?" she says. She sounds exhausted.

"Hi," I stammer. "It's Piper..."

The mattress springs creak and the sheets rustle as she sits up. "What's wrong?" she asks, panic lacing her voice.

"I don't know. She's locked herself in the bathroom and won't open the door. She said she wants you."

"Okay." She breathes. "It's okay. She's okay." I'm not sure if she's telling this to herself or to me—or maybe both of us. "Will you stay with her until I get there?" she asks.

"Of course, Aud." I want to kick myself for calling her that. It's too intimate, too close for what we are.

"Thank you," she whispers before disconnecting the line.

It takes her five minutes to make it from the cottage to the bathroom, breathing heavily and hair a mess. She's wearing her glasses and a pimple patch, hair in a bun that's falling out. There are dark circles under her eyes, and I wonder if maybe neither of us is okay.

I step back, as she knocks on the door. "Piper? I'm here, birdie. Let me in."

The door unlocks with a click, opening just a crack. Audrey pushes it the rest of the way. She slips inside with Piper, but before she shuts me out, our eyes meet. I see my own fear reflected back at me in hers.

I walk to the piano to grab Piper's phone, and pace back to the bathroom. I lean against the wall, waiting. I don't want to leave until I know she's okay. Ten minutes later the door opens again, and Audrey and Piper step out. My heart sinks at Piper's puffy red eyes and tear-stained cheeks.

"Why don't you go home?" Audrey says softly to Piper. "I'm going to talk to Mr. Q real quick. You gave us quite the scare."

Piper's eyes fill with fresh tears. "I'm sorry," she sniffs, wiping at her nose.

"You don't have to apologize," I tell her gently. "I just want you to be okay."

She nods, staring down at her feet as Audrey rubs her back. "I'm going to go get what you need after I talk to him, okay?"

Piper nods again and shuffles away.

I glance at Audrey. "Is she okay?" I ask. It feels like something is stuck in my throat.

Audrey laughs nervously and lifts a trembling hand to push her glasses up her nose. "You scared the shit out of me."

"*She* scared the shit out of me," I say. "But she's okay?"

"Yeah. She got her period for the first time and panicked." She exhales shakily. "Thanks for staying with her," she says, wrapping her arms around herself and averting her gaze. "That was... thanks. I have to run out to grab supplies for her and..."

"I'll go," I interrupt, pulling my keys out of my pocket.

She looks up in surprise, "Ren, no. It's okay..."

"You should stay with her, she needs her mom."

She exhales. "Thank you. I'll text you what she needs. Do you know how to find tampons and such?"

"Six sisters," I remind her.

"Right. Right. You're probably better at it than I am." She still won't look at me, and I don't know whether I want her to or not. "Thank you." She turns to walk away, but I grab her wrist before she can leave.

"Aud, are you okay?" I ask quietly, in case any of her staff is nearby.

She pulls her arm away. "I'll be fine," she answers tightly.

"That's not what I asked."

She shakes her head. "It's the answer you're getting."

I nod curtly. "Got it. Thanks."

I walk around her and towards the lobby to exit before I can be foolish and say something else.

Because that's exactly what I am when it comes to her, isn't it? A foolish, foolish man.

Chapter 29

Audrey

Playlist: Can't Take My Eyes off You (Acoustic) | Nora & Will

> that's perfect, thank you

> shit, can you grab ibuprofen too? i'm out

Ren

> on it, i'll be at the cottage in like 45 min-
> utes

Audrey

> thank you again, i really appreciate it

Ren

> <thumbs up emoji>

"What is he doing now?" Piper asks, pointing at the TV. She and I are snuggled up on the couch, a microwaved dish towel across her lower belly. I don't get my period with my IUD, so I was completely unprepared for when Piper tearfully told me she saw blood on the toilet paper. I should've been prepared, considering she's fifteen and hadn't gotten one yet. I should've had pads and tampons for her to choose from. I should have *known*. Been ready.

"What is who doing now?" I ask. I'd been thinking about Ren, and I was *pretty* certain she wasn't asking about him.

"Patrick Verona, of course." I can sense Piper's eye roll as she gestures to Heath Ledger's character in *10 Things I Hate About You* serenading his love interest on the bleachers.

"Oh, sweetie." I'm about to break this poor girl's heart.

Luckily, a knock at the door interrupts us and Piper adjusts so I can get out from under her. "While you're up, can you microwave this again?" She holds up the DIY heating pad I'd made her out of a kitchen towel drenched in water and shoved into a gallon freezer bag. I should have asked Ren to get a heating pad. The DIY project works fine when I need it, but Piper's cramps are pretty bad, and it doesn't stay hot for long.

I take the heating pad from her and put it in the microwave for thirty seconds before opening the door.

"Hey," I greet Ren, who's on the porch with much, much more than the four items I'd requested.

"Hey," he responds. "I, uh. I brought way more than you asked for."

A smile spreads across my face when I notice the cat carrier slung over his shoulder. "You brought Princess Leia."

I'm not sure how, when he has at least four reusable shopping bags and a living being hanging off his arms. "Yeah... I should've asked... I brought food and stuff too, so she can spend the night, if it's okay with you."

"Leia's here?" I jump when Piper is suddenly ducking under my arm to unzip the cat carrier.

"You're in too much pain to get off the couch to microwave your heating pad," I remind her.

"Yes. But not too much to come get my best friend!" she says, lifting the fluffball into her arms and kissing her all over her fuzzy head. "Can she stay? Pleeeeeease?" She widens her eyes into a puppy dog pout, which is playing dirty and she knows it.

"Okay," I agree, meeting Ren's eyes. He's fighting back a laugh, but his eyes are sad. I know it's my fault, and I don't know how to fix it.

"You should stay too, Mr. Q!" Piper says excitedly. "We're watching a really old movie called *10 Things I Hate About You*."

"Ah, an ancient artifact," the traitor agrees. "I'm gonna help your mom put this stuff away, but then I have to head out."

Piper's face falls. "Oh," she sighs sadly. "It's okay, I guess."

"I... I mean. Maybe I can stay for the rest of the movie," Ren stammers, cheeks reddening. I roll my eyes. Is he this much of a sucker for his other students, or does Piper have some sort of evil power?

Piper goes back to her spot on the couch while Ren and I head to the kitchen to unpack the bags. He surprises me when he not only pulls out the items I'd asked for, but several other things I didn't. Ice cream, Midol, and a heating pad. My stomach flips when he pulls the last item out of the bag. It's like he knew what we needed without me telling him.

"Leia's food and bowls are in this bag," he says motioning to a colorful reusable bag next to him on the floor. "And I can come grab her in the morning if you want, or after I have dinner at my parents' if Piper wants her for longer and if it's okay with you."

"Whatever's easiest for you," I respond, pulling my phone out. "How much do I owe you?"

"Don't worry about it."

I meet his eyes, and fight the urge to look away, to hide. I spent yesterday and today, until he called about Piper, in bed having shitty brain days. It's not his fault—if he needs space, he needs space. But I don't know how to deal with the sadness from him suddenly not being a part of my daily routine anymore. I miss him.

"Ren, I'm worrying about it."

"Don't, I've got it." I want to grab him by his shirt, shake him so that perfect, floppy hair falls into his face, and tell him I need to pay him.

"I don't want to owe you."

"You don't owe me anything," he responds, a touch of frustration in his voice. "That's what I'm saying. I've got it."

"I can't let you do this for me," I insist.

"I'm not doing this for you, I'm doing it for Piper. I'd do it for any of my students if they needed. That's all this is, okay?"

"And you'd bring your cat to them too?" I challenge.

His cheeks flush. "That's not what we're talking about. Piper is important to me, and yeah. Maybe my feelings for you impacted how much she means to me, but I care. God, I wish I didn't *care*," he hisses, rubbing his temples.

"I'm glad you care," I say quietly. "I don't think you know how much I've wished Piper had more people who showed up for her. And it's my own damn fault she doesn't, right? But you showed up for her tonight, and I'm grateful."

"I want to show up for you, too," he says quietly. "I wish I could be who you want."

A small flicker of hope ignites in my chest. "Ren, I don't see why we can't... try again. We had fun. *I* had fun, at least. And not just with the sex but with everything and..."

"But I'd always be your dirty little secret. I can't be a real-life Sky to you, only existing to you when you want an orgasm. I want everything with you, Audrey. You asked if I thought there was a universe where we work out, and I think it's this one. I want to hold your hand and call you my partner and kiss your cheek in public. I want you to come to Sunday dinners and to be an emergency contact for you and Piper. I want to love you both, but you won't let me. I'm... just a guy you fucked."

He sounds so resigned, so hurt and it hurts me. "That's not true, Ren. You're much more than that. You're my best friend."

The sadness in his eyes tells me that's not enough.

"I'm staying because Piper asked, but that's it," he says, averting his gaze back to the floor. "You know what you want, and I know what I need, and they're incompatible. That's it."

The silence after he leaves me in the kitchen echoes. I force myself to return to the living room, where Ren's on the couch next to Piper, who's chattering away, explaining the plot of the movie to him with Leia tucked in her arms.

"So now you're back to having zero friends," Eva says, reading me for absolute filth.

I exhale heavily, leaning back in my desk chair. I decided to do therapy in my office today so I could be on call because of a callout. "I suppose you're right. I'm back to zero friends."

Eva doesn't say anything, just stares at me.

"And, I mean..." I continue with a hollow laugh. "Who's surprised? Not me! Me not being enough for Ren? Shocking! I've never been enough for anyone." The back of my throat burns with the threat of tears. "I want to be good enough for someone."

"I'm curious. Ren has been in your life for a little while now, and he's the first person you've let get this close to you. I'm wondering if you have feelings for him? Beyond friendship?" Eva asks.

"I don't know. I don't even have friends, remember?"

Eva hums. "What about your high school friends? Was the way you felt about Ren reminiscent of how you felt about your friends in the past?"

My instinct is to say yes. To insist that, yes, my heart beat faster around my friends as a teenager. Yes, I always smiled when I thought about them, which was all the time. Yes, touching them made me feel like my skin was on fire. Yes, this is normal friend stuff.

When I don't respond, Eva speaks again. "Can you do something for me? I want you to visualize your future, maybe five years down the road."

I sigh, but oblige, closing my eyes.

"I want you to imagine the life that makes you happy. Where's Piper? What does your relationship with her look like?"

"Piper's in college," I answer immediately. "We FaceTime once a week and she's happy."

"What do you do when you come home from work?"

"Make dinner, I guess. Watch TV and go to bed."

"Are you alone?"

I've always been alone, except for Piper and Aunt Olivia. But in this moment, five years down the road, Ren is cooking dinner with me. Kissing me good morning and goodnight. Snuggling me on the couch, his hand on my rounded belly. He gets out of bed when our toddler has a nightmare, carrying them back to bed. I can hear him, reading their favorite book to them, complete with the various characters' voices.

And I'm grateful. At peace. Happy.

I open my eyes, and a tear escapes. "No," I admit. "I'm not alone."

Eva smiles kindly at me. "You've achieved *so* much in your life. I know it doesn't feel like it, but you have. You've raised a child you're proud of, you run the inn you once wanted to give up, you worked your ass off to get your degree. If you can do that, I have complete faith you can get to where you want to be."

I sniff and swipe at my nose with the back of my hand. "It sounds scary."

"Scarier than being pregnant your senior year of high school? Or doing it all on your own?"

"Yes," I answer immediately. Eva cocks an eyebrow and I sigh, resigned. "I guess not."

"The Audrey I met fifteen years ago had a tiny little baby she felt disconnected from. A stubborn teenager who never thought she'd be okay again. Look at you now. You have a wonderful relationship with Piper. You've grown and healed and yes, going out of your comfort zone and challenging your core beliefs is always going to be terrifying. But you've done it before, and I know you can do it again."

My responding smile is shaky, but it's there. I hope one day, I can have the kind of belief in myself my therapist does.

Chapter 30

Audrey

Playlist: Deeper Well | Kacey Musgraves

After an emotional therapy session, I try to focus on work, starting with my inbox.

"Holy shit," I say, accidentally loud enough that both Hunter and Jo, who has begun to spend as much time loitering in my office as her girlfriend, glance at me.

"With a reaction like that, you have to tell us what garnered it," Hunter says in a saccharine sweet voice, folding her hands under her chin and leaning on her arms.

"I got invited to a conference in the city?" I answer.

"Are you asking or telling us?" Jo asks, taking a sip from her water bottle.

"Both?

Hunter gets up and comes behind me, leaning on my desk chair as she reads the email I received.

From: Justine Frazier <Justine@PrestigeLodgingAndHospitality.com>
To: Audrey Hinton <AHinton@SandpiperInnCT.com>
Subject: Prestige Lodging And Hospitality Conference

Dear Ms. Hinton,

We are pleased to invite you to the annual Prestige Lodging and Hospitality Conference. Once a year, we invite innkeepers from the east coast to meet with leaders in the hospitality industry, as well as networking with vendors and other folks in the hospitality industry. We also offer a yearly award with a monetary prize.

We send out representatives to stay at small inns on the east coast, and they nominate their favorites for the award and attendance at our event. We are pleased that the SandPiper Inn was found to be an outstanding experience.

The conference takes place January 13th-15th at the Windsor Tower Hotel in Manhattan. The price is $1,000, and includes access to events, room and board, and three meals per day. Alcohol is not included.

To RSVP, please go to the following website where we will collect your information and fees.

Sincerely,

Justine Frazier
Owner of Prestige Lodging and Hospitality

Hunter squeals and slaps my shoulder with excitement! "Oh my god!"

"It's probably a scam," I say, trying not to let myself get excited.

"Giovanna!" Hunter yells too loudly at Jo. "Come here!"

Jo obliges and quickly reads over the email. "Hold on, let me text one of my vendors who owns an inn on the Jersey Shore. I know they've won a bunch of awards, so if anyone would know if it were legit, it's them."

We sit in silence as Jo texts her acquaintance until Hunter hands me her phone. "I googled it and it seems pretty legit. Pretty prestigious, too."

Looking at the website she pulled up, I have to agree. It's professionally designed, with testimonials and pictures from past events. As I continue to scroll, I notice a page titled, 'This Year's Prestige Lodging and Hospitality Award nominees,' and click on it. Emotion fills my chest when I see SandPiper Inn on the list. Hunter squeezes my shoulder and I will *not* cry again.

Deep in my chest, there's a feeling of sadness along with everything. The first person I want to tell has asked for space away from me.

"Sage sent back a bunch of exclamation points, which is a promising response, I think," Jo says. "Oh, yes. Apparently it's like *the* award to win, and there's a $15,000 prize. Only past and present nominees are invited so it's super exclusive and it's their life's dream to go."

"Wow," I breathe. "That's..."

"Incredible!" Hunter squeals, clapping, as she bounces on her toes. "Audrey, this is *amazing*! We have to celebrate! Can we shout you out at the launch tonight? Can we pregame or get day-drunk?"

I laugh. Jo and Hunter are throwing the launch party for their event planning firm, Lillian Theresa, tonight at the inn. I've been invited as a guest, which is cool, but I know I'll be on boss lady mode to support my staff if needed. "I appreciate the enthusiasm, but I don't think I can go."

"Why *not*?" Jo asks incredulously.

"Because I don't have the money. If I did, I'd give raises to my staff, not use it on something silly like this."

"But this could be an incredible networking opportunity." Hunter says. "You'll meet so many people, and will be forever known as a nominee. Hell, I bet just being nominated will increase reservations."

I chew on my lower lip. "It feels selfish."

"It's not," Jo says. "It's you investing in a business you revitalized and work hard to maintain and *love*. It's a big chunk of change, but I'm learning you have to spend big on the important things to earn big."

"Is that why y'all are lowkey squatting at my inn?" I tease.

"It's important as business owners to know *what*'s worth investing in." Hunter sounds like a white dude with a podcast, or maybe herself if she was involved with an MLM.

"It's too much," I argue.

Hunter and Jo are both silent for a moment. and I can see them having a conversation with their eyes in the monitor's reflection.

Finally, Hunter speaks. "Forward me the email, I'm paying for it."

I whip my head around so fast my neck hurts. Being in your thirties is *rough*. "The hell you are!"

"Yes, the hell we are. You charge us a way discounted price for rent," Jo says, shrugging her shoulders. "We'd pay way more than this a month anywhere else in town, and now we're making money, we can actually afford to. Consider this backpay for the past few months while we got on our feet. It's our turn to support you. Deal with it."

"You can't," I argue.

"We will," Hunter counters.

"No," I say firmly. "No, I can't take any more handouts. I've always done this on my own and that isn't changing. Sometimes I have to make cuts or choices that suck because I don't have the funds, and maybe this is one of them. It's life. It's..."

"How's that hyper-independence thing working for you?" Jo asks, tilting her head to the side.

I scowl at her. "Don't try to psychoanalyze me. I already went to therapy today."

"Is it because of how everyone treated you when you got pregnant?" Jo continues. "It makes a lot of sense if it is. People screwed you the hell over, and trauma is a bitch."

I inhale shakily, thinking about the fantasy Eva made me imagine for my future. All the things I want, but have never dared to try for. "Piper wants to go to a summer program at Juilliard, and I'm not sure of what the scholarship situation is like, but tuition is... expensive." My stomach turns as I remember the website Piper texted me the other day.

"You don't have to choose between you and your daughter," Hunter says gently. "Hell, you *shouldn't*. I remember everything my momma said about every wrinkle on her face, and I'm still unlearning what she said about herself. Don't you want Piper seeing her mom going to a conference that will further the career that means a lot to her? So she knows it's okay to do the same?"

"Of course I want her to know it's okay to put herself first," I reply. "I'm just... still learning how to do that myself."

"Life is nothing if not learning and growing. And if it isn't a little uncomfy, are you growing?" Damn, Podcast Bro Hunter has a point.

"Okay." I slowly spin my chair to face Jo and Hunter. "Okay," I repeat.

"Okay?" Hunter prompts.

"Okay, you can pay. But I want to pay you back when..."

"If you try to do that I'm giving the money to Piper for her to use for Juilliard," Jo says in a voice that makes it crystal clear she's dead serious.

"No, that's..."

"You invested in our business, Audrey," Hunter interrupts. "Why the fuck wouldn't we want to invest in yours? You created something beautiful with the SandPiper Inn. It's time for you to give yourself the same TLC you've given your business and your daughter."

I blink back tears. "I don't... I don't like owing people."

"You don't," Jo says simply. "I'll have my lawyer draw up a contract if you want."

I laugh and lift my glasses to wipe at my eyes. I did the absolute bare minimum before coming to the office this morning, and the bare minimum did *not* include putting in contacts. "I... thank you."

"Can I give you a hug?" Hunter asks, spreading her arms out.

I get to my feet and embrace her. Goddamn, she's shorter than Piper.

"This is amazing," she says, voice muffled by my cleavage. "I'm at perfect motorboating height."

"Oh my god," Jo groans, rolling her eyes affectionately. I giggle. Maybe I was wrong. Maybe I don't have *zero* friends.

I arrive for the launch party early, going into the event space and making sure everything is being set up correctly. Hunter and Jo are providing various pride flag pins for openly queer attendees, so I pin a bi flag onto my lapel.

Slowly, guests start filling the room, and of course, Ren is one of the first to arrive.

Fuck.

This man is gorgeous in every situation I've ever seen him in, but him wearing a suit has me weak in the knees.

He meets my eyes, then quickly looks away and my heart sinks. I think about everything he told me, about everything I talked about with Hunter and Jo.

I have no idea what to do.

Chapter 31

Ren

Playlist: Strawberry Wine | Noah Kahan

Audrey is unbelievably breathtaking tonight.

It makes me want to vomit.

"Hey." I slide next to Leo, who's leaning against the wall, eyes on his phone.

"Hey," he responds, staring at his phone. He and Izzy both came home from college to celebrate, and Alex surprised us by flying in from LA this morning. For the first time since Kat's wedding, all eight of us are together. Including Kat, who's here without her asshole husband. Her presence and his absence have convinced me of the existence of a god.

"What's his problem?" Alex asks, gesturing towards Leo. Her hair is shorter than the last time I saw her and she has a nose piercing, and it's so silly, but it makes me sad to realize how little I interact with her compared to my other siblings.

Leo finally looks up and narrows his eyes at her. "I can *hear* you, you know."

"Okay," Alex says, absentmindedly swirling her flute of champagne. "What's your problem?"

"I don't have a problem!" Leo says, loud enough that Hunter glances over at us. I smile and wave at her to signal everything's fine. She shouldn't have to deal with whatever has Leo's knickers in a bunch.

"He and Stelly are fighting," Izzy says, appearing out of nowhere. Finn's back at college, so she, like her twin, is riding solo tonight.

"Can you *not*?" Leo moans.

"At least you're not married," Kat says, from behind Alex. How the hell are my siblings so stealthy? "Because then you don't have a way out." She takes a long sip of her champagne.

We stare at her in uncomfortable silence.

"What?" she snaps.

"Are you okay, Meow?" I ask cautiously. I've been calling her Meow since I was a toddler, and I'm the only sibling allowed to do so. Family lore says I decided all cats were named Meow, so Kat and our actual household feline were confirmed as "Meow."

"I'm fine," she snaps. "Obviously."

"No, no," Leo says, pushing off the wall with renewed energy. "This is great. Let's focus on Kat."

It's like he doesn't know us, because trying to take the attention off yourself in this family is the only surefire way to make sure you have it.

"Tell them what's going on," Izzy encourages.

Out of the corner of my eye, I see Kat snag another glass of champagne. I'm not sure what instinct kicks in, but I reach over, snatch the flute and toss it back.

"*Lorenzo!*" Kat shrieks. "That was *mine.*"

The rest of my siblings stare at me, and I don't blame them. I'm usually a one and done kind of guy when it comes to alcohol.

"I'm... gonna go say hi to Jo and Hunter," I say slowly. "Sorry you're sad about your boyfriend and wife."

"Husband and girlfriend," Alex corrects gently. "You okay there?"

"I'm fine," I insist stubbornly.

"Sure, buddy," Leo says as Kat pats my shoulder sympathetically.

My god, they're onto me. I'm usually better than this.

It's probably because Audrey's wearing the same perfume she wore when we went to the symphony and it's making me lose my sensibilities.

As I walk to the bar, I pull out my phone.

I stare at her as she straightens a centerpiece before she pulls out her phone and glances at her screen. She does a double take, then scans the room.

I wink at her when she finds me, and she scowls before locking at her phone again.

Ren

> sucks to have someone treat you like a toy, doesn't it?

I watch Audrey stare at her phone after I send the last message, her face falling even more before she looks up at me. She shakes her head the same way I picture her shaking her head at Piper when she's not mad, just disappointed, and pockets her phone.

Ren

> i'm sorry, that was a shitty thing to say

Delivered.

I exhale shakily and take another glass of champagne from a waiter, thanking them. I keep my phone in my hand, willing Audrey to text back.

I take a swig before walking over to Jo and Hunter to congratulate them. Jo is wearing black, like she always does, and Hunter is wearing a Barbie pink sparkly dress that makes her look like a human-sized disco ball.

I, as a dutiful younger brother, annoy Jo, and she attempts retaliation with a wet willy. I yelp and jump away at her wet finger in my ear, causing champagne to slosh out of the flute and onto my shirt, and me to drop my phone. Jo bends to grab it, but I beat her to it.

"That's shady," Hunter says, eyeing me suspiciously.

Why does everyone think I'm being weird tonight? I'm usually much better at pretending I'm fine, I'm really losing my touch.

"It's not," I argue. "If she was your sister, you wouldn't want her touching your personal belongings, either."

"What's that supposed to mean, Lorenzo?" Jo asks, planting her hands on her hips and glaring at me menacingly. I try to pat the top of her head, but she swats at my hand and pulls away.

"Don't worry about it," I reply. "I'm proud of you."

Jo's come so far from the depressed and closeted teenager who had my parents worried sick. Within the last year, she survived a failed engagement, reunited with a childhood love who turned out to be the love of her life, and she's thriving in a business she worked hard to build.

She's also the reason I decided to go to therapy. I was home from college for Thanksgiving one year, and she'd had three glasses of merlot. She was talking about how mom and dad made her go to therapy in high school because she was depressed. I asked how she knew she was depressed, and she told me she didn't realize the symptoms weren't normal. When she listed out a bunch of them, there were so many of the same things I was struggling with. Since my scary big sister did therapy, I thought I might give it a try, too.

Jo was the first of our siblings to come out as queer, and it shook up our entire family dynamic. In a good way, but change, even positive change, isn't always easy or painless. Since then, Nic and Alex have come out as bi, and Millie's out as pan, making half of us openly queer.

Then there's me, demi and pan but not knowing if I'll ever come out to my family. While I'm sure they would be fine with it, I feel like I've spent too long perfecting this persona I have with them. I can't reveal anything that might jeopardize how they perceive me.

I deposit my empty champagne flute onto a tray and head to the bathroom to clean myself up. I dab at my shirt with a dampened paper towel, relieved to see I hadn't spilled too much on myself. I put my suit jacket back on and look in the mirror.

This is the Ren I want people to see, the one without flaws. Perfectly dressed, no tattoos visible. I don't recognize myself, because I'd become comfortable being myself around Audrey.

Audrey.

The idea of being in the same room again sounds like hell, so after fixing my hair, I head to the baby grand in the lobby. I sit on the bench and flex my fingers before placing them over the keys and starting to play. I don't know what I'm playing, and there's no rhyme or reason to it. I used to do this a lot, usually when my feelings got too big, or I had my heart broken. I let my emotions guide me in the music.

So that's what I do with these too big feelings, this all-encompassing heartbreak. It feels like the notes dance around me, a devastating number, and for a moment, I'm not in the lobby of an inn. I'm not pretending to be someone I'm not. I simply *exist.*

"Birdie?"

I still when her voice breaks through my trance, and I'm violently yanked back to reality when I see Audrey frozen by the front desk. She stops in her tracks when our eyes meet.

"Shit, sorry. I heard the piano and Piper's really the only one to play it, so I thought it was her..."

I shake my head. "It's your inn. You don't have to apologize."

The silence hangs over us like the threat of rain—uncertain, but present all the same.

"I'm going to go back," she says. "I'm sorry for interrupting. But it was beautiful."

It feels like someone takes an icepick to my heart, and it shatters. "You... don't have to leave. If you don't want to," I choke out as she turns. She stills, and for a moment, I allow myself to dare to hope.

"I really, really don't want to go." Her response is so quiet I think I imagine it. Last time, it was me saying that to her. That I wanted to stay with her, in her bed. I could be petty, but when she turns back to me, I slide to the edge of the bench to make room for her.

She sits next to me, the hips and thighs I dream about pressed against mine. It's devastating.

"Keep playing," she whispers, and I do. She's silent as I let the music speak for me. It's like running, but instead of exerting physical energy, it's emotional energy. As I continue to play, I almost forget about Audrey until she makes a noise. I stop playing and look at her, taken aback by the tears streaming down her face.

"Aud," I say, but she cuts me off.

"I'm scared," she whispers, eyes meeting mine. "I'm so scared, Ren."

"I know, sweetheart," I say softly. "I am, too."

"I don't think I know how to be brave," she chokes out.

I stare at her in disbelief. "You're the bravest person I know."

"Not brave enough to let myself be happy. Not brave enough to be honest."

Not brave enough to be honest.

I can be brave for her. For this. "I can't fucking sleep," I whisper after a moment. "I barely eat. I haven't gone on a run because I think about the first time you brought me coffee whenever I pass the seawall. My new scripts are shit because my reality was better than anything I can imagine. And I miss you, Audrey. I didn't tell you, when you said it, but you're my best friend, too."

"I never meant to lead you on. I never wanted you to feel used or that you weren't important to me. Because that's not true."

I cup her cheek and wipe away her tears with my thumb, knowing it's risky. "I can't give you pieces of me, and I don't want pieces of you. I want so much fucking more. You already have all of me, because you... you saw me without even trying. And I want all of you, too. Even if you're scared and can't do it right away. I want us to at least *try*."

She leans into my hand, and the pressure is like coming home. "I'm scared I won't do it right, and I'll keep hurting you. I haven't told you everything about what happened when Piper was born. But I texted her dad, who was away at college, that I was pregnant, and he wanted nothing to do with it, so I planned on getting an abortion."

She inhales shakily. "The nurse from school called my parents to tell them about the pregnancy because she knew them from church and wanted them to know before word got out. They sat me down and *told* me they made an appointment for the abortion, and if I didn't go, I would be kicked out. And you know Piper, how hard-headed she is. I was worse. Hearing them say I *had* to abort..." She gives me a watery smile. "I decided to continue the pregnancy out of pure spite, and I left before they could kick me out."

I don't know what to say. I didn't know all this, I just knew it wasn't easy when she was pregnant, but I didn't know the specifics.

"I... um. I never wanted you to know this part. But I need you to understand where my fear comes from." Her voice is barely audible and my heart sinks, unsure if I'm ready for what comes next. "After I left, I went to your house. Kat and I already weren't talking, but I thought your family would help.

"Your mom answered the door and I told her what was going on and asked if I could stay with you. And... um, she told me there were consequences to the choices we make. She didn't want me to be a negative influence on you and your siblings. It hurt more than my own parents' rejection."

A raging sea of anger grows in my core. "What the hell?"

"My aunt was the only person who didn't define me by my pregnancy. Then we lost her, and I've been so, so afraid of letting anyone in, because I don't think I'm worth staying for. And that was okay, because no one was worth the risk of being abandoned again.

"But then you showed up." Her voice cracks. "And you kept showing up. I've never felt this way about anyone, and it scares me, Ren. Because I already know how your parents feel about me, and how they'd feel about someone like me dating their son. What happens if they still don't want me around, or when you realize what a mess I am? When you realize you can do better? What happens to me? What happens to Piper?"

My eyes burn with the threat of my own tears. "I didn't realize how many people failed you, and I hate that I became one of them. I'm scared too, because this incredible woman I feel so much for wants different things than me, and I've lost myself trying to love others many times. It's not that I don't want to do casual, it's that I *can't*." I exhale roughly. "I told you I'm demisexual, but I'm also pansexual, which means the stereotype is I want to fuck everyone, but it means my attraction isn't based on gender. I need a strong emotional connection to be attracted to someone. So that first night? I was already all in. I kept sinking deeper and deeper, and I realized if I kept going I was going to drown. I had to save myself."

I force myself to meet her eyes, my heart lurching at the pure expression of grief.

"I understand, especially the stereotype. I'm bisexual, so I am a victim of it to an extent, too. But I'd never want you to lose yourself," she whispers. "I didn't realize that's what I was asking you to do."

"I didn't tell you."

"I didn't *ask*. I'm going to keep hurting you, Ren, no matter how much I don't want to. Because I'll always be waiting for you to have enough and leave. I'm trying to challenge that belief, you know? I want more from life."

"Hey." I take the biggest risk of my life when I press my forehead to hers. "What if I stay? What if the people who abandoned you were the problem? What if that's not how you deserve to be treated? And yeah, you can always wonder what happens if I leave... but what happens if I don't? What happens if I stay? What happens if you let me be on your side?

"What if you've protected Piper so well that no matter what happens, she'll be okay? Give me a chance, Aud. Let me prove I'm not going anywhere, that you're worth wanting everything with. I'll go as slow as you want to, I'll do anything." I'm well aware that I'm begging, and honestly I don't care. I mean every word. "My life is empty without you and Piper, and I need..."

I'm cut off when she throws her arms around my shoulders and presses her lips to mine. Simultaneously, we exhale in relief as I pull her in closer to me.

This is where I belong. With her, in her life.

"I've missed you," she whispers after breaking the kiss.

I brush a strand of hair out of her face. "I missed you," I echo. "It felt like I was dying."

"You're okay going slow?" she asks anxiously. "I don't want to push you away further."

"Slow is good. Slow dancing, slow sex, slow mornings..." My hands trail down her sides, settling on her waist. "I want to take my time with you, Audrey Elise. I want slow."

I bring her lips to mine, kissing her soft and slow and languid to prove this is what I want. That she's what I want.

Chapter 32

Audrey

Playlist: Delicate | Taylor Swift

Ren comes over after the event, and I finally tell him everything about my pregnancy and raising Piper on my own. I tell him what it was like being *the* pregnant girl my final semester of high school. How teachers and students alike suddenly stopped talking whenever I was near. How I ate lunch alone in the nurse's office while she ignored me. How I took my finals in April and finished early, because Piper was due in early May. How when they sent my diploma, I threw it away. I tell him about the depression that plagued me after she was born, how I'd cry during the sleepless nights, begging her to latch or to sleep, depending on the situation.

I tell him what it was like working the front desk of the inn with a tiny Piper in a bouncer seat next to me. How she started showing autistic traits at a pretty young age, and I brought her to a psychologist to be diagnosed. I admit how ashamed I still feel for wishing she weren't autistic at first. I tell him how I still struggle with how my body's changed, and how *guilty* I feel for struggling. I tell him about the encompassing grief that overtook when Aunt Liv died. How I felt numb when I found out she left me not only the cottage as promised, but the inn, too. How I planned on selling, but couldn't go through with it.

And Ren... well, he's Ren. He's steady and comforting as he listens. He holds me when I sob, rubbing soothing circles on my back. He asks all the right questions about what Piper was like when she was younger, and wipes away tears when I tell the story of her first steps.

He stays until 2 a.m., or maybe even later. All I remember is commenting on the time, and waking up the next morning in bed, my glasses folded neatly on the nightstand with a glass of water and a post-it note next to them.

> *Thank you for letting me in. I went home so I wouldn't be here when Piper comes back this morning, but that doesn't mean I'm not staying. I am.*
> -R

For the first time, the idea of him staying doesn't seem impossible.

Chapter 33

Ren

Playlist: Growing Sideways | Noah Kahan

Jo

so we got the pictures back from the launch party… and guess who's missing from the FIRST FAMILY PHOTO INCLUD-ING JOSH AND HUNTER.

Nic

why, could it be lorenzo and emilia, giovanna?

Jo

why yes nicoletta, yes it could.

i hope you jerks leaving the most important night of my life early was worth it.

In. Out. In. Out. In… Fuck.

I forget to breathe, because there she is: on the coldest morning of the year so far, thermos in hand, and bundled up with a light blue hat with a pom-pom on top. Audrey and I reconvened our daily walks after we decided to officially date a few weeks ago.

I had assumed she wouldn't come this morning due to a dramatic overnight drop in temperature. But here she is.

"Hey," I huff, slowing to a stop and pulling out my earbud. "I'm surprised you braved the cold today."

Audrey peers at me. Her scarf is wrapped so thoroughly around her face that only her gray eyes framed by her glasses are visible. "I hate the cold," she says, voice muffled by the scarf. She gets to her feet. "I want to be inside. With a mocha. And a good book. Not outside. But I *am* outside because some sexy lunatic thinks it's cool to run in the arctic tundra."

I smile and cup her waist, pulling her into me as I peel down her scarf. I silence her gasp when I capture her mouth with mine.

"*Ren,*" she gasps, looking around after breaking the kiss.

We're still keeping our relationship to ourselves right now, and I know she's nervous about anyone seeing us together, and what that would mean for me.

Personally, I think it would mean I'm the luckiest son of a bitch in the world.

"No one's here," I reassure her instead kissing across her jaw and down her neck. "Though I wish there was, I want everyone to know goddamn lucky I am. But unfortunately, they're all inside with a mocha and good book…"

She grumbles and pulls away. "Dammit. You were being sweet and then you ruined it. Jerk."

I pull her back to me, wrapping my arms around her waist. For as feisty as she is, her body relaxes against me, and she loops one arm around my shoulders. "Whatever you say, dear," I murmur into her ear. "As long as I'm your jerk, *and* your sexy lunatic."

She pulls her away and playfully shoves my chest while retching.

I laugh. "Too corny?"

"*Way* too corny," she agrees, wiggling her nose. "Corn casserole level."

"Speaking of corn casserole," I say, reaching forward and tugging her scarf over her nose. "What are you and Pipe doing for Thanksgiving?"

"Cheesecake for breakfast, a viewing of *Miracle on 34th Street*, and I go and cover breaks at the inn while Piper plays piano in the lobby. We do the same on Christmas, too."

"Would you... um. Would you two want company?" I ask, staring intently at my cup.

"You don't have plans with your family?" she asks, surprise lacing her voice.

I shrug. I don't want to tell her I'm not too happy with my family after finding out how they treated Audrey when she was pregnant. Mom's texts have gone unanswered, and I muted the sibling group chat. My dad called me last night, which is weird in itself, and I sent it to voicemail.

How am I supposed to look them in the eyes and act like everything's normal when I learned they turned a pregnant teenager away? Not just any pregnant teenager, but a girl who trusted them to support her? A girl they welcomed in our home frequently until she was pregnant. The entire concept of the religion that is so important to them is built on the back of a pregnant teenager.

When I was growing up, being a good Catholic meant being like Jesus. Being kind, not excluding people, looking out for one another, praying... not literally refusing to help someone they were more than capable of helping. While I don't put my parents on a pedestal, I always admired how their faith wasn't something they used to harm others, even when I stopped practicing. Learning I'm wrong is a mindfuck.

"If you want to join us, you're more than welcome to," Audrey says gently, tilting my chin with the crook of her finger. "But I don't want you to choose between us and your family."

But what if I want you and Piper to be my family, too? I hold it back. That's too much right now. We've done a really good job at moving slow, physically and emotionally, and I don't want to make her feel rushed.

"I'm not really talking to my family," I say slowly.

She cups my cheek with her mittened hand, and I can't help but lean into the safety and security of her touch. "Ren, please tell me it's not because of me."

I exhale heavily. "It's not. Not really. I'd be pissed to find out they treated *anyone* the way they treated you." *It's unbearable because it was you.*

She pulls her hand away, and I immediately miss her touch. "I don't... Ren. You'll resent me one day if you let me pull you away from your family. What happens when you realize that it was..." she trails off.

"It was what?"

"A waste. That I'm a waste of your time."

I take a step towards her. "And what if I don't?" I ask. "Let's challenge that thought like you've been working on with Eva. What if I never think you're a waste of time and next year you're stuck watching the *Star Wars* holiday special with me?"

"The *what*?"

"Lorenzo?" Audrey and I jump apart like two high schoolers caught making out at the way-too-familiar voice. I give Audrey an apologetic look, hoping she can read my true remorse in my eyes. "Is that you?"

"Hi, Mom," I say, turning on my heel, and plastering my 'Ren is always happy!' smile on. My parents stare back at me, pickleball paddles in hand. Why they're playing pickleball in this weather is beyond me.

"You haven't texted me back," is the next thing out of my mother's mouth, and I have to go into overdrive to make sure my smile doesn't falter. A faltering smile gives too much away.

"Right," I say. I'm not certain if my cheeks hurt from smiling or the biting cold. Probably a little of both. "Sorry. Been, uh, busy..."

"Buddy, are we interrupting something?" My dad is pointing his paddle at Audrey, and I fight the urge to reach out and slap it out of his hand. "Are you going to introduce us to your friend?"

Damn my father's overly friendly demeanor.

"No." Now I fight the urge to slap myself because I answered *way* too fast.

"Lorenzo, baby. What's going on?" My mom's suddenly cupping my cheeks. "Is something wrong? Are you sick?"

"I'm fine, Mom." My cheeks burn with embarrassment of being babied in front of Audrey. I'm a grown man, for god's sake. "I've been—"

"Hi, Mr. and Mrs. Quinn," Audrey says, stepping out from behind me. "It's good to see you."

I exhale, and face my parents. "Mom, Dad, you remember Audrey?"

Mom and Dad stare at Audrey, mouths agape as recognition sets in. "Audrey?" Mom says, blinking rapidly.

"Audrey!" Dad exclaims, a big grin spread across his face. "I knew I recognized you. It's good to see you, sweetheart." I watch in complete horror, still trapped in my mother's vise-like grip, as Dad steps around me, arms outstretched to Audrey.

I pull out of Mom's grasp and grab his shoulder to stop him. "Get away from her," I snap.

"Okay, buddy," Audrey says, placing her mittened hand on my shoulder. "I need you to chill out a degree or two, okay?"

I flush, knowing this is the voice she uses when Piper has big feelings. She's gentle-parenting me in front of my actual parents, who are currently staring at me like I've grown another head. That's fair, I kind of feel like I have. A second head that is filled to capacity with Audrey's smile and the way she holds her breath right before she...

"Audrey?" My mom asks, eyes darting between the two of us. "I didn't know you knew Ren."

"You mean Kat's former best friend who was always around when I was a kid?" I throw my arm around Audrey's shoulder and pull her into my side. "Yep. Her daughter is one of my private students." *The daughter she was pregnant with when you threw her out to the wolves, assholes.*

"I thought you weren't teaching private lessons anymore?" Mom says, and goddammit, of course that's what she's gonna focus on.

"I made an exception for Piper," I answer calmly.

"Piper?" Mom asks, her gaze turned to Audrey. "Is that...?"

"My daughter," Audrey finishes, and my heart breaks at the forced smile on her face. "Sorry to cut this short, but I should be going. I have a lot of laundry to do and..."

"Come to Thanksgiving dinner," my mom blurts out, and judging by the expression on her face, I can't tell who's more surprised by the words that came out of her mouth—her, or the rest of us.

"Oh, I..." Audrey stammers, her fingers tapping nervously against her ceramic mug.

"The three of us will be working at the inn that day. Audrey owns the SandPiper Inn—did you know that? We'll be working because it's tradition for her and Piper to eat cheesecake for breakfast and then work so more of her employees can have the day off. I'm doing that too this year." I breathe deeply once I've finished word vomiting.

Mom's eyes are sad, and I have to avert my gaze. "You're not coming to Thanksgiving?"

"Kat doesn't come to Christmas Eve anymore because they spend it with Steve's family. Alex will stay in LA. You don't need me there, and believe it or not, not everyone wants Audrey to suffer on her own," I snap, daring to meet my mom's eyes. Her eyes widen as she realizes what I'm saying, what I know. And that just eggs me on. "Not everyone is—"

"Lorenzo." Audrey's voice is muffled beneath her scarf and barely audible above the pounding in my head and the crash of the waves of the shore. She slips her hand into mine and squeezes gently.

God, I'm an asshole, aren't I? She doesn't need a protective, macho man to rescue her from a dragon. She deserves a partner who stands beside her, helps her navigate the flames, and avoid getting burnt in the future.

I glance at our hands, at her black mittened hand in mine. *Mine.*

I inhale deeply. "We're spending Thanksgiving at the inn, but if Audrey wants to, maybe she and Piper could come for dinner tomorrow?"

I look at Audrey, gauging her reaction. She uses her free hand to pull her scarf beneath her mouth. "Piper and I would love to come for dinner, Mrs. Quinn." She squeezes my hand again and I need my parents to leave so I can tell this woman how brave she is, how her bravery makes me want to be braver, too.

I sneak a glance at my father, who is doing a hilariously bad attempt at hiding a smirk behind his fist.

"That would be lovely," Mom says, and I have to hand it to her, she sounds genuine, but I still won't be letting Audrey or Piper out of my sight that night. I need to know they're safe and are being treated with the kindness they should have received fifteen years ago. "Lorenzo, you must be freezing. Why don't you wear pants when you run?"

Aaaaaaand overprotective Italian mom strikes again.

"I will," I say to appease her. But Audrey squeezes my hand, and I find that desire to be brave once more. "Actually, I'm fine in shorts and a hoodie right now. I appreciate you looking out for me, but I can take care of myself."

I feel the reassuring squeeze of Audrey's hand again, and this time, I know it's her telling me I did good.

My therapist is gonna be so proud of me.

Finally, my parents continue on their way to the courts where they're meeting friends for a few games of pickleball, and I turn to Audrey.

"We don't have to go tomorrow," I tell her gently. "I don't want you to feel obligated to spend any time with them."

"Ren."

God. I love her voice. Maybe I can convince her to make me a recording I can get off to, or fall asleep to, or...

"I always admired how close your family is, how much you care about each other. I always thought one day I'd grow up and get married and create a family that loved each other that much. I don't want to be in between you and them. I'm not going to tell you not to spend Thanksgiving with us, because to be completely honest, I'd love to show you the ropes at the inn and to spend it together. But if it's possible to mend something instead of throwing it away altogether, shouldn't we put the effort into that? Instead of coming between you and your family, I'd like to see if maybe Piper and I can become part of it."

Her mouth is still uncovered, so when I pull her soft body into mine, I'm easily able to kiss her long and hard. "You make me want to be better," I say after breaking the kiss and burrowing my face in her shoulder. "You make me...god. I don't know. You make me want to be kinder and more patient, and as good as you. As brave as you."

Because why wouldn't I want to be more like the person I love? To encompass everything she is?

She laughs. "Are you serious? *You* make me want to be braver."

I go to kiss her again, but she cups my cheek. "Ren," she says slowly. "How would you feel about telling Piper?"

My heart is a stone skipping on the surface of the ocean. "About us?" I clarify, and she nods. "Are you sure? I promise there's no rush."

"I trust you, and I trust her. I'm scared, but like I said: you make me want to be brave."

My heart is in my throat when I rest my forehead against hers. *I love you*, my pounding heart screams. *I love you. I love you.* I'm almost certain she can hear the pounding in my chest.

"Let's tell her before dinner tomorrow."

Audrey's returning smile is radiant. "She's gonna be so happy," she whispers. "*I'm* so happy."

Happy feels too small a word for the way my chest is expanding.

Piper and I are on the couch waiting for Audrey. We were supposed to leave twenty-two minutes ago, and Piper's ignoring me because she's mad I didn't bring Leia. She keeps glaring at me out of the corner of her eye when I bounce my leg, and it's been happening often. I don't know why I'm concerned about Audrey taking a long time to get ready. People are allowed to take a long time. It's no big deal.

But it's Sunday and I'm taking her and Piper to dinner at my parents'.

I'm a nervous wreck.

Not about her, obviously, but about how my family will behave. How they'll treat her. But mostly, I'm nervous about sharing Piper and Audrey with them. This is the first time mine and Audrey's relationship won't solely be *ours*. Other people are being let into our little world.

"Do you want to go check on your mom?" I ask Piper in what I hope is a casual tone.

"No, but I think *you* want to go check on my mom," she responds, eyes trained on her phone.

"I want to make sure she's okay," I argue, cheeks flushed from her call out.

"Then go make sure she's okay," she answers, slumping further down on the couch.

"I think I'll—"

"Mom!" Piper yells, making me jump. "Are you okay? Mr. Q's nervous."

"I'll be out in a minute!" Audrey responds.

"I think, uh. If you want. You can. Uh. You can maybe... uh. Call me Ren?" I say, nervously rubbing my chain between my fingers. "Since, you know, we see each other outside of class quite a bit. I feel like I'm less your teacher and more your..."

"Dad?" Piper finishes, peering up with hope in her eyes.

Fuck.

I don't know what to say, because how do I tell her that yes, I care about her differently than any of my other students. I feel a grief at missing most of her life, like I belonged there in the first place. Sometimes I wonder if this is how Dad feels about us.

"I..."

"Sorry, sorry," Audrey says, coming into the living room and I try not to moan when I realize she's wearing the perfume again. "My hair wasn't behaving."

"I can tell," Piper says dryly, finally looking away from her phone to look at her mom.

Audrey's hand flies to her hair. "You can?"

"Be nice," I warn teasingly, playfully, knocking my shoulder against Piper's.

"Stop being my mom's knight in shining armor," she teases, nudging my shoulder back.

I peer at Audrey, who smiles softly while watching us, a cardigan draped over her arm. "You two are such drama llamas," she says affectionately, ruffling Piper's hair.

I meet her eyes. "Ready?" I ask.

She nods and sits on the other side of Piper. "Birdie, we want to talk to you about something..."

"Oh my god." Piper drops her phone in excitement. "Oh my god," she repeats, eyes wide as she pivots her head between the two of us. "It's happening. It's happening and you didn't bring Leia!"

Audrey laughs and Piper scowls at her. "You're excluding one of your daughters from the conversation—and you're *laughing*?"

Audrey looks at me, her bottom lip clenched between her teeth to stifle her laughter.

"Wait, what's happening?" I ask, confused.

Piper lets out a long-suffering sigh. "You're finally telling me you're more than friends and are actually dating. Duh."

Audrey's attempt at not laughing is valiant, but ultimately fruitless as she once again bursts into laughter. Piper scowls at her.

"Are you okay with that?" I ask her. "Me dating your mom?"

"Oh my god, *duh*. Why do you think I've been at Annika's so much? I could invite her over but I needed to make sure you two got together *somehow*." Piper takes one of mine and Audrey's hands in hers and squeezes. "You've both been happy. More than happy. And I'm happy, too. For you, but also for me, because you are two of my favorite people in the world. Except for Leia, of course."

I try to blink away the threat of tears stinging behind my eyes. "Leia's not a person..."

Piper yanks her hand away and gets to her feet. "Fuck you. I take it back."

Audrey and I stand, and we all head to the door. I reach around her to grab her coat, helping her put it on.

"So," Piper says as she unlocks the door. "Can someone remind me why we're going to eat dinner at this place when they were mean to Mom?"

"Because we're trying this new thing where we try not to live in the past," Audrey explains, trailing behind her and holding the door open for me.

"Right," Piper says sarcastically. "It's not because you want to make a good impression on your future in-laws."

"*Piper*," Audrey and I warn simultaneously. We make eye contact, and she smiles at me while my heart explodes into sunbursts.

Piper, meanwhile, is horrified. "He says it in the same tone of voice now?! You've *got* to be kidding me."

I ruffle her hair and she jerks away, scowling and smoothing her bangs. "If you weren't being such a menace, you wouldn't have to worry about me using my teacher voice, pipsqueak."

"I regret everything," Piper mutters, shaking her head sadly.

Audrey smiles at me, and my heart melts like ice cream on a summer day. "I regret nothing," I respond.

Chapter 34

Audrey

Playlist: "Slut!" (Taylor's Version) (From the Vault) | Taylor Swift

I regret everything.

It's a five minute car ride to Ren's parents' house, and I spend the entire time with my hands fidgeting in my lap.

Ren keeps glancing over at me, and at one point takes his right hand off the steering wheel, covering mine. It doesn't fix everything, but this small action reminds me I'm not alone in this, that he's on my side.

Piper is jabbering in the backseat about how excited she is for Christmas break, despite Thanksgiving break not starting until Tuesday. Apparently, she and Annika have big plans of starting a cat sitting business, and she asks Ren to be a reference.

"I don't know if he'll recommend the person who is not-so-subtly trying to catnap Leia." I tease.

Despite my pathetic attempts to act like everything's fine, my heart sinks lower and lower as we get closer to the Quinns' and I begin to recognize houses and landmarks. They send me back to the last time I was here.

I don't want to go back to that moment. I want to move forward.

My stomach sinks further when Ren has to park on the street in front of the house because their huge driveway is already full.

"Are we the last ones to arrive?" I ask as I unbuckle my seatbelt. God, my voice is shaking, and I hate myself for it. I need to be better for Piper, for myself, for Ren, and the steps we've taken towards the future we could have. The future I want more than I've ever wanted anything in my life.

Ren puts the car into park and squeezes my hand, like he's trying to transfer his effortless confidence and charisma he has to me.

Except it's not effortless. It's a role he works extraordinarily hard to perform well, a role that's taken so much from him.

"You'll be great," he murmurs. "It's them I'm worried about."

I squeeze his hand back. "You love them. I loved them, too. You and I don't love carelessly."

He turns his neck and searches my eyes. I wonder if he can hear what I'm not saying, but what I mean.

I love you. And it's scary as shit because I've never loved anyone like I love you. I never thought I'd have the opportunity to. I want to do it right, but I don't know how.

"Is this my life now? You two, not even trying to hide the goo-goo eyes you make at each other?" Piper interjects from the backseat.

I bite my lip as I try not to laugh, but Ren isn't as subtle. His laugh is loud and lovely and warms me the same way he's warmed the cold parts of me I've avoided facing for so long. "Yep. Sorry, pipsqueak. You get to have *two* adults embarrassing you now. And Pipe," he adds, voice suddenly serious, "if you are uncomfortable or if anyone says anything less than kind to you..."

"I'll punch them in the face," Piper finishes, way too seriously for my liking.

"Piper!" I scold, turning my head to narrow my eyes at her.

"Sure," Ren says, and I want to shake him. "I don't normally condone violence, but they'll deserve it."

I can't help but laugh as Piper climbs out of the car. I've barely gotten out of the car when I'm greeted by a high-pitched noise and a mass of pink and blonde flying at me.

"*Oof!*" I say, stumbling and trying to keep my balance as Hunter's body collides with my own.

"You're *here!*" she screeches directly in my ear. "At Sunday dinner! This is the best day of my life!"

"Christ, Hunter." Ren's beside me at vampiric speed. "Give her space."

"Space doesn't exist in this house." It's another masculine voice this time, and I try to peek through Hunter's lion mane to see who it is. I don't recognize him at first, but he's a few inches shorter than me with red hair and a mustache. If I had to guess he was five years or so older than Piper.

That's when it clicks.

"Baby Leo?" I gasp, and Hunter mercifully detaches herself from me. "My god, you're *old.*"

Ren snorts. "He's a sophomore in college, if you can believe it."

"Oh my god. *I'm* old."

"You? Never. You don't look a day over twenty-five," Leo responds with a wink.

I blush. "Oh, I wish. You're too sweet."

"I only speak the truth," Leo says, so earnestly I'm convinced I truly look like I'm in my mid-twenties.

"Are you *flirting* with her?" Ren asks in bewilderment.

"And if I am?" Leo challenges his older brother with a smirk. "She's not attached, right?"

Oh. Actually, this might be fun, seeing Ren's siblings rag on him a little.

Ren shoves Leo's shoulder with a little more force than what I would consider playful. But then again, I'm not around siblings very often. "*You're* attached, asshole."

"I'm not *actually* flirting," Leo whines, rubbing at where Ren pushed against him. "I'm a really likeable guy who knows how to give a compliment! Try it sometime!"

Ren rolls his eyes. "Whatever," he grumbles, and him being jealous of his brother is the cutest thing I've ever seen in my entire life. His arm is still slung over my shoulder as we walk to the door and I'm literally obsessed. "We'll talk later."

"Nothing to talk about," Leo says quickly, bounding up the stairs behind Hunter and Piper. He calls over his shoulder, "I mean, I have nothing to talk about. *You,* however, look like you have quite a lot to talk about, pretty boy."

I smirk, and pinch Ren's cheek. "You are such a pretty boy, aren't you?"

Ren's face turns scarlet. "Fuck. Me," he whispers, suddenly removing his arm from my shoulders and gently grabbing my hips to move me in front of him.

"Wait, what's happening?" I ask in confusion.

In lieu of a verbal answer, he presses against me, like he did in the kitchen all those months ago. And like that time in the kitchen, he's astoundingly hard.

I glance over my shoulder at him in surprise. "Where did *that* come from?"

"That did it for me," he answers sheepishly.

"*What* did it for you? Me calling you a pretty boy?"

He groans and grips my hips again, guiding me toward the stairs. "Apparently? Because all I want is for you to sit on my face and tell me what a pretty boy I am when I'm drenched in your come."

I stare at him, mouth agape.

He winces. "Too far?"

"Use that in an audio," I say after finally being able to close my mouth. "You should… uh. Definitely use that in an audio."

"Are you coming?" Leo hollers from the front door.

"I wish," I sigh, only loud enough for Ren to hear. He coughs in an attempt to mask a laugh. "Get that thing under control, Lorenzo, or else your family will really think I *am* a slut."

He puts his hand on my lower back and gently pushes me forward, which immediately has fireworks going off and spreading fire throughout my entire body. I take off my coat as we enter the house, immediately enveloped in the scent of garlic and onion, and the loud noise of a family that loves each other.

I grieve for the time when this was my second home. When Mr. Quinn would make us grilled cheeses after school and every Sunday meant Mrs. Quinn's Italian food.

Ren senses my discomfort and takes my hand in his, squeezing gently. "We can leave right now, if you want to."

I want to. I want to put my coat back on, find Piper, and speed back home so I can crawl beneath my covers and hide from the things that hurt me, from my past. But that's what I've spent my entire life doing, and Ren has me wanting to do things differently.

"Are you going to introduce me as your friend?" I ask, squeezing his hand back.

He smiles. "I can, if you want. But I need to warn you: I refuse to hide the way I feel about you, to pretend you're not the most important person in my life. I can't go back to treating you like a friend."

"How would you want to introduce me instead?" I ask, throat thick with an emotion I'm not ready to name.

"I'd introduce you as mine," he says simply. "Because they need to understand you're here to stay and if they want me, they have to want you, too."

We break off from the rest of the group, Ren guiding me into the front parlor. The room looks the same as it did sixteen years ago, with a baby grand piano and floral furniture. I wander to the piano, tapping on C sharp.

"I learned to play on this bad boy."

"I remember. Can you still play *The Imperial March* while staring menacingly at whoever pissed you off?" I tease.

He scoffs. "Can I still play *The Imperial March*? What a silly question, Audrey."

I run my fingers lightly across the keys, soft enough they don't make a sound. Part of me wishes we could just stay like this. Me, Ren, and Piper in our own little world, without anyone else. I whisper, my eyes cast down to the piano, "What if they don't want me?"

"If they don't want you, then the love they have for me isn't as unconditional as they claim it is." He shrugs and leans casually against the piano, like he's not talking about cutting off the family he loves. "They're family, but you're home, Aud. You and that persnickety blonde with a penchant for sarcasm and catnapping. You're where I want to begin and end my days, where I'm safe and known."

I stand on my tiptoes and press my lips to his, heart pounding in my chest. *I love you.* My heart screams in rhythm with my heartbeat. *I love you, I love you, I love you.*

He turns us, pressing my ass against the keys and creating the worst sound I've ever heard in my life.

But I can't find it in me to care, because he's kissing me like he loves me, too.

"Ren, are you in... oh, shit."

Ren and I spring apart like we've been electrocuted. "Hey, Dad," Ren says sheepishly, hand going to his chain as we turn to face his wide-eyed father. "You remember Audrey? My..." He trails off and looks at me. "Girlfriend?"

"Right. Right." Mr. Quinn is nodding vigorously, like he knew we were dating, which, to be fair, he probably deduced from our prior interaction. "Right. Right. Right. Audrey's your girlfriend."

Piper comes sliding into the room in her socks. She wasted no time in making herself at home, and I love her for it. "What the *fuck*? It took you like fifteen years to tell me you were together and you tell *him* right away?" She glares at Mr. Quinn like he's the bane of her existence. "I don't even know who he is!"

"This is my dad," Ren says. "Dad, this is Piper, Audrey's daughter."

Somehow, this seems to break Mr. Quinn out of his ongoing frantic nodding and he beams at Piper, who scowls at him, arms folded across her chest. "It's nice to meet you," he says, holding his hand out for Piper to shake. "I'm Sean."

"I don't care," Piper says, making no move to shake his hand.

I give her a death glare, but am taken aback when Sean throws his head back and howls with laughter. Ren and I look at each other in confusion.

"I like you," he says to Piper after quieting his laughter. "You're funny. Have you met Nic? Nic hates people too. Nic!" he yells over his shoulder into the house. "Come here."

A short woman, around Piper's height, with Ren's complexion and a curly pixie cut comes into the room, a scowl etched on her face. "I was *busy*, Dad." she complains, crossing her arms across her chest so her posture mirrors Piper's. "What?"

"This is Piper. She's scary like you."

"You're short for a full-grown adult," Piper says to Nic.

"Fuck you," Nic responds, and Piper grins at her.

"I like you," Piper says decidedly. "I'm Piper and my mom is fucking Ren."

"No... that is *not* how we're introducing ourselves now, birdie," I stammer.

Piper ignores me, setting her eyes on the woman. "Who are you?" she asks.

"I'm Nic. The guy who's fucking your mom is my annoying little brother," Nic responds flatly.

"Can we not reduce Audrey and I to our sex lives? Is that a possibility?" Ren asks, raising his hand.

"No," Nic and Piper say simultaneously.

Nic eyes Piper. "Goddammit," she sighs. "I think I like you too, kid. This sucks."

Nic and Piper wander off, yammering about how annoying it is that they like each other which... okay. That leaves Ren, me, and Mr. Quinn lingering in the parlor.

"Do you want something to drink?" Ren asks, turning to me before his dad can say anything. "Wine, beer..."

"A white wine would be great," I say.

"On it," Mr. Quinn says with a salute. He zooms further into the house toward the kitchen.

Ren takes my hand and leads me into the family room, where a pink-haired woman sits with her legs tucked under her next to a redheaded woman with some of the most intricate tattoos I've ever seen covering her arms. They immediately stop talking when we enter the room. "Hey, Mills," Ren says, and the red-head waves back without looking at him. "This is my girlfriend, Audrey. Audrey, this is Millie and her best friend, Poppy."

"Hi," I wave awkwardly. "You probably don't remember me, but..."

"Of course I do. You're the reason I didn't sleep for a week, and why I tattooed Ghostface on my arm when I was eighteen," Millie points at me in a way that feels slightly threatening. "Thanks for that."

With her right arm extended, I can see the Ghostface tattoo in question. It's around two inches big and below the dimple of her inner elbow.

"Um. You're welcome?" I answer, oddly touched and confused by the interaction.

"So, that's like... what, half of my siblings?" Ren says, wrapping an arm around my waist and gently directing me away from Poppy and Millie. I hear them whisper when my back's to them, and my instinct is to worry if it's about me.

"But you, like... were careful?" One of them whispers to the other.

"I mean, it broke, but we took care of it. So it shouldn't matter... but I think it might," the other responds, voice tense.

I want to eavesdrop more, but I'm distracted when someone says my name.

My old name.

"Audrey Price."

This time, I recognize the voice without looking. It's a voice I used to know better than my own.

"Hi, Meow," Ren says, turning us to face her.

Kat Quinn—Holt now, I guess—looks pretty much the same. Long, wavy chocolate brown hair and menacing brown eyes. Full lips, and the lightest scattering of freckles across the bridge of her nose. Now, there are faint wrinkles at the corner of her eyes, and I'm suddenly filled with a grief I didn't expect at the years I've missed in her life. At the years she's missed in mi ne.

Kat ignores Ren, crossing her arms over her chest and giving me a judgmental once over. "Had to see it to believe it. You're dating my brother?" She scoffs and rolls her eyes. "Really? Couldn't find anyone else?"

"Shut up, Kat," Millie yells from her spot on the couch. "Just because you're miserable doesn't mean the rest of us have to be."

Kat shoots a death glare at her sister. "I'm sorry, was I talking to you?"

"No, you were talking to my partner," Ren says coolly. In a stark contrast to his icy tone of voice, my body fills with a warmth I've rarely experienced. Everything about him makes me feel new.

Kat's face softens when she looks at Ren, and I can tell she has a soft spot for her brother. Even when we were younger, Kat was the one Ren would go to when he had a homework question. He'd always knock on her door and stick his little bespectacled face into her room to ask for help with a word problem, or how to spell something.

Maybe it was less about his admiration for Kat, and more about his big-ass crush on me, but it's still evident Ren is important to Kat.

"Your brother is the most incredible man I've ever met," I say quietly, appealing to her love for Ren. "I can't believe he wants me..."

Kat scoffs. "Neither can I."

"That's enough, Kat," Ren says, raising his voice enough to show he's not fucking around. "I love you, but you need to back off if you want any sort of relationship with me."

Kat opens and closes her mouth like a fish. "I just want to protect you," she says feebly.

"For what it's worth, she was like this with me, too," a blond bearded man says, stepping next to us. He grins at me and sticks his hand out for me to shake. "I'm Josh, Nic's boyfriend. You're Audrey, right?"

I smile as I shake his hand, grateful for an interaction that isn't an interrogation. Maybe knowing Kat was like this with him should make me feel better, but it doesn't. The reason Kat's acting this way towards me goes beyond the fact I'm dating her brother.

It's because I'm me.

"Ren!" Another voice says. This family has too many people.

"Hi, Ma," Ren says as Mrs. Quinn approaches. She wraps him in a big mom hug, and even though I see him trying to remain stiff, part of him still melts into her.

"And Audrey!" Mrs. Quinn breaks away from Ren and suddenly she's hugging me, too. I look with panic at Ren, taken aback by the physical contact, and he places his hand on her shoulder and gently pushes her back.

"Ma, give her some space," he says softly, and I'm impressed by his ability to remain cool, despite his face clearly showing his annoyance.

"Right, right. I'm sorry, dear." Mrs. Quinn steps back and appraises me as I shift nervously on my feet. "I just met your precious daughter. She's a spitting image of you at that age, but she did ask me if I was nuts when I tried to hug her."

"Piper's autistic," I explain, forcing a smile onto my face. "She's particular about physical touch."

"She did a wonderful job at asserting her needs," Mrs. Quinn says sincerely, reaching out to pat my arm before seemingly remembering what Ren said and pulling it quickly back. "She's delightful."

My eyebrows shoot up. No one has *ever* referred to my daughter as delightful.

Mrs. Quinn insists we go into the dining room and sit, so Ren and I oblige. Piper and Nic—who is enthusiastically explaining her favorite TV show to my daughter—are the only ones at the table, and slowly the room fills with more Quinns and the savory aroma of Mrs. Quinn's legendary lasagna.

Hunter claims the open seat next to me, and Josh takes the seat next to her.

"Have you met Josh?" Hunter asks. "He's Nic's boytoy." I laugh as Nic cackles and Josh's face turns strawberry ice cream pink.

"I'm... no. Not... no," Josh sputters. Nic grins and pulls him down to kiss him on the cheek. It's like he forgets he's embarrassed the way he stares at her with heart eyes.

My entire body tenses when Steve Holt, Kat's husband, sits between her and Ren. I'm not saying this family is quiet—in fact, they're anything but. However, he's somehow even louder than the rest of his family, his voice echoing above the rest.

Kat always acted like she was above the noise, and she'd never admit it, but she could be as loud and brash as the rest of her family. "You have to be loud sometimes," she explained when I called her out one time. "Otherwise, nobody will hear if you have something important to say."

Steve is beyond loud and seemingly clueless to anyone but himself. Mrs. Quinn is staring in the distance and nodding absently as he talks about a client he golfed with last week, and Piper's expression is one of unbridled disdain.

"Audrey, do you want salad?" Mr. Quinn asks, raising his voice and the salad bowl so I can hear him over Steve's incessant yammering.

"Yes, please," I say at the same time Steve takes a breath and is quiet enough to hear, apparently.

"Audrey?" he says, drowning out my response. "Who the fuck is Audrey?"

I lean forward to look past Ren and smile. "I'm Audrey."

He narrows his eyes at me. "Do I know you?" he demands, like this is his home, and how *dare* someone he's not familiar with step into his domain.

"Audrey went to high school with us," Kat says quietly. I notice her plate is still full, and she's pushing her food to the edges with her fork. "She was in my grade."

"Are you sure? I think I'd remember her." The way Steve's eyes move over my body make me feel like spiders are crawling under my skin. I cross my arms over my chest in discomfort.

"No, it's true. I remember you," I say awkwardly. I don't say exactly what I'm thinking, and keep the "unfortunately" to myself.

Steve grins. "Well, that I believe." He laughs before lifting his beer to his mouth and taking a drink. Kat is still pushing her food around, eyes intent on the floral pattern swirling around the edges of the plate.

When Steve lowers the bottle, he somehow misses the table and it tumbles off the edge, spilling onto Ren's lap.

"*Shit*," Ren yelps, leaping to his feet.

As I look around the table, I'm filled with the realization everyone at the table seems to be done with Steve's bullshit. Especially Mr. Quinn, who's rubbing at his temples the same way he did when he caught me sneaking back into their house one morning. Kat is a close second, her lower lip trembling like she's about to dissolve into tears.

Steve, however, is staring at Ren's crotch like he doesn't understand it.

I'm taken aback when the scrape of a chair against the hardwood floor fills the air. "Excuse me," Kat says, voice shaky before she exits the room. In my peripheral vision, I see Mr. and Mrs. Quinn exchange an anxious look.

Steve gets up and follows her out of the room, as the rest of us are silent.

"*Drama*," Piper says in a sing-song tone, and I turn to tell her not to joke, but Nic and Josh are already openly laughing.

"You chose a good day to come," Nic tells her. These two are already thick as thieves, and I wonder if Nic is the autistic sister Ren told Piper about at the beginning of summer.

"Can I borrow a pair of pants?" Ren asks with a heavy sigh, tossing his napkin onto the table. I wonder who he's talking to, until Mr. Quinn gives his assent.

Ren smiles at me before leaving the room, and it's not his full smile, which is so bright and full of joy, like staring directly at the sun. Instead, it's this nervous, embarrassed smile with its own charm, its own light.

As he leaves, Steve re-enters the room, typing something on his phone. Since he's distracted, he misses the dirty look Ren shoots him, but I don't. It's one of the hottest things I've ever seen.

I can't believe this man was ready to abandon his family because of me. He loves them *so* much. I can never be the reason for any division between them.

I know what I have to do.

I make eye contact with Mrs. Quinn, seeing so much of Ren in her: in the way her nose is slightly turned up at the end, in her long eyelashes and the shape of her mouth. In the shape of her dark chocolate eyes and the way she seems to understand what I need without saying it.

"I think I left the salad dressings in the fridge." she says, getting to her feet. "Audrey, would you mind helping me?"

"Yep," I say easily, standing and following her into the kitchen.

"We literally have five different salad dressings already," Leo mutters.

Mrs. Quinn goes to the sink to wash her hands, and I inhale shakily preparing myself for what I know I have to say.

"I think I'm in love with Ren."

Okay, *whoa*. That was not what I thought I was going to say.

Mrs. Quinn, however, seems unmoved by my impromptu and personally shocking love confession. "I can tell," she says, turning off the sink and reaching for an embroidered hand towel to dry her hands. "You came to dinner even though you didn't want to."

Her back is still to me, and I think not being able to see her face makes me braver. "I think he could love me, too."

As I say the words, it violently hits me how true a statement it is. How easily I could see Ren waking up next to me every morning, his face buried in my neck. How natural the thought of him cooking with me is. How mine and Piper's girls nights would become family nights. How his and Piper's relationship feels like it's filled a hole in my heart that I didn't know existed.

"I know he can," she responds, like it's the most obvious thing in the world, and maybe to her, it is. She knows the Ren who drops everything to help his family. The Ren who is always smiling and always there for everyone who needs him. She doesn't know the Ren who's crumbling beneath the weight of everyone's perceptions of him.

The last thing I want is to become another person he feels like he can't let down.

"And... and he loves you. All of you," I say, a giant lump in my throat. "So much. The way he talks about you is..."

"Is this about what I said to you all those years ago?"

I freeze, heart pounding so hard I feel it in my head. It is, but I didn't expect her to even remember. I expected it to be something inconsequential to her, just another Wednesday.

"I... yes. I told him about what happened." A wave of shame fills my body. I don't *want* to get between Ren and his family, especially not his mother. But he deserves the truth, especially when he's bent over backwards to come across as perfect for people. "He wanted to know why I stopped coming around, why I left town, then came back in hiding. I told him the truth."

Mrs. Quinn finally turns to face me. "What did he say?" she asks. Her voice is calm and even, and I can't tell if it's because it's a genuine curiosity, or if she's holding back more anger towards me.

"He was furious," I admit, remembering Ren's reaction. "He didn't understand why... why..."

Mrs. Quinn sighs heavily. "I fucked up then, and I'm fucking up now."

I blink at her. I don't think I've ever heard this woman say *fuck*. "Uh..."

"I was a dick." She says it matter-of-factly and it catches me off guard. Not that I don't agree, but *dick* is, once again, a word I didn't think was in Mrs. Quinn's vocabulary. "It's not *not* an excuse, but I was trying to do right by the church, by my community, by my family. I was so worried about the rules and what other people would think that I forgot why these things are important to me... and you were a casualty. I failed you, and myself, and I'm so sorry, Audrey."

I finally look up, and her brown eyes are swimming with tears. My throat is thick with emotion when I try to swallow. "I thought you'd help me."

"I should have," she says quietly. "I was so worried about following the rules perfectly that I forgot the rules are supposed to help us best love God and His people. Turning you away did neither of those things, and what's worse is it took *years* for me to realize I did something wrong.

"You have every right to hate me," she continues, "and the guilt I feel is necessary because I did something wrong. I hope more than anything that one day you can forgive me, but I understand if you can't."

"I hated you for what you did. I hated everybody, to be honest." My voice is shaky, but I continue to talk. My younger self deserves to be heard. "When I became a mom, my anger grew because I couldn't imagine turning my daughter or any of her friends away if they found themselves in a similar situation. I couldn't imagine not loving them as hard as I could.

"But if I had such strong convictions about something, even if they turned out to be misguided, I can understand wanting to keep Piper away from that. While teen pregnancy isn't one of those things, I think I can understand why you did what you did. But I'll never stop wishing you had let me stay."

"I wish I could do it over." Mrs. Quinn smiles shakily, wiping at her eyes. "I hate that I hurt you. I'm learning I've hurt a lot of people and while I can't change the past, I can certainly take ownership in the present, and be better in the future."

"That shows a lot of growth," I tell her earnestly. I pause for a moment before speaking again. "Could I hug you? Would that be okay?"

In lieu of a verbal answer, Mrs. Quinn steps forward and wraps her arms around me. "Thank you," she whispers. "I don't expect your forgiveness, but thank you for coming, and for talking to me. You've grown up to be a wonderful woman, and a mother to a wonderful girl. I'm so grateful you and Ren found each other again."

"I am too," I rasp, slowly softening into her embrace. Her hug reminds me of Aunt Liv, and my heart aches at the reminder of how much I've lost. While that's true, I've also found and gained so, so much. Piper. Ren.

Myself.

Chapter 35

Ren

Playlist: Everywhere, Everything (with Gracie Abrams) | Noah Kahan

"Unghhhh."

I'm currently pantsless in my parents' closet, while there's apparently a ghost in the room.

"Uh, hello?" I call.

The ghost responds with another groan. I step out of the closet, a pair of sweats in hand and my jeans under my arm, and jump in surprise. "Jesus *Christ*, Leo."

"Hnnghhhh," Leo, who is currently sprawled face down across our parents' bed, turns his head to the side and smirks. "Would you look at that, you're a boxer briefs guy. What if I told you that's a family..."

"Stop."

He turns his head until his face is pressed into the mattress, letting out a long-suffering sigh.

I pull the sweatpants on, and head toward the door to leave.

"*Wait*, you're gonna leave me here in my fragile emotional state?" I turn to see Leo's flipped to his back, limbs spread out like a starfish.

"Uh..."

"How are you so good with girls?" He whines. "You're such a nerd."

I blink at him. "Thanks?"

"Not a compliment," he specifies.

"Thanks for the clarification," I sigh, rubbing a hand over my face. My parents raised eight children, but somehow, getting Leo to be a functioning adult is what's going to get them canonized to sainthood. "What's going on with you and Stella?"

Leo does the most un-Leo-like thing and is silent for a few seconds. He then lets out another long-suffering sigh and sits up. "I don't know."

I've never heard him sound so sad and dejected, and it's disconcerting as fuck. I walk to the bed and sit on the edge, waiting for him to continue. "I don't know if you heard," he starts to say, fidgeting with a friendship bracelet on his left wrist, "but her mom has stage four uterine cancer."

"Fuck," I breathe.

"Yeah. Um... they thought it was treatable at first, but recently, her insurance said they wouldn't cover the necessary, aggressive treatment doctors were recommending since it's stage four and... it feels like I'm losing her. No, it feels like I've already lost her, and I don't know how to get her back. She barely talks to me, and I get it. Her mom's her priority, but I want to be there for her. I told her I'd take the semester off to support her and she got *so* angry. I don't understand why she got so angry." His voice quiets with each word in his last sentence until it's barely a whisper.

"She's going through a lot right now," I said gently, placing my hand on his shoulder. "Try to give her the time and space she needs."

"I hate that she's doing it alone," Leo mumbled, staring intently at his tightly clasped hands in his lap.

"Sometimes people need to do things alone."

"Quinns don't," Leo says, so confidently wrong it makes me laugh.

"Maybe Leo Quinn doesn't. But the rest of us have had to, at one point or another. There's no right way. Everyone deals with life differently."

"What if she breaks up with me?"

Leo and Stella have been together for years. She's part of our family. It *is* weird when she's not with him.

There's no guarantee a relationship won't end, and sometimes, it's best they do. That's not what he needs to hear right now.

"If she breaks up with you, you'll be heartbroken." I say simply. "You'll grieve and it'll hurt like hell, and you'll be okay."

Leo sniffs and swipes at his nose with the back of his wrist. "You're supposed to promise she won't break up with me."

"I'm not going to tell you what you want to hear, Leo. Not if I don't know it's true. That won't help anything."

He narrows his eyes. "Who are you and what have you done with my brother?

"What's that supposed to mean?" I ask with a laugh.

"It *means* that's exactly what you do. You're the optimist, the one who says the cup is half full when the rest of us are convinced it's half empty."

I'm taken aback by his words, but I shouldn't be. He's right, I *have* always told people what they want to hear, whether it's true or not.

"I'm turning over a new leaf," I say slowly. "I'm trying this thing where I don't jump through hoops to make everyone happy, and seeing if I'm still worthwhile if I'm not a show pony."

"Are you kidding me?!" Leo looks absolutely horrified by my words. "We don't like you because you tell us what we want to hear. We love you because you're one of us. One of the best of us, as much as it pains me to say. You could provide nothing and guess what? You'd still be my favorite big brother."

"I'm your only big brother," I remind him.

He ignores this. "Why do you love people? Because of what they do for you, or because their presence in your life is a fucking delight?"

"Whose existence is a fucking delight?" I stand and turn to see my dad leaning against the door frame.

"This pretty boy here," Leo coos, squishing my cheeks between his hands from behind.

"Please don't call me that," I beg, words muffled by Leo's squishing. That just became my new favorite phrase, but only when Audrey uses it.

"Leo, can I talk to your brother alone for a second?" Dad asks, stepping further into the room.

"Oooooh. Pretty boy's in trouble," Leo teases, finally freeing my cheeks from his imprisonment.

"I *will* kick your ass," I warn.

He scoffs. "No, you won't."

"I'll ask Nic to kick your ass."

"Okay, well, that's uncalled for," Leo stammers, face paling.

"Boys," Dad says in the warning voice I haven't heard in a good decade. "Be nice to your brother."

"Sorry," Leo and I mumble unenthusiastically.

Once Leo leaves, Dad smirks at me. "He's a little shit, isn't he?"

I laugh. "You *cannot* just be realizing this about him."

"Eh," Dad says, stepping around me and sitting on the edge of the bed. He pats the mattress next to him, motioning for me to sit beside him. "I think you'll realize soon enough you have a blind spot when it comes to your kids."

I eye him suspiciously as I sit. "What does that mean? You mean like my students?"

"No. I mean you look at that girl the same way I look at you." My face must adequately communicate my confusion, because Dad continues. "Piper. You look at Piper the same way I look at you and your siblings."

My throat is thick with emotion and I find myself staring at my hands. "Is that a bad thing?" I wonder.

"No," Dad says quickly. "I think it's a really good thing. I'm proud of you, you seem happy, and you deserve that."

I force myself to meet my dad's eye. "Did you know about what Mom told her?"

My dad is taken aback, but averts his eyes. My heart sinks.

"It was a mutual decision," he admits. "A wrong one. I'm sorry."

"I'm not who you should be apologizing to."

"No, I owe you an apology, too. I always wanted to be someone I'd be proud to see my sons be like, and I wasn't. I let you and your siblings down. I will apologize to Audrey, too, because she deserves it. I can tell she's really important to you."

"No one's ever mattered to me as much as she and Piper do," I admit.

He clasps my shoulder. "I'm glad you have them, and I'm glad they have you. You're a good man, and even though I made mistakes along the way, I can't help but be proud of my kids and the people they are."

As we return downstairs, I see Will arrived during our absence and Millie excitedly fills him in on the drama. Next to her, Poppy is the only person in the room not chattering, staring in silence at her wine glass.

When I sit, I realize the chair to my left is empty, as is my mom's. My stomach sinks, and I'm back on my feet and heading to the kitchen, where Mom and Audrey are facing each other, because of *course* Mom had to corner Audrey while I wasn't here.

Mom notices me first, and instead of looking like she fears me, which she *should*, she breaks out into a joyful smile.

"Hey," I say through clenched teeth. I place a protective hand on Audrey's lower back and she immediately leans into me. "What are you talking about?"

Audrey tilts her head up and presses her lips to my chin. I hate myself, because I'm immediately melting into a pile of Ren goo, absolutely smitten with this sweet woman. "Mom stuff. We're okay, baby."

I no longer can try to intimidate my mom, because now my insides are doing a complex cheerleading routine. She called me *baby*.

God, I can't even be protective for fifteen seconds before this woman has me giggling and kicking my feet.

"You're okay?" I repeat, lightheaded from the euphoria that her calling me *baby* elicited.

"Mmhmm. I wanted to talk to her," Audrey says, leaning her head against my shoulder.

I meet Mom's gaze. Her arms are crossed across her chest and she's smiling smugly.

It's the same face she made when Josh came over for the first time after he and Nic were official. When Hunter and Jo came to their first espresso morning as a couple, and Mom happened to wake up and catch us. When Stella and Leo snuggle on the couch, heads together as they laugh at a video on one of their phones.

She *likes* this. Likes *us*.

"I don't know, Lorenzo," Mom says teasingly as she walks to the fridge and grabs a single bottle of salad dressing that's probably been in there for as long as I've been alive. "She might be too good for you."

I meet Audrey's gaze. Her eyes are watery, but shimmering, a soft smile turning the corners of her lips upward, like she has a secret that only the two of us know.

"Yeah," I say absentmindedly as I cup her cheek. "She certainly is."

Chapter 36

Ren

Playlist: Smiling All the Way Back Home | Tom Odell

"So," I say, tapping my thumb on the steering wheel. "How do you feel about watching *A New Hope* tonight? We can stop and get Leia on our way to the cottage." I'm trying to keep my cool, but my insides are bursting at the idea of introducing my favorite film franchise to my favorite girls.

"Actually," Piper says from the backseat. "Mom, can I stay at Annika's tonight? You can drop me off on the way home."

"Pipe, tomorrow's a school day." Audrey turns her neck to look at her daughter. "Should you really stay over tonight?"

"Annika goes to school too, Mom." Piper's tone shows how silly she thinks this conversation is, and how confused she is that the answer wasn't an immediate and emphatic 'yes.'

"Did you finish your homework?" Audrey asks.

"Did *you* always finish your homework when you were my age?" Piper fires back.

"Ooooh," is my very mature and supportive response.

"That's not the point," Audrey sputters. "I also got pregnant around your age, is that your next step in your 'taking after my mom' mission you apparently have?"

"Gross, no." Piper sounds disgusted at the idea of pregnancy. "Mom, pleeeeeease? It'll give you and Ren time alone and you can bring me my backpack and a change of clothes in the morning."

When I glance in the rearview mirror, Piper's gray eyes, so much like Audrey's, are wide and her lower lip is pushed out. I a m *very* familiar with the famous puppy dog expression children give their adults. Personally, I fall for it every time.

While I don't want to insert myself into Audrey's parenting... I do want to be alone with her. Desperately.

I guess Audrey wants to be alone with me, too, because she lets out a heavy sigh. "Fine. But we're getting your stuff first because I don't want to have to bring it to you in the morning."

"Deal," Piper agrees quickly.

When we get to the cottage, Piper runs inside at the speed of light. Audrey turns to me with a soft smile on her face. "After we drop Piper off, do you want to run to your place to feed Leia and grab your necessities?"

My cheeks are as hot as the sidewalk in August. "Actually," I say slowly, "I was thinking... would you want to maybe come over?"

Audrey blinks in surprise, and I don't blame her. The only time we've spent at my apartment is the first time she invited herself over.

"Oh! Yeah, we can do that," she stammers, and I'm certain her blush mirrors my own.

"We don't have to if you don't want to," I say hurriedly. "We can come back if that's easier for you..."

"No, no," Audrey says, but she still seems anxious. "I'd, um, love to come to your place."

"Hey," I say, taking her hand in mine and bringing it to my lips. "Tell me what you're actually thinking and not what you think I want to hear."

She's silent for a moment. "I'm scared," she whispers, squeezing my hand. "It's not that I don't feel safe with you, I do. Safer than I've ever felt. But there's something about the control and comfort that comes with everything happening in my space..." She trails off, looking away from me.

"Hey." I gently clasp her chin, and turn her face back to me. "I understand. I wanted to show you the studio, but this makes sense and I'm not annoyed or anything like that, and—"

"Studio?" Audrey's eyes grow wide as she interrupts me. "You mean like... where the magic happens?"

"If by 'the magic' you mean my audios, then yes."

Audrey anxiously taps her right hand on her thigh, chewing her bottom lip as she stares out the passenger side window.

"We can come home after and spend the night here, if that's what you want."

Audrey clears her throat. "Okay. Yeah, I want to see the studio."

"I need to shower first, though. My entire crotch is still sticky with Coors Light, or whatever the hell Steve was drinking."

"Speaking of... what's going on with that? Kat seems miserable."

I sigh and run my left hand through my hair. "He's a tool. She doesn't listen to any of us and she's stubborn as hell. We've all tried to talk to her about it, but she gets so defensive."

I squeeze her hand as Piper tumbles out of the cottage, her school backpack fastened on her back and an overnight bag dangling from her left hand as she locks the door.

"I miss her," Audrey says quietly. "Your sister was my best friend for a long time."

"What happened between you two?" I ask her. It's one of the great mysteries of my life, why Audrey stopped hanging out with Kat. "Was it just you getting pregnant?"

Audrey's smile is sad. "It's not my story to tell."

I have no idea what that means, how an event she was directly involved in isn't her story to tell, but I don't say anything as Piper clambers back into the car and Audrey weaves her fingers in mine as we drive away from the cottage.

Chapter 37

Audrey

Playlist: All My Life | Kina Grannis

Sky's Sluts

SkysMainSlut: guys it just occurred to me that sky could have a girlfriend. Or a WIFE. Does that ruin the fantasy for anyone else? Knowing he could be like so happy with this other woman and we have no chance with him.

AshBash69: ...

SkysMainSlut: like he could be in LOVE! With someone who's not ME!

LadyRebel93: i say this with all the love in the world, but i need you to look up parasocial relationships and go to therapy.

AshBash93: personally, i hope he does. I hope he has someone who makes his life better than any audio he could record, and makes the words he say true. Isn't that what we want for the most part? To be loved and to love that person who gets us?

SkysMainSlut: and what if that person is me?

LadyRebel93: THERAPY. NOW.

"It's weird not breaking into this building," I observe as we climb the stairs to his third floor apartment. I'm trying to not sound like I'm about to drop dead, because *damn*, stairs are *hard*, and we've only climbed the first flight.

My hand is clasped firmly in Ren's, and suddenly, so is my waist as he spins me and pins me against the wall in the stairwell. "*Whoa*," I breathe, eyes wide at the unexpected maneuver.

But that might be my own fault, really. If I can expect anything from Ren, it's that I can never know what to expect from him. And yet, I know he'll be steady and consistent too. He's a contradiction and a thrill.

Ren drops my hand and grips my hips with both hands, pressing himself to me. I bite back a moan when I feel how hard he is already. What is this man planning to do to me in this studio of his?

"You know," he says, voice low as he leans into me, mustache brushing against the shell of my ear. It makes me shiver with want and anticipation. "I'm thinking you might actually be the bad girl they always said you were." He drops his lips to the hollow of my throat and leaves a warm, open mouth kiss. "I fucking love it."

"You know I'm not the bad girl they said I was," I correct, voice trembling as I wrap my arms around his shoulders. "I'm the bad girl you've turned me into."

He groans into my neck and squeezes my hips hard enough to hurt, but not so hard I want him to stop. "Even better—I get you all to myself."

Then the son of a bitch kisses my cheek, steps back, and *winks*. "Shall we continue?" he asks, taking my hand in his again.

"You are a sick, sick man, Lorenzo," I grumble as we continue our trek to his apartment.

"Lovesick, you mean," he teases, squeezing my hand.

"No, just sick."

We finally make it to the third floor and he unlocks the door. Immediately, Princess Leia is weaving between our legs, screaming her discontent.

"You'd think I'd never fed her a day in her life at that volume." Ren says, shaking his head as he closes the door behind us. "Or she didn't have an automatic feeder."

"*Meow!*" Leia screeches in response, staring up at us with big green eyes.

"To be fair, I believe her," I tease, nudging his side with my elbow.

"You're a *mom*, Audrey," he says playfully, stepping behind me and wrapping his arms around my middle. I lean back against his chest, the steady *thump thump thump* of his heart a soothing rhythm. "I know this isn't how you parent your daughter."

"According to said daughter, Leia is actually *her* baby, which makes her my grandbaby. Aren't parents required to throw away their parenting values when they become grandparents in favor of spoiling them?"

"I don't mean to be rude, but I really don't care or know." He buries his nose in my hair, inhaling deeply. "You smell incredible, and I want to make you come."

I dig my teeth into my lower lip, and I squeeze my thighs together, desperate for relief. "Take a shower, then you can show me the studio, *then* we can go home and we can spend the night counting how many times you can make me come."

He kisses my temple and drops his arms from around my waist. I'm immediately unsteady without his strength supporting me. I turn to face him, surprised by the intensity in his eyes.

"Audrey." He says my name so slowly, like he wants to keep the sound of it on his lips for as long as possible.

"That's me," I say quietly.

He smiles softly and cups my cheek with his hand, running his thumb over my lower lip. "Fuck, Aud. I—"

My heart is pounding harder than it ever has before. Is he going to tell me he loves me? God, I want him to. I desperately, desperately want him to say it. But instead he drops his hand, a forced smile on his face, and my heart sinks. "I think you smell good."

"You said that already," I say softly, averting my eyes to hide my disappointment.

"It bears repeating," he responds, voice low. "I'm going to shower real quick, okay? Make yourself at home."

How am I supposed to make myself at home when home's the one walking away?

When I hear the shower turn on, I let myself explore his living room. Leia followed Ren and now sits outside the bathroom, so I'm alone.

Above his couch are framed pictures of him and his family through the years. A picture of all ten of them at Kat's wedding. A picture of a teeny tiny bespectacled Ren and a grumpy Jo, I think, each holding a teeny tiny baby. I smile, remembering the day Mr. and Mrs. Quinn brought the twins home, and how excited we'd been to each hold them. A picture of him with his parents at his college graduation, and him and all of his siblings at what looks like his high school graduation.

My heart blooms as I take in how much *love* he grew up with. I know it wasn't perfect, because he received that love, and somehow thought it was something he had to earn, not his birthright. That being "good" and readily available and willing to drop anything for anyone made him worthy of love, not the fact he's him. Just him.

I need him to know he could do nothing else for me, and I'd still love him. I'd still want to live life with him. After a lifetime of isolating Piper and I to keep us safe from everyone else... I want to let him in. Let him see everything I used to hide.

I'm not sure what comes over me, but I'm moving towards the bathroom, pulling my dress over my head as I go. I'm sure I look goofy as hell in nothing but my bra, underwear, stockings, and ankle booties. But still I take a deep breath and push the bathroom door open.

"Aud?" Ren calls over the sound of the shower. His voice is like a beacon through the steam. "I'll be out in a sec."

This bathroom is gorgeous. White and gray tile, and a huge shower with a glass door. My heart pounds when he and his perfect body turn to face me, eyes widening at my state of undress.

"Actually," I say slowly, kicking off my ankle boots. "I was wondering if I could join."

It feels like his silence lasts minutes, but in reality it can't be more than three seconds. "I... uh... yeah. Of course. Do you... want to come in?"

"Yes," I say quietly, pulling my stockings and underwear down in one fell swoop. Ren quickly turns so he's facing away from me as I reach behind me to unclip my bra, my breasts sagging as the fabric pools at my feet. I take a deep breath and push open the glass door, the heat of the shower enveloping me.

"Hi," Ren says. "I won't turn around, I promise."

My heart flutters. This man is good without having to try. Even though I undressed and joined him in the shower, he's still respecting my boundaries. Still seeing me.

I move forward until my front is pressed against his back and wrap my arms around him.

"What—are you okay?" Ren asks, and I notice his eyes are squeezed shut. I grin at the fact that not only is he facing away from me, but he's keeping his eyes shut to ensure he doesn't see me.

"I'm so good, Ren," I whisper, pressing my cheek against his sculpted back. "I needed to tell you something."

He nods solemnly, like this isn't an outlandish situation. "I'm listening." He covers one of my hands with his, squeezing gently.

"I think you wanted to tell me you loved me earlier," I say, the words tumbling out one after the other. I can't stop it. "The second time you told me I smelled nice. And don't you dare tell me you were quoting *Star Wars* again, because you *do* love me, Ren. I know you do. But I also know you didn't want to say it because you don't want to scare me. Because you don't know if I love you, too." I inhale before continuing. "And I do. Love you. So much that sometimes it feels like you live in my chest and squeeze my heart for the fun of it. So much that... that I let my guard down and I'm okay with that. So much that I think you can love Piper as much as I do. So much that—"

I'm cut off when he turns towards me, cupping my face in his hands. He steals my confession out of my mouth when he tips my face and kisses me.

I love you, I think, wrapping my arms around him again. *I love you because you're you. I want you because you're you. You're good because you're you.*

"Audrey." He sighs my name when he finally breaks the kiss, pressing his forehead to mine. He cups my waist, thumb absentmindedly drawing designs on my skin. "I... I don't know what to say. You said it all. You stole my goddamn love confession."

I laugh, delighted at his frustration and the smile that spreads across his face at my laughter. "You saw right through me. Of course I love you, sweetheart. I've loved you since I was nine years old." He pauses. "Maybe it wasn't love because I was nine years old. But the thing I'm most certain of in my life is I love you today."

"You became a safe haven for us, for me and Piper. I don't think I had a choice but you love you. It was as inevitable as the tide changing.

"It feels silly, but I want to show you this. Because I know you'll be good to me, Ren. I know you won't run or be put off by me. That you'll still find me beautiful and still want me."

I inhale shakily as I step back so he can see me. All of me.

Instead of looking down like I expect him to, Ren surprises me by keeping his deep green eyes on mine. "Sweetheart." His voice is soft and filled with the devotion I've only heard in his audios. "Nothing could make you less beautiful. You're beautiful because you're you. I love your body because I love you."

That was rude as fuck because I want this man to look at my tits and get it over with but he's reciting the most romantic and loveliest poetry, words I never dreamed I'd hear.

"Is it okay if I look?" he asks, and something about him asking for my consent despite me being the one initiating breaks me. He's giving me an out.

"Yes," I whisper, and my legs tremble as slowly his eyes move downward. I watch as his eyes land on my breasts and he exhales shakily.

"Fuck," he whispers. "Audrey, you're perfect. How are you so perfect?"

It feels like my veins are filled with melted gold, spreading warmth from the top of my head to my toes. "Touch me, baby."

His hand slowly moves up my side, my breath hitching when his thumb gently strokes the side of my breasts.

"I know they're saggy and..." I begin.

"Audrey, they're breasts. They nourished your daughter and yeah, they changed because of that, maybe in a way you don't love. But when I look at you, I see my best friend, the most caring and generous person I know. The woman who gave her body for her daughter, when no one gave anything for her when she needed it. I see generosity and care and tenderness and the fact that I get to be loved by you is better than anything I could have dreamt of."

He cups my breast in his hand, and I shiver as he swipes his thumb over my nipple, which puckers and aches at the attention. "Can I kiss you here, sweetheart?"

"Mmhmm," I manage to say. He ducks his head and flicks my left nipple with his tongue while cupping the right in his hand, using his thumb to show the same care and attention.

I gasp at the sensation, so different from when I touch myself. I weave my fingers through his hair as he gently scrapes my nipple with his bottom teeth before sucking it into his mouth. I cry out. My god, I didn't know this feeling *existed* until now, and I only want to experience it with him.

He gazes at me through his unfairly long lashes as he swirls his tongue around the aching peak, and I nod frantically to show him I'll gladly take whatever he wants to give me.

He releases my nipple and lifts his head. He leans forward, brushing the tip of his nose against mine before he takes my lower lip between his.

This man makes me feel more alive and in tune with my body than I ever have.

This man *loves* me.

"Ren," I whimper. "I need you, baby. Please."

"You have me, sweetheart," he answers, and while the sentiment is so sweet, that's *not* what I meant.

How the do I tell him I need him to fuck me? I don't want to wait until we're back at the cottage, I need him inside me as soon as humanly possible.

"No, I... I want you inside me. Now."

Okay, that wasn't as hard as I'd thought it would be.

Ren freezes, and maybe I should've taken the time to find less forceful words.

"Sorry," I say, embarrassed by how fucking needy I am for him. "I should..."

"Don't you *dare* apologize for telling me what you want," he says, voice husky and deep and reminding me of Sky. But this isn't Sky, this is Ren, the man I love, who is infinitely better than my fantasies. "I left the condoms in the car. I was hoping this would happen soon and thought it would happen at your place and..." He trails off, his face reddening profusely.

I bite my lip to keep from smiling, but I don't think it works. "I have an IUD, and you said you've been tested recently, right?

"Yeah," Ren assures me. "You have, too?"

I nod.

"But I don't want you to feel like you have to—"

"I want to," I promise. "I want to feel you, all of you. Nothing between us anymore."

He groans, pressing his lips violently against mine while he reaches behind himself to turn off the shower.

"That door leads to the bedroom," Ren tells me, grabbing two towels from the linen closet and gesturing to a second door I hadn't noticed. He wraps me in the fluffiest towel I've ever felt, and I shuffle into his bedroom, a smile spreading across my face when I see even more *Star Wars* LEGO sets displayed. God, I love this man.

"Go lay down for me, sweetheart." He presses against my back, using one hand to rest on my towel-covered belly, and the other to sweep my wet hair off my right shoulder. It gives him access to my neck, which he immediately starts leaving wet, open-mouthed kisses on. I'm cold, but quickly warmed by him.

"How can you tell me to do that when you're doing *this*?" My playful whine is quickly transformed into a gasp when he fists my hair at the roots and pulls my head back until our eyes lock.

"You're going to lay down for me," he says slowly, his voice deep and commanding, "because you're such a good girl, aren't you?"

"Yes, sir." My response is involuntary, and dripping with neediness the way my arousal is currently dripping down my thighs.

His cock hardens against my ass and I teasingly wiggle my ass against it.

"*Fuck*," he groans, tilting his own head to the ceiling. "I think I like 'sir.'"

"Silly boy. I've known you liked 'sir.'" I step away from him and turn to face him. As I walk backwards towards his bed, I slowly untuck the towel, letting it fall to the ground. He curses, and his eyes are absolutely feral.

This is going to be so much fun.

Chapter 38

Audrey

Playlist Options: No Plan | Hozier

I push myself back to the headboard and recline onto my back while Ren stands at the foot of the bed, gorgeous cock erect and eyes dancing over my body. He exhales heavily and runs his hand over his face. "I can't believe I get to love you," he says, voice disbelieving. "You're the most beautiful thing I've ever seen."

I shake my head. "You took your contacts out before showering, and you're not wearing your glasses. You can't possibly have an accurate view of me."

He scoffs and reaches for the pair of glasses neatly folded on the bedside table. His breath hitches as he looks at me after putting them on. "It just made the view clearer, and I've truly, honestly, never seen anything as beautiful as you."

I swallow the lump in my throat. "You make me feel that beautiful."

"Good." He sits on the bed, and runs his hand over my hair. "I need to ask you a very serious, very important question."

"Anything," I whisper.

"Will you please sit on my face?"

I roll my eyes. "You're incorrigible."

"It's not my fault I can never have enough of that pussy." He follows the filthy comment with the sweetest puppy dog pout I've ever seen in my life.

I bite my lip. "I'm not thin, Ren."

"Yes, I've officially seen you naked," he agrees, a cheeky smirk on his face. "I can use lots of words to describe your body, but 'thin' is not one of them. Voluptuous. Curvaceous. Heavenly. Miraculous. Jaw-dropping…"

"Ren, I can't sit on your face. I weigh too much." I have to interrupt his list of adjectives he'd use to describe my body, apparently. I have to admit, it is making my cheeks pink.

He raises an eyebrow. "Not to make things weird, but I've done this with partners bigger than you without any problems. I'm not worried about you hurting me, Aud. If you don't want to, that's fine, but don't let it be because you think I can't handle that perfect pussy on my mouth. I can. I can handle all of you, I promise."

I exhale, reminding myself this man has done nothing but give me reasons to trust him. I sit up as he climbs on the bed and rolls onto his back, fluffing the pillow beneath his head. I straddle his hips and we both moan as my cunt brushes against his cock.

"You should take your time getting up here," he teases, smirking cheekily as he bites his lower lip.

"You little brat," I tease.

"Sweetheart, you know nothing about me is little—*shit*." I cut off his gloating with a firm grind of my hips, and his hands find their way to them as well. "Never mind. Fuck taking your time. I need to taste you."

I crawl up his body until I'm hovering over his face. His breath is hot on my cunt as he uses his thumbs to spread me. I shiver at the contact as he exhales a swear.

My thighs are already trembling when he wraps his arms around my thighs and buries his face in my pussy.

"Grab onto the headboard, sweetheart," he says, voice muffled and vibrating against my already sensitive clit. The sensation makes me almost collapse. "I *know* you've listened to the audios I've done and know how to do this right. Stop hovering."

I lower myself further onto him, because bossy Ren has melted my brain into goo, and any dominant streak I've had vaporizes. He groans as I lower my weight onto him, and while I'm *obviously* enjoying it, I think he may be enjoying it even more.

He licks and sucks, nips and circles, and digs his fingers into my thighs, all the while moaning with pleasure. I loosen my grip on the headboard and lean back to watch him, planting my hands on either side of his thighs. I can barely see him over my breasts and belly, but can see his eyes are closed and his hair is mussed. He's fucking blissed out. He opens his eyes, a hazy yet animalistic expression in them.

"Pretty boy," I praise, digging my teeth into my lower lip. "This is what you wanted? To be smothered by my pussy and told how pretty you are while doing it?"

He groans again, eyes widening as he nods as best as he can in our current position. No one can say he's not enthusiastic.

God, his enthusiasm feels good. Both for my body, but also my self-esteem. This man not only loves the essence of me, my heart and everything else someone means when they say they love someone... he loves my body and pleasing it. The same body I've hated, the same body that's created life and nourished it, the body that's carried me and taken care of me for over thirty years. He sees what I haven't, and he loves it so earnestly I think maybe I could learn to love it, too.

Ren lifts me off his face. "Fuck, sweetheart. You taste so good," he gasps, beard and mustache soaked with my arousal.

"You've tasted me before," I say, voice shaky.

"Not when you've loved me," he says, that crooked smile back on his face. "Everything is different when you love me."

My heart twists in my chest. He's right. It *is* different when I love him, when he loves me. It's like our love is fusing with lust and becoming one new emotion, one new desire. While letting him find my fragile heart has been one of the most terrifying things I've ever done, he's protecting that part of me well. We're both taking care of my heart now.

He makes me new, makes me want new things Old things, made new.

"Ren... I want you. Inside me," I beg, absolutely hopeless for him.

His expression softens, no longer feral and animalistic. "You sure you don't want me to wear a condom?"

My hand finds his hair, and I rake my fingers through his unruly waves. "I only want you."

"I've never... uh. I've never had penetrative sex without a condom before." His cheeks redden at the confession, like his face wasn't just buried in my pussy.

"Oh!" I say, my own face heating. "That was... presumptive of me. I'm sorry, we can totally..."

"I want to, with you, though," he interrupts. "Only you."

I nod. "Me too." I scoot myself backward until I'm straddling his hips, and he sits up, eyes never leaving mine. He cups my cheek gingerly, running his thumb over my lower lip. "Can I have you, sweetheart?" His voice is so gentle and earnest and it makes me want to implode.

"Yes," I say, lowering my face to his and kissing him. It's urgent and slow, languid and desperate, rough and gentle. A kiss made of contradictions and impossibilities. Kind of like us.

"Yes," I repeat, his fingertips tracing my curves until they curl around my hip.

"How do you want me?" He murmurs, brushing his nose against mine. "Do you have a favorite position?"

I pull away from him, fighting the urge to roll my eyes. "Ren, I've only ever done cramped missionary in the backseat of a Honda Civic. Anything different sounds amazing."

He barks out a surprised laugh, deep and delighted.

"I think I can do that," he says. "Any position in any audios that piqued your interest? "

My entire body is heated by the blush creeping down my neck. "I've... I've always been curious about being fucked from behind," I admit. I hate the shame filling my entire body with my confession, like the shame I experienced when pregnant is returning and filling me to the brim.

Ren notices, wrapping his arms around me and pulling me into his chest, and running his hand down my hair.

"I hate that sex can still make me feel like this," I whisper, fighting the tears filling my eyes. "I hate it."

"I know," he soothes, his hand moving from my hair to my upper back, rubbing calming circles on it. "We don't have to do anything tonight if you're not ready. I'm willing to wait until you're comfortable if you—"

"I'm tired of letting fear and shame and anxiety call the shots," I interrupt, voice cracking. "I'm sick of hiding and not doing the things I want to do, live the life I want to live."

"The things you want to do? Liiiike me?" he says in a teasing tone, and I can't help but crack a smile.

"I certainly want to do you. But, like... even going out with you in public. Or going out in public in general. Loving you. Letting myself be loved by you." I melt even more somehow when he presses his lips to the crown of my head. "I want to live, Ren. I want to love and…"

"Laugh?" he offers.

"What?"

"You want to live, laugh, love?"

This time, I don't try to stop the eyeroll. "Dweeb."

"I wanna make you smile, Aud. Your brain's being so mean to you, and I want to love you and make you smile through it."

I lift my head and meet his eyes. "I want to have sex with you. I don't… my anxiety is the one that doesn't."

"Are you anxious you'll get pregnant again?" he asks, voice kind.

I think about it for a moment, surprised at the answer I find. "No," I say slowly. "No… I've always wanted more kids, always wanted someone to build a family with. I couldn't do it on my own again, but I'm not on my own anymore. I have you."

I cup his cheek with my hand and he leans into it, the pressure of his presence calming. "I mean… I'd rather wait a bit. Like, maybe when Piper's in college. But I think that's something I might want. With you. If you want it. And the thing is… the unexpected seems less terrifying when I have you to hold my hand when I navigate it."

"I want that with you, too." he says softly, and my heart blooms in my chest. "I'd get you pregnant right now if you'd let me."

"Okay, breeding kink," I tease. "Settle down."

His smile is radiant. "I told you, I'll wear a condom if you want me to. But I'm gonna be honest with you, Aud, the idea of filling you and watching your body grow our next baby." Ren exhales heavily and shakes his head. "It's doing it for me."

I kiss him to shut him up, because to be completely honest, it's doing it for me, too.

"Also, I should let you know I'm not going to fuck you," Ren murmurs against my lips. "It's gonna be slow and luxurious. I'm going to take my time giving you *exactly* what you need, learning what makes you make those pretty noises for me. I'm going to learn your body the same way I learned the piano, discovering what sound each touch elicits."

I shiver, unbelievably turned on by this man and his filthy mouth. The filthy mouth that makes so many people come, gives so many people pleasure.

Tonight, he's all mine.

Chapter 39

Ren

Audrey is currently naked in my bed. Hands pressed to my chest, her legs bracketing my hips, and her pupils dilated. Because of *me*.

I've definitely had a wet dream about this before.

She squeals as I flip us, her stormy gray eyes wide as I take in her body yet again. "I think I need to get my glasses again..."

"*Ren*," she giggles, planting her hands on my chest. "Please. I need you."

I climb off the bed, grasping my dick in my hand and firmly tugging as she rolls onto her belly, wiggling her perfect ass and making my cock drip with pre-cum.

I reach to the head of the bed and grab a pillow. "Lift your hips for me, sweetheart," I murmur.

She groans as she does what I ask. "God, I've *definitely* heard Sky say that in an audio," she groans while doing what I ask. "Was it the one where he runs into his ex at her shithead ex's party and sneak into the shithead ex's room and fuck..."

"On his bed?" I finish, sliding the pillow beneath her hips. "Damn, you may be his biggest fan."

"Ren's biggest fan? Undoubtedly. Sky's? According to the Reddit thread, that's definitely debatable."

"Ah yes, Sky's Sluts."

"You *know* about Sky's Sluts?"

I scoff. "Of course I do, sweetheart. I'm checking the subreddit at least twice a week."

She's quiet for a moment. "If you ever figure out my username, please ignore the feral replies I may have made in the past."

"Oh, I will *not* ignore those, MeetMeInStarsHollow." I tease.

"*Goddammit,*" she groans. "This is humiliating. When did you figure it out?"

"When I realized that user stopped posting around the same time we started dating. I'd never really paid attention before, but as soon as I understood the reference, I looked through your old replies. I'd know my girl anywhere." Her entire body shivers and breath catches as I run my index finger along the curve of her spine. I climb back onto the bed and slowly drape my body over hers, my chest pressed to her back and cock just above her ass, so she knows without a doubt what she's doing to me. I run my tongue along the side of her neck, tasting her salty-sweet sweat and earning the whimper I've become obsessed with. "You manifested us, sweetheart."

She turns her head and kisses me, slipping her tongue into my mouth and stroking mine with a silky touch.

I'll be careful with you. I promise with my kiss. *I'll be careful with your body, your heart, your life, your daughter. I promise.*

"You're gonna take such good care of me, aren't you?" she murmurs as she breaks the kiss.

"I don't think I've ever wanted to take care of anything as much as I want to take care of you."

She tries to hide her smile by turning her head, but it's no use. It's too bright, and you can't hide the sun. "Then get to taking care of me already, Lorenzo."

"So needy," I murmur, kissing her right shoulder blade.

She wiggles her ass and I swear into her soft skin as she rubs against my cock. "Right," she says sarcastically. "You're the one with the cock harder than stone and *I'm* the needy one."

"Woman," I warn, though it sounds more like desperate worship. With the pillow beneath her hips, her pussy is at the perfect level for me to sink into her.

I drape myself over her again, and guide myself to her entrance. "Spread those perfect thighs for me, sweetheart. Let me in." She does, and it's perfect. *She's* perfect. I exhale shakily as I press the head of my cock to her slick opening, cursing loudly as I slide in.

"*Fuck*," she curses, just as loud. Her head's turned to the side, cheek pressed into the mattress and eyes closed as she fists the sheets.

I still my movements. "You want more?"

"Please," she begs. "Give it to me."

I oblige, slowly pushing into her, and *god*, she feels incredible. So hot and wet and tight, like our bodies were made for one another. I pause the few times she tenses, pulling out, leaning forward to kiss her back, and praising her before slowly pushing in again. I repeat this until I'm fully seated in her, completely surrounded by this incredible woman.

I don't think I belong to myself anymore. My body, my heart, my future, it belongs to the perfect woman who's moaning my name.

"*Ren.*"

I slowly pull out of her, immediately missing the feel of her around me, and thrust back in. "*Fuck.*" I slide my left arm under her, cupping her breast and thumbing her nipple, and my right under her belly, pulling her closer into me.

"Just like that, sweetheart. You're taking me so well." *Well* doesn't cover the cacophony of feelings she's giving me, not even a little bit.

She squirms beneath me, twisting from side to side as she cries out with pleasure, the pleasure *I'm* giving her. I lean forward, and she turns her face. "Eyes on me," I encourage. Her lids flutter open, and her gray, hooded eyes are on me. "You're being such a good girl for me."

"I love you," she gasps, her body clenching around me. "I... fuck. I love you. Too much. Unsafely so."

I kiss her, letting her words soak into my body, reminding me how much she's trusting me with. How many of her fears she's facing for this, for me, for *us*.

I want to be gentle with her, but when she's moaning into my mouth and grasping at the sheets, it's *hard*.

"More," she gasps, pulling away from our kiss. "I need... more. Please..." Her sentence trails off with a moan when I thrust in with more force. Her sounds are loud, but not loud enough to mask the sound of our skin slapping together, and I'm obsessed with how filthy and natural it all sounds.

I move my hand from her belly to her thigh, my fingers digging into her stretch marks, her skin marked by her love. She rocks her body back to meet my thrusts with the same frantic energy I feel in my bones. She slips her hand beneath her body, gasping when her fingers circle her clit.

"Touching yourself for me, sweetheart?" I gasp, somehow able to form words in this state.

"Ungh." Her response is muffled and unintelligible. "No. Touching myself for me," she gasps, movements becoming jerkier and more desperate.

I bury my smile in her shoulder blade. "That's my girl" I praise. "Do it for you, sweetheart."

"Gonna come for you, though," Audrey says, words garbled. "I'm close."

I squeeze her nipple between my index finger and thumb, her responding cry an electrocution through my bones.

And then she's gasping, body tensing around me as she falls apart.

"Aud," I gasp, tightening my grip on her thigh and pulling her closer to me. "I can feel you coming, sweetheart. You feel so good."

She cries out, and my balls clench as I come inside her, filling her body. I want her to feel me everywhere, the same way I feel her everywhere. I drop my hand from her breast, wrapping my arm around her and gently rolling us to the side so we're spooning, my cock still pulsing inside her. She rests her head on my arm, breath heavy as I kiss the freckles on her back. There's a handful of them, like whoever created her took care to place these marks only where they were needed, like they had a "less is more" mindset. Maybe they were right, because I'm able to kiss each and every one multiple times while we catch our breaths.

"So. Good," Audrey breathes, and my chest inflates with pride at the fact this woman, who only looked at the sexual encounters of her past with disdain, is currently trembling with the aftershocks of her pleasure in my arms. That Sky's audios made her give herself the pleasure she missed out on all those years, and that I get to give it to her now.

"So. Good," I agree, exhaling shakily as I press my forehead to her shoulder. "So. Good."

I'm not a scholar, but I am a reader. Even in romance, a genre that can be considered lowbrow, a plethora of words exist for everything. Synonyms for love, for beautiful, for *good*… and despite having read over fifty romance books in the last year, good is the only word I can think of to describe how it feels to have her tucked into my front like this, how it feels to still be inside her. But maybe there's a contradiction in the simplicity of the word, kind of like the contradiction in the simplicity of the word "love." How can a word meaning so much, meaning something different to every human to exist, be so simple? So unoriginal?

Maybe that's what this is. Having the woman I love, and the woman who loves me, in my arms is simply *good*.

Chapter 40

Audrey

Playlist: Late Night Talking | Harry Styles

Sex with Ren was so mind-blowing that—dare I say it?—it was worth waiting a decade and a half for.

While I'm desperate to stay in the post-coital quiet, Ren reminds me I have to pee after sex.

Which is something my reckless ass *never* did after sex in high school, so Ren mansplains why it's important I do it.

"Don't get up yet," he says, flustered as he nudges me back against the sheets. He runs to the bathroom, a damp washcloth in hand. "Let me help clean you up."

I adjust myself to watch, but instead of cleaning, he just stares. He put his glasses back on, and it takes me back to when he saw my toy for the first time.

"Speechless?" I tease, weaving my hand into his hair.

He nods and reaches his hand between my thighs. Instead of wiping away his cum, he uses his fingers to push it back into me. I gasp at the sensation, my pussy sensitive from his thorough fucking.

"I read that in a book once," he murmurs, eyes fixated on my cunt. "Always wanted to try it."

After going to the bathroom, I come back into his room wearing my glasses and an oversized black t-shirt with the phrase "Musical puns are my forte" across the front.

He does a double take when I enter, and I'm certain I do the same. He's shirtless, his tattoos a dark contrast against his flushed skin, gray sweatpants hanging low on his hips and highlighting the V on his lower belly. Sky has tens of thousands of listeners, and *I'm* the one who gets to see Ren like this.

"Where did those come from?" Ren asks, blinking in confusion at me.

"You gave me the shirt," I remind him, peering down at it. Ren's four inches taller than me, so while the shirt is tight across my chest, it hangs to my mid-thigh. He's staring at my face, and it dawns on me. "Oh!" My hands fly to my face, touching the wire frames of my glasses. "These?"

He scoffs. "Yeah, *those.* 'Those,' she says, like the damn things didn't appear magically on her face," he mutters to himself.

"I keep contact solution and an extra pair in my purse, as well as extra meds. Did you think I came over tonight ready to raw dog it?"

The dopiest grin spreads across his face. "I mean... we *did* raw dog it..."

"Oh my god." I roll my eyes and continue into the room.

"I thought you wanted to see where the magic happened?" he says as I begin to climb back into bed.

I raise a brow. "Was that not here? Is there someplace else where you have incredible sex you want to show me?"

Ren smirks. "Something like that. I want to show you where I record..."

"Oh, *hell* yes," I hiss, scrambling off the mattress. I'd forgotten the whole reason he took me to his apartment. "Show me."

He chuckles softly and envelops my hand with his before leading me out the door.

"*Meow*!" screams the little fluffball sitting outside his door.

"Not now, Leia," Ren says absentmindedly, pulling me past her and further down the hallway. "Daddy has to show Mommy the magic."

"*Mommy*?" I tease. "Piper would throw a fit if she heard that."

Ren stops us in front of a closed door. "She'll get over it," he responds, still absentmindedly. "You are entering a space no one but myself has entered before."

"Lucky me," I tease.

"It's my sacred place, a place where I shed everything Ren's supposed to be and am just Sky."

My heart flutters in my chest. "Okay," I tell him quietly. "Thank you for letting me in."

"*Meow*?" Leia asks while weaving between my feet.

I look at Ren, who's gazing at his cat child with a furrowed brow. "I think she wants to come too."

He sighs heavily. "*Fine*." He bends over and scoops Leia into his arms. She rubs her face along his, purring happily at being held by him, and what is *wrong* with me? Am I jealous of a goddamn cat?

Ren turns the doorknob, and honestly, I'm disappointed at the lack of a code or lock. I was imagining his studio to be akin to Dexter's laboratory.

But no, it's a simple spare room with a fiddle leaf fig in the corner and a monstera next to the door. It has a big bay window, a large desk and a plush armchair, and a bunch of recording equipment set up. There's a laptop and a monitor, post-it notes stuck on the desk with notes like "come harder?" scribbled on them. Next to the desk is a rolling cart equipped with a pink sparkly pencil case, a brown leather belt, and other random objects. A small succulent lives in the corner of his desk, right next to a large pair of lilac wireless headphones with the 4Play logo on each ear.

"So, this is where the magic happens," I say, stepping further into the room. I drag my finger along the edge of the desk, reading more of the colorful sticky notes stuck to his desk. " *mask kink script?" "practice whimpers to make more realistic." "look through subreddit for listener feedback." "call millie for her birthday."*

"Is Millie's birthday soon?" I ask, tracing the edge of the post-it note.

"That's from last month," Ren answers. "I haven't gotten around to throwing them away." He's fidgeting with his St. Anthony medal with the hand that isn't holding Leia, whose satisfied purrs rival the volume of a motorcycle.

Me too, girl. Me. Too.

"Tell me about this mask kink note," I say teasingly. "What inspired that?"

His blush deepens. "Nope, I'm not telling you."

I tilt my head to the side. "What! Why not?"

He narrows his eyes. "You know exactly why, you unrelenting woman."

I bite my lip to stifle my giggle. "Will I make fun of you for it?"

"Most definitely."

I clasp my hands and put them beneath my chin, blinking at him pleadingly. He groans. "What if I promise not to?" I ask innocently.

"Then you would end up breaking your promise."

I wince. "Damn, that bad?"

"That bad," he confirms.

"Does it have to do with *Star Wars*? Are you wearing a Carrie Fisher mask and wearing that skimpy bikini..." I trail off at the look on Ren's face. He seems intrigued, and that worries me. "Stop making that face. That's not a fantasy you have." If I demand it, it makes it true, right?

"I mean. That's not what the audio was gonna be about, but now that you mention it..."

As he rambles about his newfound fantasy of dressing in the costume most straight men fantasize about their female partner wearing, something in the rolling cart catches my eye.

"Oh my fucking *god*!" I shriek.

The noise startles both Leia and Ren, the former wrestling her way out of Ren's arms and leaping over his shoulder onto the floor. She sprints out of the room as I lunge for the cart, clenching my fist around the black fabric.

"Jesus *Christ*, Aud. What the..." He's silent when I turn around, a Ghostface mask in my hand.

"Please tell me it's because we started watching *Scream*," I beg, nearly vibrating with excitement.

His face of horror morphs into a self-satisfied smirk. "Ah, you're into it."

"I never said that." I toss the mask to him, and he catches it, shit-eating grin still in place. "Put it on," I demand.

Ren takes his glasses off and places them on the edge of the desk. He slips the mask over his head and looks at me. "You have a mask kink. I was right."

"Sure," I say, biting my fist to keep in my laughter. I can see how this image would definitely work for a lot of his listeners, cat scratches red on his chest, tattoos on full display, and those evil gray sweatpants hanging on to his hips for dear life. "Will you read the script for me?" I ask, batting my eyelashes despite the fact his vision is currently impaired by both his lack of glasses and the mask.

"You can't make fun of me when I enlarge the font," he says, closing the office door.

"I wouldn't dream of it," I agree.

He sits at his desk, mask still in place, and turns the computer on. He opens a file folder and clicks around until a document is pulled up. I keep my word, not laughing when he enlarges it to a forty-eight-point font.

"Hello, slut," he says, lowering his voice to Sky's. *Oh, we're just going there.* "I bet you didn't expect to see me..."

"No, I didn't," I respond.

He turns his masked face to me. "Aud, you don't have to answer. It's like... rhetorical."

"Oh. I guess I'm used to answering when I'm alone with my headphones and toy..." I sigh wistfully and trail my nails over his shoulder.

It doesn't elicit a single goosebump. Not one shiver. "I get it, but... it's kind of taking me out of my Sky mindset, you know? Like I have to stay in the zone to record and stay in character and..."

I bark out a laugh. "Okay, diva."

He wraps his arm around my waist and rolls closer to me, burying his face just below my breasts. He says something, but with the mask covering his mouth *and* his face buried in the t-shirt, I have no idea what it is.

"What?"

He sighs and straightens. "I don't mean to be a diva, but it's how I do a good job. That's what it is, you know? A job. I enjoy it, but it's not something I'd do if I weren't being paid. It's not arousing or sexual or pleasurable for me. I love that it is for so many people, but that's not what it is for me."

I hear what he's saying, I respect it, and I know he's serious. But he's still wearing that damn mask.

I gently take it off him and search his eyes. "That's fair," I tell him, dropping the mask to the floor. "And I can literally continue to not be involved with the process if that's what you need."

"I mean... I'm not aroused when I record," he says. "And I don't want to be, the idea of thousands of people listening to me in such a vulnerable state?" He shudders.

"What if you recorded something just for the person you want to be aroused with?" I say carefully.

He frowns. "You mean... you?"

I bite my lip to hold in a giggle. "Yes. Me."

He licks his lower lip, and I have to mentally hold myself back from leaning forward and nipping at his tongue. "Would you like that?"

I can't help the shiver wracking through my body at the thought of an audio just for me. Of Ren, not Sky, in my ears while I pleasure myself. Of me pleasuring him while he records an audio that no one but us will hear.

He raises a brow. "Oh, you *would* like that."

"Maybe a little," I admit, cheeks flushing.

"You want me to record something for you like I'm alone?" he asks, his hand wandering from my waist to my ass and squeezing. I squeak and he grins. "Just for us?"

I nod. "I want to make it clear I don't have an issue with what you do. I'm proud of the work you do, actually. But I also really like that there's parts of you only I get to see. Like the fact you want to wear a skimpy bikini and..."

He groans and pushes away from me. "It's my own damn fault, isn't it?"

"Yep."

He puts his glasses on before clicking around on his computer and messing with the microphone.

I squeeze my thighs together, desperate for even the tiniest bit of relief from the ache in my center.

"I can see you." This motherfucker is too smug, smiling at his own reflection on the monitor. Someone needs to take the wind out of his sails.

Oh. I guess that's me.

I slip my hand between my legs, gasping when my fingers make contact with my clit. Suddenly, he's not smiling anymore.

"Wait, wait." Ren frantically clicks around on the computer before meeting my eyes. "It's recording. Come here."

I pull my hand away and step toward him. He's impatient and needy, though, and fists the hem of the shirt and pulls me closer.

"Show me your fingers," he demands, and like the desperate slut he turns me into, I obey, lifting a hand that is literally dripping with my arousal.

"All that for me, sweetheart?" He palms his cock through his sweatpants, the outline obvious and straining against the fabric.

"There's something else I'd rather put in my mouth," I say sweetly, tracing my lips with my own arousal. He lets out the sluttiest little whimper for me.

I love how desperate we are for each other, how absolutely unabashed our attraction and desperation is. I lick my bottom lip, enjoying the fact I'm the one tasting the salty-sweetness of myself when he so obviously wants to. Without breaking eye contact, I slowly lower myself to my hands and knees.

"Move back," I instruct him, and the speed at which he pushes his armchair backwards is almost comical. I crawl beneath the desk, making sure to move slowly enough he's tortured by the sight of my bare ass and cunt.

It works, and he reacts with a choking, unintelligible noise that makes my nipples harden. As much as I love him taking charge and taking care of me, I love making him desperate and pathetic just as much. I adjust myself and sit on my heels, eye level with his straining length. There's a wet spot on his sweatpants, and I'm *delighted* by it. I trace the outline of his cock with my fingertip. He swears and jerks in his chair, and more pre-cum smears on the fabric.

"Audrey, *please*," he begs.

Like I said. I *love* when he's pathetic.

He moves one hand from the arm of the chair and reaches into the front of his sweatpants to pull out his cock, but I stop him. "Don't touch," I instruct, wrapping my hand around his wrist and moving it back to where it was. "Just watch."

He moans, throaty and deep. "You're trying to kill me, aren't you?"

I smirk and lean forward, licking along the length of his bulge. I can tell he wants to touch me, to pull his cock out and fuck himself, but he doesn't. "Look at you, keeping your hands to yourself," I say, pulling the front of his sweatpants down until his cock springs out. "You're such a good boy when you're losing your mind over me."

He starts to say something, but it turns into a loud cry when I spit on his cock, wrap my lips around the head and suck the way I know he likes. "Come on, pretty boy," I say as I pull away, a string of spit between my mouth and his cock. "Tell me how good it is. You're excellent at giving the people what they want."

"I... fuck," he stammers as I take him in my mouth again. "It's so good, Audrey. It feels so good." I moan around him, bobbing my head and taking him as deep as I can. I guess I'm doing a good job, because after that, he only moans and whimpers for a few minutes, until his hips start thrusting to meet my movements.

I stop and pull away and he swears. I crawl out from under the desk as he pants heavily in his chair. I straddle his lap, cup his head in my hands, and kiss him as hard as I can.

"Come on, baby," I murmur, grinding my soaking cunt against him. "I need your cock."

His hands are clumsy when he grasps himself with one hand and my hip with the other. I love the way he touches the parts of my body I don't always love. The way it feels for his fingers to dig into the dimples and stretch marks and softness of my body. The way it feels like not only can he handle all of me, but he delights in it.

Ren notches the head of his cock at my entrance, and I slowly sink down until I'm taking all of him. He buries his face in my neck, inhaling deeply like he wants to commit the smell of our sex to memory. His hands roam my back, hips, and thighs, and I cover them, trying to restrain them behind his back. I'm inspired by an audio Sky did earlier this year, but unfortunately, it's a much more difficult task than I expected.

The brown leather belt he keeps with the rest of his props catches my eye, and I lean back to grab it. When I make eye contact with him, his eyes are wide and glistening with excitement. He gently squeezes my hips before putting his hands behind his back, like he can read my mind. I reach around him, looping the belt around his wrists to secure them between his back and the chair.

"Are you comfortable?" I ask, slipping my index finger between the belt and his hand.

He wraps his hand around my finger and squeezes gently. "It's perfect. You're perfect."

I nod and move my hips in a circle, testing the waters. The water is just fine apparently, because Ren's eyes flutter closed when I clench around him. "*Fuck*. You feel so good, sweetheart."

I slowly lift my hips up until only the head of his cock is still inside me.

"*Audrey*," he whimpers. "Please, sweetheart. Please."

"Please what?" I tease. "Please stop? Please get me some water? Please untie my hands? Please *what*, Lorenzo?"

"Please ride my cock, hard. I need you. I need this pussy. Use me to make yourself come." God, I almost come right then from the pure need in his voice. "Please..."

I drop my hips, enveloping him once more. Our mutual moans of pleasure make a beautiful duet, and I do exactly what he begged me to do. I ride him, hard.

I loosen my arms around his neck and lean back, snaking one hand down my breasts and belly until I find my clit, swollen and sensitive and aching.

"Yes, yes, yes," he chants. "Touch your clit. Please, I need you to come again."

He sucks at my neck as I frantically rub my clit, internally begging my body to let me have this, let me have what he's giving me.

"Please, please, please." It takes me a minute to realize I'm the one chanting this time, that I'm begging my body to work the way I so want it to.

It's fast and unexpected when my orgasm comes, like a single firework exploding in the sky instead of steady, continuous explosions. I cry out his name, slumping against his chest as I clench around him, triggering his own orgasm.

For a few moments, the only sounds are our heavy breaths and the heartbeat I can clearly hear with the side of my face pressed against his chest.

"Sweetheart? I don't want to interrupt but I need you to free my hands. I really, really need to hold you right now." Ren's voice is pained, like it's causing him physical harm not to have his hands on me. Considering what he told me about his need for aftercare our first night, that very well may be the case.

"Oh!" I exclaim. "Right. Yes." I reach around him and unfasten the belt. He pulls his hands free quickly, wrapping his arms around me and squeezing me to him. Like he's a plant and I'm the sun keeping him alive. I kiss the top of his head.

"I love you," he breathes, words slurred, and I'm not sure if it's because of the fact his face is buried in my neck or because of his hazy afterglow.

"I love you too, pretty boy." My voice is teasing, but I know he feels how true it is, too.

Chapter 41

Audrey

Playlist: The Bones - with Hozier | Maren Morris, Hozier

The next morning, I drool as Ren gets ready for work. I don't think we went more than three hours sleeping before one of us woke the other, needy and feral.

It was fun, but now I want to stay in bed and see how desperate I can make him. I mean, this man is standing in front of a mirror, whistling the *Bluey* theme song while tying a neon pink tie with swirling music notes around his neck.

My ovaries are losing their shit, and I think I get the breeding kink thing.

"Call in," I demand for what must be the six hundredth time.

He grins at me through the mirror. "But sweetheart, the winter concert is in two weeks, and it would be unbelievably cruel to put a poor sub in that position."

"I need you to get me pregnant immediately," I respond.

He laughs. "Okay, well, I'm otherwise occupied at the moment, so that will have to wait." He walks to the bed and sits on the edge. I'm still blissfully bare and tangled in the sheets that smell like him. "You can stay, if you want," he offers before kissing me. "Listen to that audio we made last night again..."

My nipples harden at the thought and I sigh. "Since you're being a responsible adult, I probably should, too."

"Adulthood is a scam," he murmurs, pulling away from me. I don't let him go far before grabbing the front of his shirt and pulling him in for another deep kiss.

Ren takes me home on his way to school, and I force myself to shower before going to the inn. Doing such routine things without him feels wrong—he's ingrained himself into so much of my life. I'm finding that after years of choosing to be alone, of choosing not to let anyone get close enough to become part of the day-to-day, life isn't as exhausting when I spend it with the person who makes it better.

When I open the door the night before Thanksgiving, there's Ren, homemade pie in hand, and a cat carrier on his shoulder. "Hey," he says, stepping through the doorway and leaning in to kiss me. I let his lips press to mine, for just a moment, before I take the pie from him and Piper runs in for her routine catnapping.

"Mom made the pie," he tells me as he walks into the kitchen. "It's blueberry. She insisted I bring it."

His hands wrap around my waist, trapping me between him and the countertop. He ducks his head to kiss the side of my neck, one hand moves to grip my hip, and the other slides down the front of my belly.

I stiffen, and without giving it much thought, snag his wrists and step out of his way, pulling my big, threadbare t-shirt down farther.

"Aud?" he asks, and I hate hearing his worry.

"Sorry," I say, turning to him, but refusing to meet his eyes. I try to smile as I wrap my arms around my middle. "Just warm in here because I've been cooking. The pie sounds great though, Piper's gonna love it."

He doesn't seem to buy my lie. His gaze looks me up and down, and I feel nauseous that he sees me the same way I saw myself in the mirror this morning.

"What's wrong?" he asks quietly, because of *course* he knows something is wrong.

"Nothing," I lie again. I continue making the cheesecake we'll eat for breakfast tomorrow, hoping he'll drop it. "Was Piper happy you brought Leia?"

He's quiet when he stands beside me, beginning to tackle the dishes piled in the sink. Then, he speaks again. "Talk to me, sweetheart," he encourages softly. "What's going on?"

Tears threaten to spill. How annoying that he's able to see through me.

"It's not important," I say, voice trembling.

"*You're* important and so is the way you feel. Please, Aud? I want to try to understand."

"When I got home, I took a shower," I whisper, "And when I looked in the mirror, I hated what I saw. Most days I'm fine, but some days, it's hard. And when I think about how you could have any woman you wanted but you're stuck with me..."

"*Stuck* with you?" Ren turns me around, confusion on his face. He cups my face. "Audrey Elise," he says sincerely, "it's the honor of a lifetime to love you. I know I said I'd love you no matter what your body looked like, and that's one thousand percent true, but I *do* love your body. All of it. I understand you don't sometimes, and that society has ridiculously impossible beauty standards for women, but you're a goddamn goddess, sweetheart."

I sniffle. "I doubt goddesses feel like this."

He grabs my hand. "Come on."

"What are you doing?" I ask, confused as he pulls me out of the kitchen and down the hallway. He opens my bedroom door, closing it once I'm in the room.

"I'm not doing anything," he says simply, turning to face me. I bite my lower lip as I scan his body. God, this man calling me a goddess when he's in front of me looking like that? All grumpy-looking with his unruly hair in his face and slutty little glasses on and sleeves rolled up to his elbows.

He looks positively scrumptious.

"You, however," he continues, "are going to be stripping."

"What?" I squeak.

"Can I show you how I see you?" he asks gently, stepping forward and rubbing my arms. "Do you think we can look at your body in a nonjudgmental way, sweetheart?"

I hate the idea. I hate it and I want him to know I hate it.

But more than that, I want to feel better. This shame I feel is a vicious cycle: shame about my body, then shame about feeling a certain way about my body when I have a daughter who looks to me for guidance.

"I can try," I say, mouth dry and voice hoarse.

He presses his lips to my forehead and it feels like he's trying to siphon out the bad thoughts in my brain and replace it with the way he feels about me.

I strip out of my clothes, and when I'm just in my underwear, Ren steps behind me and plants his hands on my shoulders. He gently guides me until we're in front of the full-length mirror attached to my wall.

My stomach churns as I run my eyes over my body, my eyes immediately drawn to the lines and dimples, the rolls and dips. The cellulite on my thighs and upper arms, and the way the waistband of my underwear digs into the fat of my stomach. They scream at me, reminding me why I'm not good enough.

Ren gathers my hair, sweeping it over to one side to rest his chin on my shoulder as I instinctively raise my arms to cross over my body. He catches my hands, lacing our fingers together and bringing one hand up to kiss the back of mine. "Can you tell me what you don't like?" he asks without an ounce of judgment in his voice.

I blink back tears. "I... my stretch marks. They're everywhere." I watch in the mirror as his eyes move down my body, stopping at my breasts, my hips, my thighs.

"What else?" he asks.

"The rolls on my sides and back," I tell him, voice wobbly. He doesn't say anything, only surveys my body.

"Keep going."

"There are these dimples right above my elbow. And my breasts are so saggy and my belly so wrinkly. It hangs down, too." I want to point to them, but Ren's grip on my hands is tight. I hate that he knows if he lets go of my hands, I'm going to cover up. "And my thighs and upper arms jiggle and have cellulite."

He squeezes my hands encouragingly. "It sounds like your brain is being really fucking mean to you."

I let out a sob, the dam finally breaking. "Yeah," I say, voice cracking.

He turns my body towards him, wrapping his arms around me and holding me as I cry. He doesn't say I'm wrong for feeling this way, but lets me feel with no restrictions, no conditions.

After a few minutes of him rubbing my back and telling me that it's okay to cry and to feel this way, I take a step back and wipe my eyes. "I feel like such a bad person, such a bad mom." I admit, shame washing over my body. "I'm raising a daughter whose body will change, and this is how I am about my own changing."

He puts his hands on my waist and pulls me in a little closer, pressing his forehead to mine. "You are *not* a bad mom or person for feeling very human things about your body," he tells me, tucking a strand of hair behind my ear. "You're a person doing her best in a world that idealizes a certain type of body. It's not your fault you don't fit in a tiny box, the box should have space for bodies like yours, and so many others."

"Says the male beauty ideal," I say tearily, hoping my joke lands. I poke one of his abs.

"Hey." He cups my face and adjusts my head so he's looking directly into my eyes. "My body isn't better because society says it is. My body isn't better, *period*. It's a body that could change, like yours has. Like my sisters' have. I am not *better* because my body type fits in the tiny box, and no one is worse because theirs doesn't. You're not magically going to love your body, even if I do. That's okay. You don't have to love it. I just don't want you to hate it, because your body..." He exhales heavily. "...Aud, you make me want to go back to church, because whoever created you deserves to be worshipped as much as you do."

He drops one of my hands, tracing his own over the stretch marks. I inhale sharply, and his eyes find mine in the mirror. "I love these marks," he murmurs, eyes intent on mine. He's taken to wearing his glasses more often and it makes me weak in the knees. "I love them because they represent your body changing to accommodate the growth of one of my favorite people in the world."

Hearing him refer to Piper as one of his favorite people in the world brings tears back to my eyes.

His touch is gentle as it moves upward, resting over the loose skin on my belly, his fingers spreading to cover it. "She grew right here. Your body did what it had to to keep her, and you, safe. It expanded with your universe to make room for Piper."

Tears are streaming down my face as his hands move again, lightly tracing the sides of my breasts. "You literally nourished her with this body, Aud." He says it like he's witnessed a miracle. "Your body took care of her, *and* you." He gently turns me towards him, cupping my face and leaning forward to kiss away my tears. "Can you look at yourself that way? With a neutral attitude towards your body's functionality?"

I peer out of his embrace, making eye contact with myself. I try to see myself the way he described me, see my body as something that created my favorite human, the body that allowed me to nourish and hold her and stroke her hair when she's sad.

While I don't feel one hundred percent better, I can acknowledge what my body has done not only for me, but for the daughter I love so much.

I squeeze Ren tighter and bury my face into his chest, inhaling the scent that is as safe and familiar as my own home. "Thank you," I whisper.

"I know it doesn't fix everything, but I hope it helped a little," he says, kissing the top of my head.

"It did," I tell him, tipping my head to peer at him. "But honestly, when you told me to strip, I expected it to be sexual."

He blinks at me in surprise. "Would me sexualizing you while you sobbed about your body have been helpful?" He sounds genuinely curious, like he's making note of how to deal with the situation in the future.

"No, but I'm not sobbing now, am I?" I say slowly, because what's more arousing than an emotionally intelligent and sensitive man? I drag the tip of my index finger along his sternum, knowing my cheeks are tearstained and eyes puffy beneath my glasses.

He rests his hands on my hips, squeezing gently. "You want me to tell you the parts of you that make my cock ache, sweetheart?"

I dig my teeth into my bottom lip to stifle my moan. Is it ridiculously embarrassing that I'm horny as hell after my little mental breakdown?

Yes, but that doesn't stop me.

"Can I take your bra and underwear off?" Ren asks, slipping his finger between my shoulder and bra strap.

"Please," I say, not caring how desperate I sound. I *am* desperate. I reach behind me to lock the door. "Was Piper wearing her headphones?"

"Yes," he answers breathily, reaching behind me and undoing my bra.

"Excellent," I respond as I lower my arms, the fabric falling to the floor.

Next comes my underwear, which he gets to his knees to pull down. I lift each foot and shudder when he lifts the fabric to his face, inhaling deeply.

"I like when you do that," I admit, feeling my blush covering my body.

"Good," he says simply, looking at me like I'm the sun appearing after a rainstorm. "I like doing it."

I open my mouth to say something, but he's on his feet, angling my head and kissing me hard enough to make me wonder if my lips will bruise.

"This mouth," he murmurs, tracing my lips with his thumb after pulling away. "This mouth kisses me like I've never been kissed. This mouth sucks my cock like she's trying to suck out my soul."

My cheeks burn and I glance away, but he firmly clasps my chin in his hand, forcing me to look at him. "Uh-uh," he says darkly, and I know he's in charge. "You wanted this, sweetheart. You're gonna take it for me like a good girl."

"Yes, sir," I promise.

He kisses me again, one hand tracing down my body, the other on my waist. I gasp and jolt when he cups my pussy and gently squeezes. "This cunt? The prettiest, tightest cunt I've ever fucked."

I bury my face in his neck. "*Ren.*"

He spins me so I'm facing the mirror, moving his hand from my waist to my neck, squeezing with the perfect amount of pressure to make me even wetter. "Look at yourself."

And I do, I see chest heaving, body flushed, nipples peaked.

I see myself how he sees me when he fucks me.

I look *hot*.

Ren parts me and uses one finger to circle my clit, not quite touching me where I'm desperate for him. He lifts his hand and I take his fingers into my mouth. "Sweetest pussy I've ever tasted," he murmurs into my ear, and I shiver, releasing his fingers.

"Your ass, your hips, these goddamn thighs..." He groans, tracing over each part of my body as he says it, the wet warmth of my spit on his fingers lingering after his touch. "I can't believe I get to touch them, hold them while you fuck me."

He hesitates, his hands lingering below my breasts. I love him so much when his eyes meet mine in the mirror, uncertain and waiting for my consent. "Yes," I breathe, and his hands cup my breasts, gently squeezing and massaging. He traces his thumb over my already hard nipples, somehow making them tighten even further.

"Your breasts..." I can't tell if his voice is awestruck, or pain stricken. Maybe both. "I will never forgive the piece of shit who made you think these are anything less than perfect. That *you* are anything less than perfect. It feels like my hands were made to hold them. Like my mouth was made to kiss them." He pauses, like he's not sure if he should say what he wants to. He leans in closer, his facial hair scratchy against the shell of my ear. "My cock made to fuck them."

My knees go weak at his words, and thank god this man is holding me, because otherwise I'd be a boneless heap on the ground. "*Fuck*," I moan, leaning my head against my shoulder.

He smirks, playfully twisting my nipples. "You like that, sweetheart? You want me to fuck those pretty tits of yours?"

"Yes," I whimper helplessly. "So much."

"One day I will," he promises, kissing my cheek.

"Why not today?" I ask, and he freezes mid-nipple pinch, his face buried in my hair.

"What?" he says in the highest pitch I've ever heard come out of his mouth.

I feel so empowered after that, sensual and sure of what my body does to him. I step out of his embrace and turn to face him. His eyes are wide and face pale.

"You want to... now?" he squeaks.

"Is my pretty boy all talk?" I tease, reaching to cup his face in my hands.

He shakes his hands frantically. "No, I meant it. I really meant it." His eyes drift towards my breasts, and I angle his face to mine. He gulps.

"Be a good boy for me, baby," I say sweetly. "There's lube in my nightstand drawer."

I'm certain it takes less than a second for him to get the lube and come back, white knuckling the small bottle in his hands.

I get to my knees, tucking my hair behind my ears as he sits on the edge of the bed. "I've never done this before," he admits bashfully.

I smile at him, running my hands over his thighs. "Me neither," I whisper. "It's kind of cool we still get to be nervous about a few firsts together, huh?"

He leans down to capture my lips with his, gently sucking on my lower lip. He shakes his head in wonder as he pulls away. "I can't believe this is real. I can't believe *you're* real."

I push my breasts together, lifting them as I arch my back for him.

He opens his mouth, running his tongue over his bottom lip as he grips his length through his jeans. "You're sure?"

"Please," I whimper, losing grip on any control I had.

Breath heavy, Ren frees his gorgeous cock from his pants, hard as hell and pre-cum dripping from the head. He leans forward, drizzling lube on the tops of my breasts, and watching in wonder as I spread the liquid.

"I can't believe you're real," he repeats, shaking his head as I lift my breasts again.

"You've said that already," I whisper, my smile crooked.

"It bears repeating. Over, and over, and over again." He bites his lip and fists the base of his cock. I lean forward, enveloping his hardness between my breasts, both of us gasping at the sensation.

I gaze up at him as I squeeze my tits around him, lifting and lowering them, a thrill running through my entire body at the ecstasy on his face. I want more of it, more of his pleasure, more of him losing his mind.

The next time I lower my tits, I take the head of his cock between my lips, eyes still intent on him as he lets out a strangled moan.

I release his cock with a *pop*. "You have to be quiet, baby," I say. "Noise cancelling headphones aren't foolproof." I dig my hand into his pocket, pulling out the lacy underwear I indulged in a few weeks ago.

Ren immediately catches on, taking the fabric from me and putting it in his mouth. "Good boy," I praise, pumping his cock with my tits before I suck on the head again. He groans muffled by my underwear, and leans back on his elbows, fisting the comforter so tightly his knuckles turn white.

This man continually has turned me on, but I can't remember the last time I was this wet. I can feel my arousal dripping down my inner thighs, my cunt screaming for attention. My movements become more frantic, and, god, he loves it, whimpering and gasping. "Eyes on me," I instruct. "I want you to watch when you come on my face."

His eyes widen as a mix between a whimper and a groan escapes from his mouth. When I think he's about to come, he's lurching forward, pulling my glasses off my face. I'm so surprised by the action that the spurts of cum take me by surprise, landing on my cleavage and face.

He pulls me onto the bed with his superhuman strength. I squint through my cum-covered lashes as he whips his shirt over his head and uses it to wipe my face.

When he's finished, I open my eyes and my gaze immediately meets his. His face spreads into the softest, warmest smile.

"You stole my glasses!" I tease, jabbing my index finger into his bare chest.

He rolls his eyes and returns my glasses to me. "I mean, *personally*, I'd hate getting cum on mine, but I'll remember you don't hate it for next time."

I smirk at him. "'Next time'? You're so confident there's a 'next time' you'll come on my face?"

He doesn't answer right away, tracing my collarbone with his thumb and bringing it to my lips. I open to take it into my mouth, but instead he rubs the cum from his thumb onto my lips. When he pulls his hand away, I lick my lips, tasting the saltiness.

This time, it's his turn to smirk. "Yeah, sweetheart," he murmurs, pulling me into him and pressing his lips to my forehead. "I'm pretty sure there will be a next time. But for right now…"

I gasp as he buries his head between my thighs. This time, I'm putting my underwear in my own mouth to keep myself quiet.

Chapter 42

Ren

Playlist: Glittery - From the Kacey Musgraves Christmas Show | Kacey Musgraves [feat. Troye Sivan]

December

Over the next few weeks, Audrey and Piper become a part of my daily routine. One Thursday in early December, I get a text from Piper asking for a ride home because she doesn't want to take the bus. I agree, but regret it when we find ourselves in an argument about Hayden Christensen's performance as Anakin in the prequels.

"Just because he's attractive doesn't mean he's a good actor," Piper argues as she uses her free arm to unlock the front door to the cottage. Leia is happily curled in her other arm, because Piper somehow convinced me to go back to my apartment and pick up Leia. I'm convinced Piper has weird mind control powers, because suddenly I was unlocking the door to my apartment with no recollection of driving there.

"I'm not *saying* he's a good actor because he's attractive," I respond, closing the door behind me. "I'm *saying* he's a good actor *because* he's a good actor. He also just so happens to be attractive."

While Piper launches into her rebuttal, I head to the kitchen, kissing Audrey on the cheek before washing my hands and cutting the vegetables on the counter.

"But you know who's hot *and* is a good actor? That dude who plays Obi Wan," Piper shouts from her spot on the couch.

"You're right," I agree, mostly so I can talk to Audrey. "What's for dinner?"

That night, when Audrey and I brush our teeth side by side, I realized she never asked me to stay, and I never asked if I could.

I just... did. Like we both have decided this is where I'm supposed to be.

"Mom hates Christmas," Piper informs me in the middle of class a few weeks later. The two of us are sitting at the piano at the inn, while Audrey's reading a romance I gave her at the front desk. When I glance towards the front desk out of the corner of my eye, Audrey flinches, like Piper's words cause physical pain.

Similarly, I can feel the chasm in my heart at that moment.

"She's always sad, but pretending she's not," Piper continues, and I turn my attention back to her. "And she says she's not crying on Christmas morning, but her eyes are always puffy and red when she finally comes out of her room for presents..."

Piper's voice fades as I look back at Audrey and meet her eyes. She smiles, but I know she's forcing it.

That night, I ask her about it after she unties my hands from the headboard.

"Did you let me sit on your face to butter me up, Lorenzo?" she asks teasingly, playing with my chain.

"You know I didn't. It's a coincidence you're soft and satiated in your afterglow."

She's silent for a beat before speaking again. "I used to love it. I loved any excuse for decorations and celebration, and for most of my adolescence, I'd insist to my parents we hang our stockings the day after Halloween." She exhales heavily, refusing to look at me. "And then I got pregnant."

I grab her hand, kissing the back of it as I weave our fingers together.

"Halloween is easy," she continues. "Pumpkins and skeletons and apple cider and handing out candy. Christmas is hard. Thanksgiving was easy to make our own, with the tradition of working, but Christmas was when the questions came. Why didn't she have a dad? Where were her grandparents? Why did other kids get more expensive gifts?"

I swallow roughly, the image of Audrey in her early twenties trying to give Piper the best life she could, feeling like she never was doing enough. "That sounds hard," I say earnestly.

"It was," she whispers. "Aunt Olivia tried to make it as special as possible, and we came to the cottage and made our own little traditions... but the season was a stark reminder of what I didn't have, of what I used to. It's gotten worse since Aunt Olivia died, because now Piper remembers what used to be different, too."

"What was your favorite tradition?" I ask, and it feels like my heart is filled with helium as a soft smile makes her face glow.

She tells me about how she and her parents would cut their own tree at Miller's Tree Farm, a small farm an hour northwest, then get hot apple cider before driving home. Her dad would set up the tree in the living room, and they'd spend the evening eating pizza and watching Christmas movies while decorating the tree.

"I always put the angel on the top," she reminisces wistfully.

The day before Christmas Eve, I text Piper.

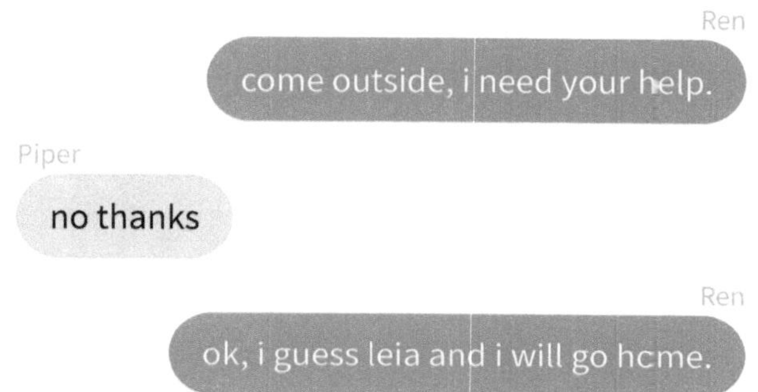

Piper's bolting down the porch steps exactly thirteen seconds later, skidding to a stop when she sees my car.

"No. Way." Her eyes are wide as saucers.

I grin. "Way. Think you're up to the challenge?"

"Hell, yeah," she says decidedly, cracking her knuckles. "Let's do it."

An hour later, Audrey comes home from work, freezing in the doorframe as she takes everything in. To be fair, her boyfriend and daughter wrapping lights around a seven-foot-tall tree in her living room while wearing footie pajamas and singing along with *The Muppets Christmas Carol* is a lot to take in.

"Mom!" Piper shouts excitedly, hopping down from the chair she's standing on. "We saved the angel for you! And your pajamas are on your bed!"

Audrey's staring at me, face unreadable, and I begin to fidget with my St. Anthony medal. "I'm sorry, I didn't think we'd have time to get it together, so I drove to Aurora Falls myself and got it and—*umph*!"

I'm cut off by Audrey throwing her arms around my neck and pressing her lips to mine.

"Oh my *god*!" Piper yells behind us. "This is a *family* establishment! Leia, cover your eyes!"

I chuckle against Audrey's lips before pulling away and tucking her hair behind her ears, lost in her eyes that glisten with unshed tears.

"Merry Christmas, sweetheart," I tell her, voice hoarse.

The next evening, the three of us head to my parents' for Christmas Eve dinner. It's loud and obnoxious, even without Kat and Steve there. Audrey drinks a little too much white wine and is giggling with Jo about something. Try as I might, I haven't been able to follow their conversation.

After dinner, we gather in the living room for presents.

"All right," Leo says, clapping his hands and rubbing them together enthusiastically.

"I'm afraid your days of being the youngest in the family are over, son," Dad says.

"Oh my god," I say before I can stop myself. "Is Mom pregnant again?"

"Lorenzo! I'm not pregnant!" Mom scolds while my siblings and I let out a simultaneous exhale of relief. "But Piper gets to go first, because *she's* the youngest."

Before I can say anything, Nic is rummaging under the tree and depositing a stack of wrapped gifts at Piper's feet. Piper stares down at them, wide eyed. "These... are for me?" she asks, voice barely audible.

"Did you do this?" Audrey whispers, voice shaky in my ear.

I shake my head, throat tight as Piper opens her first gift. "I didn't know," I said honestly.

That's when I notice everyone, except my parents, who are diligently documenting Piper's gift opening experience on their phones, is staring at me, grins on their faces.

And I think they know by taking care of Piper, they're taking care of me, too.

Every single one of my siblings got Piper a small but unbeliev-ably thoughtful gift—even Kat and Alex, who aren't here. Nic and Josh got her some fidgets she likes, Jo and Hunter gave her a gorgeous embroidery piece of the baby grand in the SandPiper Inn lobby, and Kat got her a classical composers calendar.

"No way!" Piper screeches as she unwraps her last gift, a long, rectangular package in silver wrapping paper. "Is this a..."

"YAMAHA 88-key Weighted Action Digital Piano with Sustain Pedal and Power Supply?" Dad finishes, obviously read-ing from his phone. "Sure is."

"Holy shit," I say, mouth agape. My parents *never* got me anything as expensive as one of those.

"The salesperson at the music supply store told us this was top-of-the-line," Mom adds anxiously, either taking pictures of or filming Piper's shocked reaction.

Piper's suddenly on her feet, throwing her arms around both of my parents' necks and pulling them in for a group hug. Audrey bursts into tears next to me, and my parents exchange over-excited looks over Piper while my siblings whoop and clap.

And me? Me, I never knew happiness like this could be e-ffortless.

Chapter 43

Audrey

Playlist: Oh shit...are we in love? | Valley

January

"Okay," I say, zipping the suitcase closed. "I think I have everything."

My train to the city leaves in half an hour, and I'm mentally running through the packing list I made for the conference. Ren lounges on my bed, legs stretched out in front of him and crossed at the ankle while he reads a smutty book on his e-reader. He offered to help me pack, but I told him the best help he could give me was his presence. He blushed, smiling bashfully, and it was damn precious.

"You have the stockings you want to wear with the green pencil skirt?" he asks, swiping his finger across the screen to turn the page.

"Fuck," I mutter, turning and rummaging through the open dresser drawer for my sheer black stockings. "What would I do without you?"

"You've spent years doing just fine on your own," he says, eyes still on his e-reader. "You're able to breathe because you don't have to anymore."

I shove my stockings into the front pocket of my suitcase before joining Ren on the bed and snuggling my face into the side of his neck.

"Piper's staying with Annika, right?" he asks, putting his e-reader down and kissing my temple.

"Mmhmm," I agree. "She rode her bike over a little earlier."

"With her stuff?" Ren asks, seemingly impressed.

"She'll come back and switch stuff out as she wants." I snuggle closer into him. "I have a great idea."

"Is your great idea to skip the conference and stay in bed instead?"

"You said it, not me."

He tilts my chin and kisses the tip of my nose. "Nope. You have to go be a badass and think about how needy you'll be the next time I'm in your bed." He nips at my lower lip.

"Brat," I grumble.

"Come on, Aud. Let's get you to the city so you can show everyone how magical you are." He reaches around me to grab his car keys from the bedside table. I, meanwhile, make no attempt to move.

"I don't feel magical, I feel like a potato. A potato going to a gathering of sweet potatoes and trying to pretend it's as pretty and sweet as the rest of them on the inside."

"Hey." Ren tilts my chin up, forcing me to meet his eyes. It's fucking sexy of him. What a dickhead. "I don't want to hear you shit-talking potatoes again. Or yourself. Potatoes are magic, and so are you. Potatoes are versatile and resilient. Like you. Also I'm only happy if I have you or some sort of potato dish in my mouth."

I pull away. "You're weird as hell."

"We've always known that, sweetheart. What does it say that, despite me being weird as hell, I can still make you come so hard you cry?"

"Okay, that was *once*," I sputter, cheeks reddening.

"Yeah, literally this morning," he counters. "I had to make sure you would be able to feel me the whole time you were away."

He drives me to the train station and kisses me before I make my way to the platform. I take a deep breath, both terrified and eager to see what comes next.

Chapter 44

Ren

Playlist: Never Let Me Go | Florence + The Machine

Audrey's been gone less than forty-eight hours, and I'm already dead inside.

I'm pathetic.

"You think you're in love with her, then?" Will asks, cursing as he's hit with a blue shell.

I know he's talking to me in an attempt to distract me from the race. He always does, and usually I'm better at ignoring him and not giving him what he wants.

But he isn't usually asking about Audrey.

"I love her," I say, like it's the most simple, straightforward thing in the world. And in a way, it is. "She's it for me."

"But are you ready to be a stepdad... *fuck*." Unlike me, Will can't multitask, and slips on a banana peel. I smirk as his chosen character, Donkey Kong, flails in distress, watching Mario, Waluigi, and Daisy speed past.

"Sucker," I snicker. "But, I mean. I'm not marrying her tomorrow." *Though I would.* "And Piper and I have a good relationship..."

"You piece of shit," Will interrupts, shaking his head in disgust as I cross the finish line, securing first place.

"I parent you and Leo more than I'd have to parent her," I joke, picking up my phone. "Speak of the devil, she just texted me."

I bark out a laugh as Will crosses the finish line, finishing in a respectable eleventh place. He looks at me questioningly and I show him the phone.

"This is the kid?" he asks, eyeing the screen like it has cooties.

"Piper," I affirm as my phone starts ringing. I smirk to myself before answering. "Are you dying?"

"Yes," Piper answers without even a hint of a beat. "I'm dying of Leia withdrawal. Let me in."

"The lock is broken on the front door, and I'm in apartment 3A. You can take her to Annika's for the night if it's okay with her parents," I sigh, knowing exactly what she wants.

The door squeaks as she pulls it open. "Wow, if I were a serial killer, you'd be dead," she says, sounding way too pleased by the idea.

"Well you're not, so—" I roll my eyes when I realize she already hung up on me. She's banging on the door less than twenty seconds later.

"We have a custody agreement! Don't make me call my lawyer!" Piper shouts between knocks.

"Door's unlocked," I call, and she pokes her head in, brow furrowed.

"I'm a little concerned about your mental health, if we're being honest," Piper says, helmet under her arm. "The lack of locked doors is worrisome. Do you have a death wish—who the fuck are you?"

"Will." He responds in a tone that shows he's staking his claim and right to be losing pathetically to Mario Kart in my home.

"Ren's never mentioned you," Piper fires back, crossing her arms over her chest.

This is untrue, but I'm unable to remind her of this before they're bickering again.

"He talks about your mom more than you," Will snaps back.

"I'm a *minor*, loser. That's a really fucking good thing."

"Piper, do you want to borrow Leia for the night? Also, you met at Sunday dinner, stop being weird." I raise my voice so she can hear me over the dying car noises coming from Will's mouth.

"Yes. Thank you," Piper responds, walking to the couch with her arms outstretched, all thoughts of her roasting a grown-ass man evaporated. Then she freezes, eyes widening. "Ren. What is that?"

I look behind me at where she's staring. "Oh. Uh, my guitar?"

"You're cheating on the piano with a *guitar*?" She truly looks like I've done something unforgivable.

I shrug. "I play both, and usually, I really only play the guitar at school..."

"It can't be *that* important to you," she interrupts. "Because like that guy over there, you've never mentioned it."

"I don't like you. You're mean," Will grumbles, crossing his arms over his chest.

I sigh. "Are you going to take Leia or are you going to continue berating me for playing multiple instruments?"

"Multiple?!" she gasps. "There are *more*?"

I hold Leia out to her, hoping to distract her from her distress at my infidelity. "Look how cute Leia is, Pipe."

It works, and Piper grins before collecting Leia and putting the harness and leash she bought for her on.

"I don't like her," Will says as soon as Piper closes the door behind her.

"She's a literal child," I remind him, eyeing him. "Please don't beef with a child."

"A *mean* child," he mutters.

After I beat him in six more races, and let him win the last one, Will leaves. It's a pretty routine Sunday; chores, recording, editing, and dinner at my parents.

"Where's Kat?" I ask as we sit for dinner. My mom glances around the table, brow furrowing when she realizes my eldest sister isn't present.

"Probably sulking over her latest Spoons loss," Nic says smugly. According to an excited text from Nic in the group chat, she "pummeled" Kat in Spoons on New Year's Eve. Josh eyes her with an expression that is somehow both admiring and nervous. He knows my sister perfectly.

I notice another empty seat. "Mom, Piper's not coming this week."

"I know, she texted me earlier," Mom says easily, serving Dad salad. I almost knock over my Guinness at the revelation that my mother and Piper text each other. "Josh's friend, Brandon, is coming this week."

"He's also our accountant," Hunter adds. "Josh hooked us up, and now... well. Jo's in love with him." Hunter sighs dreamily, resting her chin on her open palm and batting her eyelashes at her girlfriend.

"He makes taxes and bookkeeping so easy!" Jo whines.

"You're a lesbian," Izzy reminds her.

"Me not having to worry about taxes is not in contradiction with my sexuality," Jo bites back.

"Ren, did you hear I beat Kat in the annual Spoons tournament?" Nic says.

"What kind of salad dressing is there?" Hunter wonders.

"Do you people ever communicate by not talking over each other?" Poppy asks, talking over everyone else.

"Emilia, is something wrong with the salad?" My mom asks over Izzy and Leo bickering over something asinine. The doorbell rings and Josh and Jo both jump to answer it.

"I... um, I'm not feeling great," Millie stammers, wiping her hand across her forehead.

"Where the *fuck* is she?" The room falls silent again at the echoing voice. Steve stampedes into the room, eyes wild, and a piece of paper clenched in his hand.

"Steve's here," Josh says awkwardly from the doorway. "Also, this is Brandon."

Brandon is a white man an inch or two shorter than my pretty-much-brother-in-law, with dark hair that's graying at the temples. He smiles politely, and Hunter pretends to swoon while Jo sits back down. "I think I met most of you at the launch party…"

"Where is she?" Steve yells again, at a volume that makes Mom startle in her chair. Dad and I are both on our feet, Josh next to us.

"Let's talk about this outside instead of yelling, okay?" I say in my best teacher voice, putting my hand on my brother-in-law's back to guide him away from the dining room.

He violently pulls away from me, stumbling into Josh, who's a little less gentle when he clasps Steve's shoulders. "Outside. Now," he says through clenched teeth, shoving Steve towards my dad, who's holding open the front door.

Leo's scrambling towards us. "Can I take a swing at him?" he asks excitedly, the argument with his twin forgotten.

"Wait. Millie?" Brandon is staring at my sister, who's staring back, eyes wide and face sheet-white. "What are you—"

He doesn't get to finish his question, as Millie promptly vomits on her untouched salad.

"*Ew!*"

"Millie!"

Instead of shoving Leo back towards the chaos like I'd initially planned, I grab him by the collar and pull him out the door with me.

"You need to calm down or leave," Josh is telling Steve. My sister's boyfriend is a big guy, but I've never seen him use his size to intimidate… until today. He's towering over my brother-in-law, shoulders squared, and honestly, if Nic doesn't marry the guy, I might.

"I'm not *talking* to you," Steve spits, shouldering Josh. Except it doesn't do anything, and Josh doesn't budge.

"We don't know where she is," my dad says, voice calm. "Why don't you and I take a walk and you can tell me what's going..."

"Sean, Leo filmed him refusing to leave. He can be arrested for trespassing." I turn, and sure enough, Will and Leo stand side by side, Leo's phone capturing the interaction.

Steve points menacingly. I'm sure he thinks it's menacing, at least. It looks like one of my students is tattling on another student, in my opinion. "I'll find out where she is," he tells Josh, like Josh might suddenly pull Kat out of his pocket. "She's my *wife*."

Josh shakes his head in disgust as Steve stomps towards his BMW, slamming the door shut as he starts it. "It's way hotter when a grumpy guy stuck in a marriage of convenience says 'my wife,'" Josh grumbles.

"Indeed," I agree, remembering the scene from the contemporary marriage of convenience Audrey and I read the other night.

"If anyone knows where Kat is, I think it's best you keep it to yourself." Everyone's eyes are on Dad's, whose brow is furrowed as Steve runs the stop sign at the end of the street.

I pull my phone out of my pocket to call Kat and ask her what the fuck is going on when I notice I have almost a dozen missed calls, and four missed texts, all from Audrey.

Audrey

ren call me

its an emergency

My heart is in my throat, the hustle and bustle surrounding me muting into a buzz as I call her back.

"Ren?" Audrey sobs when she answers the phone. "Ren, it's Piper."

My bloodstream freezes, and I'm filled with ice. "What happened?"

She doesn't answer at first, just sobs quietly, and I've never hated myself more than I do for missing her calls. "She was in an accident. She's at the hospital."

"Which hospital?" I ask, and it feels like I'm pleading. Begging. *Not Piper.*

"Bridgeport. I'm taking a cab to Grand Central, but she's alone and..."

"I know, sweetheart. I'm going."

Her thank you is barely audible before she hangs up. I turn back to my family and Will who are all silently staring at me. I open my mouth to say something when Leo's running out of the house, and pressing my keys into my hand.

Dad squeezes my shoulder. "*Go.* We've got this." Josh, Will, and Leo nod seriously in agreement. They can't possibly know how much them taking the weight right now so I can be with Piper means to me.

I nod once, throat too scratchy to form a proper thanks before walking to the Corolla.

I make the twenty minute drive to Bridgeport Hospital in thirteen minutes. I can't help but speed; all I can think about is Piper alone in a hospital bed.

Audrey sends a text letting me know Piper was in the pediatric emergency room, and when I get to the front desk, I'm out of breath from running.

"Piper... *wheeze*... Hinton... *wheeze*."

"And what's your relationship to the patient?" the nurse at the desk asks, eyes unmoving from the monitor in front of her.

Shit. How do I answer this? Her mom's boyfriend? Piano teacher? Hopefully future stepfather?

"Mr. Quinn?" I turn to see a short, Eastern Asian doctor with a hijab and soft smile addressing me.

"Yes," I respond, still panting.

"Piper told us her dad was coming. You can follow me." My stomach is doing somersaults in my belly as I follow her further into the emergency department.

After a few minutes of twisting hallways, the doctor pulls back a curtain to reveal Piper reclined on a hospital bed, a black boot on her right foot and a yellow cast on her left arm. She's trying to feed herself chocolate pudding, but her spoonful ends up on her chin when she sees me.

"Dad!" Piper exclaims, giving me a look that very obviously means she expects me to show my acting chops.

"Hello... offspring," I reply.

You know what? I tried.

"Her MRI is clear, but make sure you keep an eye on her for any sign of head trauma. I'll be back in a few minutes with the discharge paperwork," the doctor says, a kind smile on her face. She closes the curtain around us, and I pull the guest chair to Piper's bed.

"So," I say, sitting and clasping my hands in my lap. "You scared the shit out of me."

She grimaces. "Sorry. I was in the MRI tunnel of hell when they called Mom and I wasn't able to talk to her until I got out, and by that point, she'd already called you. In an absolute panic, I'm sure."

"What was the MRI for?" I ask.

"My helmet broke when I fell, so they want to make sure my brain is okay or whatever. I swear to god, if it's not, I'm suing the helmet manufacturer for all they're worth." Truthfully, I expect nothing less from this kid.

"And the casts?" I ask, motioning to her arm with my head.

"Arm and foot broke when I fell. I think I hit a patch of black ice, it was nasty. Phone broke too. Luckily, someone saw it happen out their window and called 911..." She trails off, fidgeting with the blanket with her non-broken arm. "Ren... Leia was in my basket when I fell, and she ran away. I tried to chase after her, but my foot hurt..."

My heart sinks, and I'm immediately filled with anxiety. I've had Leia since she was a tiny, rage-filled kitten.

But right now, Piper is staring at me, eyes filled with tears, and I know I can't let myself feel what I want to, because Piper's already feeling it.

I force a smile, and move to sit on the edge of the bed. "Hey, I'm just glad you're okay," I say, meaning every word. While I'm absolutely devastated at the possibility of Leia being gone, I don't know if I could survive if something worse had happened to Piper.

Piper's lip trembles, and the movement causes the chocolate pudding to drop from her chin to her lap. I take a napkin and dab the remaining pudding off her face. "Do you hate me?"

"I don't hate you," I promise. "Piper, when your mom called... I was terrified. You're so important to me, and the idea of you alone, and not knowing if you were okay..." I clear my throat, frantically blinking away the tears filling my eyes. "It was one of the most terrifying moments of my life."

"I'm sorry I told them you were my dad," she whispers. "I was scared they wouldn't let you in otherwise."

"God, Pipe. I would have caused a scene if they didn't. Full on Karen, throwing papers and demanding a manager."

This at least gets a small smile out of her. "That sounds like what a dad would do," she says cautiously. "Even if you're not biologically my dad. But Luke would do that for Rory if she needed it. I've never had one, so maybe I'm wrong, but sometimes it feels like you're my dad. It didn't feel like I was being dishonest."

It takes everything in me to not dissolve into sobs. Instead, I smile tearily at her. "You're right. That does sound like something a dad would do."

Chapter 45

Audrey

Playlist: Happy Accidents | Saint Motel

My heart is breaking, and it's lying in Bridgeport Hospital while I'm desperately trying to get back to it. To her.

I can't even find it in me to care that I'm leaving the conference early. While I had a wonderful weekend and don't regret going, my family will always come first. That's where my heart is.

I trust Ren, but he's never had to deal with a crisis like this on his own. When Piper got her period, I was able to get there quickly, but this time, I had no choice but to trust he'd take care of my girl until I could. I know he's a teacher and he's responsible for groups of children on a daily basis, and I've been trusting him with Piper during lessons.

But for so long, I kept Piper and myself hidden because I didn't trust anyone not to hurt us. I've never not been there for her during an emergency. But part of trusting Ren with my heart means trusting him with the daughter who owns so much of it.

After an Uber ride from the train station, I'm quietly unlocking the door to the cottage, in case Piper's sleeping.

"We should be looking for Leia," Piper says from the living room. I freeze and, like a terrible mom, listen into their conversation.

"I told you. I'm not going anywhere," Ren responds. Even in one of the worst moments of my life, his voice is a balm. "And you're certainly not going anywhere, either."

"But we have to look for her! It's all my fault that she ran away! If I hadn't fallen, she wouldn't be missing. I'm *scared*, Ren."

My stomach sinks as the pieces come together. Leia must have been with Piper when she crashed, and got away. Poor Ren, he loves that damn cat.

"I'm going to be honest with you," Ren says, and the couch springs squeak as he adjusts himself. "I'm scared, too. I love Leia as much as you do, and I'm scared something happened to her. She has a microchip, and my family and Will are putting signs up around town, but besides that, there's not much I can do. What I *can* do, however, is remind you to take your meds at the right time and elevate your foot. Leia matters to me, Pipe. But you do, too."

"Would you still be here if you weren't embarrassingly in love with my mom?" Piper asks, and I bite back a smile.

"Yes," Ren responds, not missing a beat, unlike my heart, which has missed several in the last few seconds. "Because I love you, too. And one of the reasons I'm embarrassingly in love with your mom is because you're a part of her.

"So much of her heart belongs to you. Her love for you and your love of her helped make her the woman I have the honor of being in love with. She's her because you're you, and because you're hers. And it feels like... you're mine too."

The tears are plentiful as I eavesdrop, every fear I felt on the way home washing away and being replaced with gratitude. Hope. Joy. Love for this little family we accidentally became.

I wipe at my eyes before clearing my throat and continuing into the living room. "Hi, birdie," I say, still teary as both Ren and Piper's eyes light up when they glance over their shoulders. "Next time, wait to crash your bike until I'm in the state."

"Mom!" Piper exclaims, scrambling like she's going to stand.

"No!" Ren and I both yell and he throws his arm in front of her, keeping her safely off her feet.

"I'm coming to you," I promise, dropping my bags to the floor and walking around the couch. Ren stands, and I smile in gratitude before taking the vacated seat and pull Piper into my arms.

"I broke my phone," Piper mumbles, voice muffled by my shoulder. "And my helmet. Also a few bones. Also my heart."

"We'll figure it out," I promise, rubbing circles on her back. "I'm just glad you're going to be okay."

"I won't be able to play piano until my arm heals. It will probably be a few months and it's going to be a lot of hard work to get back to where I am now," she says, voice drenched with grief. "I've worked so hard, Mom. *And* I lost Leia."

I meet Ren's eyes, remembering how he responded to her. How he'd put his own fear and grief on the back burner to hold space for and validate Piper's. "That sucks," I tell her, because what else do I say? It *does* supremely suck. "But I know you can do it, birdie."

Piper pulls away, and I kiss her forehead. It isn't until then I finally notice what she and Ren were watching on TV.

Gilmore Girls.

"Ew, stop crying," Piper says, disgusted by my sudden heaving sobs.

"I love you so much," I wheeze between sobs.

"I love you, too, but at least *try* to keep it together."

"Hey," Ren says, gently placing his hand on my shoulder. "Be nice to your mom. She's had a long day."

Piper groans and slumps against the back of the couch. "Traitor. I should have known you'd take her side."

I place my hand over Ren's and gently squeeze. "It's nice to have someone on my side." He smiles, and my heart melts. "Are you hungry?" I ask Piper.

"Can I have ice cream for dinner?" she asks hopefully, turning her head and clasping her hands under her chin as she bats her eyelashes.

I wearily examine her, bandages on her face and casts on her lanky limbs. "You're using your injuries to your advantage, aren't you?"

She sticks out her lower lip. "This is the only positive I'll get from them."

I sigh and stand up. "Fine. I'll go grab you a bowl of Moose Tracks."

"I'll come, too," Ren says, squeezing my shoulder as I get to my feet.

When we're in the kitchen, I can't hold myself back anymore. I spin to face him, throw my arms around his neck and pull him down, pressing my mouth to his. He seems taken aback by this, freezing for a moment until his body softens against mine and his arms are around my waist, pulling me closer into him.

"Thank you," I murmur against his mouth, heart so full it could burst. "Thank you."

"Don't thank me," he responds, pulling away slightly and pressing soft pecks across my face. On the corner of my mouth, my chin, my forehead, the bridge and tip of my nose. "Thank *you* for trusting me with her."

"I'm sorry about Leia," I whisper as he presses his forehead to mine, both of our breaths heated and frantic. "I'll help you look for her. I'll do everything I can..."

"She's chipped, and posters are hung all over town. If anyone finds her and brings her in, they'll call me. I'm devastated, but it was an accident. They happen."

"They do," I whisper, thinking about how Ren accidentally stumbled into my life, into my heart. If Piper had chosen another instrument as her special interest, or if Ren had refused to do private lessons last summer like he intended, this man wouldn't be holding me in the kitchen. Piper, too, was a happy accident. The two people I love most are in my life by accident. Accidents happen.

Thank god they do.

Chapter 46

Audrey

Playlist: Crooked Smile | The Weepies, Deb Talan, Steve Tannen

The next morning, I insist Ren go to work, and Piper insists I go to the inn.

"You're making me claustrophobic!" she whines, burrowing beneath her weighted blanket on the couch.

I remind myself she needs space as I smile at Caroline, one of our front desk employees, when I walk in.

"How was the conference thing-a-mabob?" she asks when she sees me approaching, pausing her scroll to place her phone face down on the desk.

My stomach flips. "Good. I had to leave earlier than planned, but I'm glad I went."

Caroline grins. "Hell, yeah. We already got a booking from a guest who found you on their website."

"That's great," I reply, grabbing a stack of mail and turning toward my office.

"Oh, also," Caroline calls. "There's a guest who checked in yesterday and specifically asked to speak to you. Said she was an old friend of yours."

I turn and stare at her in confusion. Old friend? I don't have old friends. "Who is it?"

Caroline clicks her mouse until she finds the booking. "Sidney Prescott."

"Sidney Prescott, like... Neve Campbell's character in *Scream*?" I don't think I've ever been more confused in my life.

Caroline picks her phone up and shrugs. "I guess?"

I shake my head in bewilderment. "You can tell her to come to my office if she wants to see me."

I'm making my way through my bottomless email inbox when Caroline knocks on my open office door twenty minutes later.

"Boss lady, Ms. Prescott is here." Caroline steps to the side, and I choke on my coffee.

"Thank you," Kat Holt says quietly. Caroline closes the office door and Kat peers at me, our eyes meeting. There are dark circles rimming her dark brown eyes, and she's wearing sweatpants. Her appearance reminds me of myself when I'm depressed.

"Kat, I... hi," I stammer, slapping my chest to clear my airway. "What are you doing here?"

"Can I sit?" she asks, motioning to the chair across from my desk with her hand.

I nod, and watch as she flops into the chair. I never thought I'd see the day where Kat did anything that could be described as "flopping."

We sit in an uncomfortable silence until she speaks again. "I know you don't want me here, but I didn't know where else to go," she says, barely audible as she stares at her hands in her lap.

"You have like the biggest family in the world," I say, dumbfounded.

She shakes her head. "They'd laugh at me."

"Respectfully, what the hell is going on?"

"I left Steve," she blurts out, lifting her head, eyes watery. "I can't do it anymore. I can't be his wife, can't be who they want me to be."

"Who's 'they'?" I'm surprised I can get the words out, honestly. I'm shocked by her revelation.

"My parents. God, my whole family. I did everything I was supposed to. Got married, got my law degree, and I think it broke me. My parents will be so disappointed, and divorce is a sin, and my siblings will laugh at me because they've always hated Steve, and they hate me, and, *god,* I don't blame them. I hate me, too."

I hand Kat a tissue as her voice cracks, tears escaping from her eyes. "I can't speak for the rest of your family, but I know for a fact Ren doesn't hate you," I say softly. "He loves you."

She shakes her head. "He wouldn't understand. No one would... only you."

I furrow my brow. "Kat, we're not friends. We haven't been friends in well over a decade. Why do you think I'd understand you over your family?"

"Because you're the only person I know who was brave enough to do the opposite of what was expected of her. Because I want to be like you. And I think you're the last person who knew me—like, really, truly knew me—before I became Steve's."

My stomach drops. "He hurt you." It's not a question, and she knows it.

But still, she shakes her head. "No, he never touched me..."

"Abuse is more than physical harm. He hurt you, emotionally."

She nods in resignation. "Yeah. We've been trying to get pregnant for a few years, but were never able to conceive. With every negative pregnancy test, he became angrier and more aggressive. It's like he married me to use me as an incubator, and when I couldn't fulfill my purpose, I was worthless to him."

I swallow the lump in my throat. "You can stay free of charge as long as you need to," I promise. "You're safe now, okay? But you need to at least tell Ren that you're here so he can tell your family you're safe. No one else needs to know, but I can't lie to him, and they deserve to at least know you're safe."

She shakes her head. "Okay. But, Audrey, I can't stay for free."

"You're going to tell me Steve doesn't have access to your finances?" I ask.

"I withdrew cash to pay for my stay."

I shake my head. "I don't care. I'm not charging you. You're going to need money for the divorce."

"Audrey," Kat meets my eyes and my stomach sinks when I realize what she's going to say. "I'm sorry. I'm so, so sorry."

"I need you to say why," I say, mouth dry. "You owe me that, at least."

She nods. "I'm sorry for kissing you. I'm sorry I kissed you and blamed you for it and pushed you away. I'm sorry I didn't reach out when I heard about the pregnancy, or said anything to you at school."

The memories replay like a movie. The night we'd been watching *Vampire Diaries*, laughing and joking around when she'd suddenly cupped my face and planted her mouth on mine.

I was so surprised. She was my best friend... but it felt good. Right. I kissed her back. When she pulled away, she looked at me like I was disgusting. Like she hadn't initiated the kiss. She demanded I leave and I obliged, too confused and hurt to fight back.

This is the first time we've spoken since.

"That was a fucked up thing to do." I say in response, because honestly? I'd dreamed about saying it to her for sixteen years. "I never would have done that to you, and you know it."

She winces, but nods. "You're right. And I don't have excuses, but I am sorry I did it. I was so scared about what it all meant."

"What did it all mean?"

"I don't know," she admits feebly. "I still haven't figured it out. I've been too busy trying to be the perfect wife, but that obviously didn't go the way I'd hoped. None of it went the way I hoped."

"It's not too late for things to go the way you hope," I say, thinking about how long it took for me to truly be happy with my life. God, it feels too new to be happy. Too soon. "You just have to open yourself to the possibility."

Chapter 47

Ren

Playlist: Carry You Home (feat. Ella Henderson) | Alex Warren, Ella Henderson

Piper takes an aggressive bite out of her burger, and I eye her cautiously.

She stayed home from school, but kept herself busy by continuously texting me things she needed. What she "needed" was burgers from Queenie's and about twelve different types of ice cream. "I hate this show," she grumbles through her mouthful of food. I nod to placate her, deciding not to mention the fact that *Gilmore Girls* was on when I got here.

I check my phone, pleased to see a text from Audrey.

"Ooooh, someone's crush texted him," Piper teases as I grin at my phone like a damn fool.

"Shut up," I mumble, maturely and paternally.

A few minutes later, there's a loud cry and a thud from outside. Piper and I exchange confused glances.

"Stay right here," I tell her warily. I walk outside, finding the contents of Audrey's bag strewn across the porch, and Audrey sprinting down the driveway.

"Aud!" I yell after her, but she doesn't so much as look over her shoulder. I shove my feet into my shoes, and hurriedly tell Piper I'll be back, before taking off after Audrey.

I follow her down the driveway, but she has too much of a head start for me to catch up. I wonder if she's been secretly running every morning, too. She runs without responding to my calls for a few blocks before turning into a yard. Finally, I catch up to her. Christ, you'd think I didn't run ten miles a day, but the shoes and clothes *really* make a difference. "Aud," I wheeze. "Why are you praying to a shed?" That's the only reason I can think of as to why my girlfriend is prostrated next to this decrepit shed.

"Leia!" she coos, and I stare at her, somehow even more confused.

"What?"

"Leia was on the porch when I came home," Audrey says before meowing. "But she ran away and I followed her here."

"Oh my god!" I exclaim, lowering myself to my belly and joining her on the ground. "Are you sure?"

"Random cats aren't a frequent occurrence on my front porch." She meows again and I'm immediately taken aback when I hear an answering *meow* from under the shed.

"Leia!" I call, my heart swelling with hope. "Come out, baby girl."

"*Meow,*" Maybe Leia responds.

After a few more seconds of calling her, she comes out from under the shed, a tiny gray kitten dangling from her mouth. I sit up, and Definitely Leia climbs into my lap. She drops the kitten onto my thigh, glaring at me like I'm a deadbeat dad who's hours late for our agreed-upon visitation time.

"She had a baby," Audrey says softly, pushing herself off her stomach and scooching in closer to me.

"*Meow,*" the kitten adds, blinking at me in confusion. I run my index finger along their tiny head, and they knead their paws on my thigh, hard at work making biscuits.

"Leia's fixed, but maybe she found a kitten without a mom and has been taking care of them."

Leia purrs and nudges me with her head. I scratch behind her ears.

Audrey grins. "God, Piper's gonna love this."

I smile. "Yeah?"

"She's been begging for a cat of her own for *years*. And your damn cat led me right to a tiny kitten?" She shakes her head in disbelief. "If I don't let Piper keep them, I'll be cursed by an ancient spell. It's fate."

I scoop the kitten off my lap and put them in Audrey's cupped hands. "What were you saying about accidents last night?"

She smiles up at me. "That sometimes life is better because of them. Because sometimes you get a baby. Or a kitten. Or a hunky dude."

I laugh and kiss her, grateful for every accident that led me to this, to her.

Chapter 48

Audrey

Playlist: Mess Is Mine | Vance Joy

August

Sky's Sluts

AshBash69: so, should i reach out to Sky to let him know he got me pregnant again?

SkysMainSlut: my therapist would say no, i think. but congrats!

MeetMeInStarsHollow: i've been meaning to ask! how's therapy been?

LadyRebel93: holy shit she LIVES

SkysMainSlut: broooo you disappeared like...a year ago.

MeetMeInStarsHollow: it's only been a few months!

AshBash69: your last comment was on August 6th of last year.

MeetMeInStarsHollow: wait really??? it does NOT feel like it's been that long. Maybe because i've kinda been kept up to date on stuff.

LadyRebel93: have you been silently lurking?

MeetMeInStarsHollow: well, not exactly. My partner keeps me up to date.

SkysMainSlut: wait wait wait, rewind. PARTNER???

LadyRebel93: ARE YOU GETTING DICK? OR PUSSY? OR BOTH?! NO JUDGMENT.

MeetMeInStarsHollow: ...yes. And it's really. really good.

SkyOn4Play: thank you, sweetheart, but you're just gonna give me a big head

SkysMainSlut: WHAT THE FUCK

LadyRebel93: NO. WAY.

AshBash69: WAIT ARE YOU BONING SKY???

SkyOn4Play: boning feels a little crass.

MeetMeInStarsHollow: <eyeroll emoji> oops. Anyway, i promised my partner i'd listen to his new audio before he drops it next week.

SkysMainSlut: sky please don't tell my therapist but i want to have your babies so bad please respond to this.

AshBash69: ...yeah i think they're both gone for good now.

SkysMainSlut: too much?

LadyRebel93: toooo much

"Fuck." I arch my back, gasping as Ren's teeth scrape against my collarbone. He slowly pulls out and re-enters me before I can catch my breath. Parenthood means setting an alarm so you can get a pre-workday screw in.

"Naughty girl," Ren teases as he pushes my knees back towards me, opening me more for him. "I told you, you need to be quiet."

"I'm... trying," I gasp. I'm not lying, I'm truly trying my hardest to stay quiet, because Piper's getting ready for the first day of school. "I can..." I gasp loudly when Ren gently wraps a hand around my neck, squeezing with the perfect amount of pressure. I fumble with the bullet vibrator I'm holding to my clit, cursing loudly.

"*Quiet*, sweetheart," Ren coos, his other hand dropping my leg. I wrap my legs around his middle, desperately trying to pull him in closer to me. He cups my cheek, pressing his thumb against the seam of my mouth. I open, and suck his thumb into my mouth. "That's it. You're gorgeous with my cock inside y ou."

I run my hand along his back, squeezing his perfect ass before sliding between his ass cheeks and massaging the area behind his balls. This time, he's the one having trouble keeping quiet, so I bring my hand to his face, slipping my index finger between his lips. His eyes are intent on mine as his tongue circles my finger in a way that has me clenching around him. Moments later, we're both moaning as I press the same finger into his ass, crooking it to find the spot that makes him lose his mind. His head falls to the crook of my neck and shoulder, teeth clamping down on my clavicle and it's a good thing his thumb is in my mouth, because I surprise myself with my yelp at the sting.

My orgasm is instantaneous, and I'm whimpering helplessly around his thumb as my body tightens.

"That's right," he praises, breath ragged. "You take your pleasure perfectly, sweetheart."

His own climax follows moments later, and his body collapses onto mine. "Fuck," he breathes.

"Fuck," I agree. "That was..."

"Amazing. You're the best sex of my life, and that's not even what I love most about you."

My hand strays down his back before squeezing an ass cheek. "Personally, this ass is what I love most about you..."

He barks out a laugh before flipping us over so my body drapes over his. I rest my cheek against his heart, the thing I *actually* love most about him. The steady beat is soothing, and I run my thumb over one of the newest tattoos on his right forearm, the first ones he doesn't try to hide. Over his pulse point is a little sandpiper he said he got for his "other girl." Piper rolled her eyes when he showed her, but her trembling lower lip gave away her true feelings.

My fingers drift to my tattoo, marigolds and cosmos for my birth month. He's made us permanent, keeps us on his body for everyone to see.

"I don't want to go to school," Ren groans, fingers tangled in my hair. "I should play hooky."

"You're the teacher," I remind him. "*And* it's the first day. You were excited about it yesterday." I force myself to sit up, and Ren lets out an appreciative whistle. I blush, still flustered by his appreciation and attraction.

"You make pancakes for the first day of school, right?" he asks offhandedly, like every time he remembers something about the life Piper and I built, it doesn't make my heart jump with joy.

"Mmhmm," I confirm. "I have ingredients to make chocolate chip pancakes, banana, blueberry... what's your favorite?"

Ren sits when I climb out of bed and shrug on my robe. "What's Pipe's favorite?"

Pipe Pipe Pipe Pipe. Ren's been in our lives for a year, and still my heart repeats her nickname with each beat whenever he says it. "Not what I asked, pretty boy," I tease. "What's *your* favorite?"

The poor man's entire body blushes. He grabs a pillow and holds it to his chest, burying his face in it. "Blueberry," he answers, voice muffled.

I run my eyes down his body and grin to myself. Yep, pretty boy still gets him. He's hard again. "Cold shower," I say with a cheeky wink.

"We'll revisit this later!" he says as I turn to face the mirror. I silently recite the few affirmations I wrote on post-it notes in therapy and stuck to the mirror. My body image issues aren't fixed, but every day, I look in the mirror and remind myself that my body is a good body.

When I finish, Ren's in the bathroom, so I head out to the kitchen. Piper is assembling ingredients for pancakes next to the stove, her hair perfectly styled and headphones on. She's wearing the new white sneakers Ren took her to get last week when I had to stay at the inn late, and the music note necklace he got her for her sixteenth birthday a few months ago. She looks so grown-up, and I take a moment to take in the fact my life is better than I'd ever let myself hope for.

Piper smirks when she sees me and lowers her headphones. "Someone seems happy. More than happy, actually. Hmmm, I swear someone told you that would happen." She taps her chin with her index finger, pretending to be deep in thought.

I playfully nudge her with my shoulder. "Good morning, birdie. Go sit down, you don't have to do this." I gesture towards the ingredients she's assembled.

"I know. I wanted to let you guys have more time together. You've both been busy lately and I know you've missed each other."

With tourist season in full swing, I spent the majority of my waking time at the inn, and while Ren visited when he could, he's been busy himself. Sky is still the most popular

4Play creator, and while he outsources most scriptwriting and editing nowadays—except for the occasional script we work on together—it's still something that takes up a lot of his time. He's also been spending a lot of time helping his family out after his sister gave birth last month. Piper's helped too, as did the rest of his family. It's been so special to see all of them step up for the new parents, but even more special to see Ren supporting his family, without feeling solely responsible for them.

"I have missed him," I admit, "But I may or may not have reserved a room for us at the inn next weekend so we can spend time together." I measure the flour and pour it into the bowl, sighing when I see Piper smirking out of the corner of my eye. "Don't."

"You didn't spend enough time together when you both were sooooooo tired last night and went to bed early after casually asking if I was going to have my headphones on?"

"That's enough from you," I say, cheeks pink.

She snickers, but blessedly respects my request. "When are you meeting with the architect?" she asks, bending over to scratch Luke, our newest family member, behind her ears.

The kitten Leia found was a girl, but by the time we found out a few days later, Piper had already named her Luke and refused to change it.

"This week," I say, trying to remember the exact date. While Ren still *technically* lives at his apartment, he only is there to use his office to record. Otherwise, he and Leia are completely moved in. We had a long talk about our next steps together, and decided to have the cottage renovated, adding a second floor, expanded kitchen, and other features to accommodate our new family, the family we want to grow.

Twenty minutes later, Ren comes out of the bedroom, and kisses my cheek when I hand him his plate of blueberry pancakes. The three of us eat together, Piper and Ren sharing what they're looking forward to in the new school year. Piper is a junior, which I'm pretty sure is actually illegal, and is excited for AP Music Theory. Ren is excited his least favorite student finally moved up to middle school.

"What about you, Mom?" Piper asks, spearing a piece of pancake and shoving it into her mouth. "What are you most looking forward to this year?"

I think about it for a moment. Where to even begin? "I'm excited about so many things," I tell her. "Renovating the house, joining the PTA and small business association, starting weekly trivia nights at the inn…"

"Damn," Piper interrupts. "Adulthood sounds boring."

I glance at Ren, who's resting his chin on his hand, eyes shining behind his glasses as he looks at me with pride. "I don't think so," he says. "It sounds wonderfully exciting to me."

"You're both dorks," she mutters.

"Okay, time to go." Ren gets to his feet, and Leia leaps onto the chair, stealing his spot. "You still want a ride to school, Pipe?"

"Yep." Piper stands. "My hair looks good as hell, and *someone* makes me wear a ugly as hell helmet when I ride my bike." She gives me a pointed look.

"That ugly as hell helmet is the reason you didn't have a brain injury after your accident," I remind her, rolling my eyes.

"Ugh, whatever," Piper says, slinging her backpack over one shoulder and walking toward the door. "You don't have to rub it in!" she calls over her shoulder.

"Wait!" I call out, scrambling to my feet. "I want to get pictures!"

Piper groans. "*Mooom*. I'm too old for first day of school pictures. It's cringe as hell."

I look to Ren. "It's Ren's first day of school, too, and he's older than you. He doesn't think they're cringe as hell." I look at Ren as he ducks his head. It's a valiant attempt, but doesn't hide his grimace. "*Wooooow*," I draw out the word. "You're supposed to be on my side."

"I am!" Ren says quickly. "That doesn't mean I can't find this thing in particular cringe as hell."

I sigh. "Would you two humor me if we included the cats?"

Less than a minute later, Ren and Piper are standing on the front porch steps, a cat nestled in each of their arms.

"Say cheese!" I squint at my screen, shading my eyes so I can see through the glare.

"Cheese!" Ren says, beaming.

"This is cheesy!" Piper says.

I scroll through the pictures I took and sigh with relief. "Okay, we got at least one usable one."

They put the cats back into the house before heading to the car. Piper climbs into the passenger seat, but Ren hangs back, his hand light on my waist.

"Have a good day," I tell him as he bends to kiss my cheek. "I can't wait to hear all about it."

"I love you," he whispers. "Every day is a good one with you. The best one, even."

"Okay, loverboy," I tease. "Go to work."

He smiles bashfully, and in that crooked grin of his, I see our future. The future looks like our present, but with its own unique challenges and joys. Challenges and joys we'll experience together, hand in hand. I don't know what exactly the future brings, but for the first time, I don't mind the uncertainty. In fact, I can't fucking wait.

Acknowledgements

Two years ago, I was beginning the process of self-publishing my debut. It's wild to look back and see how much I've changed, but also how much I've stayed the same. So like I have for every book, I'd like to start by thanking myself. Thank you for hanging on when times got tough. For being soft and stubborn, and easily hurt. I'm forever proud of who I am because of these books.

To my family: thank you for believing in and supporting my dreams. For coming to signings and excitedly bringing attention to me and my books during them. It means the world to know I'm making you proud.

To my alpha readers: Cait, Kae, and Emily. Thank you for loving the Quinns as much as I do, and for your friendship and support. Your friendship is one of the best things to come out of publishing.

To my beta readers: Bekah, Kelsie, Valentina, Paige, Cait, Myra, Vic, Ricki, Kae, Annie, Erin, and Amy. Your unhinged comments kept me giggling through the editing process, and your feedback was invaluable in making Audrey, Ren, Piper, and their story the best it could be.

To my editor: thanks for the late-night editing sessions, and talking through alternative words when I couldn't find the right one.

To my proofreader: thank you, thank you, thank you. I'm so appreciative of your friendship and willingness to help me out.

To my girlfriend: I got to fall in love with you while I wrote about Audrey and Ren falling for each other, and I see our story all over theirs. Thank you for the encouragement, and being the best little spoon in the world, except for when it's my turn. Yes, yes. I know we're cute as shit.

To everyone who donated and shared my GoFundMe: this wouldn't be happening again if it weren't for you. Thank you for believing in me and the stories I want so desperately to tell.

To Vic: what the hell would I do without you?? From beta reader, to sticker and brand designer to beloved friend, I am just so freaking grateful for you.

To my artists: Paige, each cover and artwork is better than the last. I always love working with you! AJ, I'm absolutely obsessed with the bonus artwork you did. It's prettier and better than I ever hoped! Emily, thank you for the family trees and page break graphics, AND for helping me with my website. You make my books prettier, and life more manageable.

And last, but certainly not least, to you, my readers. Whether it's your first time hanging out with the Quinns, or your third, I'm so grateful you're here. Romance books healed, changed, and, in a way, saved me, and being able to write books that I hope heal and change you is the greatest honor of my life. Thank you for taking a chance on me, and for allowing me to continue writing stories for you.

About the Author

Katie Duggan (she/they) is a New England transplant currently living in Northern Virginia. She writes romance novels that give fat, neurodivergent, and queer characters spicy happily-ever-afters. When Katie's not writing or being kept up at night by her characters, they can be found drinking Doctor Pepper, going to therapy, convincing people to read her favorite books, and doing whatever hobbies give their neurospicy brain the most dopamine at the moment.

Email: KatieDuggan.Writes@gmail.com

Instagram & TikTok: @KatieDugganWrites

Also By Katie Duggan

The Quiblings Series

From the Start (Nic & Josh)
Back to Me (Jo & Hunter)
On My Side (Ren & Audrey)
Book 4 (Spring 2026)

Standalone Holiday Novella

Ice Cold Witch (November 19, 2025)